Roaring Flames

MATED BY FIRE
BOOK TWO

KATIE MAY

EXPRESSO PUBLISHING, LLC

Copyright © 2024 by Katie May

All rights reserved.

No part of this book may be reproduced in any form or by any electronic or mechanical means, including information storage and retrieval systems, without written permission from the author, except for the use of brief quotations in a book review.

No parts of this book or cover were created by using AI. Katie May does not give anyone the right to use this novel in any AI-training databases.

Edited by Lindsey Loucks of Midnight Library

Cover by Laura Soica-Clarke of Covers by Aura

To you, the person reading this book and—who is that behind you? Whatever you do, don't. Turn. Around. Seriously, don't.

Contents

Foreword

This is book two of a why choose/reverse harem series where the FMC won't have to choose between her love interests at the end. Though this book takes place in high school, all of the characters will be over the age of eighteen before any sexy times commence. Triggers include:

- Past sexual assault
- Attempted sexual assault
- Mental health issues
- Self-harm through reckless actions
- Death

There will absolutely be NO cheating. All of the guys are one hundred precent devoted to the FMC from the second they see her (though some may need to get their heads out of their asses first).

One

IZZY

Wolves.

Mates.

Fate.

My head reels, spins, somersaults, and a headache threatens to rip apart my skull. There's a strange sluicing sound between my ears as well, drowned out by the pounding of my feet against the earth. Twigs snap. Leaves crackle. Dried dirt crunches. But all of that is background noise to my tumultuous thoughts.

Wolves.

Mates.

Fate.

The wind is brutal today—keen, almost, as if I'm being stabbed by a thousand tiny knives—but the slice of it against my skin makes me feel alive.

I need to feel something.

Anything.

Without breaking my stride, I begin to scrub at the mark on my arm, half expecting for pain to spiral through me at the touch. Yet, despite the distinct texture of my skin, there's no ache.

Wolves.

Mates.

Fate.

Those three words ricochet in my head like pinballs —bouncing off every wall, hitting every surface, and eventually falling into tiny holes before re-emerging and beginning anew.

Wolves.

Mates.

Fate.

I know I shouldn't have run out of Mr. Montgomery's office the way I did. That's not me. I don't run from my problems.

The old Izzy would've laughed in the vice principal's face. Maybe even suggested he see a shrink.

Who the fuck believes in werewolves?

And yet...

I can't deny the sincerity in his words. The sheer possessiveness that emanated from his red eyes. The slightly sharper than normal canines that dug into his lower lip.

Wolves.

Mates.

Fate.

Water pricks my eyes, but I'm not sure if it's tears

or sweat. Despite the chill in the air, I've been running for who the fuck knows how long. All I know is that I have to get away.

From the school.

From Mr. Montgomery.

From the secrets that seem to be pressing down on me, burying me alive.

I draw in a shaky breath as I finally stumble to a stop, placing one hand against a tree to steady myself.

Now...where the hell am I?

Sunlight slants through the tree branches and illuminates the path I've been running on. Probably designed for cross-country or track. I take a smidgen of comfort in the fact that I'm not lost in the woods after everything that has been going on—namely, the two murders.

Was it stupid of me to head out on my own? Quite possibly.

But I couldn't stay in that stuffy school a second longer.

Using the tree for support, I lower myself to the ground and spread my legs out in front of me. I will my rampant heartbeat to return to a normal pace, but no matter how many deep breaths I take, the organ continues to pound relentlessly.

I've always suspected that there is more to this world than what meets the eye, but this?

Absently, I run my fingers over the strange markings and swear I feel a surge of heat in my stomach.

Wolves.

Mates.

Fate.

"You belong to the wolves now."

That's what Mr. Montgomery said.

The wolves...

As in him and Ashton?

What about Ethan, Emery, and Reid?

Grayson?

Is that why I haven't been able to get in contact with my best friend? Is he somehow tied up in this mess?

I place an arm across my forehead as I struggle to get my thoughts in some semblance of an order. They continue to swirl like a roulette table, never stopping, never slowing down.

I have so many questions and no idea where to start.

Wolves.

Mates.

Fate.

Christian will know, I reason, resolve settling in my gut. Instinctively, I ball my hands into fists, my nails digging into my fleshy palms. *Christian will have the answers.*

And yet...

Thinking about Christian inevitably reminds me of the strange, inappropriate thoughts I had about him just before I ran from his office.

What his lips would feel like against mine.

How his stubble would feel grazing my chin.

How wonderfully delicious it would be to have his body pressed against my own.

What the fuck is wrong with you, Izzy? I mentally berate myself for the one hundredth time.

He's the damn vice principal. An authority figure. I shouldn't be lusting after him or thinking about his perfect body or imagining running my fingers through his dark hair.

And I definitely shouldn't be remembering how *right* it felt to hear him call me his.

He's mine, my inner voice growls with startling ferocity.

I shush her.

Strange feelings aside, Christian Montgomery has the answers I'm so desperately looking for.

Now I just need to gather the courage to *talk* to him.

And hopefully not jump his bones in the process.

Two

CHRISTIAN

You fucking idiot!

With a snarl, I sweep my hand out, tossing everything off my desk and onto the floor.

What a fucking idiot!

Shame wars with anger in my chest.

How could I have been so dumb?

But I know the answer to that, even if I don't want to admit it.

I wasn't in charge during my conversation with Isabella.

My wolf was.

He still is, if I'm being completely honest. I can sense him pacing in my mind, his teeth bared, his eyes glowing red, his nostrils flaring, desperate to catch a whiff of her.

Mate, my wolf snarls, that one word bursting with

possessiveness and need. Raw, unencumbered need that borders on obsession.

No!

I run both of my hands through my hair as I try to think things through, try to get myself out of this shit show I found myself in.

Isabella can't be my mate, dammit. She's a student here. I'm the vice principal. It's wrong. Taboo. Forbidden.

But you're not really a vice principal, a dry voice retorts in my head.

I ignore the voice and continue pacing, weaving a pathway around the wayward items I threw in my hissy fit.

How could this be happening? How?

Sure, it's not unheard of for a lone wolf to find a mate, but it's also not typical either. Mating a lone wolf can only ever lead to heartbreak and destruction. And for a *human* to be mated to one? That's a recipe for fucking disaster.

No. Not happening.

I refuse.

My wolf growls viciously in my head.

Mate, he repeats.

No.

Anger coils in my stomach, a serpent waiting to strike, as I wear down the carpeting in my office.

This can't be happening. No. This can't be fucking happening.

Most lone wolves are isolated from others in the community—and for good reason. Without a pack to keep them grounded, most of them turn feral. Insane. It becomes impossible for the human to differentiate themselves from the wolf. Years ago, a lone wolf refused to leave town, and he ended up slaughtering five different humans and two of his fellow shifters.

The thought of that happening to Isabella...

Bile scorches my throat, and my pacing picks up speed, as does my heart.

I never should've left the forest. Never should've returned home.

Maybe then this wouldn't have happened.

You need to stay away, Christian, I tell myself firmly, ignoring my wolf's vehement howl of protest. *For her safety. For your sanity. This is wrong. You know it's wrong.*

She can't be my mate.

It's impossible.

Not when she's already chosen for my brother and his friends.

Fuck!

For the billionth time in the last few minutes, I fork my fingers through my hair. I don't need to see a mirror to know the strands are wildly disheveled. My father would have a field day if he were to see me like this, looking less than meticulous and perfect.

Fuck. Fuck.

Fuck!

A tentative knock sounds on the door, and I pause mid-step, my ears straining. Heart hammering. Lungs burning in a desperate bid to take in oxygen.

But I don't need to hear her voice to know it's her. My wolf sensed her long before I did. Already, he's sitting at attention, wagging his tail, utterly besotted by the endearing female.

Obsessed with her.

Until he loses his mind and rips her apart.

I flinch at the mere thought.

Fuck. Fuck. Fuck.

I need to get her away from me.

So why do I move towards the door and open it, inviting her inside?

Izzy stands on the threshold, her hand raised in the air as if she planned to knock again, her jaw clenched tightly. I swallow heavily at just the sight of her.

She's so fucking beautiful, and I feel like a creep for noticing, despite being only a couple of years older than her. Golden curls tumble around a heart-shaped face with full, generous lips and sharp cheekbones. Her blue eyes are framed by the darkest, thickest lashes I've ever seen. She wears jeans and a sweater that slides carelessly down one shoulder, revealing the strap of her bra.

Mine, my wolf growls possessively.

I ignore him and step aside so Izzy can enter, which she does in a flurry of anger, stalking towards the front of my desk while I remain by the door.

Now that I'm not ogling her like some fucking

pervert, I notice the tension radiating off of her in almost palpable waves. A furrow lines her brow, and her tiny hands are balled into fists. Her gaze—usually warm and slightly teasing—is hard. Stony. Angry.

Fuck.

"I'm surprised to see you back," I say, keeping my voice casual despite my turbulent emotions.

I gently shut the door and flick the lock. I don't want to risk anyone overhearing this conversation.

"I have questions. You have answers. Seemed like a no-brainer to me." She shrugs a single shoulder as she whirls to face me. "So talk."

My lips twitch instinctively. "You didn't ask any questions."

I know I'm being a smart-ass, but I can't help it. This girl gets under my skin, a splinter that can't be plucked out or sanded away.

Izzy makes a strange noise that would make most wolves proud—a combination between a growl, a snarl, and a whine. Her hard, angry eyes remain fixed on my face.

"You want a question?" Each word is slow and succinct. "Fine. Which questions should I ask?"

Ah. Smart girl.

Smart and beautiful, a voice remarks in my head.

And a student, I rebuke. *And, more importantly, human.*

I fold my arms over my chest and lean against the door. "You should ask what I am. What my brother is.

What his friends are." I pause, considering, before adding, "What *you* are."

"Fine." She throws her arms up in the air. "What are you guys? What am I?"

"You're human." A fact that flays me open. "We're not."

She bares her teeth at me. "Then what are you?"

"You guys call us werewolves, but that's not an accurate description. Not really."

No one knows how the legends of werewolves began. Some theorize that years ago, a human stumbled across a group of us shifting and concocted that ridiculous story. Others claim that one of the other supernatural species started the rumor as a way to confuse the humans.

"We can shift whenever we want, not just during the full moon. Silver doesn't harm us. We don't need to eat human flesh or anything like that to survive. Oh. And we don't imprint on babies."

Self-satisfaction courses through me when Izzy's lips twitch upwards for a fraction of a second. I've never actually watched the *Twilight* movies or read the books, but you would have to be an idiot or living under a rock not to know the entire plotline from beginning to end. And I know Isabella hates being compared to the protagonist of that story.

Ironic, considering she's surrounded by supernaturals.

"So werewolves are real?" Her voice is a breathy murmur.

"Shifters, yes." I push away from the wall and move towards my desk.

She pivots on her heel to keep her eyes on me the entire time, enveloping me in warmth.

"There are other animal shifters out there, but the majority of them are wolves."

"Why is that?" For a moment, her anger subsides, replaced by curiosity.

"I can't say for sure, though there are theories." I recline slightly in my chair and place my folded hands on my stomach.

Her gaze drops for a fraction of a second, resting on my toned abs beneath my shirt, before she swallows and focuses once more on my face.

"And those theories are?" She infuses her voice with just the right amount of sass to make me want to spank her ass.

No, I mentally berate myself, frowning. *Fuck.*

I shake my head vigorously in an attempt to clear my thoughts. A futile attempt, but an attempt all the same.

"Do you know how shifters came to be?" I ask, though the question is more rhetorical than literal. I know her answer will be no.

Even still, Izzy shakes her head, her lips firming.

I begin to tap my fingers against the table.

Every young wolf knows the history of how our kind came to be. It's common knowledge.

Facts.

Facts, I can deal with. It's when emotions become involved that things get messy.

So I pretend I'm in one of the few classrooms at Council headquarters, discussing the origin of our species with the younger generation. It's what I used to do when I was still in high school.

Before I discovered I didn't have a pack.

Before I became a lone wolf.

Before I moved away from everyone I loved and found a home for myself deep within the forest, far away from civilization.

Closing my eyes helps. I don't have to see Izzy's frowning face and puckered brow then.

Even as I think that, I snap my eyes open and home in on her. I can't look away, despite how badly I want to.

Fuck.

I take a deep breath, open my mouth, and tell the truth about our kind to quite possibly the only human who's aware of us.

Here we go...

"Legend has it that, thousands of years ago, a powerful witch lost her Blood Companion," I begin, tapping my foot to a rhythm only I can hear.

"Blood Companion?" Izzy interrupts, obviously

having picked up on the importance of those two words.

"A Blood Companion to a witch is what a Heart is to a shifter." I hesitate briefly, tapping my fingers on my desk. "Humans would probably refer to them both as a person's soulmate."

Her breath hitches, and I wonder if she's remembering my words from before. When I used the word "mate." When I claimed she belonged to the wolves.

Fuck, how could I have been so dumb?

I hurry to speak before she can put the pieces together. I'm terrified of the final image they'll create.

"The soulmate principle stems from the belief that every person is defective until they find their other half. That their souls aren't complete until then. Based on that, witches and warlocks believe that their Blood Companion holds the other half of a person's magic. Once they form the bond, they'll become immensely powerful."

Her brows dip low. She opens her mouth, and I just know she's going to ask about Hearts and mates and shifters. I fucking know it.

So I take the coward's way out and continue speaking before she can.

"Thousands of years ago, a powerful witch named Letty found her Blood Companion—a warlock named Juan. Now, let me preface this by saying that witches and warlocks are different from humans. We all are, but them...more so." I lean forward and rest my arms on the desk, holding Izzy's stare. "The magic users receive prestige and privilege by being the most powerful. It doesn't matter if you're rich or poor, young or old, pretty or ugly. If you have power running through your veins, you're at the top of the food chain.

"It's why some witches and warlocks will spend their entire life searching for their Blood Companion. Not because they believe in true love or any of that crap —but because they want to be whole again. They want their *magic* to be whole again."

Now, this... This is the part I don't want to tell Izzy. This is her first look into the paranormal world, and I hate that it's so bleak and despairing. Yet, she needs to know the truth.

The sooner she learns about the monsters that lurk in the shadows, the quicker she can figure out how to fight them and survive.

"As I said before, power trumps everything for magic users. A lot of times, the witch or warlock will kill their Blood Companion to claim the magic for themselves."

It's a sad truth of not only their history, but their present as well. Though the murdering of Blood Companions is illegal nowadays, a lot of witches and warlocks will still do it and just pray they don't get caught.

The thought of hurting my mate, hurting Izzy, makes me physically nauseous.

Izzy's mouth drops open in shock. "That's fucking horrible."

"It is, but it's the way of their kind." I clear my throat and hurry to get us back on track.

It won't be long until my brother and his friends come sniffing around, searching for Izzy.

And I'm certain that's the last thing she wants.

Hell, it's the last thing *I* want, as much as I hate to admit it.

"Anyway, Letty and Juan broke the mold when they fell in love. Letty's family members—all powerful witches in their own right—were appalled by her decision. If she were to kill her Blood Companion and claim his power for her own, she'd be unstoppable. But Letty refused. She loved him too much. And she thought Juan loved her as well.

"No one was more surprised than Letty when Juan attempted to kill her. We can't be sure what changed for him. I'm sure the witches and warlocks have extensive records of this entire ordeal, but we've only received verbal testimony.

"A lot of shifters believe that Juan became paranoid. Perhaps his own family was whispering in his ear that Letty planned on killing him. Or maybe he always planned to attack her. The *why* doesn't matter. All we know for certain is that Juan attacked Letty in their shared bedroom with an ax.

"She fought him off and begged him to stop, but he was consumed by rage and fear and confusion.

Those emotions... They can control you if you're not careful. Consume you."

I would know, after all. I'm experiencing all three of them in spades right now.

"And then what happened?" Izzy seems entranced by my story. Her eyes are wide and guileless and brimming with questions.

"She killed him," I answer without preamble. "She used her magic to fling him off of her, and he hit his head against the bedside table. Died instantly. She became consumed by grief and pain and retreated in on herself, refusing to show her face to the world.

"All she wanted was her mate back. She became so lonely and despondent that she came up with an idea —what if there was a way for her to not be so alone anymore? Witches can't bring the dead back to life, but they can dabble in soul magic...if they're powerful enough."

Soul magic has been a point of contention between witches and warlocks for centuries now. The current leaders—the Maiden, Mother, and Crone—have chosen to outlaw the practice of it. Too unpredictable. Too dangerous. Too unnatural.

I, personally, believe they banned soul magic simply because none of them could perform it. They hate the prospect of someone having more power than them. I can't prove my theory, of course, but it's the only one that makes sense.

Magic—regardless of the type—isn't inherently evil. Only the way you wield it is.

"Soul magic?" Izzy cants her head to the side.

Sunlight reflects off her golden hair, creating a tapestry of color in the blonde strands. White and brown and even red.

Beautiful.

So fucking beautiful.

I clear my throat again. "Soul magic is...well... It's complicated. It's been outlawed for centuries now, so not a lot of research has been done on it. Rumor has it that warlocks and witches who possess this type of magic can see auras, gauge intentions, talk to wayward spirits, sometimes even hear thoughts."

Izzy shudders. "That's fucking terrifying."

"It's tame compared to some of the other magic witches and warlocks can perform." I chuckle darkly and then pick up where I left off. "Legend states that Letty searched the beyond for her lover's soul but couldn't find it. Perhaps Juan didn't want to be found. Or maybe the universe decided he didn't deserve a second chance."

I shrug. "Either way, after weeks of fruitless searching, Letty was about to give up. It was only then that she felt a presence with her. It was a female, and someone Letty was positive she never spoke to in her life. This presence could barely talk coherently, but the two of them forged a bond.

"Both of them were lonely—one stuck on Earth by

herself; the other stuck in a strange plane of existence. So Letty did what she thought was best for both of them. She tugged on the entity's soul and brought her to Earth so they both wouldn't be alone anymore.

"Letty realized then that she felt strange. Different. There was a voice in her head that wasn't her own. A beast, so to speak. She had instincts she never had before. Letty realized that she *did* bring the beast back with her—by trapping the creature in her body."

"A wolf..." Izzy breathes in awe.

I nod once. "That's right. The wolves are actually creatures from a different plane of existence—a different world, so to speak—that traveled to Earth. They can only survive when they're in a host's body. Think of it as a...parasite." My wolf snarls angrily at being compared to something so demeaning. "We could probably survive without our wolves, but our wolves can't survive without us.

"Over time, the bond between the human and wolf evolved until the two became virtually the same person. They have the same thoughts, wants, fears, desires." I offer her a brittle smile. "We are the wolf now. They are us. I'm not sure we'll ever be able to unbraid ourselves from each other."

And I'm not sure any of us want to. Despite my fear of the future—my fear of turning feral—I can't imagine life without my wolf. He's a part of me, the good and the bad.

"Are you all descendants of Letty?" Izzy asks, frowning.

"No." I shake my head with a tiny smile. "Apparently, when Letty pulled her wolf to Earth, she also transported all of the other animals as well. Wolves and horses and cheetahs and lions and even a creature that resembles a dragon. They all latched on to the nearest witch or warlock they could find—only humans with magic in their veins can survive the merging." I spread my arms wide. "And thus, shifters came to be."

Izzy seems to be processing the story. Her chin is tilted upwards in contemplation, and her brows are furrowed.

After a moment, she lowers her gaze back to me and says, her tone carefully neutral, "Why did you refer to me as yours? And what does a mate mark mean?"

Oh...fuck.

Three

IZZY

Mr. Montgomery stares at me as if I just whipped out a blue, tentacled, alien dildo and then taped it to my forehead like a unicorn horn. A potent combination of disbelief, horror, and reluctance lines his handsome face.

But I don't back down, despite his silence. I refuse to.

My head reels from all of the information thrown my way. Wolves? Witches? Warlocks? Blood Companions? Hearts? This feels like something plucked straight out of a bad romance-turned-horror movie.

Instinctively, I lower my gaze to my arm once more. I can't stop myself. I *need* to see the brand on my skin. Because that's what it feels like—a brand. Owning me. Possessing me. Claiming me.

My sweater, however, obscures the mark from view.

Which is probably a good thing, considering I'm less than a second away from being homicidal.

Christian clears his throat and focuses on some of the papers scattered across his desk. There are even more on the floor, almost as if a tornado tore through his office before I arrived.

As I watch, my arms now folded over my chest, Christian begins the painstaking task of straightening the pages. His gaze doesn't stray my way. Not even for a second.

"As I said before, a wolf's Heart is similar to a witch's or warlock's Blood Companion. A fated mate, so to speak."

An uneasy feeling swirls in my stomach. "And do these wolves...kill their fated mates to gain power?"

Christian's head snaps up, and shock splays across his face. "God no!" He shakes his head vigorously. "No. It's not like that. Wolves treasure their Heart."

He blows out a heavy breath while simultaneously dragging a hand down his face. After a long moment of silence, he pushes the papers aside and focuses on me once more.

Being the object of his full attention is unnerving, to put it mildly. Unnerving...and arousing. A flush starts in my neck and creeps up to my cheeks.

"Explain," I say at last, grateful when my voice doesn't crack.

"As you probably guessed, wolves form packs when

they reach a certain age. They can be as small as two and as large as ten or more. Most of these packs live together in a community—"

"Like this one," I interrupt.

Christian's lips nudge upwards a quarter of an inch. "Like this one," he agrees. "When there are a lot of packs in one place, they usually elect the most powerful pack to settle disputes. We call them the Council. They also deal with all matters concerning nearby supernaturals. They're the spokespeople on behalf of the wolves, so to speak."

I purse my lips as I think this through. "And who is your Council?"

A strange, indecipherable emotion flickers across Christian's face. It's too fleeting for me to gauge, but it almost looked like...grief.

"My parents' pack, actually." He pauses and then adds, "Well, they *were* the Council. Now, it's my dad and a different pack."

I feel as if there's more to the story than what he's saying, but I decide to drop it for now. I have a feeling that this is one wound that hasn't yet scabbed over.

"So what do these packs have to do with the Heart?"

Christian runs a hand through his dark hair, ruffling the black strands. "When wolves are of a certain age, they form a pack. Usually that's signified by a mark forming on their skin." He absently runs a finger across his wrist, a forlorn expression marring his face before he masks it. "A lot of times, a wolf will receive a second mark as well—a mate mark."

"A mate mark," I repeat, feeling oddly numb. Empty. There's a hollowness in my chest that refuses to abate.

"Not all pack members will have a mate. Some wolves within the same pack will have different mates. Only strong packs will share a mate—what we call a Heart, though that term is often interchangeable with mate. It's believed that the Heart will strengthen the pack, make it more cohesive and unified. Wolves will know if they're a Heart by their eighteenth birthday. Before then, they'll just believe they're a mateless wolf."

"Only wolves are Hearts?" Something akin to jealousy climbs insipidly inside of me.

Christian casts me a strange, unreadable look. "Usually, but not always. Sometimes a witch or warlock can be the Heart of a pack. Sometimes it's a vampire or a succubus or a—"

"Wait, wait. Wait a fucking minute. Back up." I hold my hands up as if I can somehow fend off his words, yet they continue to come at me, a knife that's all blade and no hilt. "Vampire? Succubus?"

Christian offers me a smile that's almost pitying. It instantly pisses me off.

"There's a lot you need to know, Isabella." He hesitates, his lips firming. "But I'm not sure I'm the one who should be telling you all of this. Your...your *mates* should." He speaks through clenched teeth.

"Mates?"

And you're not one of them?

He seems to realize what he said a second too late. His eyes widen in panic.

"Izzy—"

"I have *mates*?"

"I didn't mean for you to find out like this."

"Who are they?" I demand, but I know. I fucking know.

A wave of anger capsizes any rational thought in my head. All I know is rage. Rage and betrayal and fear —all three of them so potent they threaten to drown me.

Before Christian can answer my first question, I follow it up with, "Do they know? Do they fucking know that I'm their so-called Heart?"

His silence is answer enough.

Those cunt-licking, ass-kissing, dildo-fucking assholes! Why didn't they tell me?

And why does Ashton continue to push me away and hurt me if he knows?

I feel like an idiot.

A stupid, oblivious dumbass.

"How is this even possible?" I explode, throwing my arms up in the air. "I'm human. One hundred percent human."

"Perhaps—"

"Perhaps?!" I'm afraid to admit my voice rises to an embarrassing level. I'm sure scientists haven't even discovered this particular sound wave yet.

"We should sit down with Hale and Gerry—"

"Hale and Gerry?"

They know too?

Out of everyone, their betrayal hurts the most.

But can you even call it a betrayal?

What right did you have to know?

I place my knuckles against my forehead and groan.

"I'm fucking this all up, aren't I?" Christian's voice is tired. Weary.

"You're certainly not making this any better," I snap.

I don't know how I feel. What to think. How to process.

On one hand, it feels as if my entire life is a lie. Everyone knows this humongous secret while keeping me in the dark. They simply moved me where they wanted me to go—a puppet on strings. A pawn on a chessboard with no checkmate in sight.

On the other, what would I have done if I knew about this earlier? Freak out? Run away? Call them insane? If I didn't quite literally see my skin change and distort, I probably would've laughed in Christian's face.

So what does this all mean for me?

I don't get a chance to ponder.

The handle on the office door shakes once, twice, three times, but the lock holds.

Then Ashton's voice calls out, cocky and belligerent, "Christian? What the fuck are you doing? We need to talk about Isabella."

And I *lose my shit*.

Four

ASHTON

Never in a million years did I expect to receive a text from Desiree freaking Harper demanding I *Get my ass to school right this second or else I'll cut off your balls and feed them to you.*

I spent the last few hours in my father's office, poring over all of the details of the case while he watched. Exhaustion clings to me now, and my body feels heavy and leaden. It's a miracle I can keep my eyelids open for longer than a second at a time.

But as my father always says, our kind doesn't *get* tired.

We're the superior species.

The superior breed.

The superior...everything.

I'm not sure I ever willingly believed his rhetoric, but I also didn't argue against it. Not as much as I should have.

Dragging a hand down my face, I pause outside of Christian's door. If anyone were to know where Izzy ran off to, it'll be him. Even at a young age, my brother made sure to be keenly aware of all of the players on the board. He was like me, in a sense. Constantly studying the game so he could emerge victorious.

It's ironic that, in the end, he lost so spectacularly.

Christian Montgomery.

I'm surprised I didn't make the connection sooner. Montgomery is our mother's maiden name, after all.

An uneasy feeling swirls in my stomach as I hover my knuckles above the door, not daring to knock.

My relationship with my brother... It's complicated, to put it mildly. Not as volatile as the one between the twins, but definitely not loving either.

We used to be everything to each other, but that changed when Christian was revealed to be a lone wolf and not a member of my pack. He withdrew in on himself—that's the only word I can think of to use. *Withdrew*. The fire in his eyes dulled to a burning ember, and his smiles became less and less frequent.

Then, without a word, he disappeared. Father told me he chose to travel deep into the forest in order to protect the community.

I didn't want to believe it.

Christian wouldn't leave me behind without even a goodbye, would he?

For years, I imagined something horrible happened to him, and that's why he left. I read the obituaries every morning with a macabre sort of fascination, searching for any descriptions of my brother.

But there was no need.

He's alive and well, apparently.

And he didn't even bother to tell me he was back in town.

Betrayal sinks like a boulder in my gut, but I work to blank my expression.

That's another thing my father taught me—men in power shouldn't show their emotions. Because every time they do, the enemy gets another tool to use against them.

Power.

You have all the power here, Ashton.

Not him.

Not her.

Not your father.

You.

Taking a deep, shuddering breath, I lower my hand and twist the knob, determined to barge right on in.

Locked.

I frown and wiggle it again, but the door refuses to budge.

What the fuck?

Why would Christian lock his door?

Even if he were in a meeting, he wouldn't lock it. That's highly inappropriate, especially if he's with a student.

"Christian?" I tug ineffectually at the knob once

more before releasing it with a huff. "What the fuck are you doing? We need to talk about Isabella!"

I fold my arms over my chest as I wait for him to open the door and let me in.

A part of me doesn't want to see him.

The rest of me wants to run into my big brother's arms and demand that he take me away from here. Protect me. Tell me that I'm doing an okay job leading my pack.

But that little boy who constantly sought validation died a long time ago. I no longer need my brother to protect or look after me. I can do them both myself.

I no longer have a choice in the matter.

The door opens, and I brace myself, the muscles in my stomach tightening.

But it's not Christian staring back at me.

It's Isabella.

Her blue eyes are electric with fury, and red splotches explode on both of her cheeks. There's a noticeable tremble reverberating through her body as she points an accusatory finger at my chest.

At first, I think something happened. Was she hurt? Is it the killer? Then I fear Christian did something to her—and instantly feel like a piece of shit for having that thought in the first place.

I don't have to wait too long for an explanation.

"You motherfucker!" she hisses, the noise coming through heavily clenched teeth.

I refuse to let my mask slip. "I don't believe I fucked any mothers as of late," I deadpan.

"When were you going to tell me?" She once again jabs a finger at my chest, and a tiny thrill shoots through me at the connection.

Warmth seems to emanate from her, as if she houses an internal fire.

"Tell you what?" I ask.

Now I'm confused. I glance at Christian over her shoulder and arch an eyebrow, but my older brother looks away with a frown.

"Tell me about shifters and witches and mating bonds and Hearts!" Her voice rises in pitch with each consecutive word she says, and I'm suddenly grateful I didn't spot anyone lingering nearby when I walked through the hallways.

I don't know how we'd explain a screaming female to the faculty.

Then her words register, and all thoughts of secretaries and principals overhearing us vaporize.

I open my mouth, close it, and then open it again. I can't find the words to speak. I think this is the first time that has ever happened to me. I'm always eloquent, always articulate, always the first with a quip or a comment to ease the tension.

But not now.

"Care to explain this?" Isabella rolls up her sleeve and thrusts her bicep into my face, and all I can do is gape at her branded skin.

I've seen this image more times than I care to admit every time I look in the mirror.

I dip my gaze to my own arm for a fraction of a second before focusing on her—this tiny female full of unfettered energy, violence, and anger. She truly is a hurricane contained in a woman.

"It seems as if you don't need any explanation," I say carefully. Slowly. Cautiously.

I feel as if I'm approaching a rabid dog, one that's foaming at the mouth and snarling. If I move too quickly, she'll attack, and I'll feel the full impact of her bite.

"You truly are an asshole. You know that?" Tears well in her eyes, but she doesn't let them fall.

They hang there suspended, crystalline shards that refract the artificial lighting in Christian's office.

"I've been told that on more than one occasion." I cross my arms over my chest as I study my mate intently.

She's everything I've ever wanted in a woman—strong, fierce, protective of those she cares about, and kind. So, so kind, despite the shit hand she's been dealt so far in life.

But I can't have her.

None of us can.

She's Little Red Riding Hood, and we're the big, bad, scary wolves intent on chewing her up and spitting her out. What kind of life can she have with us?

We're beasts, monsters, creatures of the night, and she's…innocent. Pure. Sweet.

I remember my father's words from only two nights ago. At the time, I hadn't thought anything of them, but now I can't help but wonder if he knew, somehow, what Isabella is to us. To me.

"There are humans, and there are monsters," he says, sipping idly from his teacup. Though his words are addressed to me, he doesn't look away from the newspaper he's reading. "And sometimes they overlap." At that, he lowers the paper and gestures towards an article detailing the sexual assault of a college student. "But if you force a human to play with the monsters, what do you think will happen?" He chuckles, the noise devoid of any genuine mirth. "They'll have no choice but to become one just to survive."

He couldn't have been referring to Isabella, could he?

My father says weird shit all the time—trying to divulge life lessons before I take over the Council for him.

And yet…

I don't want Isabella to turn into a monster.

This world isn't safe for her. *I'm* not safe for her.

What the fuck was Christian thinking telling her the truth?

Idiot.

Maybe he thought he was helping me out. Or maybe his years in the forest fucked with his head.

Either way, he put me in a predicament I'm not sure how to get out of.

Hurt her.

Send her away.

You don't need her.

You don't want her.

I clear my throat and push back my shoulders. I tell myself I don't have a choice. Christian brought Isabella into this mess; I'm the one getting her out of it. I repeat that until I'm blue in the face, but I don't believe a word of it.

It's not selflessness driving my actions, but something inherently darker, almost sinister.

"I never intended on telling you the truth," I tell her blandly, ignoring her sharp intake of breath. "Because I never intended on mating with you. Still don't, if I'm being completely honest."

Hurt flickers across her face, there and gone before I can even fully register it. Her lips compress in a straight line, but she doesn't tell me to stop talking. She doesn't cry and beg and plead for me to change my mind. She just stares at me with hard blue eyes, a multitude of emotions swarming in their depths.

"AJ..." Christian steps forward, but I hold my hand up to stop my older brother.

"This has nothing to do with you," I say to him, not bothering to pull my attention off of Isabella.

"He's right," Isabella says dryly, still keeping her

gaze on me. "It has to do with us. Though... There is no us, is there?"

A lump manifests in my throat. Swallowing it down proves to be impossible. "No."

"Because you're...what? Are you rejecting me or something? Is that a thing?"

I will my heart to harden and frost over. It's the only way I'll get through this conversation in one piece. Later, when I'm alone, the organ will shatter, but I'll be the only one who will face the consequences. The only one who will feel the pain of my insides slicing me to ribbons. The only one who will bleed out.

"We don't want you, Isabella." I keep my voice cold and my expression neutral.

Even still, she flinches as if I screamed those words at her. I wonder if she picked up on the plurality of my statement. I know I shouldn't make this decision for my brothers, but they're so blinded by her charms that they can't see how dangerous this pairing truly is. For her and for us.

"I don't know how much you know—"

"I know enough," she snaps.

"But you're human." I allow my upper lip to curl away from my teeth derisively. "And we're not."

"Ashton!" Christian's voice is sharper than I ever remember hearing it before. Even when he used to scream at Dad over something stupid... He never got this angry. My older brother's expression is practically thunderous as he glares at me, his hands fisted by his sides. "What the *fuck* are you doing?"

"This"—I hold up Isabella's arm so her mating mark catches in the light—"is a mistake."

"A mistake," Isabella repeats numbly.

"My pack has already chosen a mate." God, I just can't help myself, can I? I need to stab the knife even deeper into her back. Need to make her bleed the way I am. The way my brothers will when they discover what I've just done. "We'll be mated to Desiree after graduation. We chose her."

I hate myself.

I really, really hate myself.

Isabella stares at me for a long moment, and her eyes glimmer with so much pain that I almost take back the words. But I don't. Because I'm an asshole and a coward and a leader. I need to do what's best for my brothers and our mate—even if that means breaking all of our hearts in the process.

Tears well in her eyes, but just like before, they don't fall. Her lower lip begins to tremble, though, despite her best efforts.

"Desiree?" she rasps out shakily. "As in, my *friend* Desiree?"

I sneer. "Why do you think she wanted to be friends with you in the first place? No doubt scoping out the competition."

I know that isn't the truth—Desiree is as repulsed by us as we are by her and seems oddly entranced by

Isabella—but something is broken inside of me. I just want everyone in this world to hurt because maybe that will heal something inside of me.

I'm a sick, twisted bastard.

Never claimed to be anything but.

"I see." Isabella's face goes carefully blank.

And I know then that I fucked up. I desperately wish I could take everything back and apologize for what I just said. There'll be no coming back from this. She'll never forgive me. My brothers will never forgive me.

Yet I don't take the words back.

I don't apologize.

I don't say anything as she pushes past me and stalks out of the office, her little hands balled into fists and her chest heaving.

Christian stares at me, his eyes brimming with unfettered hatred, and a little piece of me dies inside. Or maybe I'm already dead inside. Who the fuck knows anymore?

"What the hell did you just do?" Christian breathes in horror.

But I don't have an answer for him.

Because honestly? I don't know what the hell I just did.

I just pray I made the right decision and my brothers will forgive me in the end.

Five

IZZY

I don't even notice Desiree until I practically plow into her.

"Woah there." She places her hands on my shoulders in an attempt to steady me, then she pauses when she gets a good look at my face. Her brows crease, and a frown touches her lips.

Lips that Ashton and the others have probably tasted.

I feel dizzy and sick just thinking about it.

And I hate the fact that I have a reaction in the first place.

"Iz, are you okay?" she asks with concern.

Or, at least, I think it's concern. Ashton's words replay on a continuous loop in my head—a never-ending racetrack that I can't escape from no matter how fast or far I run.

Is Desiree just using me to get close to the guys?

Does she see me as competition? Why is there always this mentality that women need to compete against each other to win the affections of a man?

"Iz?" she repeats, squeezing my shoulders.

"D-don't touch me." I stumble back a step, and her arms fall to her sides as hurt flickers across her face.

We stand just outside Christian's office. She must've been waiting for me.

Or for Ashton.

Good. She can fucking have him.

Even as I think that, my traitorous heart pinches painfully. I despise Ashton with an intensity I've never felt before, but at the same time, I desire him just as much.

The conflicting emotions swirl around and around in me like a tornado, collecting debris and broken furniture and worn-down bricks. Soon, the tornado will dissipate, and all of the trash will crash down on everyone in the immediate vicinity, burying them alive.

Burying *me* alive.

"What the fuck is going on?" she demands, placing her hands on her hips and scowling.

I open my mouth to answer but then immediately snap it shut when the office door behind me creaks.

I don't even need to look to know that it's Ashton. I can sense him standing there, the heat he emits almost palpable. My stomach twists into a dozen knots, and I inhale sharply.

"Desiree. Thank you for waiting." Ashton shoulders past me without a word.

Grabs Desiree's shoulders.

Spins her to face him.

Lowers his head.

And I take off in a sprint, hating him, hating her, hating everyone in this godforsaken town. There's so much fucking hate in my heart that I feel as if I'm dying. It's a corrosive acid wreaking havoc on my insides, destroying everything it comes into contact with.

Someone says my name, but I don't know if it's Desiree, Ashton, or even Christian. I wouldn't look back no matter who it is.

Fuck them all.

I'm done with the secrets and the lies and the tiny voice in the back of my head telling me I'll never be good enough. A tiny voice that sounds suspiciously like Ashton's, if I'm being honest.

I feel the burn of tears in my eyes, but I know they're a product of my growing anger and frustration —not sadness. I don't know Ashton well enough to be heartbroken. And Desiree? Yeah, that stung like a bitch, but I'll get over it.

I always do.

Even still, another piece of my heart crumbles to dust in tandem with my steps.

Away. Away. Away.

I need to get away.

Farther down the hall, I spot a familiar shock of golden hair framing an angular face and high cheekbones. A pair of glasses rests on his nose, a startling contradiction to the tattoos on his arm.

Ethan.

He smiles and lifts his arm to wave.

Nope.

Not today.

Because with all of the revelations I just discovered, I don't know what I'll do if I were to come into contact with him. Scream at him for keeping me in the dark? Demand to know why he pretended to be my friend if he planned to leave me for Desiree? Cry?

I have a feeling it'll be the latter, and that'll piss me off.

Pivoting on my heel—and ignoring the confused expression on his handsome face—I stomp towards the back exit of the school.

I don't have a particular destination in mind, but as long as it's *away from here*, I'll survive. I'm not sure if I can even go home. Knowing that Gerry and Hale kept this from me...

What about Jake, Lissa, and Seth? Do they know too?

My heart fissures at the prospect. Jake has become my best friend. If he knew this entire time and didn't tell me—

I shake my head to clear it of the errant thought.

No. I can't make any assumptions. For now, I have

to assume that Jake and my other foster siblings are as oblivious to this new world as I am. I can't assume everyone is in on this conspiracy—I'll go insane if I do.

There has to be at least one person still on my side.

I greedily inhale lungfuls of fresh air as I step outside. The stench of pine and stagnated mildew clogs my senses as I skirt around the edge of the school.

I don't have a car, but that's okay. There's a collection of stores and restaurants not too far from school where I can set up shop while I get my mind in some semblance of working order. Then I can pick apart what Christian and Ashton told me and—

Someone grips my shoulder, and I react without thinking.

I whirl, reaching for the wrist of my attacker and squeezing it hard enough to bruise. Then I thrust my leg out in a swooping kick that catches the backs of his knees. He falls to the ground with a pained "oomph," and I collapse on top of him, still holding his wrist.

Ansel blinks up at me in surprise.

Some of the adrenaline riding my system dissipates as I stare into his face.

Oh...

Oh fuck.

Not again.

"Ansel?" I quickly scramble off of him, panic fueling my movements. "I'm so sorry. I didn't know it was you, and you startled me—"

"Did you just...dropkick me?" He continues to stare up at me incredulously.

"I wouldn't necessarily say I *drop*kicked you, but..." I anxiously run a hand through my tangled curls. For some inexplicable reason, *this* is what thaws those pesky tears. A few traitorous ones cascade down my cheeks. "I'm sorry. I didn't mean to... I'm sorry."

Away. Away. Away.

I stumble backwards a few steps, not taking my eyes off my fallen classmate. His brown hair—normally meticulously combed—is disheveled. His shirt is slightly askew as well, revealing a sliver of his pale neck.

What the fuck is wrong with me?

I'm losing my damn mind.

Everything just seems to be converging on me at once. I feel scared and overwhelmed and confused. Every time I think I have an answer, a new question pops into existence. The people I thought I could trust turned out to be frauds.

I could handle not knowing about shifters and witches and other supernaturals. That has nothing to do with me, and I understand their wariness to tell a stranger.

However, what I can't handle is being smack dab in the middle of this mess and still being left in the dark. I'm apparently *mated* to some of these men.

What the hell does that even mean? Am I going to be forced to choose one?

I don't want any of them, if I'm being completely honest. Ashton can burn in hell.

I'm not as mad at the other three, but their betrayal still smarts. I've begun to trust Ethan and Emery. Open up to them. And this entire time, they've known exactly who I am to them.

Reid's a different story. I realize that I don't feel any way towards him, good or bad. On one hand, he kept this a secret, but he also didn't pretend to be my friend.

So am I less mad at Reid than the others?

Images bombard me.

Reid tackling Grayson to the ground in my bedroom, his face distorted in fury.

The sheer possessiveness radiating from his eyes when he stared at me.

The growl that left his lips.

No, I'm equally mad at Reid, just for a different reason.

And what about Grayson? What part does he play in all of this? He's dating the twins' sister. Does that mean he's her mate? Then why did he kiss me? If he knew about this the entire time, I'd *never* forgive him. Never.

"I saw you stomping through school." Ansel winces as he sits upright, and I instantly feel like shit. "You looked upset. I wanted to check in on you."

"So you're not a hall monitor prepared to drag my ass to detention?" I tease, though my voice wobbles near the end, betraying my true feelings.

Ansel's face turns ten shades of red. "Um…" He absently pulls at his shirt collar. "I'm technically off duty—"

"No fucking way." Some of my anger dissolves in the face of this new discovery. "Hall monitors are actually a thing? I thought that was just something I saw in shitty pre-teen shows."

Even sitting down, he manages to lord over me. He has this air of superiority that commands respect, made even more prominent when he pushes out his chest like a preening peacock.

"I'll have you know that it's actually an esteemed position—"

"Do you wear vests?" I quip. "Sashes? Please tell me you have a walkie-talkie."

Ansel's cheeks burn crimson. "Shut up."

"Do you have a weapon? What is it? A ruler that you spank disobedient kids with?"

He gracefully moves to his feet and brushes at a few loose pebbles sticking to his pants. He attempts to tame his hair, but that lone chocolate strand refuses to cooperate, continuing to flop forward.

With a sigh, he gives up and focuses on me. "If you keep being a brat, then I won't show you the surprise."

Something about his words causes a strange heat to spiral through me. Probably being referred to as a brat.

Kinky bitch.

"A surprise?" I take a step closer to him, my curiosity piqued.

His face is still pink, but he manages a tentative smile, some of his earlier bravado fading. "You looked upset. I think I have an idea how to help with that."

He begins to move towards the parking lot, and after only a moment of hesitation, I follow him.

"The great Ansel is skipping school," I say in feigned horror. "What would everyone think?"

"That I've gone mad," he mumbles under his breath.

The words are so soft, I'm not sure if he intended for me to hear them.

Even still, I can't help but say, "That makes two of us."

He pivots on his heel and extends his hand out for me to take. His fingers are long and graceful, almost as if they belong to a piano player. I can picture them running up and down the ivory keys. And up and down my body...

"What do you say, Isabella Martin? Do you want to skip school and go on an adventure with me today?"

Six

IZZY

"What is this place?" I eye the tiny building dubiously.

It's smack dab downtown, nestled between a diner and a clothing store, with wood siding and two opaque windows. The sign above the door reads *Rage Room* in huge block letters.

Ansel simply grins mischievously, an unfamiliar twinkle entering his eyes, and holds the door open for me to step inside. A bell jingles above, announcing our arrival.

At first glance, I can't tell what business we just walked into. There's a counter against the far wall, but there's no menu that I can see, nor are there any products. A hallway leads to several smaller rooms farther away. The walls are a dark blue, which contrasts with the white-tiled flooring.

A door I didn't notice before—located directly

behind the counter—opens, and a huge man steps forward. His gray hair is pulled back in a loose pony, a few strands tumbling wildly around his wrinkled face. His beard is long and thick. He looks as if he'd be found in a biker bar.

Despite his intimidating look, he offers Ansel a sly smile. "Shouldn't you be in school, kid?"

"Shouldn't you have a wife, Uncle?" Ansel shoots back—obviously addressing an inside joke I'm not a part of.

Wait...uncle?

The man chuckles and leans on the counter, his muscles straining against his leather jacket.

I try to search for a resemblance between the two men—straight-laced, meticulous Ansel and this rugged biker—before remembering that Ansel's adopted.

"You have a room available?" Ansel asks, pulling out his wallet and handing over his card.

The man waves Ansel away. "You know I don't accept your money."

He reaches beneath the counter and grabs a key ring. Twirling it between his fingers, he ventures down the hallway.

I glance at Ansel hesitantly, a stone of trepidation lodging in my throat, but he simply offers me a timid smile that instantly soothes my frayed nerves. I return it.

And when he offers me his hand? I take it.

Ansel's uncle stares at the two of us for a long

moment, his bushy eyebrows touching his hairline. A part of me wants to be embarrassed, though I don't know why. It's not as if we're doing anything wrong.

"Ahh. I see now." He flashes Ansel a knowing grin, and the tips of Ansel's ears pinken.

"Umm...Uncle Ted, this is Izzy. Izzy, meet my uncle."

"Nice to meet you, girl." Ted's withered face splits into a huge grin as he clasps my hand in both of his, giving it a decisive shake. "Is my nephew treating you well?"

"Do you have to speak?" Ansel gripes.

Ted ignores him and keeps his focus on me. "Because if he's not, I'll beat some sense into him."

"It's not like that!" Ansel sputters, appearing horrified.

Someone else may have been offended by how disgusted he seems by the prospect of us dating, but I know Ansel doesn't mean it like *that*. The brightness of his cheeks is just another indication of how uncomfortable this conversation is making him.

I decide to put him out of his misery. After all, he played hero for me. It's only fair I repay the favor.

"Ansel is being a perfect nineteenth-century gentleman," I assure Ted, adopting a haughty, Victorian accent. "He took me out for tea and crumpets." Lowering my voice to a conspiratorial whisper, I add, "I even allowed him to look at my ankles."

Ted throws his head back in raucous laughter. I

can't help but compare him to a huge grizzly bear. And that, in turn, makes me think of shifters and Christian and Ashton and—

"So you two are...what's the word...courting?" Ted asks once he's gotten his laughter under control.

"We'll see." I wink at first Ted and then Ansel, who's blushing profusely.

When he meets my eyes, he slowly shakes his head, even as a tiny smile unfurls on the corners of his mouth.

"Grab the items you want," Ted instructs, opening up one of the doors at the end of the hall. "And get the protective gear on."

Ansel drags me into a room dominated by metal shelves. There's barely room to stand side by side. On one shelf, I see televisions, radios, computers, and iPads. On another are more miscellaneous items—a copier, a printer, and an overhead machine I used to see in school.

Ansel points out items at random to Ted as my confusion grows.

"What...?"

"Trust me?" His earnest eyes ensnare my own.

I don't have any reason to trust him, yet...

I do.

Slowly, never taking my gaze off his, I nod.

The smile that erupts on his face is radiant. Heat and butterflies vie for dominance in my stomach.

"Come on." Ansel leads me towards the far wall of

the room while Ted remains behind, grabbing the items Ansel indicated.

Ansel first hands me a navy jumpsuit.

"Um..."

"Just put it on, Izzy." Ansel rolls his eyes like my hesitation is ridiculous and annoying.

I step into the hideous jumpsuit and begin to pull it over my clothes. "Are you arresting me or something? Is that what this is? Because let me tell you...I won't survive long in prison. I don't have the face for it."

"Yes. You caught me. I'm taking you to a secluded location to put you in a jumpsuit and then ship you off to the nearest women's penitentiary," he deadpans.

"Oh, he jokes."

"Oh, she listens," he retorts, moving to stand in front of me.

He helps me pull up the suit the rest of the way. His fingers graze my collarbone, exacerbating the goose bumps already present there. A shiver that has nothing to do with the cold rushes through me.

I just pray Ansel doesn't notice.

Once the jumpsuit is in place, he steps away and returns with green gloves and a glass shield mask.

"Okay, now this is getting weird," I tell him as I take the objects and put them on. I feel ridiculous and clumpy. "Is this some kind of kink you're secretly into?"

"What?" He blushes and quickly lowers his eyes from mine. "No! Of course not!"

I lift my hand to cover the laugh that threatens to bubble up. Ansel seems to understand sarcasm and jokes...unless a sexual innuendo is involved. Only then will he take my words literally and blush brighter than a nun in a porn shop.

"I'm joking," I tell him, pushing up on my tiptoes to place my hands on his shoulders. I can practically feel his muscles relax. "But are you going to tell me what this is?"

"Have you never heard of break-room therapy before?" he asks, eyebrows lifting.

"Why does that conjure up images of a bunch of stuffy businessmen and women sitting around a table, eating their lunches and discussing the weather?"

"Not that type of breakroom, pretty girl." Ansel gently grabs my wrists and removes my hands from his shoulders.

Did he just call me pretty?

Warmth winds its way down my spine.

"Then what...?"

"Come on." Ansel once again guides me forward. "Let's go watch you break the shit out of stuff."

Seven

IZZY

Apparently, all a girl needs in life is a single hour of destroying the ever-loving shit out of a dozen or so items.

Every second that passes seems to lift a weight off my shoulders. The tension doesn't completely abate, but it's no longer as suffocating as it once was. I can almost...breathe.

After the last item has been thoroughly destroyed, I step out of the room, remove my safety clothes, and thank Ted profusely.

"Come back anytime, kid." The older man flashes me a wink before slapping his hand down on Ansel's shoulder.

He whispers something to my new friend—too low for me to hear—and Ansel's cheeks erupt into flames. Both men flick their eyes to me before quickly looking away.

"What was that about?" I ask Ansel as soon as we step outside.

The air is chilly, but the sun does its job well, reaching out with spindly rays to warm my skin. I still need my jacket, but the weather isn't as bad as it could be.

"Nothing," Ansel answers quickly. *Too* quickly.

I arch an inquiring eyebrow at him, but he focuses straight ahead with steadfast determination. However, instead of heading immediately towards his car, he surprises me by skirting to the side and stopping in front of another small building that reads *Rosie's Diner*.

"Hungry?" he asks me.

I place a hand to my stomach, which suddenly resembles a bottomless pit. "Starving," I confess. "Who knew destroying computers could work up such an appetite?"

Ansel grants me a shy smile as he opens the door for me to step inside.

The restaurant is nearly empty—no surprise, considering the time of day—and boasts red booths, checkered floorboards, and jukeboxes. A middle-aged waitress in a pink blouse and white skirt nods her head in greeting from where she stands behind the counter.

"Take a seat anywhere, and I'll be with you two in a moment."

Ansel instinctively grabs my hand—*ohmygawd, he's holding my hand*—and leads me to a booth farthest away from the few patrons present. He slides into the booth, realizes he's still holding my hand, and then releases me as if I burned him. A rosy flush paints both his cheeks as he grabs the menus out from behind the napkin dispenser.

"Errr...sorry." He practically shoves a menu at me as I claim the seat opposite him.

A part of me wants to tease him and relish the red coloring his face, but I decide to change the subject.

"So...have you been here before?" I scan the menu quickly.

It's early enough that they're still serving breakfast, so I settle on pancakes, eggs, and bacon.

Ansel seems relieved at the topic change and closes his menu to give me his full attention. "Unfortunately more often than I'd like. I went through a period last year where I would spend most days with my uncle. He would come here every day after work. I think I have the menu memorized by now."

There's a lot to unpack in that statement—mainly why he would spend so much time with his uncle—but I push the questions aside for the time being.

"So what's good? I was going to get the pancake platter, but—"

"Go with the French toast," Ansel interjects. "I'm not normally a French toast type of guy, but I have to say that Freddie in the kitchen has a magic touch—"

"That sounds dirty," I deadpan, and he throws me a look.

"You need to get your mind cleansed, Illy." He chuckles softly, and my brain short-circuits.

Not because of what he said, but because of what he called me.

Illy.

I can't remember the last time anyone used that nickname with me.

Ansel's brows furrow, and he leans forward, resting his forearms on the table. "You okay? You look like you've seen a ghost."

"Just...that nickname." I try to wave away my strange reaction the way one would a pesky mosquito buzzing around their head. "My mom used to call me Illy."

A pregnant silence stretches between the two of us, but it's not an uncomfortable one. I can see Ansel turning over that information in his head, piecing together everything he knows about me and my past—which is, admittedly, not much.

"I'm sorry. I didn't know. I won't call you that anymore—"

"No, it's fine," I rush to reassure him. And this time, *my* cheeks are the ones to heat. "I-I like it when you call me that."

"You do? Because if it makes you uncomfortable, I don't have to—"

"No. I promise." I wave another flippant hand in the air. "Sorry for being a weirdo for a moment there."

"You're the exact opposite of a weirdo," Ansel tells

me with a snort. Then his expression softens, turning gentler. "You don't really talk about your birth family much."

"You don't either," I point out instinctively, before realizing how bitchy I sound. I wince and backtrack. "Sorry. That was rude."

"You make a fair point, though." Ansel folds his hands together on top of the table and tilts his head to study me closer.

His light-brown hair is brushed in such a way to emphasize his high cheekbones and chiseled jawline. He really is a beautiful man—almost too beautiful. His perfection intimidates me, if I'm being completely honest. I feel utterly inadequate beneath his perusal.

"Cards on the table," Ansel says, a frown touching his lips. "I don't know my birth parents. My mom and dad adopted me when I was a child, after a few years in the foster system. Then my dad died..." Sadness flashes across his face, shadowing his ethereal features, those plush lips of his curling downwards. He looks as if he's going to say more before changing his mind. "Well, anyway...I don't know my birth parents."

He punctuates the last sentence with a sheepish shrug.

I don't blame him for not wanting to talk about his adoptive parents. I met his mom only once, and that moment...

A shiver works its way down my spine as I remember the vitriol she aimed my way. The raw, unencumbered hatred. She blamed me for the death of her husband, as strange as it sounds. I never even met the woman before, let alone her lover.

Conversation ceases as the waitress comes to our table to take our orders. She teases Ansel about being here with a girl—much to his embarrassment—before leaving with promises to return shortly with our drinks.

Alone at last, I remove my silverware from my napkin and begin to idly rip it apart. I have no idea why. I just need to move my hands, to find an outlet for all of this restless energy skittering just beneath my skin.

Ansel doesn't push me to talk, which I appreciate, and I use the silence to get my thoughts in some semblance of working order.

"My parents died when I was young. Maybe four or five," I confess in a rush. "I don't remember them that well, but I know that my mom always used to call me Illy. When they died, I was put in the foster system, and I've been there ever since."

Ansel begins to tap his lean fingers against the table. "When do you turn eighteen and age out?"

I smirk. "Today, actually."

The color drains from his face. "T-today?"

"You didn't know? I thought that was the reason for this whole spontaneous adventure." I wave a hand in the air to emphasize what I mean.

Ansel shakes his head adamantly. "No. I didn't... I

didn't know. If I would've…" He scratches absently at the nape of his neck. "I just saw that you were upset and wanted to make you smile."

A plethora of butterflies releases in my stomach.

"I…I *was* upset, so thank you."

Ansel opens his mouth to respond but pauses when the waitress returns with our drinks—a coffee for me and a Coke for Ansel. Only when she leaves does Ansel resume our conversation.

"Why were you upset?"

"I…" What can I tell him? Certainly not the truth. He'll think I'm insane. Hell, even *I* think I'm insane. There's nothing crazier than believing the paranormal exists and that you're connected to it. "I discovered some of my friends were keeping secrets from me."

His brows lower. "Secrets?"

"Secrets that involve me," I explain. "And when I confronted one of them about it, he made me feel like it's all my fault in the first place. Like I'm the problem."

A thunderous expression crosses Ansel's face. "Let me guess. Does this 'friend' have a name that starts with Ash, ends with Ton, and rhymes with Ass-ton?"

A wry chuckle escapes me, especially at his use of my own nickname for the asshole. "That obvious?"

"I know that you've been getting…close to him and his friends. But Illy…" Ansel hesitantly reaches across the table until he brushes his pinkie against mine. Heat emanates from where he touches me, as if he houses some internal fire. "If he's treating you badly, then throw his ass to the curb. You deserve more than that."

Those damn butterflies return with a vengeance. I can feel them flapping about in the pit of my stomach.

"Trust me. I don't want anything to do with Ashton and his dumbass friends. Not until they apologize and beg for my forgiveness."

And even then, can I forgive them? We're apparently—god, this sounds insane, even to my own ears—mates. What does that entail? Sex? Am I going to be forced to be with them like *that*? In the carnal sense? Ashton hates me, Reid is indifferent to my presence, and the other two...

I don't want to think about that. About them. I still have free will, and right now my mind is screaming at me to run as far away from them as I can. They lied to me. Hurt me.

Who's to say they won't do it again?

Perhaps there's a way to break this so-called mythical bond.

I make a mental note to speak to Christian about it. He may just be the only person—wolf shifter, whatever—I can trust when it comes to the paranormal.

"Good." Ansel's pinkie brushes mine again for a fraction of a second before retreating.

A tendril of heat unfurls in my chest.

He clasps his hands together and straightens nearly imperceptibly, adopting picture-perfect posture that makes me feel like a troll in comparison. "Now...what big plans do you have to celebrate your eighteenth birthday?"

Eight

EMERY

I glance for the one billionth time today at the tiny velvet box in my hand.

Fuck, am I making the right decision?

Boyfriends give their girlfriends jewelry.

But friends don't give friends jewelry unless they have ulterior motives.

Is that what Izzy's going to think when I give her her birthday gift? That I have ulterior motives? That I want more from her than what she's willing to give me?

Obviously, I want more from her, but I also recognize that she's not ready for that, ready for me. She doesn't trust me yet, and I can't say I blame her. She doesn't know me from Joe, and we haven't spent enough time together to change that.

And of course, there's the whole Grayson thing...

A tremor works its way up my spine when I think

about how close that damn Hunter got to Izzy. He could've hurt her. Killed her.

But why he would want to hurt her eludes me. She's human, as far as I can tell, and the only connection she has to the paranormal world is...

I wet my lips with a sound of regret.

Could she have been targeted because of us?

Because of the mating bond?

How did anyone discover the truth?

Questions tumble around in my head as I wait impatiently at Izzy's locker for her to arrive. I didn't see her in the morning, but that's not completely unexpected. She's probably surrounded by friends and family wishing her a happy birthday. My girl has only been at this school for a short while, and already she has a plethora of friends who love and care for her.

The bell rings, signaling the beginning of my next class, and I reluctantly push away from her locker. I'll just have to give her the present during chemistry.

But when I arrive at the class a couple of hours later, I don't see Izzy anywhere. Ansel isn't there either, but knowing that asshole, he's probably off getting his anus bleached or something equally appalling.

An uneasy feeling swarms in my stomach as I claim my usual seat beside Ethan.

My brother looks as shitty as I feel. Dark smudges line both of his eyes, making me think he hasn't slept in a while. He runs a hand through his disheveled blond hair, then he removes his glasses to pinch the bridge of his nose. I know he always does this when he's fighting off an impending headache.

I want to ask him if he's okay but quickly decide against it.

Ethan's fine.

He's always fucking fine.

When chemistry ends, I hurry out of the classroom before anyone can stop me and make a beeline towards Jake in the cafeteria. The quarterback is joking with two of his friends—Kain and Dec—but their laughter immediately dwindles when I step up to the table.

Kain gives me a sour look, but Jake smiles good-naturedly and holds his fist out for me to bump.

"Hey, man. What's up?" he asks.

There's no point beating around the proverbial bush. "Do you know where Izzy is? I haven't seen her all day, and I wanted to give her something for her birthday."

Dec chuckles obnoxiously, muttering something under his breath about me being whipped, while Kain rolls his eyes. Assholes.

Jake, on the other hand, frowns in concern as he digs out his phone. "Yeah. I'll text her. We drove into school together, so she should be here. But come to think of it, I haven't seen her since this morning."

"I texted her a few times but haven't received a response." My words come out low—almost a growl.

I hate being separated from my mate on the best of

days, but today? On her birthday? It's like a punch to the gut. I should be with her, dammit, celebrating.

"That's weird. I wonder if she left her phone—" Jake breaks off abruptly as his phone pings with an incoming text. "Huh. She just responded."

A strange combination of jealousy and hurt arrows through me at the fact that she replied to his message and not any of mine.

"And?" I ask, feeling impatient.

I'm vaguely aware that Ethan has joined us, though he stands a little bit behind me. Still, I can tell he's hanging on to every word, just as eager as I am to hear about his mate. My mate. Our mate. Whatever.

Jake takes a huge bite of spaghetti while typing something out with his free hand.

"And." Jake shrugs casually and drops his phone. "She's not here."

I'm going to fucking strangle him.

"Where is she?" Ethan interjects from behind me.

He ventures a single step closer, and I tense, feeling as if I've just been electrocuted. I want nothing more than to crawl out of my own skin just being in his presence.

"Away," Jake answers evasively.

I narrow my eyes at my friend. "Away where?"

"Look." Jake's smile falls from his face, and he swivels completely on the bench to face us. "I don't know what the fuck you did or said to her—"

"What are you talking about?" I demand.

"—but she specifically asked me *not* to tell you or any of the other merry band of idiots her location." Jake's eyes promise murder as he glares up at me—a startling contrast to his jovial look from only moments before. "I swear to fuck if I discover you hurt her—"

"Jesus," Ethan murmurs, once again removing his glasses to wipe at his forehead.

"—I'll cut your bodies into tiny pieces and toss them into the ocean. You hear me?"

"That's disturbingly graphic," Dec drawls lazily.

"I think it's the perfect level of graphic," Kain muses, grinning from ear to ear.

He looks particularly pleased by this turn of events, and I have to wonder if he knows more about our situation than what he's letting on.

If he knows the truth of who Izzy is to us.

Jake focuses back on his lunch, effectively dismissing us, but I can see the rigid tension that lines his shoulders. He's pissed, and I have to wonder what Izzy told him to elicit such a reaction.

Honestly, I'm flabbergasted. I have no fucking idea what could've happened to make her mad at us. Is it because I didn't wish her a happy birthday first thing in the morning?

You know why she's mad, dumbass, a snarky voice retorts in my head. *You had her friend arrested last night.*

Fuck.

A cyclone of emotions—all of them bitter and

toxic—unleashes inside of me. The most prevalent of them all is self-loathing.

I hate the fact that I hurt her, but if I had to go back in time, I would do it all over again. Doesn't she understand that Grayson's dangerous? That he hurt people? She may not know about the supernatural world, but she would have to be deaf not to hear about the string of murders in town.

And if Grayson's behind them...

But what if he's not? the same voice asks. *What if he's innocent? You have no idea why he had those pictures on his phone. For all you know, he was investigating the deaths.*

I ignore the voice and focus, with great reluctance, on my brother. He looks just as lost as I feel and has yet to put his glasses back on. They dangle from his fingertips by his side.

"This is about Grayson, isn't it?" he asks, his voice too low for anyone but me to hear.

At least, I think that until Kain perks up like a dog scenting a bone. His dark eyes slide in our direction.

"Not here," I hiss, gripping my brother's sleeve and dragging him towards our usual table.

I half expect to see Izzy already there, waiting for us, her pink lips curved into a beatific smile.

But she isn't.

Desiree, however, stands directly beside our usual table, a fierce scowl on her face and her arms crossed over her chest, crinkling her blouse. She stares at me like I'm a piece of shit she had the displeasure of pushing out of her asshole.

Graphic description, I know, but fitting.

"How'd you sneak out from under the house that fell on you?" I ask caustically as I move to stand in front of her. "I don't hear any munchkins screaming in terror yet. Do they know you're still alive?"

Desiree doesn't rise to the bait—which pisses me off, because I could definitely go for a few rounds in the verbal sparring ring.

"We need to talk." Her scowl deepens, a feat I didn't think was possible.

"About?" Ethan asks cautiously.

"Izzy." Desiree aims her glare at him, but it lacks its usual heat. She just seems...tired. "And your fucking idiot of a friend who may have ruined everything for all of us."

"Ashton?" Something cold spirals through me. It feels as if the Grim Reaper himself is breathing down my neck. "What did he do?"

"Let's take this conversation elsewhere, shall we? I don't want the two of you wolfing out and eating the poor humans when you hear what I have to say."

Nine

ETHAN

"He did what?!"

I've never seen my brother so pissed before. Not when our mother grounded him from his PlayStation after he was caught cheating on a math test in seventh grade. Not when our older sister called him a worthless piece of shit during a particularly nasty fight. Not when Ashton's father told the both of us that we'll never amount to anything and don't deserve to rule the Council.

Not even when I lied to him about being clean and risked both our lives.

Raw, unencumbered fury distorts Emery's face until he doesn't even look like my twin anymore. His eyes glimmer amber with the power of his wolf, and he bares his teeth in a snarl.

Desiree, for her part, appears unaffected in the face of Emery's wrath. She folds her slender arms over her chest and cocks her hip out to the side, exuding an aura of feigned nonchalance.

"Your idiot packmate decided it would be a swell idea to lie to Izzy and tell her that we're dating." Her nose crinkles in disgust. "He even started to kiss me. Fortunately, he stopped as soon as she left the room, but the damage was done. Izzy thinks that the five of us are in a...relationship."

She shudders dramatically.

Emery collapses onto the desk in front of him as if his legs can no longer keep him upright. Some of his anger has been chased away, replaced by a combination of pain and surprise. Maybe even betrayal. It's that last emotion *I'm* feeling, a sucker punch straight to the chest.

Why would Ashton do this?

How *could* he do this?

Izzy's our mate, our Heart, and should be revered and protected, not pushed away. Not discarded.

Another headache is fast approaching—the fiftieth one today. For what feels like the billionth time in the last hour, I remove my glasses and attempt to rub out the muscles in my forehead.

It doesn't help.

The three of us are in an empty classroom directly across from the cafeteria. Desiree remains standing near the front of the room—eerily resembling a teacher about to lecture and scold her misbehaving students—while Emery sits on a desk in front of her.

I remain by the door, making sure no one interrupts us.

And making sure that no one gets the wrong fucking idea.

What would Izzy think if she were to see us now? Locked in a classroom with Desiree?

Everything Ashton said would be confirmed, even if it's the farthest thing possible from the truth.

Emery's head snaps up abruptly, and he levels Desiree with a penetrating glare that would make most wolf shifters shit their pants. Desiree simply appears bored.

"And you had nothing to do with this? This isn't some ploy to get Izzy away from us?" he asks, his words bordering on a growl. "Because even if we continue with this sham of a mating, that doesn't change the fact that you're a lone wolf, Desiree. You don't belong with us. You don't belong anywhere."

Ouch.

I may not like the girl, but even I can admit that crossed a line.

Desiree flinches as if he physically slapped her and then forces herself to adopt an impenetrable mask.

She straightens her shoulders and points an accusatory finger in Emery's direction. "Hurting Izzy is the last thing I want to do."

"And why is that?" I find myself asking, unable to bite my tongue a second longer.

Both Desiree and Emery turn towards me in surprise, as if they forgot I'm even in the room.

I push away from the wall and venture a step closer. "When you touched Izzy, you saw something, didn't you? A vision?"

Some shifters are given special gifts that go beyond merely shifting into an animal. She has what our scholars call "the sight," meaning she has visions of the future. Usually, these visions pertain to herself, but sometimes, they can feature others.

Desiree's expression clouds over, turning unreadable. "What I saw doesn't matter—"

"It fucking does matter if it has to do with our ma—" Emery cuts himself off before he can say the word "mate," but I can tell the damage is done.

Surprise flashes across Desiree's face for a fraction of a second before she manages to get herself under control. She clears her throat and moves until she's perching on the teacher's desk in front of Emery.

"It doesn't matter because it doesn't concern you," Desiree tells us firmly.

"But it concerns Izzy?" I ask, though I already know the answer to that.

Desiree flinches nearly imperceptibly. "Yes."

"What did you see?" Emery's suddenly in front of Desiree, desperation painted across his features. He grabs her shoulders and gives them a shake. "Is she in danger? What?"

Very slowly, Desiree flicks her eyes towards the

fingers crinkling her snow-white blouse. They frost over, turning glacial. "Remove your hands from me before I cut them off and feed them to you."

"It seems as if it's a trend to threaten bodily harm today," I murmur, thinking of Jake's threat from earlier.

Both of them ignore me.

"Tell me," Emery growls, baring down on her.

A low chuckle sounds from behind us, just as a camera clicks ominously.

Oh...fucking ducks.

All three of us whirl towards the intruder standing in the now opened doorway, a shit-eating grin on his face and his camera phone held directly in front of him.

Kain smirks and lowers his gaze to his phone screen. "I wonder how Izzy will feel when I send her this picture of the two of you alone in a classroom with Desiree."

He tsks his tongue in mock disapproval before turning the phone in our direction.

The picture... It looks damning. All I can see is Emery's back as he towers over Desiree, who's perched on the desk looking up at him. His hands are on her shoulders, and their faces are so close that only a few inches separate their lips.

Emery growls so ferociously I wouldn't be surprised if half the school heard it. "Delete it!"

Kain flashes him a smug smile, types something in

his phone, and then responds with a flippant, "Fine. It's deleted."

Suspicion hovers in the air, a needle-sharp blade.

"You did?" I ask.

"I did," Kain confirms, running a finger over his jawline. He pauses for a moment before adding, "After I sent the picture off to the lovely Isabella, of course."

He releases a low chuckle that makes me want to rush forward and slam my fist in his face. I'm not a violent person by any means—I'll save that for the other members of my pack—but just now, I wish for the ceiling to freaking fall on his stupid head and bury him alive.

"He's lying," Desiree snaps. "He doesn't have her number."

Kain offers a one-shouldered shrug. "I don't...but Jake does. And it was surprisingly easy to snag it from Jake's phone when he wasn't paying attention."

"What the *fuck* is your problem?" Emery snarls, advancing on the other wolf shifter.

Kain holds his ground, appearing oddly unbothered by the imminent threat. If anything, he almost seems amused.

"I just think Izzy should know that her mates are cheating on her with her new friend."

His claim—as ridiculous as it is—isn't what stops me dead in my tracks.

No, it's his use of the word "mate" that causes the

fine hairs on my arms to stand at attention. Emery goes perfectly still, his head cocked to the side with rigid tension.

"What did you just say?" I ask, panic crashing through me.

How the fuck does he know? He couldn't. It's impossible.

"You must think I'm an idiot, don't you?" Another chuckle escapes him. "I would have to be blind and stupid not to realize that Isabella—a human, might I add—is your fated mate. At least...for now."

"What the fuck do you mean by that?" Emery demands.

His eyes flash amber in tandem with his growing anger. Fur begins to sprout on his arms, and his chin lengthens, resembling a muzzle.

Fuck. Fuck. Fuck. Fuck.

Kain waves a hand in the air. "Doesn't matter." He turns to leave but pauses with his hand on the door-knob. Smug confidence radiates from him in tangible waves as he smirks at us over his shoulder. "I'd be more careful about spending alone time with your mistress if I were you. I wonder how many chances our lovely Isabella will give you?"

His laughter chases him out the door...as does a growling, rabid Emery.

He lunges for Kain, death written across every visage of his distorted face, but I'm there before he can attack the other wolf. I wrap my arms around my twin's stomach and attempt to hold him back.

Desiree, wisely, jumps to the side. She knows as well as I do that Emery will not react kindly to her presence.

"You need to calm the fudge down," I snap, automatically reverting to my child-friendly swearing. It's instinctive at this point. Half the time I don't even realize I'm doing it. "Kain isn't worth it. Do you know how much trouble you'll get in if you're caught fighting at school, let alone fighting as a freaking wolf?"

Emery snarls something unintelligible and bucks against me.

I simply tighten my grip on him.

"We both know that what Kain said isn't true. We're not having an affair with goddamn Desiree. Nothing happened today. We all know it. We can just tell Izzy our side of the story. And as for Ashton—"

Emery practically roars at the use of our packmate's name, and I wince at the noise. Probably shouldn't have mentioned him.

"We'll deal with him and his lies. I promise you. Everything will be okay. Everything—"

It's at that moment the classroom door opens, but this time, it's not Kain who steps inside.

No.

It's much, much worse than that.

"Guys! Emergency! Grayson was released. I don't

know what..." Ashton pauses and eyes the two of us with concern before taking a step forward. "What happened?"

Emery breaks free of my hold and lunges at Ashton.

Ten

IZZY

I can't turn away from the photo on my phone. All of my worries... All of my fears...

They all come crashing down on me in a tsunami I can't escape from, pulling me under and tossing me around like a rag doll.

In the photo, sent from an anonymous texter, Ethan and Emery are in a classroom with Desiree. I can't see Emery's face, but the tattoos on his bare arms, that messy blond head, and those strong shoulders are unmistakable. He has his hands on Desiree's shoulders and is leaning down as if to kiss her. She's staring up at him with wide eyes.

I can only see half of Ethan's face, but I swear I see...heat in his eyes. Lust, maybe?

Jealousy threatens to capsize any rational thoughts or emotions. I have to remind myself repeatedly that I'm not dating either of the twins and a mating bond doesn't mean we have to be together. They obviously chose Desiree.

Everything we've been through has been a lie. And not just with the twins, but Desiree too. She pretended to be my friend, and for what? To keep an eye on the competition? Perhaps she truly was my friend until I got in the way of her relationship with the guys.

My emotions swirl around and around in my chest —a toxic, acerbic vortex that tastes like ash on my tongue—and it takes considerable effort to lower my phone back to my lap.

Ansel glances at me out of the corner of his eyes. "Everything okay?"

A part of me wants to snap at him and say that I'm fine.

But he's been wonderful today and doesn't deserve any of my misplaced ire.

I squeeze my eyelids shut and whisper, "I don't want to talk about it."

I feel rather than see him place his hand over mine. He gives it a single squeeze before releasing me.

We drive the rest of the way in silence.

I only reopen my eyes when the car begins to slow down.

"Izzy?" Ansel's voice is rife with concern.

"Yeah?"

"Are you sure this is the right address?"

We've stopped in front of a dilapidated apartment complex that has seen better days. Mold covers the roof, and overgrown weeds line the front entrance. Most of the windows are either broken, boarded up, or missing entirely.

I can see why Ansel is concerned.

"I can't go home to Hale and Gerry right now," I whisper, a ball of tension crawling up my throat. "I just...can't."

"And this place is better?" One of Ansel's elegant eyebrows touches his hairline. "If you don't want to go home, you can stay with me—"

"Do you really think your mom will allow that?"

"Who cares what she thinks?" Ansel's fingers begin to tap rapidly against the steering wheel, a clear indicator of his agitation. "We can get a hotel or something on the other side of town. Anything will be better than this."

Before I can think better of it, I lean across the center console and plant a chaste kiss on his cheek. Ansel stops tapping immediately, and a ruddy flush explodes across his face, turning even the tips of his ears a bright, neon pink. A muscle bobs in his throat as he swallows.

"You're sweet, Ansel, but I'll be fine. I've been here before."

"Do you know someone who lives here?"

"My friend does. My *best* friend."

Though Grayson won't be here for me to take comfort in.

Fuck, where even is he? When will he be home? Why did Ashton and the others take him away?

What if he's injured? Hurt? Dead?

What if—?

I swallow down the sharp spike of fear. It'll do me no good focusing on the "what-ifs."

A strange look inches across Ansel's face before he gives a reluctant nod.

"All right. But can you just..." The blush that dissipated during our conversation returns with a vengeance. "Can you just text me every once in a while? So I know you're okay?"

Heat and butterflies vie for dominance in my stomach, and I wonder what Ansel would do if I didn't just kiss his cheek...but his lips too. His firm, plush lips that look as if they're made for kissing—

I clear my throat, trying to ignore the surge of energy shimmying down my back.

"I will. I promise. But Ansel, I'll be fine. I can take care of myself."

"I know." There's not a hint of duplicity in Ansel's voice. He says those two words as if he's stating a fact. "You're the strongest woman I've ever met, Illy. Just be careful, okay?"

"Always." Warmth snakes through me as I hold his gaze.

His eyes dip towards my lips, and I wonder if he's thinking about kissing me. Do I even want him to kiss me? After the day I had, and all I learned, the answer to that question should be no, but the heat ravaging my body suggests otherwise. I'm a vibrating mass of knife-edged molecules, and all of them are inching towards him.

But then Ansel turns away and focuses his attention back out the windshield once more.

"See you tomorrow?" he asks as both disappointment and relief settle in my stomach.

"Yeah, of course."

Even if I want nothing to do with the four assholes who claim to be my mates, I refuse to drop out of school. I need to graduate, receive my degree, and then I'll get the hell out of this town. Fuck the paranormal.

"And...happy birthday, Illy. I hope it ends better than it started."

Me too, Ansel. Me too.

Ansel waits until I'm inside the building before his car slowly pulls away. I watch until it disappears around the corner before taking the steps two at a time. The damn elevator in Grayson's apartment is always out of order. I keep telling him he should move somewhere else, but he says it doesn't matter where he lives, only that he's near me.

When I reach his apartment, I half expect to find Grayson sitting on his bed, waiting for me.

I'm only marginally disappointed when I find the room empty, the lights off.

I don't have anything with me except for my backpack and the clothes on my back, but that's okay. I started over with less than that on more than one occasion. I can do it again.

I toss my backpack onto the bed and then take a moment to return some of the text messages I've received throughout the day. I'm furious at most of the people in my life, but I'm not a complete bitch who wants them to worry unnecessarily.

HALE

Your teachers told me you skipped classes today. Decided to have an early birthday celebration? LOL! Happy birthday!

HALE

You're still not home yet. Is everything okay?

HALE

Isabella, call me. We're worried.

IZZY

I'm fine. I'm safe. I just need to be by myself for a little bit to get my head on straight.

Before I can even click out of the message, Hale shoots back a reply.

HALE

Is this about what happened yesterday? With your friend?

Yes. No. Maybe.

How do I tell Hale it's *everything*? All of the lies

and secrets and deceit? I'm not ready to have that particular conversation with him just yet.

I leave his message unanswered and then flick to Gerry's messages. He sent me a standard happy birthday message with a plethora of GIFs. His most recent one is a simple...

GERRY

You okay, kid?

IZZY

I will be. Just need to take some time for myself. I'm safe. I'll be back soon.

Ethan, Emery, and Desiree have all sent me over a dozen messages each, but I ignore them all. There's nothing from Ashton—no surprise—but there is a text from Reid. Curiosity makes me click on it, despite my trepidation.

REID

Happy birthday.

REID

Sorry.

REID

About yesterday.

REID

I'm an asshole.

I snort before I can stop myself.

IZZY

Yeah, you kind of are.

REID

Never claimed not to be.

There's a pause, and then my phone chimes once more.

REID

You doing okay?

IZZY

Why wouldn't I be?

REID

You weren't at school today.

IZZY

You're never at school.

REID

Because I'm an asshole.

A bark of shocked laughter escapes me before I can stop it. Damn him.

Izzy

What does that have to do with skipping school?

REID

Don't know.

REID

Felt relevant.

REID

Can we talk?

Reid...wants to talk to me? About Grayson?

Or is it about the mating bond? Is he aware that Christian told me the truth? Does he want to tell me he's secretly in love with Desiree? That Michelle chick?

I don't respond to his last message, mainly because I don't know what to say to him. Reid is the most mysterious of them all, and also the most elusive. He's surrounded by cement walls, and those walls are reinforced with barbed wire and prickly thorns. Trying to scale said walls will lead to nothing but pain.

I'm just about to exit out of my phone when I see a message from Silas, my boss at the movie theater.

SILAS

Can you work tomorrow? 6-11?

SILAS

Oh happy birthday

IZZY

Yeah. I can be there. And thank you for the happy birthday message!

Silas doesn't respond, but I'm not surprised. He doesn't seem like the type of person who would spend a lot of time on his phone.

Sighing, I plug my phone into Grayson's charger and then belly flop onto the bed. I'd like to say that the blankets are still warm from Grayson's body heat, but that would be a lie. They're actually cold to the touch.

But they smell like him.

I can't help but inhale deeply, wishing he were here with me. Holding me. Promising everything will be okay.

Then I instantly feel guilty for having that thought to begin with.

He's not mine, no matter how much I wish he were. I have to let go of this childish crush or risk ruining our relationship once and for all.

God, I hope he's okay.

What even happens to people in...paranormal prison or whatever? And what did Grayson even do? What involvement does he have with this strange new world I've found myself in?

I shift on the bed, twisting so I'm no longer on my stomach but staring up at the ceiling while on my back. I place my hands on my chest and will my breathing to even out. I fear that if it doesn't, I'll pass out or spiral into a full-blown panic attack.

Deep breath in. Deep breath out. Deep breath in. Deep breath—

Something moves in the shadows by Grayson's window.

I jerk upright in bed with a gasp just as the figure lunges for me.

Eleven

IZZY

I kick out instinctively and then roll myself over the intruder so he's now underneath me. I brace myself over him, my heart hammering like a spooked rabbit, violence in my blood—

"Grayson?" I gape in disbelief as I stare into the face of my best friend.

My best friend...who I last saw being carted away by a bunch of wolf shifters.

"Izzy." His raspy voice is a balm to my bruised and tattered soul.

Tears instinctively spring to my eyes.

"How are you...? What happened? I thought..." I rub at my eyes with the back of my hand and release a slightly hysterical giggle. "How are you here?"

Grayson hesitates, an indecipherable emotion inching across his face, before he says, "They let me go."

"They let you go? What? God, I'm so confused. What did they even think you did? Why did they take you?" I belatedly realize that I'm still straddling him, my legs on either side of his lean hips and his hands on my waist, but he doesn't push me away or tell me to get off of him.

If anything, his grip on me tightens until I fear he'll leave behind finger-shaped bruises.

"Izzy, there's so much I need to tell you..."

Any hope that Grayson wasn't aware of the paranormal world evaporates. I can see it in his eyes, hear it in the unsteady thrumming of his heart against my palm.

He knows.

Fuck, he knows.

"About how the supernatural exists?" I ask with feigned nonchalance, watching his reaction carefully. "Like warlocks and witches and shifters and vampires?"

I have the great pleasure of seeing shock splay across his face, quickly followed by disbelief and confusion. His mouth opens, shuts, and then immediately opens again, though he doesn't release a single word. It seems as if I stole his ability to speak.

"How did you...?" He breaks off and coughs.

Immediately, I reach for the water bottle he always keeps by his bedside table and hand it to him. I make a move to get off of him, but he simply tightens his grip around my waist and pushes himself upright, resting his back against the headboard.

This position brings his crotch flush against my most sensitive area. I can feel how hard he is, even with the barriers of clothing between us.

A lump manifests in my throat, making swallowing impossible, and a wave of dizzying heat rushes through me.

"I know that the supernatural exists," I say, ignoring...that *thing* between his legs. Maybe if I don't focus on it, don't think about it, it'll go away. "Someone told me."

His brows arch downwards over glowering eyes. "Someone told you? And who is that someone?"

I have no idea what the rules are about spilling the beans to humans. The last thing I want to do is get Christian in trouble—or put him in harm's way. Just the thought sends icy terror careening down my spine.

"It doesn't matter." I lick my lips, struggling to find my next words. After a moment of silence, fraught with tension, I blurt out, "Are you...one of them?"

"One of them?"

"You know, a magic person thingy." I wiggle my fingers in the air to emphasize my point.

A wry grin tugs up the corners of his lips before he stifles it. "I'm not a warlock or a shifter, if that's what you're asking."

"Oh. Thank god. I thought—"

"I'm a vampire."

My brain short-circuits.

For the longest time, I'm not sure I heard him

correctly. Surely, he can't mean what I think he means, can he? Because if he means what I think he means, then he's meaning what he means, and that's what he can't mean because it's what I don't want him to mean.

And...

Now my brain is broken.

Completely and utterly broken.

I stare at him, unsure of what to say, unsure if words are even necessary, and he watches me with that cool intensity I've come to expect from him.

Slowly, giving me ample opportunity to pull away, his fingers travel up to my neck.

To the pendant he gave me for my birthday.

He tugs on it lightly, a strange expression crossing his features.

"Your heart is racing, Izzy. Are you...scared?" Disbelief is evident in his tone. Disbelief...and hurt.

His eyes shadow over, turning unreadable.

"You're a vampire?" My voice is a breathy whisper. I'm not sure if he's even able to hear it. It's almost drowned out by the sound of the air conditioning unit kicking on overhead.

"I wanted to tell you for years." He gently lowers the locket until it rests snugly between my breasts. There, his hand lingers, exacerbating the goose bumps that have sprouted on my arms. "But it wasn't safe—"

"I...I don't know what to say." I swallow around a sharp spike of bitter disappointment. "I'm so fucking sick of people keeping things from me and claiming it's for my protection."

"I know, baby, and I'm sorry."

"How are you even here?" I demand, grasping my anger and holding tight. I'm afraid of what will happen if I let it go, if I give in to one of the dozen other emotions percolating inside of me. "Why did they take you away? What did you *do*, Grayson? Why did you—?"

Grayson cuts off my ramblings, but not with his words.

No, just like before, that night in the forest behind Hale and Gerry's house, Grayson kisses me.

And my world explodes into fireworks.

Twelve

GRAYSON

This kiss is different from the last one we shared.

That one...

That one was fucking amazing. *She* was amazing. It was everything I never knew I wanted but now crave with the entirety of my being.

But this...

This is something else entirely.

I swear my soul claws its way out of my body in a desperate bid to merge itself with Izzy's. I can feel her inside of me—her essence oozing through my veins, filling every part of me. Even without the necklace, I know I'd feel her heartbeat. Taste the sweetness of her desire mingled with the bitter flavor of her fear. Hear her shallow breaths as she pants against my mouth. Smell her desire.

I'm not just one person anymore. I'm me...but I'm also her.

Mate.

My mate.

My heart jackhammers in my chest as I deepen the kiss, tangling my tongue with hers.

I always knew Izzy was different, but never in my wildest fantasies did I expect *this*.

Mates for vampires are immensely rare. So rare that most people think the bond is an urban legend. A myth.

Our Elders believe that all vampires have shifter blood in them—but the blood is diluted, having not been prevalent for generations. They claim that the first vampire was a product of two lone wolves mating. Their offspring became a creature that could only be satisfied by consuming blood.

I don't know for sure if that's true, but I do know that vampires used to experience a mating bond similar to the one shifters have with their Heart.

And this...

This incessant tugging in the center of my chest...

This merging of souls...

This heat that's sweeping through me like a forest fire...

I know without a shadow of a doubt that it's a mating bond.

Izzy. Is. Mine.

I always knew it, always felt it, but could never articulate it with words. From the very first moment she looked at me with those striking, fearless blue eyes, I was a goner. And I've fallen harder each and every day.

Joy explodes inside of me.

Mate.

My mate.

But then Izzy's next words douse the growing elation like water thrown on a bonfire.

"Wait. Wait. Wait." She pushes at my shoulders, and I immediately pull away, my lips swollen from the force of her kisses.

Izzy looks beautifully flushed in the moonlight snaking through the blinds in silver ribbons. Her blonde hair is disheveled from my fingers, and her pink lips are puffy. Satisfaction reverberates through me at the sight of her so unkempt.

Then I focus on her words.

"You need to explain things to me, Grayson. How long have you been a vampire? How did you get free of the wolves? Where even *were* you? Did you do what they accused you of? What about your girlfriend?"

The last thing I want to do is answer any of those questions—not when the majority of them can see her harmed or even killed. There's a reason I kept this secret from her, and it's not because I'm an asshole. I've wanted to tell her for years now about the supernatural world, but vampires are different from shifters.

We're volatile.

Angry.

Bitter.

Bloodthirsty.

My mom—may the bitch burn in hell for all of eternity—once told me that vampires are so wrathful because we're disconnected from our animal counterpart. According to her, we all have dormant beasts deep inside of us struggling to rise their way to the surface.

I think she's full of shit. I haven't felt anything resembling a wolf in my entire life, let alone any other animal.

All I know is that I need blood to silence the voices in my head, to create some semblance of order out of the dissonant chaos.

Like the wolf shifters, the vampires are ruled by a Council as well—what we call the Elders. All of them have been alive longer than I can comprehend and hate humans almost as much as they hate shifters.

If they knew about Izzy, about my feelings for her...

They'll kill her just to hurt me.

My position in vampiric society doesn't allow for me to have any attachments. From the very first moment I saw her, I knew I had to keep her a secret.

So I chose to shield her from the paranormal world the best I could.

But apparently that wasn't enough.

Someone told her the truth, and if I had to hazard a guess, I would say it was one of those idiotic wolf shifters who constantly hang off of her. They should be grateful I don't drain them dry and leave their corpses for their asshole parents to find.

I don't say all of that to Izzy, however. Instead, I tell her what I can.

"I didn't kill those women. I promise you." But I did unintentionally help the murderer who did. Indignant anger races through me—along with guilt—but I shove them both down before they can fester. "I work for the Elders—"

"The Elders?" She tilts her head to the side in confusion.

"They're sort of like the wolf shifter Council," I explain, reaching around her to grab my water bottle yet again. All of this talking has caused my throat to start acting up. It aches fiercely, almost as if someone took sandpaper to the skin there. "I...do odd jobs for them."

That's one way of saying I've been their personal assassin for the last ten or so years of my life.

Izzy's eyebrows scrunch together. "Okay...?"

"Someone discovered that and got a hold of me. Wanted me to dig up some dirt on a few wolf shifters." I swallow around the lump of guilt in my throat.

If I would've known that my actions would lead to those women's deaths, would I have done anything differently? I'd like to say yes, but I still remember the fear I felt when they threatened me with Izzy. Somehow, someway, they discovered what she meant to me and threatened to kill her if I didn't comply.

I don't say that to Izzy. The last thing I want is for her to feel guilt for my actions.

Izzy's eyes widen in horror as understanding dawns. "Those women..."

"They were female shifters. I swear to you I didn't know they would be killed. Once the first girl was murdered, I tried to back out, but..."

They threatened you. Told me they'll chop you up into tiny pieces and deliver each one to me every day for the rest of my life.

I take another swig from my water bottle before continuing. "That shit with Sidney... I swear to you it meant nothing. She was just a way for me to receive insight on the wolf shifters. I never kissed her or even touched her. I promise you."

There was one time Sidney tried to seduce me. I remember she asked me to meet her at her apartment before dinner, and when I arrived, she was sitting on the couch in nothing but a lacy teddy that left little to the imagination.

I turned right the fuck around.

"Your wolf...*friends* were right to arrest me. I'm sure my actions looked pretty damning." I flex my fingers on her waist before I reluctantly release her. "They took me to the Council building, and I was interviewed by some shifters. And then..."

"And then?" she presses, when it becomes apparent I'm not going to immediately continue.

"And then I discovered that my contact—the

Hunter who killed those wolves—was another wolf shifter."

Her breath hitches. "What?"

"I met with one of the higher-ranking Councilmembers. Matthew, I believe his name was. I think he's the father of those wolf shifter twins. Anyway, I told him what I knew, and he let me go."

"Just like that?" Her brows arrow downwards suspiciously, and I have to hold in my bark of humorless laughter.

No, it wasn't "just like that," but this is another thing I don't want to share with Izzy.

She doesn't need to know that they dragged me out of my cell and threw me into a separate room, which consisted of a tiny chair and a table full of torture equipment.

She doesn't need to know that I screamed myself raw after hours and hours of torture.

She doesn't need to know that only my enhanced healing capabilities helped eliminate the majority of my bruises and scars.

When Matthew eventually walked into the room, I thought this was my end. I thought I would die. But he demanded the torturer stop what he was doing at once. I told Matthew everything I knew about Kain and his involvement, and surprisingly, Matthew listened.

"I suspected something was going on for a while," he said. *"Thank you for bringing this to my attention."*

And then he let me go.

Just like that.

I don't know what to make of it. Obviously, I'm relieved to be free of that shit show, but everything felt too easy. I half expect to look over my shoulder and see a wolf shifter stalking me, watching my every move, writing down exactly who I talk to and when.

Is it possible that Matthew released me because he didn't believe a word I said, not because he did believe me? Perhaps he's hoping I'll incriminate myself in some way.

Or maybe...

Or maybe the Council knows more than what they're letting on.

"That's fucking insane," Izzy breathes.

I clear my throat against the uncomfortable tightness there and then lean forward, my lips hovering over Izzy's.

"You want to know what's fucking insane?" I whisper, swallowing her sharp exhale, making it my own. "How badly I want to kiss you again. I don't want to talk about the Council or the wolf shifters or the vampires." I lean in even closer. So close I can practically feel the heat of her breath. "So can I, Isabella? Can I kiss you? Can I make you feel good?"

Thirteen

IZZY

My body is on fire. Lava traverses my veins, but it's the most delicious type of heat imaginable, burning me alive and reducing me to nothing but ashes.

"Yes," I whisper on a breathy exhale. "Wait, no."

He's still close, too close, and I can practically feel his smirk against my lips.

"No?"

"I'm still mad at you. And there's still so much we need to..." I gasp when he lowers his face to my jawline and plants a chaste kiss against the sensitive skin there. "Ummm... We need to talk..."

"We can talk later."

His voice is always husky—a product of way too much smoke inhalation at a young age—but now it sounds completely different. Deeper, almost. Raspy. It reminds me of that first moment in the morning when you roll out of bed and try to speak, before the sun has even fully risen in the sky.

And god, the sound of it does things to me.

Decadent, delicious things that make my entire body tingle.

"I'm mad at you," I breathe out, even as I arch my neck to grant him better access.

"You can be mad at me," he assures me silkily. He kisses up my cheek, leaving trails of fire in his wake, before pausing at the corner of my lips. "You can yell at me, snap at me, hate me—"

"I could never hate you." I mean for the words to sound strident, adamant, but they're nothing but a whisper.

And then he's kissing me—or maybe I'm kissing him. All I know is I lean towards him at the same time he lunges for me. His hands are on my waist, my ribs, my cheeks, my hair. I can feel him everywhere.

I almost swear I can feel his heartbeat inside of me...

Desperation fueling my movements, I pull away to tug his shirt over his head. He obliges without complaint, and I take a moment to study his naked chest.

Fuck, how many times have I dreamed about him shirtless? Too many to count.

It isn't as if this is the first time I've ever seen him without a shirt, but it *is* the first time I've allowed myself to look. To study. To memorize every dip and crevice.

His abs are defined—a prominent six-pack—and smooth to the touch, with a tiny trail of dark hair leading down to the waistband of his jeans. I run my hands over his lean, resilient muscles as he pulls my lips back towards his.

He doesn't just kiss me. Oh no. He *devours* me. I swear it feels as if he's attempting to suck out my damn soul and merge it with his own.

And I'd let him.

Fire simmers in my veins as I clumsily remove my shirt and toss it across the room.

I've been intimate with guys before, but never with someone who matters. I feel like an inexperienced virgin, fumbling and tripping over myself.

Grayson reaches for the clasp of my bra, and I suck in a sharp breath, even as anticipation swells.

His hand pauses there, waiting, hesitant, and then he whispers, "Is this okay?"

My lust amplifies, tinged with desperation. "Yes."

Grayson's fingers tremble as he removes my bra and tosses it to the floor. For a long moment, he simply stares at me, his eyes smoldering with emotions I can't quite put my finger on, not with my brain as rattled as it is.

"God, you're so beautiful, Izzy."

Heat enters both of my cheeks as my heart pounds

dauntingly against my rib cage. I want to cover myself, to hide from his penetrating stare.

But I don't.

Instead, I meet his gaze unblinkingly, desperate to feel his hands on my flesh.

"So are you," I confess, once again trailing my gaze over him.

His dark hair is messy from my fingers, and his cheeks are flushed with arousal. Seeing him like this fuels my lust to levels I can't even articulate with words.

I remember when he told me he loves me. At the time, I didn't believe it—didn't allow myself to even entertain the possibility.

Now, it's all I can think about.

Grayson Grey loves me.

He *loves* me.

Grayson shifts our positions and then begins to kiss down my body—stopping to lavish each of my breasts with attention, his tongue circling my peaked nipples—but pauses when he reaches the waistband of my pants. There, he hesitates, his eyes burning with emotion.

In answer to his silent question, I buck my hips upwards in a wordless plea.

He slowly slides my leggings down my legs, and then my panties. When he discards both articles of clothing on the floor, he settles his muscular body between my legs, his eyes zeroing in on my core.

"Fuck, Grayson..."

He plants a chaste kiss to my most sensitive area. "Shush, woman. Do you know how often I've dreamed about this? Let me savor the moment."

"Savor my pussy, you mean?" I drawl with an insouciant grin.

"If the shoe fits..."

"Don't you mean if the cock fits?"

"Naughty girl. Get your head out of the gutter."

"Kind of hard to do when your— Oh!" I cry out as Grayson licks up the seam of my pussy lips.

"Huh." He pulls away marginally, his lips glistening with the evidence of my arousal. "I suppose that's one way to shut you up."

"You're a dick," I murmur, but the words don't hold any anger. If anything, they're tinged with desperation.

I reach for Grayson's dark hair and grip the strands tightly, guiding him back to where I want him.

His chuckle feels fucking amazing against my over-sensitive pussy.

And then Grayson's amusement dwindles, and he laps at me like a man possessed.

I buck and writhe like mad, practically arching my spine on the bed. Grayson adds a thick finger, and I swear I see stars.

Just before I can fall over the edge, Grayson pulls away and grins up at me.

I growl at him.

"What?" he asks innocently. "Did you want something, sweetheart?"

"I will castrate you if you don't let me come," I warn.

And I'm not even sure I'm joking. I don't need a dick to get off, after all. His fingers will suffice.

"Is that so?" As Grayson speaks, he stands and pushes down his dark jeans. His thick cock springs free instantly, already dripping with precum.

I rub my thighs together to help alleviate the all-consuming ache there.

"Do you always go commando?" I ask, feasting on the sight of a naked Grayson.

His cock is long and veiny with a mushroom tip. I wonder what it would feel like in my hand—all of that silky skin over solid muscle.

I've given my fair share of blow jobs and hand jobs over the years, but it's never been something I was particularly interested in. It felt more like a job to me than anything else. Half the time, it was the only way I could convince a guy to go down on me.

But with Grayson, I want nothing more than to touch him. Taste him. Run my tongue over the crown of his dick.

"Your mouth's watering a little bit," Grayson says teasingly.

I scoff indignantly and cross my arms over my chest like a brat. This draws Grayson's attention to my breasts, and his eyes heat and darken.

"Can you blame me? You have a pretty cock."

"A pretty cock." One of his brows quirks. He begins to stalk towards me like a predator approaching prey. I feel like an innocent little bunny about to be devoured by a...wolf. "My cock *isn't* pretty."

"Is that too feminine of a word for you?" I tease. "Would you like me to say it's a manly cock?"

"A sexy cock will suffice."

"A handsome cock?"

He moves another step closer. "You're being a brat, Izzy."

"I'm always a brat—" My words break off and turn into a giggle when he pounces on me, tickling my sides. "Grayson!"

He continues to move his fingers over my sides, playing my body the way he would a piano, and my laughing gradually subsides when I feel something hot and needy against my core.

This time, when I say his name, it's rife with desperation. "Grayson..."

He holds himself over me, his forearms on either side of my head, and whispers, "Are you ready for me, baby?"

In response, I pull his lips to mine while simultaneously jerking my hips up. His cock brushes against my pussy before slowly sinking inside, inch by inch.

He's big—bigger than most of the guys I've been with before—but I can't help but think he fits inside of me perfectly.

Like he was made for me.

"Fuck!" He drops his forehead against my shoulder as he stills inside of me. "You feel fucking amazing. Better than I imagined."

"Move," I beg, once again thrusting my hips.

Grayson doesn't need me to tell him twice.

He fucks me against the bed the same way he kissed me—like he wants to consume me, own me, possess me. It's a wild and desperate type of claiming, but I wouldn't have it any other way. Not after all this time. Not after years of *yearning*—a yearning I once believed to be unreciprocated.

His thumb presses down on my clit, and I finally get my wish.

I orgasm so suddenly and so intensely that I swear I black out. All I know is pleasure. My molecules are rearranged until I don't recognize who I am anymore, except for his.

I feel safer than I ever have in Grayson's arms.

There's a lot we need to talk about, but now isn't the time.

Snuggled in the embrace of the man I love, I allow all thoughts to cease, replaced by white-hot ecstasy.

Fourteen

IZZY

Grayson and I are unable to finish our conversation.

After falling asleep in his arms, I wake up to sunlight filtering through the window...and realize I'm late for school.

Grayson watches me with no small amount of amusement as I race around his apartment, attempting to make myself look presentable. I use his comb and toothbrush, and then I throw my leggings on from the day before. I don't want to wear the same sweater, so I grab one of Grayson's T-shirts from his dresser. It's long on me, coming down to my knees, but the spark of masculine satisfaction and possession in Grayson's eyes makes it worth it.

Grayson stops me just before I leave.

"Here," he says gruffly, thrusting a to-go mug of coffee in my hands.

I fucking *melt*.

Grayson offers to drive me, and I'm just about to take him up on that offer when my phone pings with an incoming text.

> ANSEL
>
> I figured you might need a ride, so I'm outside. Is that okay?

The message was sent about forty minutes ago.

Still, curiosity gets the best of me, and I move towards the window looking down onto the street below.

I spot Ansel's car almost immediately, looking out of place amongst the rusty trucks and broken minivans. The man himself stares intently at his phone in the driver's seat.

> ANSEL
>
> Is everything okay? You haven't been murdered, have you? Because I have to say, being an accomplice to murder wouldn't look good on my school transcript.

A light, airy feeling rushes through me. For Ansel to not only pick me up but to remain here well after school already began...

My heart flutters.

"Who's that?" Grayson growls from beside me, following the direction of my gaze.

Almost immediately, the butterflies inside of me

drop dead.

I just slept with Grayson, yet there's no denying my growing feelings for Ansel.

Does that make me a horrible person?

When I don't immediately answer him, Grayson places his hands on my shoulders and gently spins me around to face him. His expression is unreadable.

"Izzy, I know you. Don't lie to me and tell me he's no one or just a friend."

"He *is* just a friend," I insist.

That's the truth.

Grayson frowns. "But you want it to be more, don't you?"

I don't know how to respond. I barely know Ansel, yet I feel a strong connection to him. I love Grayson with my whole heart, yet...

Fuck, I feel like a greedy bitch.

What is wrong with me?

Grayson shuts down completely at my silence. His eyes shutter, obscuring his emotions from view.

"Gray—"

"We can talk about this later." His voice is hoarse with some indecipherable emotion.

"But Grayson—"

He stamps his mouth over mine in a possessive, claiming kiss. "I'm not mad, baby. But I think this is something we need to talk about—and not just a few minutes before you need to leave. I love you. I'm not going anywhere."

Another kiss, one that makes my toes curl.

I place my hand on his cheek, relishing the feel of his prickly five-o'clock shadow beneath my palm, and whisper, "You mean the world to me."

Yeah, I'm a coward. I can admit that. But I'm terrified of saying the dreaded L word and getting my heart shattered. Grayson already hurt me once. If he knew the type of power he held over me...

This time, I'm the one who initiates the kiss, though I don't deepen it. Time stands still as our lips touch and sparks run through me.

"Go." Grayson reluctantly pushes me away, his eyes molten. "I'll see you later. You coming back here?"

"I have to work this afternoon, but I'll be back after."

"Are you ever going to tell me why you're so pissed at your foster family? Did they...? Are you...?" Anger twists Grayson's features at some unknown conclusion he comes to.

"No!" I shake my head adamantly. "Nothing like that. I promise. This is another thing that we'll need to have a conversation about. It's a *long* story."

Grayson nods in understanding, but his jaw doesn't lose its rigid tension.

I push up on my tiptoes to peck him one more time on the lips. Now that I've started kissing him, I don't want to stop. I could spend the rest of my life with my lips fastened to Grayson Grey's.

But unfortunately, I have things I need to do—

things that don't involve continually kissing my childhood best friend.

"Text you later," I promise him as I pull away and reach down to sling my backpack over my shoulders.

"You better."

With one more glance back—his eyes reflecting the yearning that's no doubt in my own—I hurry out the door. A part of me wishes I could stay with Grayson, or at least kiss him one last time. I could use the courage his presence gives me.

I have the distinct impression I'll need it to get through the day.

Fifteen

ASHTON

"Why the *fuck* did he get released?" My father slams his fist down on his desk, causing it to shake.

I can't help but focus on the varnished picture frame directly in front of him, facing away from me. Even without looking at it, I know it's of my mother—those smiling green eyes and locks of light-brown hair that frame an angelic face.

A part of me hates that I look nothing like her.

I shift my attention towards Matthew, the only other person in the room.

The twins' father crosses his arms over his chest and sighs heavily. Today, his orange hair clashes comically with his yellow suspenders and vomit-green shirt. He looks like he just graduated from clown school.

"I told you. Grayson Grey wasn't involved in the murders," he says.

"And how do you know that?" My father stands abruptly, his knees banging against the desk.

The picture frame topples.

I just barely capture it before it can shatter. I see my mother's face for a fraction of a second—those green eyes that have haunted me for years now—before Father brutally yanks it out of my hands and settles it back on his desk, straightening it so it's facing him once more.

For a man who likes to pretend his fated mate doesn't exist, he's awfully sentimental.

"Grayson agreed to help me with an...*investigation* I started," Matthew says carefully.

Too carefully. For once, his jovial smile is nowhere to be seen.

"An investigation," my father parrots, frowning. "He's a human. A *Hunter*."

I can see how tightly he's holding on to his control. Any second now, he's going to detonate, and I'm not sure any of us will survive the blast.

"He's neither." Matthew shakes his head once, the movement causing his floppy red hair to bounce across his forehead.

For the first time since we started this meeting, I speak up. "What do you mean?"

An uneasy feeling blossoms in my stomach.

"He's a vampire." Matthew says those words calmly. Nonchalantly.

As if he didn't just throw a bomb in my lap and watch it explode.

Grayson Grey...is a vampire?

A vampire has been hanging around my mate?

Not my mate. At least, not in the possessive sense. She's not "my" anything. I made that quite clear to both her, myself, and my packmates.

So why does the thought of a vampire lurking around her fill me with such dread?

I know very little about the creatures that go bump in the night, but what I *do* know fills me with a distinct sense of unease. They're said to be killers. Murderers. Torturers. They don't just drink blood to survive—they do it for the thrill of it. Of course, all of that could be some urban legend passed down from generation to generation.

But still...

If there's even a hint of truth in that...

A vampire.

A fucking vampire.

I tighten my grip around the armrests of the chair.

"How is that possible?" My father's tone is imbued with more anger than I can remember him having in months. For once, his unflappable mask has faltered, revealing the spiteful man underneath. "We would've noticed—"

"Not if he starved himself to pass as human," Matthew counters.

Father's jaw clenches, and he reaches for the phone

on his desk. Even after all of these years, he still insists on keeping a landline. I'm not even sure if the old bastard knows what a cell phone is.

"We need to get in contact with the Elders. Now. They're up to something." Father's gaze slides to me for a moment before immediately flitting away.

He does that often. It's almost as if it pains him to stare directly at me. I wonder if he sees my mother—his fated mate—in my features. I'm dark-skinned like my father, but I have my mother's jawline and nose. At least, that's what people say. I don't see it.

"Ashton, don't you have to get to school?" he asks.

This time, I'm the one gritting my teeth together to keep from saying something I'll regret. "I think I should hear—"

"Off to school, boy." Matthew offers me a smile that doesn't quite reach his eyes. "You're not on the Council just yet. Let the adults handle this."

Let the adults handle this.

I take a deep breath, reminding myself to remain calm and nod cordially. I've perfected the art of keeping my expression utterly blank. Impassive. No one can sense the turmoil lingering just beneath the surface, demanding to be let out.

"Of course." I stand gracefully and straighten out a crease in my shirt.

Father always tells me I need to look immaculate when going out in public. Wrinkles, he claims, are for people who don't give a shit about their appearance, and that's not who I'm supposed to be.

"Please call me if there are any updates," I say.

"Of course," Matthew says, but my father remains silent, glaring at the phone on his desk.

Still, I find myself lingering, unwilling—or perhaps unable—to take that final step out of the office. "Should I keep an eye on Grayson?"

"No need." Matthew waves a hand in the air and exchanges an unreadable glance with my father.

No need?

Grayson was in a cell less than a day ago for the murder of two wolf shifters. Now he's free, and the Council doesn't want me to keep an eye on him?

What the fuck is going on?

I feel as if I'm missing something, like I've only been handed the outer edges of a puzzle and am forced to shove the pieces together.

What are they hiding?

But instead of saying any of that out loud, I simply nod once and slip out of the room.

My father and Matthew can do what they want, but I don't trust Grayson Grey any more than I can throw him. There's a reason he was released from prison, and I'm going to find out why.

* * *

The last thing I want is to go to school. To be surrounded by idiotic classmates who don't have a single working brain cell between them all.

And, more than that, I don't want to see my pack-mates or Isabella.

I still remember the fury on Emery's face as he rammed his fist repeatedly into me...

Trying to ignore the residual panic coursing beneath my skin, I lift my chin up high and stalk towards my locker. Students part for me immediately, but it doesn't bring about the usual amount of satis-faction.

Usually, one of my packmates waits for me at my locker.

Today, the hall in front of it is empty.

I am calm. I am collected.

I repeat that mantra in my head as I twist my dial combination and take out my books for the day.

I am calm. I am collected.

No one can see me break.

I did what was right for my pack—I know I did—so why does it hurt so damn much? Why does it feel like needles driving into my brain, causing my heart to pound even faster?

I am calm. I am collected.

Movement at the end of the hall captures my atten-tion. I turn to see Emery chatting with a group of guys on the football team. When his eyes meet mine, they harden instantly, turning glacial. He sneers at me.

Emery has been my best friend since we were in diapers. We've had petty disagreements over the years, but never anything like this. Not once has he ever looked at me with such raw, unfettered *hatred* before.

She did this to us.

She tore us apart.

Just as I knew she would.

Emery turns and stomps away without a single word to me, and I watch his retreating back with a spike growing in my throat. Swallowing it down proves to be impossible.

"You fucked up."

I turn to see my older brother leaning against the wall beside me, his sleeves pushed up to his biceps and his arms crossed over his chest. His dark hair is mussed in a way that makes my eyebrow begin to twitch. Hasn't the imbecile ever heard of a hairbrush before? Father would have an aneurysm if he were to see him now.

"You shouldn't be using that language around a student," I snap, something dark and insidious crawling through my chest like a venomous snake. It grips my heart in a vise-like hold and refuses to release.

"I'm not going to pretend to understand your reasoning—"

"I need to get to class." My voice is inflectionless as I begin to walk away. I don't want him to hear the anger brewing. That would mean I lost control, and I refuse to allow that to happen.

Not in front of him.

Not in front of the brother who abandoned me when I needed him most, leaving me behind with our deranged father.

"You're not just going to lose your mate but your pack as well," Christian calls to me.

His words still my feet.

I turn only my head to glare at him over my shoulder. "You don't know what you're talking about."

"I don't?" One of his eyebrows lifts mockingly. Arrogantly.

And I find I want to hurt him. I want to hurt him the way that I've hurt myself, the way I hurt my packmates, the way I hurt Isabella.

"You don't have a pack, Christian, so you can't possibly understand." I bare my teeth at him. "Why don't you retreat into the woods and lose your mind there? I'm not in the mood to deal with you and your baggage."

For a brief, brief moment, I swear I see pain flicker in Christian's eyes. But it's only for a second—no, less than a second—and I wonder if I imagined it in the first place.

Still, I can't help but feel a pang of guilt.

Guilt...and self-loathing so intense I fear I'll drown in it.

"Be that as it may, I know your packmates. And believe it or not, I know Izzy. You'll lose them all if you keep pushing them away."

Fuck. Even hearing her name is a punch to the gut.

Isabella is a perfect poison, deadly but enticing, unhealthily intoxicating. I need to purge her from my body once and for all.

I am calm. I am collected.

I am calm. I am collected.

I am calm. I am collected.

Once I'm sure I have my emotions under control, I give Christian a dry look and say, "I'm protecting my packmates."

And Isabella too.

Even if she doesn't see it.

Even if she doesn't understand it.

I'll be her villain, if that's what it takes to keep her safe.

I just pray I don't come to regret this decision in the end.

Sixteen

IZZY

The last thing I want to do is return to school and face the firing squad. Gouging out both of my eyes with a rusty spoon sounds significantly more appealing.

Ansel must see the derision on my face—or maybe he just hears my huff of annoyance—because he tosses me a glance after putting the car into park.

"You doing okay?" His long fingers tap against the steering wheel.

I focus on that, on the repetitive *tap-tap-tap* instead of his penetrating gaze I can feel burning a hole in my head.

"Not really." I blow out a breath. "It's times like this when I wish I were smart enough to get my GED and forget about school."

"You *are* smart," Ansel interjects automatically, his

124

tone colored with something akin to indignation on my behalf.

I offer him a smile—my first genuine one in the last twenty minutes. "Can you just promise me that I won't have to face any assholes today?"

His fingers stop their incessant tapping. "Unfortunately, that's not something I can promise."

"Dammit."

"Are you going to tell me what happened with the guys to make you so pissed? What exactly did they keep from you?"

I open my mouth, shut it, and then open it again. I don't know what to tell Ansel. Obviously not the truth. But I also don't want to lie to him.

So instead of saying anything, I just smile sadly and slip out of the car.

The air's cold, slicing at my skin like keen knives. The chill is tempered by the sun just beginning to rise in the distance.

Why does school have to start so damn early? Don't people know that our brains don't start working until noon? I suddenly wish I were fast asleep in Grayson's bed, nestled in his arms.

"You ready for today?" Ansel moves to stand beside me, close enough that I can feel his body heat.

A shiver that has nothing to do with the cold works its way through me.

"Remind me again what the penalty is for committing murder?"

"Life in prison," Ansel responds dryly. "Maybe a nice, old-fashioned execution."

"Do we even have the death penalty here?" I muse, tapping a finger to my chin.

"Do you want to find out?" He gives me the side-eye, and I huff dramatically.

"Nooo. Fine. No murder." I pause to consider something. "What about a little light maiming?"

"That's allowed." He tosses me a smile that makes my breath catch.

And when he reaches down to intertwine his fingers with mine? I swear the butterflies in my stomach riot.

How can I feel this way about Ansel after everything that happened with Grayson? I love Grayson. I truly do, yet...

Those damn butterflies refuse to settle down.

"Let's go inside, little psychopath." He chuckles. "We're already late enough as it is."

He tugs me into the school.

And I swear my skin continues to tingle long after he releases me.

The first member of the "asshole club" I see is Ethan. He has his back to me, moving in the opposite direction, yet he tenses as if he senses my presence. The muscles in his back flex and ripple.

And I, being the mature young lady that I am, immediately beeline down a different hallway, moving as fast as my legs can carry me.

Not today, Satan. Not today.

The next person I see is Emery, who's waiting by my locker while absently fiddling with his lip ring. Just like with Ethan, his entire body goes rigid even before I'm in his line of sight. Slowly, he turns his head in my direction, his nostrils flaring.

I promptly decide that I don't need anything from my locker and pivot on my heel, returning the way I came. All the while, my heart pounds erratically in my chest and my hands are clammy. My blood feels tainted by battery acid.

I can't avoid all of them forever, however, no matter how much I wish I could.

Third period is chemistry, the one class I share with Ethan, Emery, and Desiree. The only saving grace is that Ansel is in this class as well.

A strange, prickling heat invades my body as soon as I step through the door of the classroom. I can feel numerous pairs of eyes on me, but I purposely ignore them all as I claim my seat near the front of the class-room. Ansel is already here, no surprise, and is busy organizing his supplies.

"You doing okay?" he asks out of the corner of his mouth, straightening his mechanical pencils.

"Are they still looking in my direction?" I ask just as softly.

Ansel not so subtly looks over his shoulder and nods once. "Yup."

"Damn."

"Izzy!" a familiar voice chirps.

Mimi moves to stand in front of my desk, a wide, beguiling smile on her beautiful face.

Mimi is one of Desiree's best friends and someone I've gotten to know over the past few weeks. Her wheat-colored hair gives her an angelic look. Paired with her heart-shaped face and narrow chin, she's an absolute knockout.

"Oh my god! I was looking for you everywhere yesterday!" Mimi continues in her high-pitched, trilling voice. "I wanted to wish you a happy birthday and give you your present!"

"My present?" I frown at her in confusion.

"Of course, silly." Mimi pulls her backpack off and begins to dig through it. She releases a satisfied hum when she procures a beautifully wrapped package complete with a bow. "Happy belated birthday, girl!"

"Oh." My face feels like it's on fire, mainly because I can't remember the last time anyone cared enough to give me a birthday gift.

Except for Grayson, of course.

Hesitantly, I take the gift from her outstretched hands. I almost don't want to rip the paper. How much time did it take her to wrap it?

"Are you just going to stare at it?" Mimi places a

hand on her hip and cocks it to the side. "Or are you actually going to open it?"

Before I can do just that, Mr. Holter moves to the front of the classroom and clears his throat. "All right. That's enough, children. Take your seats."

"Later," Mimi mouths with a wink as she moves past me.

I nod and gently place the present in my backpack.

I feel...strange, and I'm sure my red cheeks reflect that.

To be completely honest, I've never had a lot of friends. It was hard to build and maintain relationships when I knew I would be passed to the next foster home as soon as my current family got sick of me. I pushed people away because it was the only way I knew how to protect myself. If I allowed no one into my heart, then it was impossible for me to get hurt.

Yet everything has changed. I have friends who care about me now. Who remember my birthday and buy me gifts. Who text me to check in. Who arrive late to school just to give me a ride.

I'm not used to this.

At all.

As I watch Mimi take her seat, my gaze collides with Desiree's. She looks as immaculate as ever in a perfectly ironed white blouse. Her brown curls cascade loosely around her face, stopping just below her shoulders. She opens her mouth as if she wants to say something, desperation etched across every line of her face, but I immediately look away.

Whenever I stare at her, I see Ashton bending down to kiss her. Emery hovering over her in a darkened classroom while Ethan watches on.

God, I feel like an idiot.

I refocus on the teacher as he drones on and on about electrons and protons and molecular mass. It's hard to focus on him, though, when I can feel Ethan's and Emery's gazes on the nape of my neck. They're directly behind me, so close that I can almost smell them, as creepy as that sounds. I wonder if it's a "mate" thing.

And I wonder if they know yet that I know.

Halfway through class, something whacks me across the back of my head. I frown at the rolled-up piece of paper but ignore it.

Ansel, however, reaches for it. He arches an eyebrow at me inquiringly, and I nod once, giving him permission to read it. He smooths out the piece of paper and frowns down at it. I can't help but peek at the hastily scrawled words out of the corner of my eye.

Izzy. We need to talk. After school?

If I had to guess, I would say the handwriting is Emery's. It's messy and chaotic, just like he is.

Ansel smirks as he grabs one of his pens and writes in big letters, ***FUCK OFF.*** When Mr. Holter is distracted, Ansel throws the piece of paper over his shoulder.

Someone releases a growl.

When class finally ends, I'm the first one out the door.

I don't look back.

Seventeen

IZZY

"So...are you going to tell me why we hate Ashton and his friends?"

Those are the first words Jake says to me when I plop into the seat opposite him in the cafeteria. Jake's best friend, Dec, looks between the two of us inquiringly, his mouth half full of meatloaf.

"We hate them?" he asks, confused.

"We don't hate anyone," I stress. "I'm just..."

Pissed off?

Annoyed?

Feeling betrayed?

All of the above?

Jake waves his fork back and forth in the air. "I don't think you understand how this thing between us works." He points the fork at me. "If you hate someone, then I hate someone, and vice versa."

"What if I told you one of the people I was mad at was Desiree?" I ask, trying to smother my grin.

Jake has had a crush on Desiree for as long as I have known him—and probably longer than that. The man has it bad.

Jake winces and rubs a hand through his sandy-blond hair. "Is there a reason why we're mad at her?"

"It's because she's fucking Ethan and Emery, isn't it?" Kain slides into the seat beside Jake with a lewd grin in my direction.

I've never liked Kain. There's something about him that makes me uncomfortable. Even now, it feels like there are thousands of fire ants crawling all across my body.

"Desiree is fucking Ethan and Emery?" Jake asks, blinking.

I take a rather aggressive bite of my sandwich. "Apparently."

Jake's entire body sags in disappointment. I feel as if I just kicked a puppy.

"Oh." Abruptly, anger distorts his features, and he throws a venomous look across the cafeteria. "Oh. That's why you're so mad, isn't it? Because those assholes were leading you on while fucking another girl behind your back. What assholes."

"Who are you glaring at?" Dec asks, frowning. "They aren't even over there."

"It's the thought that counts." Jake spins back

around and huffs. "I can't believe I defended those assholes."

"Yeah, well, it doesn't matter. I'm over it." I dab at my mouth with a napkin. "It's not like we were dating or anything."

They are just my fated mates, apparently, who are in love with another girl.

No big deal.

Oh, and did I mention that they neglected to tell me about said mating bond?

"Listen here, and listen well," Jake tells me seriously, once again jabbing his fork in the air for emphasis. "Guys are stupid. We think with the wrong head more often than not, and we do dumb shit ninety percent of the time."

"Become a lesbian," Kain says, offering me a salacious eyebrow wag that immediately turns my stomach. "Then you won't have to deal with men. And you can make a killing on OnlyFans."

"Dude!" Jake shoves at Kain's shoulder while I glare at him in disgust.

"You're horrible." To Jake, I ask, "Why are you friends with him?"

"I'm not." Jake scoffs as if the prospect is ridiculous. "The fucker just refuses to leave me alone."

"Asshole," Kain mutters.

"Speaking of assholes..." Dec leans forward as if we're about to exchange secrets. "I see that you've been hanging out with Ansel a lot."

"First, Ansel isn't an asshole," I say, feeling indignation roar through me. "And second, are you stalking me?"

Jake snorts. "The gossip mills have been going crazy lately. Someone saw you leave school yesterday with him. They claim that you found a quiet place to...you know...exchange bodily fluids."

A bark of laughter escapes me. "Exchange bodily fluids? Really?"

"Bump uglies. Do the horizontal tango. Put the pickle in the sandwich." Jake throws his hands up in the air, exasperation clear on his face. "You know what I mean."

"You had sex with Ansel?" Kain asks crudely, his eyes gleaming with excitement.

I pray to every god in existence for patience. Anything to keep me from decking this fucker.

Jake doesn't have the same restraint that I do.

"Dude." He whacks Kain across the back of the head. "Knock it the fuck off or leave. I'm serious. This is your last warning."

Kain rubs at his head while chuckling. "Dude, chill. I was just joking."

"You're being disgusting," Dec corrects.

"Sex isn't disgusting," Kain counters immediately. "It's a normal activity—"

"Seriously, Kain. Don't fucking test me..." Jake glares at his teammate, and Kain finally lifts his hands in the air in mock surrender.

"Fine, fine. I'll knock it off."

"And for the record, I didn't have sex with Ansel," I bite out. "Not that it's any of your business. We just hung out."

Kain looks as if he wants to say something—probably a lewd or perverted joke—but one warning glare from Jake has him snapping his mouth closed.

"Where is he anyway?" Dec asks, dipping his french fry into a pile of ketchup.

"Library. He had to study for a test."

Ansel apologized profusely that he couldn't sit by me at lunch, and I felt those butterflies return with a vengeance. I don't know how so much could've changed between us in a span of a day, but it did.

"I just wish you had come home last night," Jake murmurs, pouting. "I had things planned."

"Things?"

"You know...presents and cake and all that stuff. We'll just have to celebrate your birthday tonight."

My smile fades. "I don't know..."

"Did something happen?" Jake asks, concerned. "You know you can talk to me about anything, right?"

His earnest eyes ensnare my own.

Is it possible that Jake knows the truth about Hale, Gerry, and the others? Is he a part of the supernatural world as well? Or has he been in the dark this entire time, just like I was?

I want to demand answers, but now isn't the time. Kain is grinning at me with a decidedly shark-like smile

—one that clearly states he scented blood in the water and is coming in for the kill.

"Later," I promise Jake, and I'm not just talking about the birthday celebrations.

Later, we'll talk. Later, I'll get my answers. Later, he'll learn the truth.

His brows furrow at whatever expression he sees on my face before he nods once. "Okay, but I think—" A frosty scowl overtakes his features. "What the hell are you doing here?"

I don't even need to look over my shoulder to know who has just arrived. I can sense him the way I can my own limb. Heat permeates the air around me and seeps through my skin, alighting me from the inside out. I rub absently at the mark on my wrist as wave after wave of fire ripples through me.

"Izzy." Emery's voice is a dark, husky growl that reverberates through me. "We need to talk. Now."

Eighteen

IZZY

"I'd think very carefully about what you want to say next," I warn, narrowing my eyes at the ridiculously handsome wolf shifter.

Seriously, why couldn't he be ugly? It would be so much easier to ignore him if he were sporting a penis nose or had ass cheeks for hair.

Emery grits his teeth together but manages to bite out, "Can we talk, Izzy? Please?"

"Was that so hard?" I give him a sardonic smile, which causes his right eye to twitch. "And to answer your question...no."

"No?" One of his brows arches in obvious disbelief.

"You heard me. No." I swivel around on the bench to face the others once more. "Now, what were we talking about again?"

Jake leans forward and mock-whispers, "Do you

want me to kick his ass for you?" When Emery releases a sound that makes me wonder how the fuck I didn't suspect he wasn't human in the first place, Jake blanches. "I mean, do you want me to poke him with a sharp stick?"

"How did it go from kicking his ass to poking him with a sharp stick?" Dec asks, jamming a dozen french fries into his mouth at once.

"I might actually survive if I stab him with a stick and run away as fast as I can. There's no way in hell I'll survive an ass kicking." Jake nods seriously, and I smother my grin with the back of my hand.

"You don't have a lot of confidence in your abilities," Dec muses.

"I have confidence...that I don't want to die." Jake wags his fork back and forth in the air and then narrows his eyes at Emery. "But I'll stab the shit out of you with a stick if you so much as look at Izzy weirdly."

"My hero," I say dryly.

He grins and winks. "Always."

"Izzy, please."

Something in Emery's voice causes me to turn once more to look up at him. And when I do... An indescribable emotion thunders through me. It feels as if I just swallowed fire, and it's burning my throat.

His eyes are wild and desperate. I've never seen him so raw before, so open, so vulnerable. I suddenly feel lost, like a piece of driftwood on open seas, whipped around by unmerciful waves.

Why do I suddenly want to give in to him? Hear what he has to say?

Emery continues to stare at me pleadingly, unaware of the contortions my heart is putting my head through.

After a long moment of silence—the type that's rife with tension—I blow out a breath and stand.

"Fine," I hiss. "Let's get this over with."

Relief paints itself across Emery's features, his eyes widening as he briefly bows his head. "Thanks—"

"Don't," I warn him as I begin to move away from the table, leaving my backpack where it is. I'll come back for it.

"Izzy." Jake grabs my arm just before I can pass him, his touch surprisingly gentle despite the fierce glare he throws in Emery's direction. "Are you sure about this?"

"Yeah. I'm sure." I offer my foster brother a reassuring smile. "And if anything goes wrong, I know you'll always be at my back with a huge stick."

"The hugest," he agrees instantly, then he frowns. "That sounded dirty."

"Talking about your huge stick?"

He makes a face. "Ew. Stop it. I think I just vomited in my mouth a little."

"Rude."

"Izzy," Emery says again, and I notice his eyes sharpen on Jake's hand around my wrist. "Please."

I give Jake's shoulder a reassuring squeeze and then

follow Emery out of the cafeteria. I don't see Ethan, Ashton, Reid, or even Desiree. I have a brief moment of panic, wondering if they're planning to all bombard me at once, but the classroom Emery leads me into is mercifully empty.

But also familiar.

"Seriously?" I spin around to face him and place my hands on my hips, watching as he flicks the lock into place. "Do you just bring all your conquests here?"

"What?" He stares at me in confusion, but then understanding dawns and horror splays across his face. "Of course not! Look..."

He runs a hand through his spiked blond hair as he begins to pace. I can't help but notice he looks good. Real good. His hair is artfully tousled, giving him a "just got out of bed" look that drives most girls wild.

His features are beautiful, almost angelic, but paired with his tattoos and piercings, no one could ever mistake him as some godly being. His short-sleeved T-shirt clings to his muscular frame and emphasizes his biceps. His black jeans hug his hips in a way that should be fucking illegal.

Damn him.

Damn him to hell.

"I'm not sleeping with Desiree," Emery blurts, spinning to face me. "I haven't ever touched her in that way."

"But you want to."

"No!" He actually looks disgusted by the prospect,

his skin taking on a green tint. "Not at all." He resumes his pacing. "I know about the picture you were sent and what it must look like. But I promise you—despite what Ashton wanted you to believe—none of us is in a relationship with Desiree. Things with us are...complicated, and I know you don't understand—"

"What don't I understand?" I prop my hip against the teacher's desk and fold my arms over my chest. "That you guys are wolf shifters? Or that I'm apparently your fated mate?"

Time seems to stand still. I'm not even sure if Emery's breathing as he turns to gape at me, his face devoid of all color.

But I'm on a fucking roll now. "What about the fact that you got my best friend arrested for a crime he didn't commit? That you stormed into my house like a damn neanderthal? Hmmm?" My anger roils in my stomach, white-hot and blistering, and tiptoes up my neck. I ball my hands into fists. "Do you think I'm an idiot or something?"

"Who...?" He pauses, swallows, and then licks his lips. "Who told you?" Rage distorts his features into something unrecognizable. "It was that asshole Kain, wasn't it? He told you?"

"Kain?!" My voice turns embarrassingly high-pitched in disbelief. "He's a wolf shifter too?"

Emery opens and closes his mouth repeatedly. "I..."

"You know what? It doesn't matter who told me. What matters is that you *didn't*." I stalk forward until

I'm directly in front of him. I jab a finger into his solid chest. "I can understand keeping this world a secret from me. But I'm, apparently, your goddamn mate! You should never have kept *that* from me!"

"I know—"

"Do you know what happened on my eighteenth birthday?" As I speak, I twist my arm so he can see the mark on my skin. "I felt unbearable pain. It was like... It was like my body was on fire. I was confused and scared and freaked the fuck out. Nobody told me it was the mate bond coming into play!"

"We didn't know—"

"You want to know why I'm pissed at you?" I take another step closer until I'm practically stepping on his shoes. I have to tilt my head to maintain eye contact, but I refuse to back down. "It's not just because of the whole Desiree thing. It's because you kept this world-altering secret from me with no concern for my safety or well-being. What if I'd been driving when the pain came? What if I passed out and hit my head? If he hadn't been there to explain things to me, I probably would've thought I was insane."

"He?" Emery's brows scrunch together. "Grayson?"

"No," I say stiffly, refusing to give up Christian's name.

I have no idea if he'll get in trouble for telling me the truth about the guys, but I don't want to take any chances. Besides Grayson, he's the only ally I have in this new world I've found myself in. Jake and Ansel don't seem to know about the supernatural world.

Emery looks as if he wants to question me further but quickly decides against it.

Instead, his features pinched in pain and regret, he says, "Izzy, I'm so damn sorry—"

I shoulder past him and move towards the door, then I unlock it and wrench it open.

"Save your apologies, Emery." Just before I exit the classroom, I turn to him. "And you don't have to worry about having a human as a mate. I reject you, Emery. I reject your entire pack."

And with that, I leave the room.

I don't look back.

Nineteen

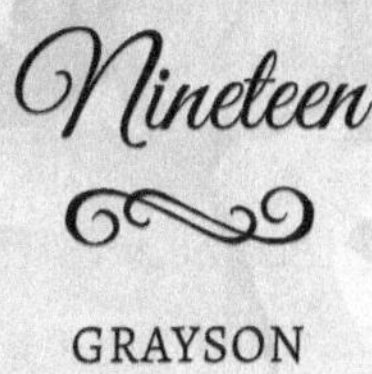

GRAYSON

The park is almost empty.

It's too cold to really enjoy it, and with school in session, there are no children to grace the play set. Still, every once in a while, I'll see a couple jog past in workout gear or a mother pushing a stroller down the sidewalk.

I don't know how long I've been sitting on the park bench when I become keenly aware of a presence directly behind me. I inhale, but with my vampire powers muted, I smell nothing but pine trees and crisp winter air. It's only when he steps closer do I detect a hint of…dog.

Matthew sits beside me on the bench, rubbing his hands together to ward off the chill.

"I came," I tell him blandly, not bothering to beat around the bush. "What do you want?"

"I don't believe you murdered those females," Matthew begins, seeming to choose his words carefully.

"I kind of suspected as much when you allowed me to leave." I lean forward and rest my arms on my legs.

Directly in front of me, a young woman jogs down the trail leading into the forest. She sort of reminds me of Izzy, and a pang reverberates through me when I think about my mate. All I want to do is be with her. Hold her. Love her.

My cock jerks to life in my pants at just the memory of her pussy milking it for all its worth.

Fuck.

Now is most definitely *not* the time to get a boner.

"What have you done about Kain?" My voice breaks on that final word, and I reach for the water bottle I always keep with me.

"Nothing as of yet." Matthew frowns. "We don't want him to think that anything is amiss."

The water I'm swallowing gets lodged in my throat. "He's still out there? At school?"

At Izzy's school?

Anger traverses through my veins like lava.

He threatened my mate.

Told me he'll kill her.

And he's with her right now?

I need to get to her. Protect her. Rip Kain's throat out—

"Remain calm, young vampire." Matthew glances at me out of the corner of his eye before facing forward once more. He, too, seems to be fixated on the jogger opposite us. "Isabella is fine."

"You don't know—"

"I do, actually." Matthew reaches into his coat pocket and pulls out two gloves. He carefully slips them onto his hands. "But we can't let him know that we're onto him. There's more at play here than you could possibly understand."

I stare at him in wide-eyed disbelief. "Are you kidding me? How stupid do you think Kain is? He knew I got arrested—hell, he visited me in my cell—and he'll know that I got released. He'll assume that I talked."

A tiny grin tugs up the corners of Matthew's mouth. "As of now, he doesn't know that you've been released, and we intend to keep it that way...at least for the time being."

"What do you mean?"

"Kain believes that you were sent away to be...interrogated more thoroughly. Or perhaps he'll believe that you're already dead. Who the fuck knows?" Matthew scratches at the stubble lining his jaw. "Which makes you the perfect asset."

"Asset?" I fucking hate that word. How many times did the Elders refer to me as their greatest asset?

"You'll be able to do some digging on Kain and the other pack members without them knowing."

"Kain and the other pack members?" I gawk at him. "You don't think Kain was working alone?"

Matthew finally turns to face me fully, his expression grave. "I don't. I believe there's more at play here than any of us can even comprehend."

"Kain was working with Hunters. He was—"

"Was he?" Matthew quirks an eyebrow questioningly. "Have you ever seen any humans with Kain?"

"No, but—"

"I want you to keep an eye on Kain and everyone he talks to." He glances at me slyly. "I heard about you, Grayson Grey. You're not just any normal vampire, are you?"

I grit my teeth together and remain silent.

"When was the last time you fed?" Matthew asks, and his abrupt change in topic makes my head spin. Before I can answer, he continues. "You have no reason to hide anymore. We know what you are, and you'll be of more use to us if you're in possession of all of your gifts."

Once again, I remain silent, not daring to speak.

Not daring to even breathe.

When I finally have my thoughts in some semblance of a working order, I ask a question that has been nagging at me since this conversation began. "What happens if Kain sees me? Or if he discovers that I'm free?"

He'll go after Izzy, of that I have no doubt. He'll hurt her to prove his control over me.

"Hopefully, the coward will run to his leader." Matthew scrubs his hands against his jeans with a wry, humorless chuckle. "A weasel like him isn't smart enough to think this up alone."

"I don't even know what *this* is," I protest.

Matthew waves a hand in the air. "Just keep an eye on Kain and his friends. And, if you're able to, see what you can find out about Gregor."

"Gregor?"

"You may remember his son...Ashton." Matthew's smile doesn't reach his eyes.

I remember being dragged into the Council room and meeting with a bunch of wolves. The tallest and most domineering one had dark skin, closely cropped hair, and a perpetual scowl on his face. He scared me more than any of the others.

"Do you think Gregor has something to do with Kain and the murders?" I demand, but Matthew is already standing, rigid tension radiating through his muscles.

He glances in both directions nervously. "I need to leave."

"Wait—" But my raspy protest falls on deaf ears as the wolf shifter hurries away.

For a long moment, I simply sit on the park bench and ponder Matthew's words.

Could Kain have been working independently of the Hunters? Why would he lie about that? No, the better question is—why would he have done that in the first place? And why would Matthew believe Gregor is involved? It isn't like they're murdering vampires or warlocks or witches or any other supernatural. The females killed were wolves.

So what is their endgame?

Or is Matthew simply creating a conspiracy that doesn't exist outside of his head?

And how will all of this affect Izzy?

Even now, my thoughts return to her. I can't help it. She consumes me.

A giddy rush of euphoria thunders through me when I think about my plans for tonight. I purchased steaks—Izzy's favorite—and a bunch of candles and flowers. Shit girls find romantic. As soon as I get home, I plan to decorate my apartment, cook a fancy dinner for her, and then tell her the truth about what she is to me.

My mate.

I've never done anything like this before. My relationship with Sidney was a sham—as horrible as that makes me. The most romantic thing I did for her was pay for her McDonald's hamburger. Suffice to say, the girl was not happy when I called and broke up with her.

But what can I say without sounding like a bigger ass than I already am?

Oh, I'm sorry, but I never had any feelings for you because I've always been in love with my best friend, who, by the way, is my fated mate.

Yeah. I'm certain that would go over well.

I pull out my phone and begin to scroll through my notes app.

Candlelit dinner. Check.

Bouquet of flowers. Check.

Box of jewelry. Check.

Anticipation swells as I finally rise from the bench.

I have a few hours before Izzy returns home from work. I need to make sure everything is perfect. She deserves nothing but the best—

Movement in my periphery captures my attention. I turn, my stomach in knots, to see a pale face and glinting red eyes.

"Grayson," the familiar man hisses. "We've been looking for you."

Before I can even think of a response, something hits me over the back of the head.

And then all I know is darkness.

Twenty

IZZY

The smell of butter assaults my senses as soon as I step into the theater.

I bypass the concession stand—where a bored-looking, college-aged woman I haven't met yet works—and step into the employee break room.

It takes me only a few minutes to change into my employee T-shirt, throw my backpack into a locker, and then clock in.

"Hey, Silas," I greet as I step behind the counter, pulling my hair up into a ponytail.

The rugged, scowling man glances up from the register. His dark hair is loose, cascading around his shoulders, but does very little to soften his features. Today, he wears an eyepatch, obscuring his scarred eye from view.

"You're late," the college-aged girl announces as soon as she sees me.

She props herself up on her elbow. Her bright-pink hair is spiky and gives her a decidedly elfin look. She has almost as many piercings as Emery—three in her right eyebrow, five in her left, one in her nose, and a hoop through her lip.

"Izzy, meet Minnie. Minnie, Izzy," Silas introduces gruffly, still bending over the register. He doesn't bother to look up.

"Hi." I awkwardly wave my hand like a total dork.

Minnie exaggeratedly pops her gum and then straightens.

Ignoring me, she turns towards Silas. "I'm heading out."

"Sweep up theater one before you leave," he instructs.

Minnie makes a face. "But I—"

"Now, Minnie."

Minnie mutters something noncommittally under her breath and then shoves past me, ramming her shoulder into mine. Abruptly, she pauses, her spine straightening and nostrils flaring. Her pierced brows draw together.

"You smell weird," she announces candidly.

"Minnie!" Silas snaps. He slams the drawer of the register shut and whirls around. His lips tighten in anger. "Now."

Minnie continues to eye me strangely, and for a brief, crazy moment, I can't help but wonder...is she a wolf shifter as well?

Stop being ridiculous, Izzy. Not every person you meet is a part of the supernatural world. Maybe you just have a bad case of BO today.

Ugh. This is probably the first time in my life I've prayed to have body odor.

"Do you know Grayson?" Minnie asks abruptly, her eyes narrowing.

The question takes me by surprise.

Does she smell Grayson on me?

What the fuck?

My theory of her being supernatural suddenly sounds more plausible.

"He's my...friend."

"Huh." Annoyance paints itself across her face, her expression turning pinched. She rubs a hand over her brow as if to ward off a headache. "He's dating my best friend, Sidney."

"Minnie. Theater one. Now." Silas points down the hallway, and Minnie blows out an irritated breath.

"Fine." She once again rams her shoulder against mine—*ow*—and stomps towards the closet where Silas keeps cleaning equipment.

I watch her retreating back with a lump forming in my throat and a lead weight in my stomach.

"You good, kid?" Silas's gruff voice sounds from directly behind me.

I glance at the large man over my shoulder to see him watching me cautiously, his eyes unreadable.

I force a smile. "Yup. Where do you want me today? Is Jake working?"

"Jake had to take off today." Silas moves towards the soda machine and washes the nobs with a rag. "Basketball tryouts, apparently."

"Football already done?"

Silas glances at me before refocusing on his task. "Nah. They have one or two more games. Maybe more if they keep winning. You going to any more games?"

I snort. "Maybe. But I won't be standing on the sidelines this time around."

"Smart idea." His lips twitch in the beginnings of a smirk before they straighten out. "Why don't you take the counter today? I'm going to be doing payroll. I'll have Reid clean the theaters."

A knot manifests in my chest and shimmies its way up my throat. "Reid's here?"

Silas eyes me strangely. "Will that be a problem?"

I force myself to keep my expression blank. "No. Not at all. It's fine."

Silas continues to stare at me as if he doesn't believe me but chooses not to comment further. However, the sudden twitching of his jaw commandeers my attention.

"If he's giving you a hard time..."

"No, no, no. It's fine." I force my lips to curve upwards. "Everything is fine."

Famous last words.

Twenty-One

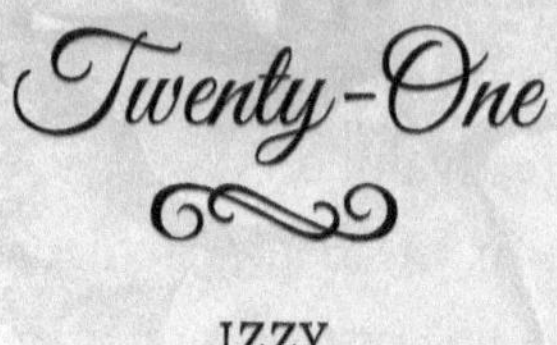

IZZY

I don't see Reid during the first hour of my shift, but I know he's here. I can sense him.

A strange heat permeates the air and burrows its way into my chest, finding a home there.

The theater isn't overly busy, but there's a steady stream of people entering and leaving. At one point, Silas comes out to work the register while I scoop popcorn and grab drinks.

"Enjoy the movie," I tell an older couple as they hobble away.

Finally, the lobby is empty. The only sound is the popping of corn and the air conditioning unit up above.

I see him a second before he sees me. He stands opposite me in the lobby, a broom in one hand and a dustpan in the other.

Reid.

His red hair is greasy, making the color appear darker, like garnet. Even from this distance, I can see the acne dotting his forehead and cheeks.

Reid is an enigma, one I can't figure out. He's gruff and broody and downright rude at times, yet he can be fiercely protective.

And, apparently, he's my fated mate.

I try to reconcile the Reid in front of me to the one I saw in the photograph from the year before. That Reid had been grinning brightly, his skin clear, his hair luminous, his eyes shining.

Rumor has it, Reid broke up with his ex-girlfriend, Michelle, and...let himself go. Stopped caring. Stopped trying. He no longer showered and rarely washed his clothes. I met Michelle once before. She was a cute girl with perfectly straight black hair, lightly tanned skin, and almond-colored eyes. I could see why Reid was obsessed with her.

Correction—I can see why Reid is *still* obsessed with her.

Yet another "mate" in love with a girl who isn't me.

At least Reid never led me on.

I snort and roll my eyes, turning away from him to focus on wiping down the counter.

But he doesn't seem to get the hint. I hear his footsteps a second before his heat seeps through my shirt, enveloping me in warmth. Prickles of awareness spread across my skin. Goose bumps form.

"You know," Reid says matter-of-factly, his gruff voice rolling over me like a cold ocean wave.

Apparently we're having this conversation...

"What do I know?" I throw the rag over my shoulder and spin around, my hands on my hips.

He's so close I can see the tiny bend in his nose—a product, I'm sure, of it being broken one too many times. A strand of greasy hair falls forward, and he pushes it away with the back of his hand. He gives me a look. You know the type.

Don't be stupid, girl.

It immediately causes my hackles to rise.

"That you're a wolf shifter and apparently my mate? Yeah, I know." I fold my arms over my chest, watching his reaction carefully.

He doesn't wince the way I expect him to, nor does his face flash with guilt. He simply watches me with the same acute intensity as I watch him.

"Someone's been chatty," he grumbles at last, turning away from me to sweep the floor.

My stomach flips as I stare at him incredulously. "That's it? That's all you have to say to me?"

He doesn't bother to turn around. "I never lied to you, Izzy, and I never led you on."

All of that is true, but...

"You beat up Grayson!" I snap, my nerves fraying.

Reid arches one eyebrow in my direction. "Because I thought he was a murderer."

"He's not!"

"Debatable."

"Reid..." My voice lowers to a growl.

Reid blows out a breath, that one single noise rife with irritation, and then spins around. He leans against his broom as he studies me. For a long moment, he's silent, his gaze traveling over my face in a way that makes me want to blush.

"Sorry for beating up your friend," he says at last, already turning away.

Once again, I blink at his back, at a loss for words. "That's it?"

"What do you want from me, Izzy?" The words are almost a whisper, but they cause me to pause. Frown.

What *do* I want from him?

What do I want from any of them?

I got an explanation—or at least, a version of one.

Do I want them to confess their undying love for me? Of course not. Do I want to be their mate or whatever? No.

So what do I want?

I flounder to come up with an adequate answer, and Reid takes my silence as some kind of confirmation. He returns to his task with a harsh scowl, one that makes him look even scarier than before.

"Don't worry about me. I won't be pursuing the mating bond or any of that shit," he grumbles.

"You won't?"

Do I feel relief or disappointment at his statement?

What the hell is wrong with me?

"I won't," he confirms gruffly. And then, in a voice that's nearly inaudible, he adds, "You don't want me as a mate."

"I don't even know what that means." I throw my hands up, but since I'm still holding the rag, it goes flying in the air, hooking on one of the rafters above.

For a long, long moment, I simply stare at the wet rag high above me. Shock holds me immobile.

Then a slightly hysterical laugh bubbles in my chest.

I hold my stomach as giggles bombard me.

Reid stares at me as if I've lost my mind before he, too, begins to chuckle. It's amazing the difference that sweeps over him. With his eyes shining the way they are, and his full lips twisted in a smile, he almost looks...handsome.

The sight stalls the breath in my lungs, and my laughter dissipates.

Reid stops laughing as well.

We stare at each other. The air between us charges with electricity. I can feel it crackling just underneath my skin. My heart pounds against my rib cage.

Reid opens his mouth, but whatever he's about to say is interrupted by the door to the theater opening and the bell overhead jingling. We both turn as a familiar girl prances inside, wearing a short white skirt and a pink blouse. Her eyes home in on Reid like two heat-seeking missiles, and a hungry, possessive smile lights up her face.

Michelle.

And just like that, my good mood evaporates.

Fuck.

Twenty-Two

REID

I don't dare breathe as Michelle saunters up to me, her dark hair swishing around her shoulders like midnight-colored silk. She flutters her long lashes up at me as she reaches for my arm.

"Reid. I missed you, baby." Her high-pitched voice grates on my nerves.

Bile rises in my throat when her manicured hand touches my bicep, gripping it in a way that feels both possessive and demeaning—like I'm a damn toy for her to show off.

But I don't dare push her away.

Not with Izzy standing so close.

"What do you want?" My words come out as a growl, despite my best efforts.

Michelle flinches at my tone but doesn't release me. If anything, she steps even closer, her tiny breasts pressing against my arm.

I go very, very still. Out of the corner of my eye, I see Izzy has tensed, her eyes homing in on the way Michelle leans against me.

"I wanted to see if you gave my offer any thought." Michelle simpers, staring up at me with hearts in her eyes. Her blood-red lips curve into a smile. "I want to give us another chance."

How deluded can this bitch be?

I almost say that out loud but stop myself at the last second. I don't dare piss her off, not with Izzy only a few feet away, watching us intensely.

My skin burns with disgust as her nails dig into my arm hard enough to make me bleed.

"Reid. Baby. I miss you." She pushes up on her tiptoes and presses her lips against the underside of my jaw.

A shudder of disgust reverberates through me.

"I'm at work." I attempt to shake her off of me, but she's like a damn barnacle.

That's apparently the wrong thing to say.

The skin around her eyes tightens, and her lips purse. Anger distorts her features into something unrecognizable. I've seen this particular expression once before—when she tried to kill a girl I befriended.

"Did you meet someone else?" Her eyes not-so-subtly slide in Izzy's direction.

I can see the wheels churning in that diabolical brain of hers.

"Course not," I snap, desperate to reclaim her

attention. Despite the way my body trembles with revulsion, I grip her chin and turn her attention back to me. "Do you think anyone will ever care about me like you do?"

Michelle made sure of that when she had her brother curse me. In her mind, if she couldn't have me, then no one could.

Her tiny nose wrinkles the longer she stares at me. "I can fix you. You know that. I just want you to give us another chance."

Another chance.

As if we've ever been dating in the first place.

"Michelle." I lower my voice to an urgent whisper. "We can talk about this later. Right now, I'm at work."

"So there is someone else!" Rage darkens her features. "I've given you everything, Reid. Everything. You're mine."

"Michelle, please—"

Her palm connects with my face before I can stop it. The slap doesn't hurt, not really, but it still causes me to gape at her shock.

Her chest heaves as she glares up at me. Both of her hands ball into fists. "You stupid, ugly—"

Her rant is cut off by Izzy sliding between us. I can't see her expression, but her shoulders are tight with tension.

"You do not get to fucking slap him," she hisses, taking a threatening step closer.

Fear grips me in a chokehold. I immediately reach

for Izzy's arm, determined to shove her behind me and protect her the best I can from Michelle's infamous wrath. But when I touch Izzy's skin—and feel the familiar prickles of heat—she simply shakes me off of her as if I'm not a two-hundred-plus-pound werewolf shifter and she's not a tiny human.

She advances on Michelle like an avenging angel—a beautiful, deadly deity plucked from the clouds to find a home amongst us mere mortals.

"Say you're sorry," Izzy growls.

Some of Michelle's initial fear evaporates the longer she stares at Izzy. I know what she sees—a human who won't be able to stand up against her magic.

Terror like I've never felt before threatens to plow me over.

"Izzy…" I warn.

She ignores me.

"So you're the bitch Reid's cheating on me with," Michelle says snottily, eyeing Izzy up and down with barely veiled disdain. Her upper lip curls. "I see he downgraded."

"Are you fucking delusional? How can he cheat on you if you're not even together?" Izzy takes another step forward, and I'm shocked as hell when Michelle staggers back a step.

"We're on a break," she snarls, regaining some of her bravado. "We belong together. He'll come back to me. He always does."

A strangled laugh threatens to escape me at her words.

"Then that's his choice. But from where I'm standing, it sounds like he told you to leave him the hell alone."

Michelle hefts her chin into the air imperiously. Her eyes flare a luminescent brown, her power shining through like a lit candle. "He doesn't mean it." She glances at me over Izzy's shoulder. "Do you really think anyone but me would ever care for you? Look at you. You're nothing but an ugly piece of—"

Izzy pulls her arm back and punches Michelle straight in the face.

Holy fuck.

Holy. Fuck.

And then, all hell breaks loose.

Twenty-Three

IZZY

I don't know what comes over me.

One second I'm standing there, watching the exchange, and the next I'm across the room. Anger thrums through me like a live wire, zapping anyone who gets too close.

And when that bitch slaps Reid and calls him ugly? I lose it.

"You stupid cunt!" Michelle screams, cradling her rapidly reddening cheek. "I'm going to fucking kill you."

"I'd like to see you try," I snarl, lunging towards her again.

An arm bands around my waist and pulls me back. I struggle against the embrace, kicking out my legs, but Reid refuses to release me.

"Izzy!" he hisses in my ear.

Is he really defending her?

Shock arrows through me, momentarily stilling my movements, before that emotion is replaced by another wave of white-hot anger.

"She hit you!"

"And you hit her, so we're even." Reid's tone is tight with something I can't quite place. Panic, maybe?

"Reid! She hit me!" Michelle's lower lip begins to wobble, and tears glimmer in her brown eyes, lightening the color to a woodsy brown.

"Michelle! Leave! Now!" Reid snarls.

The change happens instantly.

The tears dry from her eyes as if they never existed to begin with, and her lips curve into a demented scowl. Unfettered hatred radiates from her in almost palpable waves, contaminating the air just as prominently as the scent of buttery popcorn.

"I'm going to kill you," she tells me, her voice eerily impassive.

"Michelle!" Reid roars.

Blue sparks dance across Michelle's skin. At first, I don't understand what I'm seeing. They seem to skitter across her arms like electrical currents, congregating in her hands. There, it grows and grows and grows, until it resembles two blue flames resting in her palms.

"What the hell?" I whisper in shock.

Michelle...is supernatural.

What the fuck is she?

"No!" Reid roars, and then he's tugging me to the ground and throwing his body over mine.

I stay perfectly frozen, unable to compute what the fuck is happening. My brain seems to be broken. It keeps repeating random words over and over again.

Power.

Magic.

Michelle.

Reid.

"Get out!"

The roar doesn't come from Reid—who still lies on top of me, protecting me with the length of his body—but it's still familiar.

Silas.

"But..." Michelle begins, her voice wobbling, once again reverting to her tearful, weepy act.

"You know the rules about magic in my theater," he snaps.

Magic?

Silas knows about magic as well?

"But—"

"Get out, Michelle. Now."

"Fine! But I'll be back. My *brother* will have a few words to say to our little friend."

I hear the sound of footsteps. A door shutting and closing.

And then Silas leans down beside us, his mouth pressed in a taut line and his good eye unreadable. "She's gone."

Reid doesn't immediately move. Tremors run through his body.

Driven by some impulse I don't entirely understand, I reach up and run my fingers through his red hair. It's damp with sweat, but I don't feel disgusted the way I might've before. This is...Reid. Reid, who confuses the shit out of me but just protected me from his psycho ex. All I want to do is comfort him and dissipate some of the rigid tension in his shoulders.

The words fall from my mouth without conscious thought. "I'm okay. Everything is okay. She's gone."

"Good." Silas's voice is soft, but it still elicits a growl from Reid. I don't understand why. Silas isn't a threat. "Keep it up. Keep talking to him. Remind him that you're safe."

Is this some kind of wolf thing? Now isn't the time to ask one of the many questions percolating in my head.

Reaching up, I run my hand up and down his back. "I'm safe. I'm okay. You're okay. Everything is okay."

Shivers continue to reverberate through Reid's body, but he no longer holds himself so rigid above me. The arms encircling my waist loosen slightly, and he pushes himself up to peer down at me.

His eyes...

A gasp lodges in my throat.

His eyes are amber, glowing with their own personal light.

"I'm okay," I repeat, cupping his cheek. "I'm okay."

Slowly, gradually, the yellow of his eyes transitions

into a familiar shade of hazel. His breathing evens out, no longer sounding choppy and ragged, and his muscles relax.

Reid is back.

"Hey." I offer him an awkward smile.

"Hi," he says gruffly.

"All right. Get up now. Your fat ass is crushing her." Silas's words seem to shake Reid out of whatever trance he was in.

Quick as a whip, he jumps to his feet, ducking his head and scowling at the ground. I remain on my back for a moment longer, staring up at the ceiling and the circulating fans.

A large, calloused hand comes into my field of view.

"Up, kid," Silas grunts.

I take the offered hand and allow the other man to pull me to my feet. He doesn't immediately release me. His one good eye—currently as hard as granite— surveys me from head to toe. Not in a lewd or perverted way, but in a way that suggests he's checking me for injuries. Seemingly satisfied, he releases me and steps back.

"Does anyone want to explain to me what the hell happened? Why was the wit— Why was she here?" Silas folds his muscular arms over his chest and scowls.

Witch?

He was about to say witch, wasn't he?

At first, I think he's insulting Michelle, but the

more I think about it, the more the pieces begin to click together.

She's a witch.

An actual, honest-to-god witch.

A cold chill skitters down my spine.

"Reid, come to my office," Silas instructs, casting me an inconspicuous look.

Reid scrubs a hand down his face. "She knows."

The older man's brows draw together. "Huh?"

"She knows," Reid repeats with a pointed nod in my direction.

"I know," I agree.

Silas gapes at us in disbelief, seemingly unable to understand what we mean. But then that disbelief turns to shock, the shock transitions into anger, and the anger shifts into grim understanding. He absently scratches at the eyepatch on his face.

"Fuck," he mutters.

I turn towards Reid expectantly. "So your ex is a witch?"

"She's not my ex," Reid snaps, scowling.

"Tell that to her," Silas murmurs.

Reid tosses him a frosty look before returning his attention to me. "Look, what happened with Michelle is a long story, but the gist of it is—you don't want to get on her bad side. And you especially don't want to meet her brother."

"It appears to me as if Izzy is already on her bad

side," Silas interjects. He narrows his eyes on Reid. "How did you allow that to happen?"

Reid's hands fist by his sides. "I didn't allow anything to happen."

"I don't know what went down between you and Michelle—"

"Nothing!"

"But I won't allow her to—"

"I'll handle it."

"You can't just—"

"I said I'll handle it."

As the two of them continue to bicker, I allow my mind to drift.

Michelle is a witch, apparently, and a dangerous one.

Somehow, I made an enemy out of her.

A smile unfurls on my lips before I can suppress it.

I may have made her hate me, but I don't regret what I did. If I see her lift her hands to Reid one more time, I won't just punch her in the face.

I'll bury the bitch.

Twenty-Four

IZZY

To say the next few hours of my shift are awkward is an understatement if I've ever heard one.

Silas hovers around me as if he thinks I'm going to break apart at any moment, and Reid? He ignores my existence, finding every excuse possible not to come near me. When I'm behind the counter, he's cleaning out one of the theaters. When I'm in the cleaning closet, he's in the bathroom. When I'm in Silas's office, he's wiping the windows in the lobby.

It's infuriating.

When my shift finally ends for the night, and the sky turns a murky metallic gray, I clock out and wave goodbye to Silas. I feel awkward as shit around him now, knowing what I do, but I'm not mad. Unlike the others in my life, he was under no obligation to tell me the truth.

"You have a ride home, kid?" Silas asks gruffly as he wipes down the countertop.

Ansel dropped me off after school, but Grayson said he'll pick me up.

"Yeah."

I notice Reid watching us out of the corner of my eye. When he hears my confirmation, he nods once—almost to himself—and resumes sweeping.

I hurry out the back entrance and into the parking lot. Both the moon and sun are visible on either side of the sky, painting the gray in shades of white and black. I plop down on the curb and dig my phone out of my pocket. After pulling up Grayson's name, I shoot him a text.

IZZY

Hey. I'm done. Are you still picking me up?

When he doesn't immediately respond, I flick out of his name and onto Ansel's.

IZZY

Whatcha doing?

ANSEL

Ugh. Have a huge test in Stats tomorrow. Studying.

IZZY

You're in AP Statistics, right?

ANSEL

Maybe…

IZZY

Smarty pants.

IZZY

I'll let you get back to studying.

ANSEL

K. See you tomorrow. Need a ride again?

IZZY

I'll let you know.

I close out of my text messages and scroll through my social media apps. Behind me, the lights of the theater turn off, and Silas says goodbye to Reid. There's the roar of a motor—probably Reid's bike—and then silence once more.

And still no Grayson.

IZZY

Hey. Are you still able to give me a ride?

Silence.

IZZY

Are you ignoring me? Lol

When the silence continues, an uneasy feeling circulates in my gut.

I meant for my previous message to be lighthearted

and jesting, but I can't help but wonder...is he mad at me? He didn't seem to be upset when I confessed I may have feelings for Ansel, but maybe he changed his mind. Or maybe he decided that now that he's slept with me, he doesn't want anything to do with me—

No! Stop it, Izzy! Get out of your own head!

Despite my best wishes, the familiar tendrils of panic rake themselves down my spine.

I debate texting Jake for a ride but remember Silas telling me that he has basketball tryouts. I have no idea if he's still there, and the last thing I want to do is distract him.

Maybe I could call Hale or Gerry...?

But no, I'm not ready to deal with them. They'll demand we talk, and I don't yet have the words to say.

I plug in Grayson's address into the GPS and see that it's only a twenty-minute walk. Not too bad. And most of the trails are in a highly populated area of town.

My route decided, I drag myself to my feet and begin to follow the GPS down the darkened streets. The moon has fully crested the horizon, while the sun has burrowed low. The streetlights provide the only lighting.

I'm pleasantly surprised that I'm not the only person walking the streets at this time of night. I catch sight of a younger family pushing a child in a stroller and a couple holding hands. Some of the tension riding my shoulders dissolves.

I shove my hands into my pockets and quicken my pace. Without any sunlight to counter the wind, it's cold out, almost painfully so. My cheeks and nose sting.

I have a scarf in my backpack—

Dammit!

I curse when I realize I left my backpack behind in the employee break room. The good news is I have my phone and wallet on me.

I'll have to message Silas tomorrow morning and ask if he can come in early to unlock the doors before school. I have a few homework assignments that are due.

The GPS instructs I take a left, so I do, entering a side street nestled between two brick buildings. The streetlights don't quite reach this area, making the shadows appear particularly ominous.

Trepidation settles in my stomach at the unnerving feeling of eyes on the back of my head. Slowly, my heart hammering a mile a minute, I turn around.

But no one's there.

Relief sweeps through me, and I turn to resume my walk when I run smack-dab into a hard chest.

"Hey, little girl. Just where do you think you're going?"

I squint up at the man gripping my shoulders.

He's middle-aged, with red hair peppered religiously with gray. Wrinkles bracket both of his eyes, and when he smiles, he reveals yellowing teeth. He wears a loose flannel over a stained gray shirt and ripped blue jeans.

I immediately step away, allowing his hands to fall back to his sides—

Only to step into another chest.

I glance over my shoulder to see a blond-haired man standing there, leering at me.

"Where ya' going, princess?" Blondie taunts with a lewd grin.

I take a second—only a second—to analyze the situation. Ginger is in front of me, and Blondie is directly behind me. There are brick walls on either side of me. There could be people on the streets, but would I be able to scream in time for them to hear me?

"Let me through, please." I work to keep my voice calm.

Ginger licks his cracked lips. "We just want to talk to you."

"Yeah." Blondie chuckles darkly, and his hands begin to roam up my sides. "Talk."

"Let me go." This time, I allow a little bit of steel to enter my voice.

Both men chuckle.

"I don't think—"

I interrupt Blondie when I slam the back of my head against his face. Hard. He yelps and instinctively releases me. I take his momentary lapse of concentration to duck underneath Ginger's arms and race down the alley.

I know when to fight and when to run. Right now, I'm outmuscled and outmanned. I'm not willing to take a risk in a fight that I'm not positive I can win.

My tennis shoes slap against the asphalt as I push myself faster and faster and faster. I can see the end of the alley, the promise of streetlights and people and stores—

A figure moves in front of me—tall, broad, and covered in scars.

"Why are you running, sweetie?" he coos as he reaches for me.

I throw my fist back and punch Scar straight in the face. It takes him by surprise, and he immediately drops his arms, cupping his cheek.

"You bitch!"

Somebody grabs me from behind, and I kick my feet out desperately, willing them to hit something important. A scream bursts free, but a hand over my mouth immediately silences me.

"Shut up, bitch," Blondie hisses.

I bite down on his hand, hard, digging my teeth into his flesh. He tastes absolutely vile, like dirty socks and rotten eggs.

"She's fucking biting me!" Blondie screams, tightening his grip.

Scar moves until he's directly in front of me. He grips my chin in a punishing grip and forces my face up to his.

"Don't be a little brat. You should be grateful we're giving you the attention."

All three of them chuckle.

I narrow my eyes at him, even as terror floods my system.

I refuse to go down without a fight. Fucking refuse. If they want a docile female, then they chose the wrong one.

Scar's gaze trails down my body and lands on my breasts. His hand leaves my chin and slowly trails downwards—

Another shadow materializes directly behind him —an indistinct shape that I can't quite make out. Dark fingers grab Scar by the ankle and pull.

Scar flies through the alley with a scream of terror.

"What the fuck?" Ginger exclaims.

Scar's screams reach a crescendo, and I hear the sound of flesh tearing. Then there's silence.

All I can hear is the pounding of my own heart trying to burst free of my chest.

"What the fuck?" Ginger repeats, venturing a tentative step forward.

Something grabs him and drags him around the corner of the building.

More screams.

More tearing of flesh.

Silence.

"Holy shit. Holy shit. Holy shit." Blondie releases me as if my skin burned him. He begins to step away.

"Holy shit. Holy sh—" His words are cut off when someone grabs him from above and drags him into the air. I see his legs for a fraction of a second before they disappear on top of the roof. His screams are endless. They reverberate around me.

Something dark drips down the side of the building.

Blood.

Holy fuck.

Holy fuck.

I wait for the monster—because that's what it is—to grab me. Kill me. Tear me apart.

But there's only silence.

Somewhere in the distance, a dog begins to bark and a baby cries. Conversations from two girls reach me as they discuss their job.

What the hell was that?

That wasn't a goddamn wolf or anything I've ever seen before. Anything I've ever *heard* before. The shadow didn't look human...but it also didn't resemble an animal.

It was a beast, a monster, a nightmare made from shadows.

With terror still coursing through my veins, tainting my blood like battery acid, I break into a run.

And I don't stop running until I'm secure in Grayson's apartment.

Twenty-Five

GRAYSON

I groan as I lift my head and take in my surroundings.

I'm not necessarily surprised to find myself in another cell, though this one is far more degrading than the last one I was forced into. Three of the walls are constructed out of gray cement, while a fourth is composed of steel bars. The floor is cold to the touch and covered in a liquid I really, really hope is just water. There's not a single piece of furniture. All I've been left with is a scratchy-looking blanket frayed at the edges.

"Sleepy Beauty awakens," a familiar accented voice remarks.

"Sleeping Beauty," I correct automatically as I force myself to my feet and step closer to the bars separating me from my captor.

Vladimir Popov grins, revealing two rows of sharp

teeth. His red eyes gleam ominously in the darkness of my prison.

"They vant to see you," Vlad says, still smiling.

He always wanted to see me fall from grace.

I wonder if he took over my position during my... extended absence.

"They truly know how to make a guest feel welcomed," I murmur as I bring my hand to my head.

My fingers come away sticky with blood.

Instead of responding, Vlad reaches into his pocket and procures a set of heavy-looking iron keys. He sticks the largest one into the padlock and twists.

"Don't keep them vaiting," Vlad says, gesturing me forward with more contempt than courtesy.

I wobble slightly, my head spinning, but manage to regain my footing. Thank fuck for that.

Vlad eyes me with thinly veiled distaste. "So it's true."

"What is?" I don't spare the vampire a second glance as I move towards the steep staircase that will lead me to the Elder Chambers.

"You haven't fed."

Vlad's words cause my feet to freeze. Something cold and insidious circles my neck like a noose.

Unlike popular belief, if a vampire doesn't consume blood, they don't pass away. Yes, there have been a few cases where a vampire went centuries without feeding and lost function of their limbs, but they were still alive.

Blood merely enhances our powers. Makes us faster. Stronger. Smarter.

There's always a dull ache in my chest that demands I feed. It's like I've been walking through the desert for years and stumbled upon an oasis of fresh water. Only years of iron self-control allow me to resist the temptation.

I ignore Vlad's remark and continue up the staircase, noting that the door has been left ajar. Voices reach me, but they're not as clear as they would've been if I'd been well-fed. Still, I know immediately who's on the other side of that door.

The Elders.

My suspicion is confirmed when I push open the door the rest of the way and seven heads swivel in my direction.

At first glance, one would think that I've just intruded on a party. Beautiful women in long dresses mingle with striking men in suits and ties. On closer inspection, however, I can see the red of their eyes—an indication of their power. The darker the eye color, the more powerful a vampire is.

"Grayson! Welcome, my boy!" Edward lifts his arms and smiles cordially, but I could never mistake him for anything less than a shark in the water. "It's been a long time."

I don't bother to speak. Anything I say—any excuse I give or argument I make—will be used against me. These monsters want nothing more than to see my blood spilled.

I can't let them know about Izzy.

"We missed you when you...left us." Piper DeLong sniffs disdainfully, even as her eyes devour me from head to toe. She smooths a manicured hand through her mane of chestnut hair. "Where did you go?"

"Around," I respond curtly, shoving my hands into my sweatshirt pocket.

"Is that any way to treat the vampires who raised you?" Telly Montgomery asks, cocking her head to the side. A coil of black hair cascades down her cheek, but she brushes it away with a flick of her wrist.

The vampires who raised you.

Ha.

What a fucking joke.

They forged me into a monster—one who hunted and killed for them. But now this monster is free of his restraints, and he's out for blood. Only one being holds his leash, and it's not any of them.

All of this started when my mom passed away and I was thrown into the foster system. My second foster family recognized immediately what I was and contacted the Elders. They allowed me to continue living with my foster family...if I trained with the vampires at night. They taught me how to kill with a stone-cold efficiency that might've terrified me if I were anyone else.

As it was, the only thought that pulsated through my head was my need to protect Izzy. My Gracie.

If that meant killing the Elders' enemies, then so be it.

But then Kain reached out to me and threatened my reason for existence. I left the Elders without a backwards glance.

Something they're not happy about, if their dour expressions are any indication.

They consider what they did for me a gift.

I consider it a curse.

"Look at him." Piper waves a hand airily in my direction, still holding her champagne flute. I wonder if it's alcohol that she's drinking...or blood. "Look at his eyes."

"When did you last drink, boy?" Edward demands with a scowl.

Unlike the vampires here, I never drank to kill, only to survive. I needed my powers to complete the tasks they assigned me. However, when I moved to a different town and discovered that wolves inhabited it, I chose to forgo blood. I didn't want the dogs sniffing out what I am.

"Those must be contacts," Telly says, sniffing. "There's no way he hasn't fed—"

"Can't you sense the lack of magic in him?" Tika Lemont interrupts, a frown on his face.

"I suppose it makes sense." Edward scratches at the stubble on his jawline.

Despite being over three hundred years old, he doesn't look a day over thirty.

Another benefit of drinking fresh blood.

"What makes sense?" Piper licks at a droplet of red liquid that has spilled from her cup.

"He couldn't allow the shifters to discover what he was."

Edward's words cause an icy chill to skate down my spine.

How much does the powerful bastard know?

"Why was he with the shifters in the first place?" Marcus Brown frowns severely, cutting harsh lines into his pale face.

"Isn't that the million-dollar question?" Edward moves forward slowly, calculatingly, his eyes trained on me the entire time.

Every muscle in my body locks together when the stench of death and decay assaults my senses.

"Did you want to abandon your family, Grayson? Is that why you left?" His words are practically a purr —a noise that might've been seductive if it wasn't so damn terrifying.

"I heard that some Hunters visited a few wolves," Piper interjects, not bothering to hide her glee.

"Did you have a part to play in that, Grayson?" Marcus asks.

All of them are staring at me. Assessing me with their penetrating eyes.

I don't know how to respond, how to get myself out of this mess.

Edward abruptly grasps my chin, his nails digging into my skin. I don't allow any of the pain I feel to reflect on my face.

"You've always been such a good boy for me and the others, Grayson," he says, his words both a praise and a threat. Abruptly, he releases me, his shark-like smile growing until it threatens to cleave his face in two. "Maybe a good night's rest will jog your memory." He looks over my shoulder. Vlad?"

"Yes, Elder?" Vlad materializes beside me with an expectant smile on his face.

"Show Grayson back to his room, would you?"

"It would be my honor." Vlad bows his head reverently and then reaches for my arm.

I allow him to grab me, to tug me along, because what other choice do I have?

Edward's voice carries to me just before I reach the staircase. "And Grayson?"

I tense.

"Next time I see you, I want the truth. Tell me why you left, and maybe I'll allow you to live." And with that, Edward turns away, reengaging Piper in conversation.

Vlad gleefully pulls me down the staircase, his enhanced strength causing me to stumble.

Izzy, I'm so fucking sorry.

I make a vow, right then and there, that I'll never give her up, no matter what the Elders and their lackeys do to me.

I'm sorry.

Twenty-Six

IZZY

I wake to the sound of incessant knocking on the apartment door.

I blink and roll over, struggling to orient myself to my surroundings.

I'm lying in Grayson's bed, in his apartment. It's—I glance at the clock on the bedside table—just after three in the morning.

Who the fuck is banging on the door?

My first thought is Grayson. He didn't return home last night, but he sent me a text a little after midnight telling me he had to work third shift and not to worry. Did he return home and forget his key?

I roll out of bed and pad towards the bedroom door. My gaze snags on my reflection in the mirror hanging over the dresser, and I wince.

My blonde hair sticks up in all directions, and there are dark smudges beneath both of my eyes. Tiny bruises dot my chin where that asshole grabbed me, but hopefully, I'll be able to hide them with makeup.

A shiver rolls through me when I think about the night before.

Those three men.

That strange shadow.

Those agonized screams.

The blood dripping down the wall.

I squeeze my eyelids shut, desperately willing those images to dissipate, and when I reopen them, I feel calmer. More in control.

I need to talk to Christian about what I saw first thing in the morning.

Someone knocks again, and I huff out a breath as I throw on a pair of leggings underneath Grayson's oversized T-shirt. It practically engulfs my petite frame like a dress.

"I'm coming!" I call, exiting the bedroom and walking towards the apartment door.

But then I freeze as an insidious thought occurs to me.

What if the monster from last night returned?

I hesitate, my feet stilling, and someone knocks again.

"Grayson!" an unfamiliar voice screeches. "Let me in!"

Curiosity gets the better of me, and I wrench the door open.

Only to immediately wish I hadn't.

Sidney stands in the doorframe, her eyes red-rimmed from crying and her brown hair disheveled. The second she catches sight of me, her eyes narrow into thin slits.

"I fucking knew it." She shoulders past me and stomps into the apartment. "Grayson! Come out here right this fucking instance!"

I have no idea what to say.

What to do.

Never in a million years did I expect to be the other woman. Yes, Grayson told me he broke up with her—and he assured me time and time again that their relationship meant nothing to him—but seeing the devastation and anger on Sidney's face...

An uneasy feeling snakes through my stomach.

"Grayson!" Sidney storms towards the bed without hesitation.

As if she knows exactly where to go...

As if she's been here before.

Stop it! I mentally chastise myself. *Grayson told me he never slept with her, and I believe him. Hell, he promised me he didn't even kiss her.*

"*You.*" Sidney whirls on me, her eyes spewing vitriol. She lifts a trembling finger and points it at my chest. "You're the whore my boyfriend's been sleeping with."

"Ex-boyfriend," I correct automatically, and then I instantly flinch when Sidney's face flashes with rage.

"He wasn't my ex when he first stuck his dick in you," she snaps.

I wince.

I don't know if that's true or not, but it doesn't change the fact that, in some ways, I am a home-wrecker.

Self-loathing slithers its way through me and makes a nest in my chest.

"I'm sorry—"

The slap comes out of nowhere. I honestly don't see it coming.

Pain explodes in my cheek, and tears prick my eyes. I rub at the aching skin to see Sidney standing in front of me, her chest heaving, her eyes twin flames of anger.

"You're sleeping in his bed, wearing his clothes." She scoffs derisively. "How does it feel to know that you got my sloppy leftovers?"

I just stare at her, refusing to rise to the bait.

"Did he tell you that you were his one and only? That he loved you?" She laughs, but the noise is devoid of any humor. "That's what he told me—before and after he fucked the daylights out of me." Whatever she sees on my face causes her smile to broaden, turning predatory. "You didn't know that, did you? Tell me...did he do that thing with his tongue in your pussy? I taught him that. It felt good, didn't it?"

Rage sweeps across my vision in a curtain of red. My hands ball into fists by my sides, but it's like someone else is in control of my body. I'm barely aware of myself moving.

A part of me wants to punch her in the face. I totally could. Sidney may be a wolf shifter like her brothers, but I know I could take her in a hand-to-hand fight.

But...

Hurting her isn't the answer. She's in pain and taking her anger out on me.

Besides, I already won this battle, and we both know it. At the end of the day, Grayson is *mine*, not hers. Despite the little green monster inside of me peeking a single eye open, I know that all of her taunts are bullshit.

What's the point of attacking her when the war is already over and I've been declared victorious?

So, as much as I'd like to stab her in the neck with one of my blades, I restrain myself. She's not worth my anger.

Or jail time.

Sometimes it sucks having to be the bigger person.

"Tell Grayson that when he gets the balls to come see me. Or at least call me." Sidney tosses a strand of silky brown hair in a way that whips me across the face. She once again shoulders past me to get to the door. "And Gracie?" She pauses at the door frame, stopping to peer over her shoulder at me. "I'd be careful with him if I were you. Once a cheater, always a cheater. Remember that."

And with that, she stomps out of the apartment, leaving me alone once more.

Twenty-Seven

IZZY

The second time I wake up, it's to the sound of my phone buzzing.

Once.

Twice.

Three times.

Again and again and again and again.

I grab the nearest pillow and shove it over my face, allowing a scream to break free.

My dreams last night were plagued by images of a shadowy monster tearing three men to shreds, a dark-eyed witch wrapping me in her power, and a beautiful girl screaming at me for ruining her relationship.

For the first time in who the fuck knows how long, I don't dream of any of my so-called "mates."

"Who the fuck is calling me?" I murmur groggily.

Did I miss my alarm clock? But...no. It's only six

thirty in the morning. My alarm isn't set to go off until seven.

Is Ansel here already? It honestly wouldn't surprise me if he has some sort of extracurricular he has to get to early in the morning. Isn't he in, like, ten different clubs?

But it isn't Ansel who's calling me.

Five missed calls from Silas.

Seven missed calls from Hale.

Three missed calls from Gerry.

Six missed calls from Jake.

Ten missed calls from Emery.

Eighteen missed calls from Reid.

Ten missed calls from Ethan.

What the hell?

When another call comes through, I click accept, not bothering to even check who's trying to get ahold of me.

"What's wrong?" I ask immediately as a plethora of possibilities flit through my brain.

Did something happen to Lissa? Seth?

"Izzy. Thank fuck." Ethan's voice is heavy with relief—so much relief, I can practically picture him sagging to the ground. "Em! I got a hold of her! She's here!"

"Put her on speaker!" Emery demands, his voice sounding muffled.

"You're on speaker, Izzy," Ethan tells me.

"Are you okay?" Emery demands instantly. "Are you hurt?"

"What?" My first thought is that they somehow found out what happened in the alley.

Did they find the bodies? The monster?

"The theater..." Ethan swallows heavily.

"What the hell happened? You guys are scaring me."

"There was an explosion, Izzy," Emery bites out, his tone brisk. "At the theater. They found a body."

I suck in a startled breath. "What?"

"They don't know what happened yet," Ethan cuts in. "They think it could be an issue with the gas line or something."

"Oh my god." I place a hand to my mouth as tears prick my eyes. "Jake? Silas? Reid?"

"They're all okay," Ethan reassures me. "They've been trying to get a hold of you."

"What was someone doing there that early?" I ask.

The theater doesn't even open until ten on Friday.

"I don't know." Emery's voice is hoarse. "I'm just... I'm just happy you're okay."

"You should call Hale or Gerry," Ethan adds. "They're out of their minds with worry."

A lump settles in my throat, but I find myself nodding, despite knowing the twins can't see me. "Yeah. Okay. I'll do that."

"Izzy..." Emery trails off, seemingly at a loss for words.

Silence stretches between the three of us, fraught with tension, precarious in the way that glass is seconds before shattering.

"Just be careful, okay?" His voice sounds choked.

When I hang up the phone, it's with a hollow feeling in my chest. I feel aimless and adrift. Lost.

Taking a deep breath, and steeling my resolve, I shoot off texts to everyone who messaged me.

I save Hale for last.

IZZY

I'm okay. I'm still at my friend's house. But I think we need to talk.

Hale responds instantly.

HALE

Come to the house. Gerry and I will be here.

* * *

It's only as I'm getting ready for the day, my movements slow and mechanical, do I receive a follow-up text from Reid.

REID

They identified the body. It was Minnie. She was one of Sidney's packmates. Twins are with her now.

The phone slips from my hands and clatters into the bathroom sink.

What are the odds that Sidney confronted me the same morning her packmate is killed in an explosion?

I don't dare allow myself to look too closely at the connection.

I'm not sure I'll like what I find.

Twenty-Eight

IZZY

Ansel didn't ask questions when I pleaded with him to drop me off at Hale and Gerry's home. He only looked at me with one eyebrow arched and asked, "Will you be safe?"

My heart fluttered madly, even as I nodded my assurance.

Now I stand in the entryway of my foster parents' home, watching Ansel back his car out of the driveway. I wait until he disappears around the corner before taking a deep breath—willing oxygen into my glass-coated lungs—and stepping inside.

Lissa's voice immediately reaches me. "THIS IS BULLSHIT!"

I quicken my pace.

My foster family is in the kitchen. Hale leans against the counter with his arms folded over his chest. He looks tired, his eyes underscored by dark crescent moons. I swear his hair has more gray in it than when I last saw him.

Gerry stands beside his husband, in front of the stove, cleaning up whatever breakfast they had this morning. Every once in a while, the giant will brush his fingers against Hale's in a reassuring caress.

Jake and Seth both sit at the counter, watching the exchange like it's the most interesting match of volleyball they've ever seen in their lives. For once, Seth doesn't have his headphones on.

And then there's Lissa.

I remember when I first met my younger foster sister and new roommate. The only word I could think to describe her was pink. Everything she wore was pink. She had pink nail polish on. Pink lipstick. Pink headband. Pink fake highlights in her hair.

The girl standing before me is unrecognizable.

She wears a dark hoodie that's three sizes too big and obscures her body from view. She would have to roll up her sleeves numerous times to actually use her hands. Black leggings and a pair of Converse shoes complete the look.

God, what the hell happened in the few days I've been away?

Guilt niggles at me, as does a wave of self-loathing. I know it shouldn't—I did nothing wrong—but I can't help but wish I'd been here for Lissa. She's been through something traumatic, and I'm the only person here who can possibly understand what she's going through.

Lissa's eyes flick to me and harden. Her upper lip peels away from her teeth in a snarl. "Look who finally decided to grace us with her presence. When did we decide that it's acceptable to run away from our problems?"

"Lissa!" Hale scolds, but Lissa simply scowls at him, unrepentant.

"Why can't I stay here for this conversation?" she demands, stomping her foot. "You're allowing Jake to stay—"

They are?

"—but why can't I—"

"Because it's not your time to know yet," Seth says calmly, his attention fixated on the cord of his headphones.

Hale pinches the bridge of his nose as if he's begging for patience. "Lissa, please. Now isn't the time—"

"It's never the time." She throws her hands up in the air. "Sometimes I wonder if you even want me here."

"Don't say that," Gerry scolds, finally whirling away from the stovetop to face his youngest foster daughter. "You know that we love you—"

"Yeah. Okay." Lissa scoffs and reaches for her backpack. That, too, is no longer a bright pink. It's black and covered in stickers of skulls. "Whatever."

"Lissa—"

"Save it." She holds a hand up to stop Hale's protest.

Surprisingly, Hale obeys, though his face falls.

"I suppose we're taking the bus this morning?" she asks.

"We need to talk to Izzy and Jake..." Gerry begins placatingly.

But Lissa ignores him and stalks towards the kitchen doorway. She doesn't spare me, or anyone else for that matter, a second glance.

Seth doesn't immediately follow after her. He remains where he is, his glasses slightly askew and his messy brown hair flopping across his forehead.

He tilts his head to the side as if he's listening to something no one else can hear. "She won't be angry forever."

Hale offers him a tired smile. "I know, Seth."

Seth shifts on the stool and pushes up his glasses with his pointer finger. "And now isn't the time to tell her. She's not ready."

Hale and Gerry exchange an indecipherable glance. The latter opens his mouth, a question swarming in his eyes, but Seth plops his headphones back into place and slides off the stool. Like Lissa, he doesn't say goodbye as he leaves the kitchen.

The sudden silence that permeates the air is stifling.

Jake breaks it first, his gaze volleying between the two men in confusion. "Can someone please explain to me what the ever-loving hell is going on? What do you need to talk to me about? And why is Izzy here? No offense, Izzy. You know I love you. But you literally told me just yesterday that you needed space." His blond brows furrow as something seems to occur to him. "Does this have something to do with it?"

"I believe so," Hale murmurs.

Gerry sighs and scrubs a hand down his chin. Just like the first time I saw him, he wears a leather jacket that clings to his muscular shoulders, tight jeans, and cowboy boots. His red hair is long and cascades down his spine in loose waves.

"We need to talk to the two of you. Izzy's right to be angry with us. We've been keeping secrets from you. From both of you." He pauses and then says, "From *all* of you."

Jake's brows lower in trepidation. "What type of secrets?"

"Let's take this to the living room, shall we?" Hale suddenly seems older. Not just days older or even weeks, but years older. Decades. Lines bracket his eyes that haven't been there before. "This is going to be a long conversation."

Twenty-Nine

IZZY

H ale's hands tremble around the coffee mug as he tentatively brings it to his lips.

"Is this about the explosion?" Jake asks, and grief momentarily flickers in his eyes.

I realize with a start that he probably knew Minnie. Was friends with her. He worked there for years, after all.

His anguish is a physical punch to the gut, and I reach across the couch to take his hand in mine. He flashes me a grateful smile and gives my fingers a squeeze.

"What happened was a tragedy—" Gerry begins.

"Did they say what caused it?" I interrupt.

God, that poor girl. She was only a few years older than I am and had her whole life ripped away from her. Did she have a family? Friends? A significant other?

The twins mentioned that their sister knew her. Who else is currently mourning her death?

It could've been me, or Jake, or Silas, or Reid who died.

Hell, it could've been *all* of us, if the explosion happened even a few hours later.

The realization is like a bucket of ice water dumped over my head.

"They'll look into it," Hale assures us, reaching upwards to ruffle his salt-and-pepper hair. The strands are a little longer than they were the last time I saw him, almost as if he hasn't gotten them cut in a while. "They think it could be a gas line explosion."

"What was Minnie even doing there so early?" Jake asks.

"They don't know for sure, but they suspect she left something behind. Went back early to retrieve it."

I suck in a sharp gasp.

Didn't I plan to return before school began to grab my forgotten backpack? Sweat trickles down my spine, and my hands feel clammy. A lead weight drops into the pit of my stomach, sluicing the meager contents around.

"But that's not what we want to talk to you guys about," Gerry interrupts, once again steering the conversation back on track. He leans forward to run his hands up and down his thighs. The leather crinkles, the sound ominously loud in the suddenly taut silence.

"There's a lot you two don't know about this world. About yourselves."

"I know…some," I tentatively venture, flicking my gaze towards Jake.

He just appears confused, his brows drawn together.

"Know some of what?" The blond quarterback cocks his head to the side like a curious dog.

I ignore him for the time being and refocus on Gerry and Hale. "I know about the supernatural. About wolf shifters and vampires and witches—"

"Okay. Okay. I get it." Jake rolls his eyes exaggeratedly. "Is this your attempt at a joke? Because it's not funny or appropriate, considering the situation."

Hale blows out a haggard breath and scrubs a hand down his face. The lines bracketing his eyes appear even deeper than usual, more pronounced. Has he been sleeping? I swear those dark smudges weren't there prior…

"It's not a joke, Jake. There's an entire world that you don't know about—"

"Knock it the fuck off." Jake stands abruptly, his hands balling into fists. Rage distorts his handsome face into something unrecognizable. "My friend just died, and you really think now is the time to mess with me?"

"Sit down, Jake," Gerry instructs.

"No! You can't just—"

"Jake!" Gerry's eyes flash amber, the color almost luminescent in the dimly lit living room.

My breath stalls at the sight, and Jake's face drains of all color.

Slowly—never taking his eyes off of Gerry—Jake sits back on the couch beside me, a tremor reverberating through him.

"What the fuck?" he whispers, shock and horror mingling in his voice.

"I don't really know where to start this conversation—" Hale begins.

"How about the beginning?" I snap.

Hale blanches at my tone but nods once in understanding. "Right. Of course."

He blows out another breath, and in that one sound, I can hear everything he doesn't say out loud. All of his fear and anger and confusion. They meld together until I can't differentiate one emotion from the other.

"The truth is...the four of you didn't come to our home by accident."

"What do you mean by that?" Jake demands, leaning forward.

Hale and Gerry exchange an indecipherable glance, but it's Hale who continues speaking, his expression grave. "Amanda Highland finds kids who are...different and brings them to us."

A thread of trepidation unfurls in my chest. "Different how?"

In answer, Hale stands and shakily begins undoing the buttons of his shirt.

Jake's nose immediately scrunches in disgust. "What the fuck are you doing?"

"Proving this to you," Hale snaps, his tone frostier than I ever remember hearing it. "You won't listen to everything I have to say if you continue to think we're full of shit."

"Why are you stripping?" Jake asks, incredulous.

I look away when Hale pulls down his pants, but Jake continues to stare, wide-eyed and confused. His lips part in a silent O.

And then he gasps out loud, his entire face whitening until it's practically the color of the walls. I turn back just in time to see that Hale has been replaced by a huge, furry, brown wolf. His tongue lolls to the side as he cocks his head at us.

"No. No. No. This can't be fucking happening. Did I accidentally eat some pot brownies?" Jake mutters as he shakes his head rapidly from side to side, trying to dislodge the image before us.

Hale whines and places his huge head down on his paws.

Trying to make himself smaller, I realize. Less threatening.

There's a sort of keen intelligence in the beast's eyes that lets me know Hale's still inside of there. He hasn't been completely consumed by the wolf.

A part of me wants to reach forward and pet him—

the fur between his ears looks incredibly soft—but shock holds me immobile. I've known about the supernatural world for days now, but seeing it in person? That's something else entirely. I can barely get a breath out through my shriveling lungs.

"I'm hallucinating, aren't I?" Jake whispers to me.

His face hasn't yet regained the color it lost.

"If you are, then I am too," I respond dazedly.

"Maybe it's a mass hallucination."

"You're not hallucinating," Gerry says as Hale trots around the corner, his discarded pants in his mouth.

There's a shift in the air, almost like an electrical current that causes goose bumps to form on my arms, and then Hale returns, buttoning up his pants. Gerry throws him his shirt, and Hale takes it gratefully, pulling it over his broad shoulders.

"Shifters exist," Hale says candidly, "as do a plethora of other supernatural creatures. Gerry and I..." He exchanges another unreadable look with his husband. "We find children who may have been lost in the foster care system, and we gradually help them adjust to our world."

"I'm not... I'm not like that," Jake says, shaking his head. A strand of blond hair flops in front of his face, and he brushes it away with a shaky hand. "I'm not... I can't... I can't turn into a wolf or anything. You're wrong about me."

"Jake, how did your family die?" Gerry asks.

The abrupt change in subject causes me to jerk upright, alarm careening through me.

Jake tenses. "How... What... Why does that matter?"

"There was a car accident when you were a boy, wasn't there?" Gerry continues, his eyes holding Jake's hostage. "Your father and grandparents died, but you and your mom survived."

"Yes—" Jake swallows. His breathing has begun to turn ragged, shallow spurts of air that escape through chapped lips.

"But your mom committed suicide shortly after, correct?" Gerry presses.

I don't know where he's going with this line of questioning, but I hate the anguish I can feel emanating off of Jake in almost tangible waves.

"Is this really necessary?" I demand, protectiveness roaring through me.

Gerry turns sad eyes in my direction. "I wish it wasn't, kiddo, but it's time Jake knew the truth."

"I don't understand!" Jake throws his hands up in the air. His eyes are glassy with unshed tears.

"Your mom mentioned you in her suicide note, did she not?" Gerry continues, his tone gentle despite his callous words. "She said you were a mistake, an abomination."

Jake opens and closes his mouth, momentarily at a loss for words. I reach for my foster brother and wrap my arms around him, desperate to quell his pain, desperate to hold him together. I hate seeing him like this. And I hate Gerry and Hale for poking at old wounds that haven't seemed to heal.

"We're not saying this to hurt you, Jake," Hale whispers, his voice choked. "We just need you to understand."

"Understand what?" Jake grasps my arms almost desperately, as if he's afraid that if he were to release me, I'll float away and be lost forever.

"You died in that car accident, kid." Gerry's voice drips with sympathy. "Your mother made a deal with a witch to bring you back. But...nobody can bring the dead back to life. Not truly. That magic has been lost for centuries now."

Jake's already shaking his head before Gerry has even finished speaking. I don't know if he's protesting the older man's words or something else entirely, but his body trembles and convulses in my arms. All I can do is hold him even tighter, even closer, and rub my hand up and down his back in what I hope is comfort.

"The witch created a vessel out of clay and implanted it with Jake's memories. Have you ever noticed that you never get hurt? Never bleed? That you're stronger and faster than the average human?" Hale asks.

"No." It's a broken whisper.

"You're what the supernatural world calls a golem, Jake. You're not..." Hale swallows. "You're not alive.

You died back in that car accident. I'm sorry. I'm so, so sorry."

Thirty

JAKE

"This song sucks," I grumble from the back seat as I kick out my legs.

One of my feet makes contact with the passenger seat, where my mom currently sits.

She spins around and arches one eyebrow at me. "Jacob, behave yourself."

I simply roll my eyes and turn to stare out the window. Trees spin by, their branches illuminated by the white glow of the moon. There's something about the night I've always found enticing. Maybe because, in the darkness, you don't need to pretend to be something you're not. You can display all of your flaws and demons, and no one will judge you.

And I certainly have a lot of demons.

With great reluctance, I peel my gaze off of the window and focus on the back of my mom's head.

"I always behave." I punctuate my words with a scoff.

And then, just because I can, I kick the back of her seat. She whirls around to give me a scathing glare, even as the edges of her lips twitch upwards in amusement.

My grandparents, who sit behind me in the car, chuckle at my attitude.

"He reminds me of you when you were a boy," Grandma says to Dad, her tone holding nothing but fondness.

Dad throws her a look in the rearview mirror as he expertly merges the car onto the highway. "Please. Don't say that. I'm not sure I can handle a mini me."

Everybody says I look exactly like my father. We have the same blond hair, strong jawlines, and piercing blue eyes. My mother, on the other hand, has light-orange hair, green eyes, and an array of freckles on her nose and cheeks. I've always secretly wished I looked more like her than him. She's the most beautiful person I've ever met.

"This is stupid," I mutter for the one millionth time as the radio continues to blare some old-fashioned rock song.

How can anyone think this crap is good?

Ugh. If I'm going to be forced to be here, then I should at least be able to pick the music.

Mom and Dad insisted I join them for their monthly dinner with my grandparents. They all dress up, head to some fancy restaurant, and talk about boring *stuff for hours. For the longest time, I was deemed too young to accompany them, but this month is different. Instead of staying home with a babysitter, they insisted on dragging me along.*

So now I'm here, wearing a suit that practically suffocates me, wishing I were anywhere else. All of my friends are playing the new video game that just came out. Why can't I do that?

I kick out at Mom's seat again, and she spins around to face me, her eyes heated.

"Jacob, knock it off this instant. You're being rude."

"I don't want to go," I whine. "This is dumb."

"Your behavior is dumb," my dad counters immediately.

"Steve," Mom says and turns imploring eyes onto my father, "talk to him."

"What do you want me to say, Lizzie?"

"I don't know." Mom blows out a breath. "Take away his phone or something."

I gape at the back of her head in disbelief. "What did I even do? Is this just because I don't want to be here?"

"You don't want to see your favorite grandparents, kid?" Grandpa leans forward to ruffle my hair, but I swat his wrinkled hand away.

"You're my only grandparents," I retort.

My mother's parents died before I was born.

"Still your favorite, though."

"I wouldn't say—"

That's when it happens.

One second, I'm joking with my grandpa.

The next, the world tilts upside down.

I'm tumbling. Falling. Rolling. I can't differentiate up from down. Pain explodes inside of me, but I don't know where it's coming from. Everywhere. Nowhere.

A red sheen obscures my vision, like a curtain drawn shut, and a whimper of pain escapes me. Out of my periphery, I see my father, his face streaked with blood, his eyes vacant and unseeing.

Where am I?

How did I get here?

Pain.

So much pain.

Something digs into my chest, and it takes me a moment to realize it's the seat belt.

My head's foggy, almost as if it's been stuffed full of cotton balls, and dizziness threatens to consume me. The edges of my vision darken.

Then I'm aware of nothing at all.

"No. You're lying! This isn't... This can't be..." My body shakes. Trembles. Convulses.

I can't think straight. There's an incessant pounding in my head, like someone took a sledgehammer to my brain and is whacking it repeatedly.

I'm honestly afraid that I'll pass out.

Is this some kind of cruel joke?

No, that can't be right. My fathers wouldn't do that to me. Neither would Izzy, whom I have come to love like a sister.

Bile snakes its way up my throat, burning like flickering embers, and I squeeze my lips together to keep it at bay.

"We knew we needed to tell you but couldn't find the words to," Hale tells me, his voice gentle. Crooning.

It almost feels as if he's approaching a rabid dog, one snapping and foaming at the mouth. Am I that dog? I certainly feel a little unhinged, like my life has been tipped upside down, and I can't get my feet back underneath me.

"Jake..." Izzy's voice trembles as she attempts to comfort me.

"I... I need..." I jump to my feet and move to the kitchen, belatedly aware that the others have followed me.

I open drawers at random, knowing what I'm looking for but unable to remember where it is. My brain still doesn't seem to be working right. Someone put up an *Out of Order* sign and left the premises.

Finally, I grab the handle of a steak knife and whirl around.

Izzy's blue eyes are wide in her face. "Jake, what are you doing?"

"You're lying," I snap at Hale, who has come to stand directly behind her.

"I'm sorry—"

I slice at my wrist with the blade.

Izzy screams, the noise chipping away a piece of my heart, but I ignore it and focus on the wound.

The non-bloody wound.

There's nothing but a single line marring the skin.

"What the hell?" I whisper through numb lips.

"Jake, put the knife down," Gerry consoles gruffly, advancing towards me.

But I can't pull my attention away from where I cut myself.

I'm not bleeding.

Why am I not bleeding?

Why am I not fucking bleeding?

Panic grabs hold of me and shakes me around like a rag doll. My breathing comes out in stuttered, shallow gasps.

"No. No. No. No. This can't be fucking happening."

I'm not...alive.

I'm dead.

Oh god. I'm dead.

What the fuck am I?

They said... They said I'm a golem. A creature made of clay.

I need to get away. To run. To escape.

I lock eyes with Izzy, my gaze beseeching. She, more than anyone, can understand what I'm going through. I have no idea what role she has to play in all of this, but if it's anything like the one I have...

She nods once in understanding and then shifts her body so she's blocking Hale and Gerry from getting to me.

I take off in a run, ignoring their pleas for me to return. But I can't. Not yet. Not now. Maybe not ever. My brain is in turmoil, and my heart feels as if it's been squeezed through a meat grinder.

I'm not alive.

I'm not alive.

I'm not a-fucking-live.

I throw myself into the car and then slam the door shut. Gripping the steering wheel tightly, I will my breathing to calm. Despite my best wishes, it continues to escape me in uneven, shallow pants.

Almost absently, I realize I'm still holding the steak knife, the weapon caught between my palm and the wheel. I force my fingers to relax, to loosen, and the knife clatters onto the seat between my legs.

I stare at it for a long moment. The wooden handle. The sharp blade. My tear-stained reflection on the surface.

I'm not alive.

I'm not alive.

I'm not alive.

Sobbing, I pick the knife up once more and hold it to my pinkie finger.

I didn't bleed when it cut me.

But what will happen when I remove a body part?

A scream lodges in my throat, begging to break free, as I begin to slice.

Thirty-One

IZZY

I step away from Hale and Gerry when I hear the front door open and slam shut.

The last thing I want is to leave Jake alone during a time like this, but I know what it's like to want to get away. To be alone with your thoughts.

A single tear cascades down Hale's cheek as he stares after his foster son. Gerry moves to put an arm around his husband's shoulders and pull him into his embrace.

"He'll be okay," Gerry whispers, and I'm not sure who he's trying to convince—Hale or himself. "He's a strong kid. He'll be okay."

I want to yell at them, demand how they could think such a thing after what Jake was just told, but I bite my tongue. Wasn't I the one to demand answers in the first place? It wouldn't be fair for me to snap at them just because I didn't like the ones I received. Jake deserved to know the truth.

But...

How can he come back from this?

From the realization that—bile swarms in my stomach—he died years ago and is nothing but memories shoved into a clay vessel. How does that work, exactly? What would happen if the magic wore off? Is that a possibility?

Fear eclipses my horror over the situation, tainting my bloodstream like battery acid.

And what if I'm like Jake?

What if I'm a golem?

"Is that... Is that what I am?" I whisper.

Hale shifts in Gerry's embrace to face me. His eyes are red-rimmed and almost luminescent with tears. "No. No, you're not. You're...human."

"Why did you hesitate before you said that?" I demand as something icy and insidious slithers down my spine.

Gerry releases Hale and takes a single step backwards. Both men stare at me with unreadable expressions.

When the silence continues, permeating the air like a damn virus, I blurt out, "Just tell me. I can handle it."

"You're human, but you shouldn't be," Hale says at last.

My brows furrow. "What do you mean by that?"

"Let's take this back to the living room, shall we?" Gerry suggests. "I don't think—"

"Just tell me," I demand. And then, as an afterthought, I add, "Please."

I grip the granite countertop so tightly that my knuckles turn white.

Hale and Gerry exchange another one of those eloquent glances that make words unnecessary.

It's Hale who relents with a heavy sigh. He scratches absently at the beard lining his jawline as he struggles to find the right words.

"We knew your parents," he says at last.

It feels as if a bomb has just been thrown at me in a macabre game of hot potato.

I stagger back a step until my ass finds one of the barstools. I shakily sit myself down, wishing I'd taken Gerry up on his offer to return to the living room.

"What?" I'm not sure if I speak the word or only think it. My lips feel incapable of moving. Or maybe my tongue is simply too big to fit in my mouth.

"We knew your parents," Hale repeats. "Your birth parents, not the ones who adopted you."

"My birth parents?" I stare at him in disbelief. "I don't understand—"

"Izzy." Gerry moves until he's crouched in front of me, the material of his pants creaking with the movement. His long beard brushes against his kneecaps as he takes my hand in both of his. "Your parents—the ones who unfortunately passed away when you were young—were not your birth parents. They adopted you."

"No. That can't be true. No." I desperately wish to wrench my hand free of Gerry's while simultaneously wanting to throw myself into his embrace and have him hold me.

I'm in desperate need of comfort.

"They probably planned to tell you when you were older," Hale says, moving to stand behind Gerry.

He places his hand on the other man's shoulder.

"Amanda recognized you instantly," Gerry adds. "You look so much like your birth mom."

"It took her a while to finalize the paperwork so you could be housed with us. There are politics involved that go beyond what you can comprehend, especially in the supernatural community," Hale says.

"But she knew you would be safe with us, even if you never displayed any supernatural characteristics like your parents—"

"Wait. Slow down. Back the fuck up." I finally wrench my hand free of Gerry's and wave both of them in front of his face. I blink rapidly, trying to dispel the tears congregating in my eyes. "You said I look like my birth mom? Is she...?"

Sadness twists Gerry's face, a prominent line mater-alizing between his brows. "She passed away when you were a baby...which is probably how you ended up adopted in the first place."

"She was a witch, just like Amanda," Hale explains.

"Super powerful. The witches were furious when she chose to leave their community to join ours."

"To join...the wolves?" I ask tentatively, volleying my gaze between the two men.

Gerry nods. "She discovered she was the Heart of a wolf pack. She gave up everything to be with them."

Hale and Gerry exchange another one of those unreadable glances.

The fine hairs on my arms immediately prickle. There's something they're not telling me, something important. That knowledge blooms fear in my chest like a poisonous weed. Shivers scuttle all over my skin.

"She was the happiest she's ever been when she discovered she was pregnant with you," Hale whispers, his eyes glazing over at whatever faraway memory grabbed hold of him. "So all of us were shocked when she disappeared."

"We thought it was a kidnapping at first," Gerry says. "Her pack was out of their mind with worry. They searched everywhere for her. Eventually, they found the letter."

"The letter?" I ask.

Hale takes over the story, blinking away tears. "She said that she needed to leave. That it wasn't safe for her and for you. We didn't understand. Still don't, if I'm being completely honest. Some believe that she suffered a paranoid delusion. Mental illness ran in her family. Your family," he corrects.

The lead weight in my gut turns into a bowling ball, sluicing around the contents of my stomach.

"The police were called about a body found in a motel a few hundred miles away from here." Gerry reaches upwards to place his hand over Hale's, which still rests on his shoulder. "They confirmed that it was your mother's body."

I suck in a sharp gasp as pain arrows through me. Pain and grief and anger, all aimed at a woman I never met, never knew existed.

"What happened to her?"

Hale hesitates, indecision sparking in his eyes.

But I ask again, my voice curt and concise, "What happened to her?"

"They believe it was suicide," Gerry confesses. "Though her pack is convinced that she was murdered."

"You weren't found," Hale says. "There was no sign of you ever existing. Her pack thought she suffered a miscarriage."

"And then Amanda got a hold of us and claimed that she got assigned a child who looked exactly like Helena Craft."

Helena Craft.

I turn the name over and over in my head.

My *mother's* name.

Oh fuck.

I'm going to be sick.

"The witches wanted to take you in themselves.

Believed that you could have some latent magic in you, though Amanda swore she didn't sense anything. It took years of fighting, but eventually, you were able to come and live with us." Hale lifts a hand, as if wanting to touch me, but thinks better of it and drops it to his side.

"You're half shifter and half witch, yet you don't show characteristics of either species," Gerry says, scratching at his beard. "That isn't to say that you never will—"

"But usually, shifters and witches will come into their power by their eighteenth birthday, if they don't develop their gifts sooner," Hale finishes.

"The mate bonds," I whisper as realization tumbles through me. "When I turned eighteen…"

Hale and Gerry both frown simultaneously. The former releases a heavy breath, while the latter drags his hand down his face and mutters, "I suspected as much."

"It must be the latent shifter blood in you," Hale explains. "Or it could be something else entirely. It's rare, but not impossible, for shifters to mate with someone outside of their species. Just look at your mother's pack."

A new thought occurs to me, and I jerk upright in my seat. My heart, which has already been beating unreasonably fast, threatens to burst free of my rib cage. I can feel each thump of it against my breastbone.

"My mother's pack... One of those men is my father, isn't he?"

Hale's frown deepens. "It's a little different for shifters, especially ones who have a Heart. Usually, a tiny bit of all of their DNAs combine to create a child. But yes, they are your fathers."

Fathers.

As in, multiple.

My hands turn clammy, and I rub them against my jeans.

"Who are they?" I whisper, flicking my gaze from one man to the next. When they don't immediately answer, I repeat myself, my voice rising in volume. "Who are they? Who are my fathers?"

Thirty-Two

EMERY

"I can't believe this happened." Sidney hugs my twin even tighter as she cries into his neck. "How can Minnie be dead?"

Ethan murmurs something noncommittally—his voice too low for even me to hear with my wolf senses—and strokes our sister's snarled hair.

It's been a few hours since Sidney received word that her packmate and friend Minnie passed away. I can't even imagine the grief Sidney must be feeling. If I were to lose Ethan or Ashton or Reid or Izzy...

I may be pissed at almost all of them, but losing them would be the equivalent of having a limb hacked off. No, worse than that. It would be a type of death that I'm not sure I would survive—I would still be breathing, yes, but my heart would cease functioning. I'm not sure it'd ever be able to work properly again.

Almost against my will, my gaze snags on Ethan.

How can I love and hate someone so fiercely? Losing Ethan would destroy me, but allowing him into my life, after everything he's done...

I swallow the sudden lump in my throat, the coiled ball of tension that tastes like cement, and force myself to look away.

The three of us are in the living room. Ethan and Sidney have claimed the couch, but I remain standing, staring intently at the roaring flames of the fire. Their soft red and orange glow illuminates the darkened room. None of us bothered to turn on any lights when we retreated here.

And as fucked up as this makes me, all I can think is—at least it wasn't Izzy.

God, how easily it could've been her.

The mere thought splits me open from throat to navel, leaving my entrails on the ground, a disarranged mess of red and pink.

Everything with Izzy is fucked up. Our pack is made up of disparate pieces that are unable to form a coherent picture. We don't know how to act together, how to work together, how to survive together. We're no better than the lone wolves that eventually go feral.

I miss my pack.

I miss my twin.

I miss Izzy.

I barely know the girl, yet my heart craves her presence, is drawn to that effervescent grin that shatters me into pieces and reforges me into something new.

Will she ever forgive me for keeping this a secret?

I know I'm not the only one to blame, but I was her friend. I am *still* her friend, even if she doesn't consider me one. And that bond should've superseded any other.

Friends tell friends the truth.

I lick my suddenly dry lips as emotions ravage me.

Anger at Ashton and Ethan.

Grief for a life that was taken too soon.

Anguish that my sister is suffering.

Fear that Izzy will never forgive me.

And terror—a potent type of terror that steals the breath from my lungs—that our pack will never be whole.

I vow to myself, right then and there, surrounded by the ghosts of those we lost, that I'll do better. Be better. I refuse to give up on Izzy or my pack.

Not now.

Not ever.

Sometime later, Sidney drifts off to sleep, and Ethan carries her to her bedroom. The room has barely been in use since Sidney moved into her apartment, but Mom always makes sure to keep it clean.

My sister looks so small beneath the mound of blankets, so vulnerable.

My heart pinches painfully as I follow my brother out of the room, shutting the door behind me softly.

The two of us don't acknowledge one another as we bypass both of our bedrooms and take a right near the kitchen. There, we descend a long staircase that leads to a half-finished room below.

It was a project my dad started years ago, before everything went to shit. He enlisted our help in completing it. But then Dad got distracted by pack politics, and the basement never got completed. It's nothing but a concrete jungle full of pipes, padding, and rusty tools.

Ethan and I used to hide away down here whenever we wanted a break from our parents and sister. They never thought to look in the place they abandoned, allowing it to be eaten by dust and spiderwebs.

The two of us haven't been down here in a year.

Two beanbags—one red and one blue—sit in front of a dirty television that has a long crack down the screen. We found it one time in the dumpster. We think it used to belong to Sidney. Surprisingly enough, it still works, though the picture is fuzzy and sometimes indistinct.

Ethan drops himself into the blue beanbag while I claim the red. I suddenly feel like a little kid again—escaping the world and everyone in it. The only person I ever wanted by my side back then was my brother.

Ethan throws his head back until he's staring up at

the half-finished ceiling. His tattooed arms flex where he's gripping the edges of the beanbag.

"Everything is so fucked up." His voice is hoarse. Raspy with some indecipherable emotion.

I wonder if his thoughts traveled down the same path as mine did. If he thought about our crumbling pack. About Izzy.

When I remain silent, lost in the tempest of my own thoughts, Ethan prowls ahead, his voice a rugged exhale. "Izzy hates us. Ashton is on my shit list. Reid is...well...Reid. And you..." His breath hitches. "You hate me."

"I don't hate you," I snap immediately. Instinctively.

I don't know why I'm trying to comfort him, only that I am. His pain pries me apart in a way I haven't allowed it to in months. Maybe even years.

Ethan laughs, but the noise is devoid of any humor. "You can't even freaking look at me anymore, Em." He blows out a breath. "I know I messed up. I *know* that. And I know you have no reason to trust me anymore—"

"I trust you with my life. With the life of our mate," I cut in, my tone scathing. I rub a hand down my face. "I'm so fucking angry at you, Ethan. When I look at you, I just see that night all over again."

The blood.

The screams.

The tears.

A shudder works its way through me, causing the breath to seize in my chest.

"I could apologize a million times, but it won't make a difference," Ethan whispers. "I know I fucked up. I know what I did is unforgivable. I know all of that. We're tied to Desiree because of my actions, because of what I did. If I could go back in time, I would."

"Why did you do it, man?" The question has been haunting me for a while now. "I supported you. I did everything for you. How could you do this to me? To our pack? To yourself?"

Ethan doesn't respond, and I wonder if he's thinking of an answer. The silence stretches between us until it's as taut as a bowstring, but still, he doesn't respond. Doesn't offer an explanation.

But that's okay.

I'm not the one who needs the answers to those questions. He does.

"Will you ever tell Izzy about...?" I allow my words to taper off, leaving the question unspoken, hanging stagnant in the air like a plume of poisonous gas.

"I'll tell her," Ethan says, finally lifting his head to stare at me. He uses his pointer finger to slide his glasses back into place. "I'll tell her everything."

"She won't hate you," I whisper, the words tugged from between my numb lips. "That's not the type of person she is."

"We barely know what type of person she is,"

Ethan points out. "We pushed her away. We can blame Ashton all we want, but it's all of our faults. You. Me. Reid. Ashton."

"I'm not giving up on her." I don't know if my words are a warning, a threat, or both.

"I'm not either."

Both of us recline back in the beanbags and allow the silence to settle between us. It's not necessarily comfortable, but it's no longer fraught with tension. Dare I say that it's companionable?

Internally, I plan.

The next time I see Izzy, I'll prove to her how sorry I am.

We're a pack, and I'll do whatever it takes to pick up our shattered pieces and make us whole once more.

Thirty-Three

IZZY

The next week passes in a daze.

I attempt to lose myself in my home-work assignments—they have been piling up since I haven't attended school in days—but my mind is a million miles away.

I can't help but replay my conversation with Hale, Gerry, and Jake over and over in my head.

They knew my parents.

Befriended them, it sounds like.

My mom is dead.

And my fathers...

Hale and Gerry exchange an uneasy look at my question. So simple, yet the color drains from both of their faces.

"We can tell you." Hale seems to be choosing his words very, very carefully. He steeples his hands together and leans forward to rest them on his bent knees. "But we

think it's something they'll want to discuss with you themselves."

"They know I'm here?" I'm ashamed to admit that my voice comes out higher pitched than I intended.

The pounding of my heart is almost deafening, drowning out all other noise.

"They do." Gerry dips his chin in concession. "And they want to meet you. Introduce themselves. Maybe start a relationship with you. Is that something you'll want?"

The obvious answer should be yes. But…

I've been without a family for years now. I'm not sure if it's better or worse to know that there are people out there who may have loved me. Who may have taken me in, instead of allowing me to become lost in the system. Am I ready to know them? I'm not sure. My brain already threatened to implode from the sudden onslaught of information.

Wolves. Golem. Magic.

"You don't need to answer right away," Hale rushes to reassure me, his expression so painfully earnest that my stomach twists itself into a pretzel. "But when you're ready, we can make the introductions."

That conversation was days ago.

I still am not ready.

Not even close.

I sigh heavily as I stare at my reflection in the full-length mirror. I remember how excited I was to attend my first day of classes—my nerves intermixing with my exhilaration as I chose the perfect outfit.

Now I can't find it in me to give a damn.

Depression is funny like that. It's not entirely noticeable at first glance. You can adopt a smile, laugh at someone's jokes, engage in conversation, but inside... you're crying. Screaming for help. Extending a hand and just waiting for someone to grab it and haul you from the abyss. I never really understood why people call it the silent killer until now.

My life has changed so dramatically in the last few days, and it feels as if it'll never go back to normal. Maybe I just need to accept that this *is* my new normal.

Magic.

Wolves.

Witches.

Mate bonds.

Golems.

I can't even imagine how Jake feels. He returned home a few hours after he left and retreated to his room. I haven't seen him since.

Lissa still isn't talking to any of us. She's furious that we had a "private conversation" without her and demands answers. A part of me thinks she deserves to know the truth. Another part doesn't want her to live through this pain.

When I arrive at school—having chosen to walk instead of accepting a ride with one of the others—I probably look as shitty as I feel. I catch a reflection of myself in the mirror of a parked car and inwardly wince.

I haphazardly threw my hair in a braid, but a few strands have come loose, framing my face. I wear a T-shirt and jeans that aren't particularly stylish but are super comfortable. And I need that comfort today. It's my battle armor.

The hallway is still empty when I step inside, which is perfect for what I plan to do.

I veer to the right and then continue down the hall until I reach the main administrative office.

The secretary glances up from her computer and offers me a sweet smile. "How can I help you, dear?"

"I have a meeting with Mr. Montgomery," I lie smoothly, shifting from foot to foot.

Her brows crease. "I don't think he has any meet—"

"It's all right, Olive." Christian Montgomery stands in the doorway of his office, dressed in dark pants and a form-fitting blue button-up.

Like every time I see him, my breath leaves my body in a whooshing exhale. He is just too handsome to be real, too ethereal to be human. How did I not suspect him to be something otherwordly when I first met him?

His stylish dark hair is longer on the top than the sides, giving him an almost boyish look. But that sharp jawline and piercing blue eyes tell an entirely different story. Those features belong to the devil himself. Stubble grazes his jawline, and an irrational part of me wants to run my fingers across it.

I instantly squash the ridiculous thought.

Bad, Izzy. Bad.

"I forgot to add Isabella to the schedule," Mr. Montgomery continues, his eyes never leaving mine.

"Oh." Olive appears flustered, a delicate blush crawling up her neck and creating a home in her cheeks.

I don't blame her. He has that effect on me too.

"Of course. Go on in, Isabella."

I give her a tiny smile and step into Mr. Montgomery's office. He closes the door behind him with a soft click and then moves to sit behind his desk. He folds his hands together and eyes me carefully, his expression unreadable.

After a long moment, he says, "You haven't been at school in a while."

"I've been..."

Overwhelmed.

Grieving the life I once had.

Confused.

Fearful.

I don't say any of that. I just allow my words to taper off, giving him the opportunity to fill in the blanks.

He just continues to stare at me, not speaking, his eyes assessing.

I wonder what he sees.

Does he notice the cracks in my armor?

Does he realize how close I am to breaking? Shattering? Losing pieces of myself entirely?

I can pretend to be okay all I want—frozen in this superficial tranquility—but I've never felt so out of sorts before. I feel as if I'm pinned beneath a microscope and Christian Montgomery is studying me through the glass lens.

"Is this about the explosion?" Concern darkens his eyes until the sea-blue resembles a tempest in the middle of the ocean.

"No. Yes. I don't know."

I don't like to think about that either. I grieve Minnie—a girl I barely knew and wasn't overly nice to me—but I also can't help but think of the "what-ifs."

What if I had gone to the theater first thing in the morning like I planned?

What if I'd been in that explosion?

What if...?

What if...?

What if...?

The police are still investigating it, which confuses me. If it was an accident, why would they be involved? Unless...

That's one prospect that is too horrible to even consider.

"My... My foster parents told me some things the other day. Things that change everything," I blurt out at last.

The crevice between Christian's eyes deepens.

"What type of things?" he asks cautiously, leaning back in his chair.

"My mother was a witch, apparently, and my fathers were wolf shifters. Wolf shifters who are... who..." I can't find the words. I really don't know how to describe the shit show that has become my life.

Shock flickers across Christian's face, chased away quickly by confusion. "But you're human."

"I don't understand it either. I don't understand any of it." My eyes begin to burn with tears. I blink them away as fast as I can before Christian can see them. "And that's not all."

"Is this about my idiotic brother and his idiotic friends?" Christian asks warily.

"No." Quickly, I recap what happened when I left the theater a week ago.

The men. The beast. I try to skim over some of the more...intimate details of that encounter, but I can tell I don't do a good job of it when Christian's eyes glaze over in anger.

He grinds his teeth together and places a fist on the table. "Those men hurt you?"

The words come out as almost a growl.

I snort. "They tried."

My words only seem to exacerbate Christian's anger. Fur bristles on his arms, and his teeth elongate, turning into sharp points. I should feel fear being face-to-face with a creature like Christian Montgomery—a monster so innately lethal I can feel the savage brutality emanating off of him in waves. But I'm not afraid.

I'm...aroused.

What is wrong with me?

I ignore my instinctive reaction—and pray to any god that is listening that Christian isn't able to sense what his protective display is doing to me—and say, "I'm fine. I promise. They didn't hurt me."

Christian takes a deep breath, his broad chest shuddering with the movement, and lowers his gaze to the top of the desk. At first, I don't understand what he's looking at so intently, but then I realize it's a crack bisecting the wood. He focuses on that one crack, on the way it curves around his papers, and works to modulate his breathing.

While he attempts to get himself under control, I do the exact same thing but for an entirely different reason.

What are you doing, Izzy? He's your vice principal! This is wrong. You can't be lusting after him like this. He's probably your only source of information. He would be disgusted if he could hear your thoughts.

But he's only a couple of years older than you, a sly voice in my head whispers, her voice a seductive purr. *You're eighteen. It's not illegal.*

Shut up.

Make me.

He could lose his job!

If he acts on it... the voice continues. *There's nothing wrong with admiring from a distance.*

I internally shush both voices and return my attention to Christian. He has finally gotten himself under control and is staring directly at me with a quizzical expression on his face.

I shift uncomfortably. "What?"

Did he sense my arousal?

Smell it like they do in books?

God, I may just die.

"You fear us. Fear the supernatural world."

I open my mouth to deny it but instantly snap it closed. His question lingers.

Do I fear them?

I didn't think I did, but now I'm looking at everything in a whole new light.

"We're not all beasts," Christian says softly, then his gaze hardens. "Most of us aren't."

I wonder if he's thinking of the monster from the alleyway.

"Do you know what that was? The thing that attacked those men?" I ask.

"I don't," Christian confesses, and he seems annoyed with the fact. He reminds me of Ansel in a lot of ways—there's not a lot he doesn't know. "But I can ask around. Do some digging. You haven't seen it since that night?"

"No." I shake my head.

I definitely would've noticed something like that.

"It could've just been a coincidence." Christian doesn't sound convinced by his own words. He absently scratches at the stubble on his jawline, dark enough to shadow his face. "But no more late-night walks for you."

His tone turns firm. Commanding.

A shiver works its way through me.

"Yes, sir," I say, only half sarcastic.

His eyes blaze amber, his nostrils flaring, before he immediately lowers his attention back to the desk. Back to the crack running through the wood. He takes a deep breath.

"You have to know that there's no reason to fear us, Izzy. We may be different from you, but we're not evil. We have families. Jobs. Goals." He lifts his head and pierces me with a stare—a stare I feel all the way to the hollow of my bones, burrowing its way inside of me. I don't respond to his statement, but he continues on anyway. "Why don't you attend a barbecue we're having this weekend?"

His words shock me into silence. It takes me a solid ten seconds to regain the function of my brain cells.

"What?"

"A bunch of packs are meeting up and having a barbecue," Christian says. A tiny smirk dances on his lips—probably in response to my incredulity. "I think you should come. Introduce yourself. Talk to the packs. See that we're not so different from you."

"I...um..." I want to say no. With everything going

on, this doesn't seem like the time to have a damn party.

But isn't Christian right? Shouldn't I give this world a chance? I'm a part of it, after all, and the longer I bury my head in the sand, the sooner I'll suffocate.

So instead of saying no, I blurt out, "You have a pack?"

Christian's expression hardens. Turns unreadable. "No."

"No?"

Didn't he mention something about that before? I rack my brain.

"No," he repeats with a decisive head shake.

I want to ask a follow-up question, but one glance into his steely-blue eyes stops me.

"Am I allowed to attend if I'm human?" I tentatively ask.

"Of course. Hale and Gerry will be there," Christian says. "As will a few others that you know."

"Oh." I lick my lips. They have suddenly turned unbearably dry. "And...Ashton, Reid, Ethan, and Emery?"

"They'll be there too." A dark grin tugs up the corners of Christian's lips. "But wouldn't it be sweet revenge to show up on the arm of some other man?"

I almost bite off my own tongue. "Some other man?" My heart beats too loudly. I'm positive he can hear it. "As in...you?"

His smile simply widens.

Fuck, he's so beautiful, it almost hurts to look directly at him. I imagine it's a similar sensation to staring up at the sun and praying you don't go blind.

"Who else would it be?"

"Wouldn't you get in trouble?" I squeak, even as a tiny voice in the back of my head whispers, *Yes. Yes. Yes.*

And then Christian Montgomery shocks the shit out of me when he winks. Actually winks.

I almost fall out of my chair in shock, even as lust blossoms in the pit of my stomach, blooming like a flower exposed to sunlight.

"What the school board doesn't know won't hurt them. Don't you agree?"

Thirty-Four

IZZY

I'm surprised as shit to see Emery waiting for me outside the administrative office.

He's propped against the wall, his muscular arms folded over his chest and an insouciant smirk gracing his handsome face.

When he catches me staring, he stalks forward in two long strides, eating up the distance between us.

I keep my face impassive, even as his smile broadens.

Are those...?

Does he have dimples?

"What?" I ask, deadpan.

"I thought I'd walk you to class." His tongue pokes out to toy with his lip ring.

"No thanks." I move to push past him, and surprisingly, he allows me to.

But he doesn't let me get too far.

He doesn't say anything as he walks beside me, but I can feel his eyes on me the entire time, burning a hole through the side of my head. A skittering sensation ripples up my spine, and it takes every ounce of self-control I possess to keep my gaze fixed straight ahead. I grind my jaw together.

"Why are you following me?" I manage to grit out.

"I'm just walking you to class, Iz. This isn't a marriage proposal." His voice is gentle—devoid of any snark or sarcasm.

I whirl around to face him, and he immediately lifts his hands in the air in a placating manner.

"What do you want, Emery?" I growl as anger scorches my veins.

But mixed with that hostility is something warmer. Something softer. Something I don't want to look at too closely. It twists my heart into a tight knot.

The smile falls from Emery's face—disappears as if it was never there to begin with. His eyes turn solemn, the verdant green almost resembling molten emeralds in the artificial lighting.

"Do you know what a…" He glances in both directions, ensuring the hallway is still empty, before lowering his voice. "Do you know what a mate means for a shifter?"

I purse my lips. "Obviously not because you haven't told me."

"It means that you complement me. Complement my pack brothers." He takes a single step forward.

Heat emits from his body in a way that envelops me in warmth. I feel...safe.

I fucking hate that.

"You're meant for us—" Emery continues, but I cut him off before he can finish.

"I'm not meant for anyone, Emery," I snap. "I'm my own person."

I thought he'd be frustrated or even angry at my outburst, but instead, he just appears sad, his lips pinching and the skin around his eyes turning tight.

"I'm saying this all wrong, aren't I?" He forks his fingers through his tousled blond hair. "Maybe I shouldn't say that you're meant for us. Maybe I should say that *we're* meant for *you*."

My breath hitches, and a shiver steals up my spine. "I don't want that either."

"You're staring at me with pity." Emery cants his head to the side. "There's no reason to pity me, Izzy. The mating bond doesn't supersede free will or our own desires. I've heard stories of shifters rejecting their mates all the time."

His words don't fill me with the confidence I'm sure he was expecting. An uneasy feeling unfurls inside of me at the thought of any of these men rejecting me.

How hypocritical is that?

God, what is *wrong* with me?

"So you want to reject the bond?" I ask, trying to understand his point.

I keep my expression perfectly blank, not allowing

him to see the turmoil percolating just beneath the surface.

"Fuck. No!" He throws his hands up in the air. "I'm shit at this type of thing. Ethan is better at explaining things than I am."

He absently scratches at a spot on his wrist where his pack mark resides, the shade slightly darker than the rest of his fair skin. "What I'm saying is...the mate bond doesn't mean we're suddenly in love with you or anything like that. But it means that if we give each other a chance, we could be something fucking fantastic. And I want that, Izzy. I want to give us a chance. I know you're furious at me—and rightly so. I can't even begin to tell you how sorry I am. We should've told you the truth, but we were scared it would drive you away. Or that you'll think we're insane."

He huffs out a humorless chuckle.

"I probably would've contacted the mental institution if you started spouting such nonsense," I confess, my lips twitching upwards before I force them to straighten out. To become a solemn, straight line.

"Yeah. I wouldn't have blamed you. This seems like the start of a fucked-up *Wizard of Oz*. Shifters, witches, and vampires, oh my." He adopts a high-pitched country accent that's so horribly bad I can't help but laugh.

Damn him.

The noise only lasts a second—and I quickly get myself under control—but Emery's eyes gleam as if he was just handed a present the day before Christmas. A wide smile splits his face in two. Almost immediately, it fades yet again.

"And I'm sorry about Grayson. I never should've done what I did without all the information first. I thought..." He blows out another breath, the sound rife with tension. "I thought he was going to hurt you, you know? I panicked."

I haven't really talked to Grayson since the confrontation with Hale and Gerry. I texted him a few times to tell him I'm staying with my foster parents, and all I got in return was a thumbs-up. A fucking thumbs-up.

I can't help but wonder if he's still upset about... everything. Does he regret sleeping with me? He's certainly acting like it.

Maybe that's why I'm being such a coward and refusing to see him in person.

"And there is nothing—absolutely nothing—going on with Desiree," Emery insists, then he pauses. Winces. "Okay, that's not entirely true—"

"Are you kidding me right now?" I snap as hurt arrows through my chest.

"Just listen!" He grabs my arm before I can stomp away, his touch feather-soft against my skin, his fingers burning everywhere they touch. "We don't think of Desiree like that. Most of us can't stand her. But..."

"But?" I arch an eyebrow.

His shoulders deflate as if he's carrying the weight

of the world. "But—and the others are going to be so fucking pissed I'm telling you this—we're supposed to mate with her."

Shock practically plows me over. I feel lightheaded and weak at the knees. All I can do is gape at Emery, certain I misheard him. Pain whirls through me like a tornado.

I manage a choked, "What?"

"Something happened a while ago." He hesitates. "It's a story that I think Ethan needs to tell you. But anyway, something happened, and the four of us got into a lot of trouble. Desiree's dad is an influential member of the community, so he offered us a deal. He would forgive us if we mated with his daughter."

A cold chill seeps through my skin. It feels as if someone dumped a bucket of ice cubes down my shirt.

"Why?" I rasp out. "Doesn't she have a mate of her own?"

"Not every shifter does," Emery says, extending his wrist. He points to the mark that resembles a flame. "This is our pack mark. And this one? The tiny mark above it? This is our mating mark. All of us have the exact same mark on our skin, indicating that not only are we in the same pack, but we share the same mate. We got them when we reached puberty." His expression falls. "But not every wolf receives a pack mark. If someone doesn't receive one by their eighteenth birthday, they're considered a lone wolf."

"And Desiree...?"

He shakes his head sadly. "Never got one."

"What does that mean, exactly?" My thoughts stray to Christian, the only other lone wolf I know.

Emery's next words cease all coherent thoughts. "They usually go insane. Their wolf... It takes control. They can no longer maintain their human form. Most times, lone wolves are sent into the wilderness to live out the rest of their lives."

Oh...

Oh god.

Insane.

Insane.

Christian.

I think of his tiny smile, the stubble on his chin, that dark, spiky hair. My heart feels as if it's being shoved straight into a meat grinder.

And Desiree...

"And mating with Desiree will stop her from going insane?" I ask quietly, putting the pieces together.

But Emery surprises me by shaking his head. "No. As of now, there have been no known cases of a lone wolf regaining their humanity. But that doesn't stop Desiree's father from hoping."

"And what will happen if you refuse? If you don't go through with it?" Rocks tumble through my chest.

Emery's expression turns hard and unyielding, his eyes hewn from stone. "If we don't mate with Desiree, then Ethan will be locked away for a very, very long time."

Thirty-Five

GRAYSON

"Get up."

Something cold is poured over my head.

I jerk upright, sputtering and gasping, to see Vlad standing above me, his eyes burning blood-red.

A shiver works its way through me as I force myself upright, force myself to my feet. My legs tremble, but I know it's not from the chill. I'm painfully weak after days of starvation, only being granted the bare minimum of sustenance.

Well, for the most part.

Just like clockwork, Vlad thrusts a stale piece of bread into my hands, followed by a cup of tepid water. I devour both items like a man possessed, not even caring about my dignity at the moment. I need to survive and return to Izzy.

Only when I've finished drinking the last of the

water, the droplets falling into my empty stomach, does Vlad attempt to hand me another cup.

I don't take it.

I've never taken it.

"Drink," Vlad says gleefully, red spilling over the edges of the cup.

I eye the blood distastefully and then lift my icy gaze to his. Without breaking eye contact, I swat at the blood and listen to the satisfying thump of the plastic hitting the floor. Blood spills in all directions.

Fortunately, this particular room is designed for this. The floor is the only nice thing in this dank cell, the white tiles polished so meticulously I can see my reflection in them. I know, without even needing to look, that the blood has congregated towards a drain in the center of the room.

This cell was designed for blood to be spilt.

Vlad's smile widens. He has come to expect this response from me, and it always fills him with a giddy type of glee.

"So you're choosing to be difficult today, *non*?"

His thick accent instills me with a level of terror I try not to let show on my face. I didn't fear him before. But the last few days have changed that. Conditioned me to tremble in his presence.

He pushes back his sleeves, unveiling hairy forearms, and takes a step closer.

I don't move back, bracing for his punch.

His next words, however, are worse than any torture he can inflict upon me.

He holds up a rather familiar phone and dangles it in front of me.

"Who's Gracie?" he asks nonchalantly, but I can hear the undercurrent of malicious delight in that one innocent question.

My phone.

That motherfucker stole my phone.

I don't know how he was able to guess the password, but it's apparent he's been able to access it during the days I've been locked away.

I try not to let him see the terror coursing through me in blistering-hot waves. Try not to let him hear the sudden pounding of my heart, each beat slamming against my breastbone in rapid succession.

Outwardly, I keep my expression calm. Inscrutable. An impenetrable mask.

"I think she's upset with you," Vlad says conspiratorially. "She asked just the other day if you were mad at her." He tsks his tongue disapprovingly. "What did you do, Grayson? Love her and leave her?"

My heart breaks for Izzy.

What must she think now?

I slept with her. Confessed my feelings.

Then abandoned her without a word.

She'll probably think it has something to do with what we did. Or maybe she'll even believe it has to do with her confession regarding that one guy, Ansel.

"Don't worry," Vlad continues, but in his excitement, his accent makes that one word sound like "vorry." He waves the phone in the air once more. "I texted her back. Told her I needed space."

He winks then, and my heart crashes into my stomach like a one-hundred pound clump of cement.

"Good," I say lazily, feigning an indifference I don't truly feel.

But I can't let him know how much Izzy means to me. If he discovers she's my mate... I don't even want to think about it. It's too horrible to comprehend.

"She's been very clingy lately." I force my nose to wrinkle, force my lip to curl away from my teeth like I'm disgusted.

"Girlfriend?" Vlad asks, one brow arched.

"She seems to think so."

I remind myself not to change the subject too quickly. I need Vlad to believe that Izzy is just some random girl I fucked, not the love of my life.

"Got any pictures?" Vlad asks, scrolling through my phone.

My stomach twists.

Not on that one. I'm not stupid enough to leave anything overly personal on the phone I carry with me. The phone hidden in my apartment, however...

"Enough about Gracie." I level him with a glare. "How much longer do I have to be here?"

I force a tiny bit of haughty disdain into my voice.

Not enough to offend him, but enough to remind him of who, exactly, he's dealing with.

The Council's adoptive "son."

Their favorite assassin.

"Have a hot date?" Vlad asks, his lilting voice irritating my skin like a dozen ice picks.

I bare my teeth, and he chuckles.

"Don't be so dramatic." Vlad rolls his eyes. "Now come with me."

I stare at him suspiciously.

I haven't left my new cell since they forced me in here days ago. My only companion has been Vlad...and his weapons of choice.

"Where are we going?"

"Don't stare at me like that," he huffs. "You're acting like I'm about to murder you." He laughs uproariously, as if he just told the most hilarious joke, before sobering. "I need you to clean up. We have somewhere we need to be."

"Where?" I grit out.

But Vlad simply smirks at me, his eyes sparking with a savage lethality that curdles my stomach. "You'll see."

Thirty-Six

ANSEL

I receive the text in chemistry.

Trying to be inconspicuous, I slip my phone out of my pocket and hold it under the lab table.

SHELBY

Need you home ASAP.

SHELBY

There's been an incident.

Cold fear slithers through me like an insidious snake.

Shelby is my mother's nurse and has been for the last few years. The only time she ever texts me is if things are bad. Really, really bad.

"Is your phone more important than my lesson, Mr. Harthorne?" Our teacher sneers down at me from the front of the classroom.

Izzy, beside me, gives me a worried look.

I try to articulate a response, but words fail me.

What explanation could I even give?

Oh, sorry. My mom is having a mental breakdown and is probably destroying the house.

I would be teased mercilessly by the other students —even more than I already am.

So instead of saying any of that, I simply blurt, "I need to go."

Standing, I swipe everything off the table into my backpack.

Izzy's eyebrows touch her hairline.

I'm almost meticulous about the way I organize my school supplies. Everything has its place in my back-pack. Later, when I'm not consumed with worry for my mother, I'll probably panic over how disorganized my backpack is. But not now.

"You're not excused," Mr. Holter says, but I ignore him and race towards the exit.

I know Mr. Holter won't do anything to stop me. He may be a hard-ass, but I'm one of his best students. There's a reason why I'm the top of my class and plan-ning to go to college for pre-med. Science comes easily to me.

When I'm in the hall, I break into a run, not even caring when a few stragglers regard me curiously.

"Ansel! Ansel, wait!"

Izzy.

The pounding of her footsteps accompanies her voice.

She places a gentle hand on my arm, her touch sending an array of goose bumps throughout my body, and spins me to face her. Her brows dip in concern, and she eyes me from head to toe.

"What's wrong? Are you hurt?" she asks.

No, not asks. Demands. Concern undermines her voice.

"It's... It's my mom," I choke out. "I just got a text from her nurse, and..."

I don't need to finish my sentence. Izzy has met my mom. She may not necessarily understand the demons that haunt her, but she knows enough.

"Oh." Her pink lips form a perfect O. Then her brows scrunch together. "But isn't your car in the shop?"

"Fuck!"

I completely forgot about that. It's why I couldn't give Izzy a ride to school.

Perhaps I could walk. It's not too far, if I run.

Though I can't remember the last time I ran more than a mile...

"Izzy? Babe? Everything okay?" Emery and Ethan hurry out of the classroom as well, their backpacks slung over their shoulders and concern on their identical faces.

Belatedly, I wonder which one referred to her as

"babe" and why but choose not to look at it too closely. I don't think I'd like the answer.

Izzy ignores them and keeps her gaze on me. "They have a car here."

What is she suggesting? That I ask the twins for a ride to my house? That I allow them to see my most shameful secret?

But what option do I have? I have no idea what's going on. Shelby hasn't messaged me since those first two texts.

"Would they do that for me?" I ask, running a hand through my hair.

"No," Izzy confesses with a helpless shrug. "But they'd do it for me."

What the hell am I getting myself into?

Emery drives like a bat out of hell. I swear I've gripped the "OH SHIT" handlebar more times in the fifteen-minute car ride than I ever have before in my life.

Izzy sits beside me, one of her dainty hands on my knee, the comforting weight securing me to the present. I check my phone repeatedly, almost religiously, waiting for Shelby to text me back.

Nothing.

Fuck.

Ethan glances at the two of us from the passenger seat, his expression unreadable. Both Emery and Ethan are known around the school. They're two of the most popular guys—them and their little group of friends.

I never had any issue with them until I started pulling ahead of Ethan in our classes. Then I became public enemy number one.

I wouldn't necessarily say they bullied me—that's not their style—but they didn't roll out the welcome carpet either. Ethan was put out that he was no longer at the top of our class, and Emery, of course, backed his brother. Ashton tried to "ruin me" on more than one occasion. He's fiercely protective of his friends.

At least Reid ignored me. I'm not sure I would like to be on the bad side of such a big, scary dude.

It takes me a second too long to realize that Ethan isn't staring at me. No, his focus is intent on Izzy's hand still covering my knee. Her thumb has begun to move almost absently, drawing soothing circles into the material of my khakis.

I always suspected that the twins had a crush on Izzy, but this only confirms it.

Fuck.

Emery makes another sharp turn, and I slide into the window, causing Izzy to slide into me. Not that I'm complaining. I love the feel of her body molding to mine.

"Drive much?" Izzy snaps, but Emery simply laughs.

"You said you wanted to get there fast!"

"I would prefer to be alive, thank you very much."

"As if I would let you die." He tsks his tongue as if the mere idea is insane.

"What would you do if we crashed?" she demands.

"Obviously wrap my body around you and protect you from the impact."

"How would you even get to me?" She folds her arms over her chest with a scowl.

"I have moves, pretty girl. Trust me." His words are practically a purr, the salacious undertones unmistakable.

Irritation briefly burns through me, overshadowing even my fear.

What the fuck does he think he's doing, flirting with my girl directly in front of me?

As soon as that thought comes, my cheeks burn.

Fuck.

She's not my girl, no matter how badly I want her to be. I'm not even sure if we've ever technically been on a date. After all, our trip to the rage room and diner was...a hangout. Not a date.

Right?

All thoughts of Izzy and dates and obnoxious twins cease when we pull to a stop in front of my house.

When my father was still alive, we had been an upper-middle-class family, and that hasn't changed with his death. He left a hefty life insurance sum behind for me and my mother.

The home is constructed out of white bricks and boasts over a dozen windows—all ranging in sizes—

that stare out at a perfectly manicured lawn. Two pillars cradle an archway that leads to the front entrance. Potted plants line the walkway and dangle from hooks on either side of the door.

All of the lights are currently off, but that's not necessarily a surprise. Mom often prefers to leave them off, especially when she's feeling vulnerable. She hates the large windows—believes that there are monsters looking inside.

I once bought large blackout curtains, but that only made her more paranoid. She claimed that she would rather see the threat arrive than be surprised when it sneaks up on her.

Shelby's car is still in the driveway, which is a good sign. It means that she didn't need to bring my mom to the hospital.

"We can just wait out here—" Ethan begins awkwardly, but a loud crash and a startled scream interrupt him.

All of us exchange glances, then as one, we race into the house.

"Mom! Shelby!" I swivel my head from side to side as I hurry down the hallway, checking each room as I go.

The living room is empty—though I do note a broken mug on the carpeting—as is the kitchen. I take the stairs two at a time until I reach my mother's bedroom. The door is slightly ajar.

Mom is standing on one side of the bed with

Shelby on the other. Mom's face is tear-stained, her brown cheeks tinted red. She wears a too-large sweatshirt and dirty sweatpants, her bare toes just barely sticking out of the bottom. Shivers reverberate through her as she stares at Shelby unblinkingly.

It's only then that I notice she's holding a knife.

Shelby hears us first and turns, relief visible on her face.

Mom spins as well, but unlike Shelby, her expression only hardens.

"You shouldn't be home!" she screeches, brandishing her knife in the air. "You need to go away! Away! You can't let them find you."

"Mom. Please. Lower the knife." I venture a tentative step into the room, my hands raised placatingly. Fear causes my heart to pound like a battering ram. I'm sure the noise is even audible from outer space. "What's going on?"

"They've come for you!" More tears rain down her cheeks. "I can't let them take you. They know. They know what you can do."

I slyly glance at Izzy out of the corner of my eye, praying she thinks my mom's words are nothing but nonsensical ramblings.

"Mom, please." I take another step forward, and Ethan and Emery use the opportunity to enter the room as well.

I can tell they're trying to appear non-threatening,

but it's hard to do. They're both hulking men covered in tattoos.

Mom's face drains of color. Her tears dry on her face. "You brought... You brought wolves into my house?"

Disbelief saturates her tone.

I have no idea what the hell she's going on about this time.

Ethan and Emery both freeze and exchange a look. Izzy's mouth parts in surprise.

"Mom, just listen. No one's here to hurt you—"

"*You*." Mom spins towards Izzy, raw fury etched across every line of her wrinkled face. "You did this. I told you to leave my son alone. You never should've come back, Delaney."

Delaney?

"My name isn't Delaney, Mrs. Harthorne. It's—" Izzy doesn't get a chance to finish her sentence.

My mother lets out a scream of pure, unbridled rage and lunges at her, the knife extended.

Thirty-Seven

IZZY

My brain switches off, rationality replaced by panic.

All I can think is—I don't want to hurt Ansel's mom.

She lunges at me with a scream of anger, and I lift my hands up in defense. I'll do what I need to do to protect myself, but nothing more. This woman is obviously unwell.

Before she can make contact with me, however, she's knocked to the side. The knife slips free from her hand and slides across the floor.

Ethan jumps off of the woman immediately, his features pinched tight and his face abnormally pale.

"Mom!" Ansel races to his mother's side and kneels beside her.

I step forward as well—instinctively—but then

think better of it. Emery and Ethan move to stand on either side of me, their shoulders brushing against my own.

"Ansel? Baby?" His mother blinks wearily.

"I'm... I'm going to call an ambulance." The nurse appears shaken, her dark skin bleached white, but Ansel shakes his head.

"No. She's fine. Why don't you give us a second, Shelby?" Ansel says, helping his mother into a sitting position.

Shelby looks as if she wants to argue but nods once and hurries out the door. It slams shut after her, the noise ominously loud in the sudden silence that descends.

"I'm... I'm..." Mrs. Harthorne's lower lip begins to tremble. "I'm sorry. I don't know..."

She absently rubs at the back of her head and slowly turns to face me once more. I expect to see blind fury in her gaze. Hatred.

I take a step back automatically, prepared to leave the room and deescalate the situation, but her next words stop me.

"You're not Delaney, are you?" Her voice is quiet, timid almost, and wavers.

"My name is Isabella, Mrs. Harthorne," I tell her gently. "I go to school with your son."

"She's my friend, Mom," Ansel says, rubbing soothing circles on her back.

She blinks up at us, her eyes going in and out of focus, before she dips her chin once in something akin to acknowledgment.

"Friend." She repeats the word as if it had been spoken in a foreign language, as if it's something she's unfamiliar with.

"Yes, Mom. Friend." Ansel takes her arm and helps her to her feet. She sways slightly but manages to remain upright. "And these two guys are my...friends as well."

Ansel stumbles over the word "friends" but keeps his expression blank.

"Your friends with wolves?" She tilts her head to the side curiously as she studies the twins.

Emery and Ethan both still on either side of me. I'm not even sure they're breathing.

Ethan breaks the silence first, shuffling from foot to foot as he rubs his hands down his jeans. "I'm sorry for tackling you, ma'am. I just panicked—"

She waves a flippant hand in the air and perches on the bed. "Wolves protect their mates."

Every muscle in my body locks together.

What is she talking about?

Is it possible that she...knows?

Questions rise on the tip of my tongue, but I don't dare ask them. She's obviously in a fragile state, and I'm not sure what her limits are. To be completely honest, I'm not even sure I should be here. She tried to attack me, not once but twice.

"You called my friend Delaney." Ansel kneels before his mother and places his hands on her knees. She looks so much smaller than him. So fragile. "Why?"

"Ansel, you don't need to do this," I say softly.

Ansel ignores me. "Who's Delaney, Mom?"

Mrs. Harthorne slowly tilts her face in my direction. Those vacant eyes roam over me without ever sticking for longer than a second. Her tongue snakes out to lick her dry upper lip.

"You... You look so much like her. But you're not her, are you? She would be older. Much older." She rubs at her arms as if to fend off a sudden gust of cold air.

Something occurs to me then, an idea so staggeringly impossible that I feel sick to my stomach, and I stumble forward a step. "Delaney. You don't mean...? Could this be my mom?"

But no. That's not possible. My mother's name, according to Hale and Gerry, is Helena.

"You look so much like her," Mrs. Harthorne whispers.

She extends her hands as if she means to touch me but drops them back to her lap.

"Is Delaney related to a woman named Helena? Helena..." I swallow the burning ember in my throat. "Helena Craft?"

Mrs. Harthorne keeps her gaze locked on her

hands. Her fingers twist together repeatedly, the repetitive action seeming to soothe her.

When she doesn't respond to my question, Ansel gives her knees a squeeze once more, garnering her attention.

"Who is Delaney, Mom?" he asks again. "Is she related to Helena Craft?"

Gratefulness envelops me instantly. I didn't tell Ansel—or anyone else for that matter, besides Christian—about what Hale and Gerry told me concerning my birth parents. So for him to ask that question...

A bubbly sensation detonates in my stomach, buoying me up.

"I'm tired." Mrs. Harthorne pulls away from her son and lies down on the bed, curled on her side. She folds her hands underneath her head. "I'm going to go to sleep."

"Mom—" Ansel presses, but I grab his hand and shake my head.

It's obvious that Mrs. Harthorne reached her limit for the day. I don't want to push her past it, not with how fragile she is.

Ansel bites his lip but nods once in understanding.

As I watch, my heart battering my rib cage, Ansel pulls a blanket up to her chin and then kisses her forehead. The tenderness he exhibits with her...

Goose bumps erupt on my arms.

The four of us file out of her bedroom, an uneasy

silence permeating the air. I can tell the twins are fixated on her use of the words "wolves" and "mate." How did she know? Or was it merely a coincidence—the unhinged ramblings of a crazy woman?

In the living room, Shelby sweeps up the last of the glass.

She glances up when we arrive and shoots Ansel an indecipherable look. "How is she?"

"Sleeping." Ansel tucks his hands into his pockets and rocks back on his heels. "She seemed to have snapped out of it, but..."

"I'll call her doctor as soon as I'm done cleaning up here."

"Thank you, Shelby."

The nurse waves away his praise. "You four should head back to school. Everything will be okay."

Ansel opens his mouth as if to protest, but Shelby casts him a pointed look.

"Go. I got this. It's what you're paying me for, after all." She chuckles and sweeps the glass into a dustpan. "You wouldn't want to lose your valedictorian spot to that one asshole, would you?"

Ethan glares at Ansel, and the tips of Ansel's ears turn a brilliant shade of red.

"Um...I guess not."

Shelby shoos us out of the house, and the four of us meander back to the car. I can tell school is the last thing on any of our minds.

Who the hell is Delaney? Is she related to Helena? Is she a relative? These questions continue to tumble around and around in my head, but I know I won't get any answers. Not yet.

My extensive Google search into Helena Craft proved futile. I only found one article, dated eighteen years ago, that talked about her apparent suicide, exactly as Hale and Gerry described. Besides that, there was nothing. No mention of her on social media. No obituary. Nothing. Maybe I need to start looking into this Delaney chick.

But is her last name Craft as well? Is Delaney even a relative, or is she a friend? Does she even know my birth mother?

"Is it horrible that school is the last place I want to be?" Ethan asks, wincing. His words pull me out of my thoughts.

Emery places a hand to his chest in mock offense. "What is the world coming to? The great Ethan doesn't want to go to school?"

Ethan shoves at his twin.

"I really don't want to head back either," Ansel confesses.

This time, both Ethan and Emery gape at Ansel in disbelief.

"It's official. I'm in the Upside Down world," Emery says seriously.

"Do we want to play hooky?" Ethan asks, the word "hooky" sounding strange and foreign leaving his lips.

I can't imagine he has ever skipped school before, barring serious illness or injury.

All three men turn to stare at me.

Emery's eyes twinkle with a familiar mischievousness I haven't seen in way too long. "What do you say, pretty girl? Wanna skip school and get into trouble?"

Thirty-Eight

IZZY

We decide to head to the arcade on the opposite side of town. According to Ethan—who's practically bouncing in the passenger seat—the arcade has the best games in the county.

"I'm still going to kick your ass," I tell Ethan seriously, leaning forward so I can rest my arms on the center console.

"Ha. You wish!" Ethan slides his gaze in my direction, blushes, and immediately focuses back out the windshield. "You may have beat me in *Mario Kart* once or twice—"

"Every time," I correct.

"—but I am the master of arcade games."

"It's true," Emery interjects, not taking his eyes off the road. He steers the car expertly down a side street. Now that we're no longer in a hurry, he doesn't feel the need to drive like he's on a racetrack. "There's a reason why Ethan has no life or a girlfriend. He spends all of his time at the arcade like a nerd."

"Hey!" Ethan's cheeks pinken, and he whacks his brother across the head. "Shut up."

"Don't hit the driver." Emery uses one hand to rub at his head, but the wicked glint in his eyes never dissipates.

"It's not like you had a thousand girlfriends either," Ethan says with a scoff. "Actually, you've had exactly—"

"Oh look. We're here!" Emery interrupts as we pull into a parking lot.

The large brick building is nestled between a Go-Cart track and a mini golf course. A banner above the door announces an all-you-can-eat pizza buffet.

"I kind of want Ethan to finish that sentence," I say as Emery pulls the car into a parking space near the front.

Unsurprisingly, it's not crowded. Most of its clientele are still in school.

"Don't you fucking dare," Emery warns his twin.

"Emery may act like a huge player and flirt, but he—"

"Ethan, I swear to god."

"He never had a girlfriend before." This comes from Ansel beside me.

All three of us turn to stare at him, and he shrugs innocently.

"What? I hear things. The girls at school always complain that the Magnetic Four never give them the time of day."

Emery's nose wrinkles. "The Magnetic Four?"

"Wait." My brain short-circuits. "You never had a girlfriend? Neither of you?"

Ethan, I can see. He's sexy as sin but always blushes a beetroot red when he's around me...or any girl, for that matter. He prefers to spend his nights playing video games instead of partying.

But Emery? The man practically exudes sex. His tattoos, combined with his piercings and spiked hair, give him a bad-boy edge. He flirts like it's an Olympic Sport and he's gunning for the gold medal.

And it's not just with me—though I'll be the first to admit that he's only been flirting with me as of late. According to some of my friends, he used to flirt with everyone who had a pulse.

Tattoos? Check.

Sexy grin? Check.

Piercings? Check.

He's the unholy trinity of dark, sexy, and dangerous.

"Let's play some arcades!" Emery says with feigned cheer, slipping out of the car.

I exchange a "what the fuck" glance with Ansel before following him out.

"Wait. Wait. Wait. I want to hear more about this," I say, hurrying to catch up with the twins. "How is it possible that neither of you has had a girlfriend? Did you just have casual flings, then?"

Emery ignores me entirely and rubs his hands together. "I love me some arcades."

"Dude." I give him a look. "Stop saying the word arcades. I feel like you're using it as a verb, a noun, and an adjective. It's getting weird. Now answer the question."

Emery slings an arm over my shoulders and pulls me into his side.

Surprising even myself, I don't attempt to pull away.

"You're nosey."

"Yup."

Ansel chuckles from somewhere behind me.

Ethan moves to my other side and flashes me a sheepish smile. "Look, men like...us..."

He fumbles over his words, and I know it's because he can't give away too much with Ansel around. I nod to tell him I understand, and he continues.

"We usually wait until we find the one. Do you get what I mean?" His earnest eyes ensnare my own.

For a moment, I'm helpless to look away, trapped in his gaze.

Then his words register.

Is he saying...?

Do shifters wait until they meet their mates before having sex? Before dating? Would that mean...? No. There's no way.

No fucking way.

Ethan, maybe.

Emery, no. Hell no.

"That's...kind of romantic, in a way that makes me want to vomit," Ansel deadpans.

"We all know the only action you're getting is from that stick shoved up your ass," Emery snaps, glaring at him over his shoulder.

I give Emery's arm a squeeze and whisper, "Behave."

A strange tremor works its way through him. He gives me a look out of the corner of his eyes that's full of barely suppressed heat.

My stomach flips over itself.

I quicken my pace—pulling in front of the twins and Ansel—and reach the entrance first.

I'm immediately greeted by the smell of greasy cheese and sauce. In the distance, I can hear the beeping of arcade games and the laughter of children. An adult curses, and a woman giggles.

Ethan bounces on the tips of his toes like a kid in a candy shop.

Or a nerd in an arcade.

"You're kind of a geek, aren't you?" I say to him, unable to hide the fondness in my voice.

His eyes snap to mine, and a grin lights up his face. He's handsome normally, but when he smiles like that...

The butterflies in my stomach go crazy.

"As if I'm the only one." He scoffs.

"You ready for me to kick your ass at every single arcade game here?" I tease.

Something in his expression softens the longer he looks at me. "I think I can suck up my masculine pride and lose graciously."

"As if." Emery throws his arms around both of our shoulders and steers us towards the front counter, where a bored-looking attendant sells tokens. "We all know you're a sore loser."

"Am not."

"You totally cried when I beat you at bumper cars."

"I was six, Emery. Six!"

I reach behind me before we can get too far and interlock my fingers with Ansel's, tugging him closer to us. He looks moderately surprised, but then he smiles, and my heart squeezes painfully.

"You threw a toy car at my head," Emery retorts.

"I. Was. Six. And it wasn't at your head. It was supposed to be your stomach."

"Your aim is as shit as your bumper cars skills."

I pinch Emery's arms lightly, drawing his attention back to me.

"Stop teasing your brother," I say.

Emery's eyes twinkle. "But it's so fun."

"Be a good boy and behave," I warn.

Just like before, a strange heat flares in Emery's eyes, and my heart kicks into overdrive. Lava courses through my veins.

What the hell?

I try to remind myself that I'm still mad at him, still hurt and upset and confused, but the fire in my belly refuses to listen to my brain. It fizzles and bubbles and takes on a life of its own. My lungs burn.

Ansel's lighthearted teasing pulls me back to the present. "How about a wager?"

Ethan's ears practically perk up. "I'm listening."

"Whoever wins the most games gets..." Ansel taps a finger to his chin in consideration.

An evil idea occurs to me, and my smile broadens. "I have an idea about what we could bet on."

Thirty-Nine

IZZY

"You cheated!" Ethan says for the one millionth time, pouting.

I give a little celebratory dance as I step out of the arcade.

Night has fallen, and the sky is peppered with stars and a full moon. We must've been at the arcade for hours. I'm happy I texted Hale beforehand—he would've been worried sick.

I texted Grayson as well but, of course, received no response.

I try not to let that bother me, try not to let the pain of his rejection sink into me like barbs.

"Don't hate the player," I tease, walking backwards to keep my gaze on the three big losers. "Hate the game."

"I am never arcading again," Emery mutters.

Ethan pinches the bridge of his nose. "For the last time, it's not 'arcading.'"

"I think this is the first time in my life that I'm okay with being defeated," Ansel muses, canting his head to the side.

His light-brown hair flops over one eye.

"I'm not. Especially since she cheated." Ethan throws me a pointed look.

I throw my hands up in the air. "How did I cheat?"

"You know how..." His cheeks turn red, and he immediately ducks his head, muttering something too low for me to hear.

I have to bite my lip to keep from chuckling.

Because oh yeah. I totally cheated. It's amazing what being a woman can do for you around horny dogs —pun totally intended.

Take Skee-Ball, for example. The second Ethan would toss his arm back to throw the ball, I would purposely bend, showing just a tiny bit of cleavage. Once, the ball ended up on the opposite track.

Or when we were playing air hockey, I allowed my sleeve to slip down just enough to reveal a hint of my bra strap.

Or when we were playing a basketball game, I happened to drop a coin and had to bend down...

I chuckle to myself, and Ethan's eyes narrow.

"You're evil."

"Nah. I just think I'm better than you in every way." I shrug a single shoulder casually.

"She has us there." Emery throws his arms around Ansel and Ethan's shoulders and smiles at me. The moonlight catches on his piercing, causing it to glisten. "I'm more than willing to bow down to you."

"Good boy," I praise.

He bites his lip so hard, I swear I see blood.

"I still don't think it's fair," Ethan protests. "You ch—"

He freezes abruptly, his muscles locking together and his nostrils flaring. Tension lines the rigid planes of his shoulders and the granite set of his jaw.

Emery stops walking as well and whips his head to the side.

"What's going on?" Ansel asks, ducking under Ethan's arm to go and stand beside me.

A frown tugs at his perfect lips.

Ethan and Emery exchange a look and then immediately begin to herd us towards the car.

"We need to go," Ethan says briskly.

"Now," Emery agrees.

But we don't make it more than a few steps.

Out of the darkness, six people step forward, moving with a sort of elegance I could only attempt to emulate one day.

I recognize the girl closest to me immediately.

Michelle.

She smirks victoriously when our eyes connect and brushes a strand of dark hair behind her ear.

Fuck. Fuck. Fuck.

Five other people flank her—one other girl and four guys.

The man in the middle steps away from the group with an easygoing grin on his face.

"Boys. Long time no see." His smile doesn't fade, even as his eyes darken, turning flinty, two chips of obsidian refracting the moonlight.

On closer inspection, I see that he isn't a man after all. Or at least, he's not significantly older than us. He looks as if he's Christian's age, maybe a little older. His dark hair is buzzed close to his scalp on the sides but is longer on the top, sweeping forward in a stylish way. He has light-brown skin and darker eyes—so dark that they seem to swallow the moonlight.

He must be Michelle's brother. The similarities between the two of them are unmistakable.

And if Michelle is a witch, then that means he's a...

Cold fear tiptoes up my neck.

Ethan and Emery move to stand in front of me, shoulder to shoulder, blocking me from view.

Ansel may not know what they are, but he can obviously sense the threat permeating the air. He, too, shifts slightly, inching closer until only a wisp of air separates our bodies.

"Dyson," Emery greets coldly.

I can't see his expression, but I *can* see how tightly he's holding himself, like a loaded coil waiting to spring.

"How have you two been?" the man—Dyson—asks, cocking his head to the side. "It's been a while."

"Not long enough," Ethan murmurs, too low for them to overhear.

"I think you know why we're here," Dyson continues.

Michelle flashes me an evil grin and then turns to her brother, her lower lip wobbling and tears erupting in her eyes.

She sniffles exaggeratedly. "That's the girl! That's the one who punched me!"

"You punched her?" Emery's voice bleeds incredulity.

"Not hard enough, apparently." I scowl.

"I think I love you," Emery says.

I roll my eyes and then shoulder my way through the two bodies blocking me. Both immediately try to pull me back, but I refuse to cower behind them.

"I wouldn't have punched you if you weren't being such a raging bitch," I snap, putting my hands on my hips.

Witch or not, I'm not scared of her.

Okay, that's a lie.

I'm a little scared.

Michelle's eyes narrow, the tears drying up as if they never existed to begin with. "You're going to regret what you did."

"You going to have your big brother beat me up?" I taunt, unable to keep my mouth shut.

"Izzy!" Ethan hisses, his voice rife with horror.

Emery simply chokes on his own spit in surprise.

Dyson stares at me curiously, his gaze assessing, his eyes devouring me from head to toe. Interest sparks in his gaze. "This is the girl who got the best of you, Michelle?"

"She took me by surprise!" Michelle snaps, apparently giving up on her "weepy, sad" act.

Dyson continues to gaze at me intently, his expression unreadable, his jaw clenched. "What's your name?"

"What's *your* name?" I counter, even though I already know it.

I just feel like being a bitch.

He chuckles and takes a step forward, his hand extended. "Dyson. It's a pleasure to meet you."

I eye his palm like it's disease ridden and very purposely look away without taking it.

I arch an eyebrow. "Izzy."

He keeps his hand in the air, his expression amused, before lowering it back to his side.

"Izzy." He says my name like he wants to savor it, like it's something decadent for him to taste.

He goes so far as to lick his lips.

Emery growls low in his throat.

"I was curious to see the woman my sister hates so much. But I have to be honest... You're not what I expected."

"What did you expect?" I cock my hip to the side.

"For one, you're not as ugly as my sister described."

"Geez. Thanks." I roll my eyes.

"For two, you're not as...human as she described either." His eyes gleam like onyx stones as he ventures a step forward. Curiosity blankets his face. "What are you?"

Unease slithers in my stomach like a serpent. "I'm human."

"Yes, you are," he agrees easily. "But you're something else too. Something...other."

"And she's hanging around one of ours," a boy I don't recognize interjects. He jerks his chin in Ansel's direction. "I can sense the magic in him."

All six of them turn to stare at Ansel, and my friend takes a step back automatically, his face leaching of color.

Dyson cocks his head to the side. His eyes glaze over, shining like someone lit a candle beneath the surface, and he gives Ansel a cold once-over. It's not lecherous like the one he granted me.

"Interesting," he murmurs as the glow recedes from his eyes. "Very, very interesting." He turns towards the twins, his smile more of a baring of teeth than anything genuine. "Would you like to explain to us why you have an unregistered warlock hanging around you? Because I'm positive the Trinity would love to hear about this."

Forty

ANSEL

A combination of fear and panic seizes the air in my lungs.

Unregistered warlock?

What is he talking about?

I know I have these...powers, but I've never been given a name for what I am. Even my mother has been evasive when I asked about it.

Is he saying...?

I think I'm going to be sick.

I wait for Izzy to tell him he's insane, to laugh in his face, but she goes very still. Slowly, she swivels her head to stare at me.

"What is he talking about, Ansel?" Her voice is low.

A tinny, mechanical voice in the back of my head warns me to proceed with caution.

"I...I don't know," I stutter out.

"That's probably the truth." The asshole—Dyson —chuckles, though his eyes hold no amusement. "I imagine he's just as confused as the rest of us." He shoves his hands into his pockets and takes a single step forward. "Tell me... I'm sorry. I don't think I've ever gotten your name."

None of us respond to him. Emery and Ethan are coiled tight with tension, and Izzy just appears pissed. And me? I'm trying to get my racing heart under control. It tripled in speed the second he used the word "warlock" in casual conversation.

"You look like a Bart to me. Can I call you Bart?" He cants his head to the side, and his pitch-black hair reflects in the moonlight.

Again, none of us respond.

"Tell me, Bart, are you able to do things that no one else can? Things that seem impossible?" His gaze flicks to Izzy for a fraction of a second before refocusing on me. "Say...healing people?"

I stop breathing.

Stop thinking.

Fear holds me immobile.

"I fucking knew it," Emery murmurs.

Ethan shushes him.

"This happens from time to time." Dyson releases a heavy sigh. "Children will get lost in the system or raised by relatives who don't know about magic. Then, when they develop their gifts, they're confused and frightened. Is that what happened to you, Bart?"

"Stop calling him Bart," Izzy interjects, her voice tight with anger. "His name is Ansel."

Dyson grins like the cat that got the cream. I don't like the smile he offers Izzy. Not one bit.

"Ansel." He tilts his head to the side, reluctantly pulling his gaze off of Izzy to study me. "I think Bart suits you better."

"Illy." I keep my voice low so only she and the twins can hear. "I don't know what's going on, but you should leave."

"And let you face these fuckers alone?" Unlike me, Izzy doesn't bother to lower her voice. "Fuck that."

"Why don't you run off with your little pet doggies?" the dark-haired woman says, sneering.

I think they said her name was Michelle.

Izzy's smile is all teeth. "Why don't I punch you in the face and give you a matching black eye?"

Michelle gasps and spins towards Dyson. "Did you hear her? That fucking bitch—"

"Enough, sister." Dyson lifts a hand in the air, stopping her mid-rant. He returns his gaze to Izzy, his eyes sparking with curiosity and something...more. Something I really, really don't like. "We're having a civilized conversation here."

"But—"

"And if you can't be civilized, then you can go wait in the car," he continues.

"Or you can take a running leap off a cliff," Izzy mutters. "Either works."

Michelle throws Izzy a glare so full of loathing and hatred that I feel my own stomach curdle in fear.

"Ansel." Dyson extends a hand towards me. "You need to come with us. The Trinity will—"

Izzy stealthily moves to stand in front of me, the twins still on either side of her.

"Not going to happen," she says fiercely.

Dyson's grin ratchets up a dozen notches. "Is that so?"

Terror knots my heart, but the last thing I want is for Izzy to get herself hurt trying to protect me.

"Illy, it's fine," I whisper.

She doesn't spare me a glance. "No, it's not." Then, louder, she adds, "We're going home now, okay? And you're not stopping us."

Dyson gestures us forward with more contempt than courtesy. "By all means, go on right ahead."

"Dyson!" Michelle stomps her foot, but Dyson ignores his sister, keeping his gaze trained on us.

"We're not the bad guys here," he continues, his lips curling. "If Ansel doesn't want to meet with the Trinity, then that's his choice."

The Trinity?

My mind instantly conjures up images of a derelict church. A shiver of unease ripples down my spine.

Izzy grabs my wrists and begins to drag me towards the car, her eyes never leaving the six men and women surrounding us.

Dyson's smile grows as if he finds her trepidation and suspicion cute.

Emery and Ethan wait until both Izzy and I are in the car before moving as well. Scowls mar their identical faces. Normally, they're so easy to tell apart, but just now, in the darkness of the cab, I can't identify who's Ethan and who's Emery.

"I'll be seeing you guys soon. Real soon." Dyson lifts his hand in a wave.

And he continues to wave until the darkness swallows him whole.

Forty-One

IZZY

"Explain," I say to Ansel as soon as we pull out of the parking lot.

He looks distressed. Defeated. His shoulders slump, and a strand of brown hair falls forward, momentarily obscuring his right eye from view.

"I fucking knew it," Emery says again. "I fucking knew it."

I whirl to face him, my jaw clenching. "You did?"

Is this another secret he and the others kept from me?

What the fuck?

Emery's hands clench around the steering wheel, and he flicks his gaze to me before immediately looking away.

He swallows. "I didn't know for sure, I mean. I suspected."

"You suspected that the boy I've been hanging out with is a supernatural and didn't think to tell me?" Rage saturates my tone. As does hurt.

So much fucking hurt.

I feel as if someone took a meat cleaver to my body and sliced me open from throat to navel. I know I shouldn't take all of this so personally, but it's hard not to. It's really fucking hard not to.

All of these lies are piling up on me, encasing me in a coffin of cement, and sooner rather than later, I won't be able to escape. I'll suffocate under the weight—if my oxygen supply doesn't run out beforehand.

"We weren't positive," Ethan tells me from the back seat, his tone gentle. "But..."

"But at the football field when you were tackled, Ashton... He saw something." Emery's jaw clenches at the memory.

Phantom pain reverberates down my spine. There's nothing quite like getting tackled by a two-hundred-pound, muscular football player.

Okay. That's a lie. I wouldn't mind getting tackled by certain football players, but that's beside the point.

"What are you saying?" I demand.

My heart pounds in my chest. The noise is deafening. I wouldn't be surprised if the entire car can hear it.

Ansel's voice is soft when he speaks next, practically a whisper. "I healed you."

"What?" I once again whirl around to face him.

He leans forward, placing his head in his hands, and repeats, "I healed you. I used...magic to heal you."

Lightning zips through my veins as time stands still. Everything seems frozen in this superficial tranquility. But I can feel the tension pulsating.

My mind drifts back to that night—to the pain ripping me apart from the inside out. I swore all of my bones broke and was moderately surprised when I discovered I didn't even have a concussion.

Is that because of...Ansel?

I open and close my mouth repeatedly, feeling like a gaping fish plucked out of the water.

Ansel keeps his head in his hands, not meeting my searching gaze. "I didn't know there was a name for what I was, what I could do. I'm...different. Always have been. I can do things that don't seem possible."

Understanding dawns on Ethan's face. "You were adopted, weren't you?"

At Ansel's nod, Ethan and Emery exchange an indecipherable glance.

Emery slides his gaze towards me before refocusing on the road. "I've heard cases of this before. Of supernatural children finding themselves in the system and being taken in by human families."

Automatically, I think of Jake.

Me.

Even Lissa and Seth, though I have no idea what they are.

"You had no idea what you were?" Ethan asks softly, his brows creased.

When Ansel shakes his head, I feel my heart crack into thousands of pieces.

God, what must it feel like to live your life with these unexplainable powers and have no idea why you have them? Ansel must've felt so alone. So scared.

I don't blame him for not telling me. We've gotten close over the last few weeks, but that type of secret... It's life-changing. Damning, if word got out. Ansel didn't know I already knew about the supernatural world. He was under no obligation to tell me.

Unlike the furry shit brains in the car with us.

"None of you seem surprised with...this." Ansel slowly lifts his head and pierces us with a glance.

His gaze lingers on me a second longer before he drops it back to his lap.

I make a decision quickly. "We're not."

"Izzy..." Ethan warns, his voice a rumble.

"Oh, shush." I glare at him.

I won't tell Ansel what the twins are—that's not my secret to share—but I will tell him the truth about me. I can see how adrift he feels, how lost and scared, and I want him to know that he's not alone. That he has someone like him, someone who was oblivious to the supernatural world until only a short while ago.

"I didn't know about the paranormal until I arrived here," I confess, running a hand through my hair. It feels strange to say this out loud. "I only just found out. Apparently, my mom was a witch, and my dads were wolf shifters."

Ansel's head snaps up so quickly I'm afraid he hurt himself. His face drains of color, and his eyes bulge. "Wolf shifters?"

"Yeah. Multiple." I shrug. "It's a thing, apparently."

Wolf shifters who apparently want to meet me...

Unease skitters across my skin, and I run a hand down my arm as if I can rid it of that uncomfortable sensation.

Shock turns into awe as Ansel stares at me. "You're like...me?"

"I guess?" I once again shrug. "I can't really do any magic, but apparently I am like you."

I still can't wrap my head around the fact that my parents weren't...human.

How is it possible that I am?

I shake my head to rid it of that errant thought. That's a problem for Future Izzy.

"And you guys?" Ansel asks, volleying his gaze between Ethan and Emery.

Emery's lips purse in stubborn determination, and Ethan glances at me, a question in his gaze. I offer him an eloquent look that clearly states it's their choice whether or not they want to share the truth with Ansel.

"Oh, popsicle sticks and gumball machines," Ethan

murmurs, frowning. Then, louder, he says to Ansel, "We're wolf shifters."

I think Ansel is going to have a brain aneurysm. A vein in his temple bulges in a way that doesn't seem healthy.

"As in you...?"

"Can turn into wolves and eat warlocks?" Emery's smile is sharp. "Yup."

"Behave," I chastise him, glaring.

He simply offers me an unrepentant, shit-eating grin.

"I can't believe this is... God, I can't believe this is real. I always thought I was going insane." Ansel scrubs his hand through his light-brown hair and then pauses, as if a thought suddenly occurred to him. A frown touches his lips. "You guys aren't fucking with me, are you?" Vulnerability creeps into his tone. "This isn't some elaborate prank, is it?"

A strange mixture of hurt and disbelief arrows through me. "Really? You think I would do something like that to you?"

Ouch.

Ansel's cheeks pinken, and he lowers his head quickly. "I know you wouldn't. But..."

"But?"

"But sometimes it seems surreal that someone like you would want to hang out with someone like me." The blush creeps to his neck and the tips of his ears, turning them a rosy shade of red.

My heart flutters. "I like hanging out with you, Ansel."

And I like you. A lot.

But I don't say that out loud.

Emery's jaw clenches, but Ethan just glances between us, his expression curious. Before he can ask the question lingering in his gaze, Ansel pipes up.

"So who were those people? They're...witches and warlocks? They're like me?"

"That dark-haired girl is Reid's ex-girlfriend. That guy was probably her brother," I say.

Both Emery and Ethan speak as one, "She's not his ex-girlfriend."

My brows furrow.

Everyone keeps saying that, but I've seen the way the two act around each other. There's yearning in Reid's gaze when he stares at the striking girl. And Michelle obviously still loves him.

Yet...

Rage fills me when I remember the way Michelle spoke to Reid. How she slapped him across the face.

Yeah. I want to kill the bitch. Painfully. And with a variety of weapons.

"They're a dangerous group," Emery says, and I don't know if he's trying to warn me or Ansel. "I would stay away from them if I were you."

Ansel brings his pointer finger to his mouth and begins to bite at his nail. I wonder if that's a nervous habit of his. I've never seen him do it before.

"And who is the...Trinity?"

Ethan answers that question. "The Maiden, Mother, and Crone. They're the rulers of the coven."

"Every warlock and witch are required to register with them when they come of age. They have to swear loyalty to the coven and all that jazz," Emery adds.

Ansel swallows. "Are they... They won't come after me, will they? I mean, I won't get in trouble, will I?"

Ethan and Emery exchange another one of those unreadable looks. Silence stretches, fraught with tension.

Emery's grip tightens around the steering wheel.

"I would be careful if I were you," he says, the words low and rumbly, almost a growl. "Whatever you do, do not find yourself alone with a witch or a warlock. And if the Trinity tries to meet with you? Run."

Forty-Two

IZZY

Jake hasn't left his room in days.

I don't know what to say to him, how to help him. Hell, I don't even know if he *wants* to be helped. His entire life was altered irrevocably in a span of seconds.

Isn't it funny how everything can change within a blink of an eye? It doesn't seem fair. Surely, there should be some sort of buildup, some sort of gradual progression before shit hits the metaphorical fan.

I still haven't heard from Grayson, and Ansel has been...

He hasn't taken the news of what he is well.

He still attends class, but he's a shell of his former self, his eyes dull and the skin beneath them marred by purple bruises. Whenever I try to speak to him, he's cordial, but there's a gap between us that didn't exist previously. I don't know what caused it or how to fix it.

Maybe it's the fact that I kept my knowledge of the supernatural world from him. Maybe it's because he didn't tell me about his powers. Or maybe it's a culmination of everything, and neither of us knows how to handle it.

One thing's for certain—I'm floundering.

I close my locker after the last class of the day and place my head against the cool metal. Tomorrow, I'll be traveling with Christian to a wolfy barbecue. How has this become my life?

But today...

Today I just want to sleep and forget all of my troubles.

I'm aware of him before I even see him. It starts with a tingling sensation across the nape of my neck that branches outwards, engulfing me in a prickling type of heat. The tiny hairs on both of my arms stand straight up, and a flush works its way down my cheeks and to my neck.

Reid.

I don't know how I know it's him, only that I do. It must be that damn mating bond or whatever it is.

I haven't seen Reid in...who the fuck knows how long. I think the last time was at work, before the accident. He hasn't attended class since then, and I can't help but wonder if I have a part to play in that. A part of me misses his nonverbal grunts during art class.

And I wish to light that part of me on fire.

I spin around, and sure enough, Reid is standing directly behind me, a scowl on his face and his huge arms folded over his chest.

He grunts something noncommittally and then jerks his chin towards the front entrance of the school. "Come."

Come?

I gape at him and then ball my hands in anger. "Come? Are you kidding me? I'm not a damn dog."

He frowns. "Come...please?"

His gruff voice falters over that one word, as if he hasn't used it often—or at all. I can't imagine he would have a need to.

Before everything went down with Michelle, he was the most beautiful man I've ever seen in my life. He probably had girls begging to follow him like besotted puppies. And then, when he changed, he would just have to level an icy glare at someone, and they'll immediately do his bidding.

But if he thinks he can tell me to jump, I'm going to respond with a "fuck you." He can jump straight off a cliff for all I care.

Still, curiosity gets the better of me, and I find myself trailing along after him. "Um...did you need something?"

He scowls at nothing in particular. No...wait...not nothing. His gaze is latched on the disgusted face of a classmate of ours.

I glare at the kid as well, and he immediately looks away, his cheeks red.

"Need to talk." Reid absently begins to pick at the skin on his arm, tugging at a pimple until it bleeds. He frowns down at it and then lowers his hand back to his side. "Come on."

Reid wants to talk to me?

The cynical part of me wonders if he plans to take me to the middle of the woods and murder me, but that's more Ashton's MO. Reid seems more...straightforward. Like, if he wanted me dead, my brain would be splattered across the locker by now.

Not that I think Reid would ever hurt me.

There's a lot I don't know, but I am certain that none of the guys will harm me. Physically, at least. Mentally is a completely different matter.

I drove in with Ansel today now that he has his car back—the most awkward fifteen minutes of my life— but he has a student Council meeting for the next hour. I'd planned to just wait in the library and get homework done beforehand.

Apparently Reid has other plans.

I shoot a quick text to Ansel, letting him know I'm with Reid—though I don't expect him to see it until after his meeting is over—and then quicken my pace, two of my steps equaling one of Reid's. The man is a literal giant. I don't know what the fuck he's been eating, but it's working for him. Must be all those Wheaties.

Reid stops in front of a sleek, black bike. I know absolutely nothing about motorcycles, but even motionless, this baby looks fast.

"You good to ride?" he grunts out, offering a helmet and jacket to me.

The jacket itself looks as if it can fit two of me.

I've never ridden a motorcycle before, but I can't say I'm against it. Though...

"You're not taking me somewhere to murder me, are you? I dismissed that idea before, but now, I'm not too sure." I'm only half joking. Kind of. Sort of.

Reid stares at me as if he wishes to reach into my brain and pluck out what brain cells remain. I don't know whether or not I should be offended or amused.

"Just get on."

I roll my eyes but slip the jacket on. As expected, it swallows me whole. I have to roll the sleeves up multiple times just to have use of my hands.

Reid frowns down at me, then steps forward, reaches for the zipper, and tugs it up. His hand grazes my breast for a fraction of a second, and my breath hitches. His own body turns still. Something undefinable flares in his hazel eyes—the color more muddy than green today—and he takes a hasty step backwards.

"Sorry," he murmurs.

Is he blushing?

No. It must be just a trick of the lighting.

I shake off the strange, lingering sensation and

focus on what's important. "Are you going to tell me where we're going?"

His lips twitch but don't form into a full-fledged smile. "You ask that now? After you've already agreed to go with me?"

I wave a hand in the air. "I think I'm a little bit insane, to be honest. But I..." After licking my suddenly dry lips, I confess, "I trust you."

Shock widens his eyes, though that emotion is quickly chased away by something akin to awe. Then both of those emotions dissipate, replaced by his usual indifference.

"It's the mate bond," he murmurs gruffly, frowning. "It makes us...well... It's in your DNA to trust us and vice versa."

My nose wrinkles. "I really don't like the sound of that."

"You can leave if you want to," Reid tells me. "But I have something to show you."

"Is it a dead body?"

"Um...no?" Reid gives me a strange look. "What the fuck is wrong with you?"

My lips tick up before I force them into a straight line. "I really should say no and turn around."

Isn't that the truth.

"But?" Reid arches one eyebrow.

A strand of greasy red hair falls forward, and he pushes it away impatiently.

"But I meant what I said before. I trust you—

whether it's because of this damn mate bond or not." I shudder. "Seriously, this thing is creepy. Isn't there a way to remove it or something?"

Once again, Reid's expression turns unreadable, though his eyes flash with a myriad of emotions. "You want to remove the mate bond?"

"I thought that was what we all wanted?" I ask, confused.

He opens and closes his mouth, frowns, and then shoves his hands into the pockets of his jeans. His jaw clenches. "Yeah. Remove it."

"But I am curious what you want to show me," I confess. "You know what they say—curiosity killed the cat."

"Are you comparing yourself to a cat now?"

I shrug. "Maybe I am. After all, I *am* surrounded by meat-headed wolves."

"I never knew meathead could be an adjective."

"Shut up." I grab the helmet out of his hands and slip it on.

It instantly makes me feel unbalanced, like I have five hundred pounds on my shoulders.

Reid watches me struggle with amusement sparkling in his hazel eyes.

Once again, I say, "Shut up," and push past him towards the bike. Then something occurs to me, and I spin towards him. "Where are your helmet and jacket?"

The amusement fizzles out of Reid's eyes. He

shrugs, an eloquent, one-shouldered gesture that almost makes words unnecessary. "Don't need one."

"I know you're a badass wolf shifter and all, but I'm pretty sure your brain can still go splat."

He lets out a breath, as if all of my comments are irritating him. Well, good.

"Come on." He swings a leg over the bike.

"But..."

"Izzy." His tone holds a note of warning.

Grumbling under my breath about stupid, idiotic, impulsive wolf shifters, I settle on the bike directly behind him. I have no idea where to put my arms or legs. The last thing I want to do is be flush against him, but I also don't want to take a tumble off the motor-cycle either.

Fortunately, I don't have to ponder this question for long.

With sure movements, Reid grabs my knees and forces me forward until the front of my chest is against his back and my knees are on the outside of his thighs. My hands instinctively move around his torso until they're clutching the shirt over his stomach. He gives my hands a squeeze, and fireflies flutter to life in my belly.

"Hang on," he warns me, and his tone sounds huskier than normal.

"Just so you know, I told Ansel who I was with, so if I come back murdered, then he'll know it was you."

I don't need to see his face to know he's smiling. "If you were murdered, you wouldn't come back at all."

"Ghosts don't exist?" I try to tilt my head to the side but forget I'm wearing the damn helmet and nearly fall off the bike.

"Don't know. Don't care." He revs the engine. "Hold on. And whatever you do, don't let go."

Forty-Three

IZZY

I've never ridden a motorcycle before, and I can't say it's something I care to repeat.

Okay, that's not entirely true. There's something strangely appealing about being pressed against Reid the way I am, my soft curves a contrast to his hard muscles.

And it's not like I'm afraid. Oh no. I actually wish I felt a little bit of fear. That would mean Reid was driving at the speed limit.

Instead, he seems content to pitter-patter along, barely reaching twenty miles per hour, as if he's terrified I'm going to fall off the bike and break.

I've seen him drive before—more than once. He certainly didn't drive like a granny then.

At the same time, I'm relieved he's being careful, especially since I'm wearing the only helmet. I'm not sure even a wolf shifter can survive a crash on the highway.

Too soon—or not soon enough—we're pulling off the road and down a dirt path. The trees here are thinner, though a few stubborn ones still scratch at my arms as we pass. I'm grateful for the jacket.

Reid pulls the bike to a stop at the edge of the tree line, where tall pine trees transition into a tranquil lake. The water ripples in the afternoon sun like a million minute diamonds.

"Why did you bring me here?" I ask, sliding off the bike.

Before I even can attempt to remove the helmet, Reid's there, his expression grave but his hands gentle as he tugs the helmet off my head. For a long moment, we simply stare at each other. I can see the flecks of gold in his eyes, the color a startling contrast to the green and brown irises.

I wonder what he sees when he looks at me. No doubt, my hair is disheveled from the helmet. I can feel a few sticky strands clinging to my cheeks. His jacket is practically a leather dress on me. The bottom of it brushes my thighs. I'm most certainly a hot mess—but without the "hot" factor and with a huge emphasis on the "mess" part.

"Want to show you something," he says at last, turning away as if it physically pains him to stare directly at me.

He begins to walk quickly—but very purposefully

—down a tiny incline, towards the lake and the wild-flowers surrounding it.

I remain rooted to the spot, unsure of what just happened, before I remove the jacket, drape it over the seat of the bike, and hurry after him.

"This place is beautiful," I say.

I have to raise my voice to be heard over the rushing water.

He grunts but doesn't respond.

"Is that why you wanted to show me it?" I press, staring down at my feet so I don't trip over any loose roots or rocks.

I don't even realize Reid has stopped until I plow straight into his back. He immediately spins around and places his hands on my shoulders, steadying me. Just as quickly, he releases me, taking a single step away so there's space between us.

"Wanted to show you this." He jerks his chin towards the ground.

My brows dip. "This?"

I follow the direction of his gaze.

Directly between us, in a perfect circle, is...dead grass. The brown, brittle blades look out of place amongst the greenery of the forest. A single flower wilts in its own bug-riddled refuse.

My disbelief must show on my face because he folds his arms over his chest and grunts out, "It happened here."

"You need to be a wee more specific," I say, frowning.

"This..." A muscle ticks in his jaw, drawing my attention to a few scars lining the skin there. "This is where that bitch cursed me."

The implications of that statement slam into me with the force of a semitruck. I gape at him, unsure if I heard him correctly, his words playing on a loop in my head.

"What do you mean?" I ask.

At least, I think I ask. My voice is practically a whisper.

Reid looks away, his arms still folded over his chest and his customary scowl firmly in place. That expression on his face should terrify me. It probably would scare anyone else.

Yet I feel safe with him.

It's strange. On paper, Reid is every red flag I can think of. Large, gruff, mean, rude, and curt. Maybe I'm just a damn bull attracted to that color, willing to run headfirst into the unknown.

Or maybe there's more to the wolf shifter than what meets the eye.

"Michelle," Reid grits out at last. "She cursed me."

A thousand questions pop to life, but I bite my tongue to keep from asking them. Instead, I stand there, waiting for Reid to get his thoughts in order.

"We never dated," he says at last. "But not because she

didn't want us to. She became...obsessed, to put it mildly. Thought we were soulmates or some shit." That scowl of his deepens. "She began to stalk me. Hurt people. She came onto me after football practice one day." His eyes turn glazed, trapped in a memory—a nightmare—only he can see. "I was showering, and she stepped in after me, butt-ass naked. Started trying to touch me."

A shudder reverberates through him.

Blinding rage tints my vision red. My hands curl into claws at my sides. All I want to do is find this bitch and pull her eyes out.

"Reid..." I whisper, but he continues as if I hadn't spoken.

"I pushed her away. Told her I didn't feel that way about her." He turns towards the horizon, every muscle in his body held taut. "I used to come here all the time to think. Be alone. She stalked me here on more than one occasion, but I thought... I thought she understood that we were nothing. That we haven't ever been anything. I was wrong."

I venture a step closer and place my hand on his arm. I don't know if my touch provides him any comfort, but it's the only thing I can think to do.

"She confronted me with her older brother. She told him I...hurt her." He shudders again. "That bastard may have been the one to technically curse me, but it's her fault. She did this to me."

"What did she do, Reid?" I whisper.

"She took away the two things that mattered most

to me—or, at least, the two things she believed mattered most to me." He blows out a breath. "My looks and my wolf."

"Your looks and your wolf...?"

"She had her brother curse me to be this ugly, disgusting creature." He releases a sharp, self-deprecating laugh that causes my stomach muscles to tighten painfully. "And, more than that, she took away my wolf. I can't shift. I won't ever be able to until her brother lifts this curse from me."

Forty-Four

Water pelts my face as I tilt my head back, a muscle in my neck aching.

Practice was brutal today, but I don't blame Coach. We have playoffs next week, and we need to be prepared.

Coach thinks we can go all the way.

A smile tugs at my lips.

Of course, the coach is unaware that he has three supernatural beings on his team. Between me, Ashton, and Emery, we'll be unstoppable.

A hand touches the small of my back, and I spin around, my heart jackhammering.

"What the fuck?" I bellow, prepared to beat the shit out of whatever asshole snuck into my shower with me.

But it's not one of my teammates staring up at me.

It's Michelle.

She's naked, and my cock responds before I realize

what it's doing. I can't help it. The girl absolutely repulses me, but she's still beautiful, with inky-black hair, firm breasts, and dark nipples, currently puckered. She sashays forward, her hips swaying, and my gaze automatically dips towards her clean-shaven pussy and the pink lips visible.

Then I come back to my senses and squeeze my eyelids shut.

"What the fuck are you doing here?" I demand, tensing.

"Don't be like that, baby," Michelle purrs. Her fingernails drag down my stomach. "I've come to surprise you."

I snap my eyes open. I snatch her wrist before it can grab my cock and push her away.

"We're not together, Michelle. Don't fucking touch me."

She smirks slyly and takes another step closer. One of her hands inches upwards until she's able to cup her pert breast, running her finger around her nipple until it stands at attention.

"You say that, but your body seems to think differently." With her free hand, she reaches for my erect cock and gives it a punishing squeeze.

"Michelle!" I growl, once again shoving her away.

It feels as if there are thousands of fire ants crawling all over my body. I feel disgusting.

And, more than anything, I hate the fact that my body responded to her in the first place.

That it's still responding to her.

"I don't want you," I tell her, making sure to keep my eyes above her chest. "We're not in a relationship, okay? Just leave me the fuck alone."

"Are you sure about that?" She blinks up at me coyly and then drops to her knees.

Before I can even move away, she grabs my cock and forces it to her lips.

For a moment, I'm stunned, a combination of plea-sure, rage, and disgust skating through me. But just before she can take me deeper down her throat, I grab at her shoulders and push her away.

"Fuck off, you deluded bitch," I snap, hurrying out of the shower.

I grab the first towel I see and wrap it around my waist.

"But Reid—"

"Fuck off!"

I'm transported into a different memory.

Tears prick my eyes as I stare out over the lake.

I feel...disgusting. Dirty.

Violated.

Sludge coats my skin that no amount of washing can remove.

Usually, this place conjures up an innate sense of peace, but not today. I can't get my thoughts to shut the hell up.

I sit on the cold grass, my bike discarded at the edge of the forest, my legs spread out in front of me. I'm exhausted, but I'm not sure sleep will help. I'm afraid of what I'll dream of.

Michelle's face pops to the forefront of my mind, and I shudder.

God, how could I have let her touch me like that?

But...

I didn't, did I? She touched me without my consent.

Is that...?

I don't allow my thoughts to wander down that road. I'm confused as fuck. On one hand, my body responded to her the way it would around any beautiful female. On the other, I feel dirty as hell, and I sure as shit didn't want her anywhere near my dick.

I hear their footsteps a second before I see them.

The forest seems to shake with the force of their anger, the branches swaying erratically.

Dyson's face is painted in raw, unencumbered fury as he stalks forward, Michelle a few steps behind him. Her face is puffy and red, and she sniffles exaggeratedly, using the back of her hand to wipe away tears that don't exist.

"You motherfucker!" Dyson charges at me and throws a fist at my face.

I'm larger than him, but I'm still sitting down while he's standing. His knuckles connect with my cheek before I can move away.

"What the hell?" I bark, jumping to my feet.

I can feel my wolf clawing to the surface, his fangs bared. He wants blood to spill.

Dyson's blood.

And Michelle's.

"She told me what you did, you sick fuck!" Dyson roars.

What I did?

For a moment, I stand there, staring at him in confusion. It only lasts for a fraction of a second, but it's enough time for him to come barreling at me.

I manage to step out of the way at the very last moment.

"Dyson, please!" Michelle sniffs again.

"How fucking dare you?!" Dyson comes at me again, and this time, I can't hold back my wolf.

He rises to the surface with staggering intensity. Fur sprouts on my arms, and my face changes and distorts. My jawline elongates, turning into a snout.

Later, I'll discover what, exactly, Dyson believed I did: take Michelle's virginity by force and then break her heart.

Maybe a part of me doesn't even blame him for the way he reacted. If I had a sister—or a mate—I'd do the same thing in his shoes if I didn't know any better.

A flash of blue light encompasses me before I can finish my shift. It holds me immobile, locking my muscles together.

Dyson stands directly in front of me, his teeth bared and his eyes sparking with unbridled rage.

"I'm going to destroy you," he hisses. "Michelle told me about you. You only care about two things, don't

you?" His lips curl upwards then, but the smile on his face is anything but friendly. "I'm going to take them both away from you."

I try to open my mouth to speak, to plead my case, to tell him his sister is a lying bitch, but the spell keeps my lips firmly together.

A lighter wave of blue magic joins the one surrounding me. And...I can feel my body change. I don't know how else to describe it. Suddenly, my face feels itchy, and my hair hangs in greasy, limp strands around my forehead. A pungent smell assaults my nose. Is that coming from Dyson? From me? I lower my gaze to the front of my shirt, where numerous stains now dot the fabric.

What the fuck?

My wolf howls mournfully and attempts to break free, but he's...stuck. Trapped. In my mind's eye, I can see metaphorical bars crashing down, surrounding my wolf, keeping him away from me. He growls and hisses, but I can barely hear him, barely feel him.

Michelle stands shoulder to shoulder with her brother. He doesn't see the way her lips curl into a self-satisfied, sinister smile. Nor does he hear what she whispers to me, standing up on her tiptoes so her lips are directly beside my ear.

"Now no one is going to love you. You'll have no choice but to come back to me."

I'm tugged out of my memories by Izzy. Always by Izzy.

She gives my arm a squeeze.

"Thank you for telling me this," she whispers, staring up at me with fathomless blue eyes I could get lost in.

They're clearer than the lake in front of us.

I honestly don't know why I brought her here, only that I needed her to know why I am the way I am. Why I can't ever accept her as a mate.

I'm disgusting.

Repulsive.

Unlovable.

"The magic Dyson used..." I jerk my chin back towards the circle of dead grass. "It destroyed everything surrounding me."

Those brilliant eyes water. "I'm going to fucking kill that bitch."

"Izzy..."

"No, Reid. Listen to me." She positions herself so she's standing directly in front of me. "I don't know exactly what happened—and you don't have to go into detail if you're not comfortable—but I do know that she violated you. She..." Her jaw clenches. "She touched you without your consent."

"We tried talking to Dyson," I murmur, remembering those days following the curse—when I naïvely believed that this would all go away.

Dyson, of course, refused to listen to me. Even Ashton and the twins tried to talk sense into him, but he sent them on their way with threats of more curses if they didn't oblige. Ashton promised me he'll fix this, that he'll find a witch or warlock to reverse the curse, but so far, his search has proved futile.

Only Dyson or someone from his bloodline can fix what was done to me.

"I'll *talk* to him," Izzy says evasively, her eyes sparking with a malicious gleam. "I'll *talk* to him until he'll have no choice but to listen."

I'm pretty sure our definitions of "talk" are completely different.

"You need to stay away from him. From him and his fucked-up sister."

She looks as if she wants to argue, so I continue on before she can get a word out.

"Izzy, listen to me. They're fucking insane. You're already on Michelle's radar—"

"I know. She and her brother paid a visit to me the other night."

Tension floods my body instantly.

"What?" That one word is a growl.

Izzy waves a hand in the air dismissively. "Don't worry. The twins and Ansel were with me—"

"The twins were with you?"

And they didn't fucking tell me? I'm going to murder them.

No, I'm going to murder Dyson, and *then* I'll go after the twins.

"Look, Reid." Izzy pushes up on her tiptoes and cups my cheeks, forcing my gaze to hers.

I hate that she can no doubt feel the pimples on my skin. Smell the sweat that's always prevalent. See the dirt and grease in my hair. But she doesn't look disgusted the way so many have before. She just looks...determined.

"What Michelle did to you was fucking awful. I want to murder the bitch, bring her back to life, and then kill her again. You were violated in a way that no one should ever be. And to be blamed for what that bitch did?" Her hands tighten on my cheeks. "But what happened was not your fault. And you're definitely not some disgusting creature."

I release a harsh, humorless laugh. "Don't fucking patronize me, Izzy. I *am* disgusting. I saw the way you flinched away from me when you first met me in art class. Even my parents don't want anything to do with me. Did you know that? They abandoned me months ago. Left me alone with a bank account that they refill monthly. Last I heard, they were in London."

God, that still hurts, even after all this time.

I'm too disgusting for even my own parents to love. Too ugly.

"They're fucking dumb, then," Izzy says fiercely.

I try to shake her off of me, but she holds firm. "Look, I didn't tell you all of this for you to pity me. I don't need your damn sympathy." I grab her wrists and force her hands off my cheeks. "I just want you to understand why I don't want anything to do with this damn mating bond."

"Because you think you're too disgusting?" Disbelief darkens Izzy's tone.

"Because I *know* I am. I'm a big, ugly brute. You deserve better."

"Don't tell me what the fuck I deserve!" she snaps, anger tightening her features.

"I know you deserve better than me."

"Shut the fuck up."

"I'm a mean son of a bitch, Izzy," I tell her with a scowl. "And I have baggage that the others don't."

"I'm not afraid of Michelle or Dyson," Izzy says fiercely.

"You should be."

"Stop telling me what I should and shouldn't be!" She throws her hands up in the air. "You're infuriating!"

"Why can't you see I'm trying to do what's best for you?"

"Shut the fuck up, Reid," Izzy hisses, grabbing the front of my shirt.

I stumble towards her, more out of surprise than anything else, and she once again grabs my cheeks.

But instead of holding my face steady, she pushes up on her tiptoes and kisses me.

The rest of the world falls away.

IZZY

Our lips touch for a fraction of a second. His stubble grazes my jawline in a way that shouldn't feel as good as it does.

But before I can deepen the kiss, before I can take things further, Reid pulls away, practically stumbling over himself in his haste to escape me. The lightning zipping through my veins transforms into a tempest, tumultuous and all-consuming. A strange combination of panic and embarrassment seizes my lungs, especially when I catch sight of the disgust on Reid's face.

"I'm...sorry," I say, though my words feel inadequate.

Reid just confessed something horrific to me, and I immediately go and assault him. I can't even imagine what he thinks of me.

Reid looks everywhere but at me. One of his hands creeps up to absently scratch at a pimple on his wrist.

"We should go," he tells me gruffly.

I open my mouth but immediately close it. I honestly don't know what to say. I feel like shit, and more than that, his rejection *hurt*.

Reid doesn't say anything more as he leads me towards his parked bike, but his silence speaks volumes. He holds himself with a sort of rigid tension I wish I could take from him.

Without any fanfare, Reid hands me the jacket and helmet once more. I put both on without complaint.

Reid's heart beats against my palm as I curl up against him from behind, my legs on either side of his own. His large hands capture mine and give them a squeeze. The connection's brief—there and gone before I can compute it—but a fluttery sensation explodes inside of me regardless.

Instead of taking me back to school, Reid drives me to Hale and Gerry's house. He pulls the bike to a stop behind Jake's car.

Over the roar of the motor, I struggle to put my thoughts into words.

"Thank you," I say at last, pulling off the helmet and shaking out my hair. "For telling me what happened."

Reid grunts and averts his eyes, almost as if it pains him to look at me.

"And for the record..." I begin, unzipping the jacket. "I don't think you're ugly or disgusting."

At that, his gaze snaps to mine, disbelief evident on his face. He snorts and rolls his eyes.

Those eyes...

They're certainly not ugly. They're warm and expressive and open and so damn vulnerable that my breath leaves me.

"You're not," I insist, and I find that I mean it. Maybe at first, I was put off by his smell and looks, but none of that bothers me anymore. Knowing what I do, having heard about his past, I find him even *more* attractive. "I think you're sexy, if I'm being honest."

One red brow quirks. "Sexy?"

"What can I say? I have a thing for tall, dark, and dangerous." I give him an impish grin as he continues to stare at me as if I'm insane.

His throat works. "Why...? Why are you saying this?"

"Because it's the truth."

"I see myself in the mirror, Izzy, and I know I'm not sexy. Maybe before..." He shakes his head as a bitter grin tugs up his lips. "Maybe I could've been the mate you needed, but that Reid died a long time ago."

I kind of want to punch him in the face.

Why can't he see what I see?

Nothing I say now will convince him otherwise. Michelle and Dyson did more than just curse him— they destroyed a vital piece of him, the part that believes he can love and be loved in return.

I didn't think it was possible to hate the bitch more than I currently do.

"Well, I think you're sexy." I offer him a one-shouldered shrug before pivoting on my heel. "Thank you for the ride."

"Wait." His fingers catch in the waistband of my pants.

Sparks skitter up my skin where he touches my bare skin.

"Yes?" I give him a coy look over my shoulder.

At least, I hope it's coy. Knowing my luck, I probably look constipated.

Indecision splays across his face. I don't dare move—don't dare even breathe—as he wrestles with emotions I can't quite name.

Then, with an almost blistering speed, he spins me back around and wraps an arm around my waist. The sparks turn into a full-on inferno from my head to the tips of my toes. Warmth envelops me in a steaming embrace.

This kiss is different from the last one.

Everything we've been through, everything he confessed, culminates into one indecipherable emotion—an emotion I can feel skating through my veins. They whirl inside of me like a tornado as I push up onto my tiptoes and dig my fingers into his hair.

He doesn't move his hands from where they're touching my bare skin, a mere inch above the waistband of my pants. But his lips...

His lips devour mine.

His tongue tentatively tangles with mine, and I open for him, wanting more, wanting everything.

I swear when I run my fingers through the garnet strands of his hair, they feel silky to the touch. Not greasy or dirty. When his lips leave mine to trail kisses across my cheek and jawline, I don't feel the texture of blemished skin. No acne or scars.

One of his hands slowly creeps up my side below my shirt, brushing against the underside of my breast, directly below my satin bra.

I moan against his mouth.

A part of me wants to take this even further—to know what it would be like to be destroyed by Reid and then remade by his hands.

But now isn't the time or place.

We're directly in front of my foster parents' home, and who knows who's watching? Besides, there's so much I have to think about when it comes to these men.

My feelings for Ansel and Grayson, for starters.

My attraction towards Christian.

My anger whenever I even think about Ashton.

And my complicated feelings for the twins and Reid.

It takes every ounce of self-control I possess, but I manage to stop the kiss before it can escalate.

Lust tripling my heart rate, I put a hand on Reid's

chest and gently push him away. He's the size of a giant, but it takes no force at all to move him.

He stares at me as if in a daze, his eyes slightly glassy and his lips swollen.

And for a moment—for a brief, brief moment—his face is ethereal, devoid of any blemishes, and his hair is full and shiny. Then I blink, and the Reid I've come to know and care about returns to me.

No less beautiful, at least in my mind.

"Do you believe me now?" I ask, my lips quirking upwards.

I wonder if they look as swollen as they feel.

He blinks. "I...errr...yes?"

"I have to go, but I'll talk to you later, okay?"

He still seems dazed, but he manages a tiny nod. "Errr...okay."

I push up on my tiptoes and plant a chaste kiss on the corner of his mouth. Crimson immediately crawls up his neck and settles in his cheeks.

He ducks his head.

I wave goodbye as I bound up the steps to the front door, though I don't immediately go inside. Instead, I watch him, waiting for him to get his thoughts in order.

He touches his lips with a tiny smile then immediately drops his hand. Frowns. Scowls. Turns towards his bike.

And I notice that this time, just before he drives away, he puts on the helmet and jacket.

Forty-Six

IZZY

The day of the barbecue, I wake with the inexplicable tug of dread pulling at my stomach. It causes my movements to be slow and sluggish as I get ready for the day.

The weather is chilly, though nothing like it was a few days prior. Even so, I choose to dress in a loose, off-the-shoulder sweater and a pair of jeans. I call it my "basic bitch" outfit, but it makes me look pretty. I keep most of my hair down, though I do pull a few strands away from my face and twist them up into a clip.

I can't believe that I'm going to a party with *were-wolves*. Actual, honest-to-god werewolves. Though...are they really considered werewolves if they don't shift during the full moon?

It feels strange to be enjoying life after what happened with Minnie, but Hale assured me that this is completely natural. They don't have funerals for shifters—at least, not in the traditional sense. Instead, they throw parties to honor the shifter's life and perform some sort of ritual to reincarnate her wolf into a younger shifter.

Or something.

I don't quite understand all of the details.

When I mentioned to Hale that Minnie wasn't my biggest fan, he replied, "This barbecue isn't just for her."

I wonder if he was referring to the other two women who died.

Larissa, the shifter I fought in the ring, and Ali, the woman I found in the barn.

A chill skates down my spine.

It seems as if I'm surrounded by death, and nothing I do allows me to escape it.

I throw my discarded pajamas into the laundry bin and then spin around...only to have my heart jump out of my chest at the sight of Lissa sitting up on her bed. She looks rumpled, her dark hair sticking up in all directions and shadows hovering below her eyes.

"Lissa?" I blink at her. "Are you all right?"

Her lower lip begins to tremble. "D-don't...don't go to the party."

"What?" I frown.

She clumsily gets to her feet and takes a step towards me. "Please don't go."

"Lissa—"

"I think something bad is going to happen." She begins to pluck at the bottom of her sleep shirt.

"What do you mean?"

This is the most my foster sister has talked to me in...who knows how long. Most of our conversations over the past few days have been awkward and stilted—and usually end with Lissa rolling her eyes and stomping away.

A part of me prefers *that* Lissa over this one.

That uneasy feeling intensifies—the one that screams at me from all directions, clawing at my skin like jagged talons.

Lissa opens and closes her mouth repeatedly before releasing an airy laugh. "I'm being silly. Just... Just ignore me."

"You're not being silly," I tell her. "What's going on?"

She waves a flippant hand in the air. "Just a nightmare I had."

If this were a horror movie, I would scream at the main character—aka me—to trust Lissa's instincts and *not* go to the barbecue. I refuse to be the too-stupid-to-live heroine.

But then Lissa sighs and scrubs a hand down her face. "I think I'm just pissed that you and Jake are both invited, and I'm not."

A little bit of Lissa's sass returns as she scowls and

stomps her foot. Literally stomps it, like a petulant two-year-old.

"It's for adults only, Liss," I tell her gently, though that's not technically true.

It's for supernaturals...and those who know about the world.

Lissa's lips purse, but she doesn't comment. Frost seeps into her dark eyes, turning them obsidian.

Hale and Gerry need to tell Lissa the truth...and soon...before they lose her forever.

I open my mouth—to say what, I don't know—but Lissa shoulders past me before I can get a word out. The door slams shut behind her, leaving me alone in the room.

What the hell was that about?

Was Lissa's warning something...preternatural or just the worried ramblings of a depressed and confused girl?

Either way, the boulder in my stomach refuses to erode. I'm not sure it ever will.

Jake's in the kitchen when I get downstairs, and the sight stops me in my tracks. I can't remember the last time I saw him out of his bedroom.

He wears a plain white T-shirt and sleep pants, and his blond hair is artfully rumpled. Fortunately, he looks clean, as if he showered recently, which is a *huge* improvement to the last time I saw him.

He's leaning inside the fridge but straightens when he sees me. A sheepish smile tugs at the corners of his lips.

"Oops. Busted."

"I... You..." Irritation flares in my chest. "Where have you been? I've been worried sick about you! You don't leave your room, and you don't answer when I call, text, knock, or scream."

He tosses a bottle of orange juice from one hand to the other. "Are you going to hit me? Because I need to prepare myself if you are."

"I'm very, very tempted."

The smile doesn't fade from his face, though his eyes dim, the baby-blue color turning subdued. "I know you've been worried about me—"

"Damn right."

"But I needed time to think things through, you know?" He releases a dry, humorless laugh. "I don't think you understand what it's like to know that everything you believe in is a lie. I mean...I guess you do, but it's not like this, you know?"

The wind falls out of my sails at that.

I physically sag forward and place my elbows on the granite countertop.

"I can't even imagine," I confess. "I thought it sucked when I learned that my parents weren't even truly my parents, but..."

"But at least you're alive." Jake focuses on the orange juice in his hands. He continually tosses it back and forth, back and forth.

"Jake—"

"I'm not sure you should even call me that," he interrupts. "Because I'm not truly Jake, am I? He died."

Swallowing is impossible. "Don't let this change you."

He barks out another laugh. "How can I *not*?"

"I don't care what anyone says. You're Jake. You're funny and charming and annoying and protective and everything a girl could want in a brother. You're the strongest person I know. If anyone can get through this, you can."

The smile gracing Jake's handsome features turns a little more genuine. "I haven't really been a good brother, though. I've been too caught up in my own shit to ask you how you've been."

"No, Jake. Don't say that. I don't expect—"

"Did you decide if you want to meet with your birth fathers?" he interrupts, cocking his hip against the counter.

His question takes me off guard.

"I don't know," I answer honestly.

Jake nods as if he suspected as much. "Well, if you decide you want to meet them, know that I'm here for you. Ride or die, right?"

A smile tugs at my lips. "Let's hope it's not the latter."

"And let's hope the *ride* comes with Benadryl because I get motion sickness," Jake adds, his dimples making a brief appearance.

I laugh out loud at that.

Things suck at the moment, but we'll be okay.

We have to be.

Forty-Seven

IZZY

Christian arrives at the house only a few minutes later.

I honestly didn't expect him to show up. I mean, Hale and Gerry are attending the barbecue as well. They could've easily driven me.

Yet...

My heart does a strange little jig in my chest as soon as I catch sight of him. I have no idea why, besides the fact that he's the sexiest man I've ever seen in my life. Or maybe it's because he stares at me with an intensity that takes my breath away. Or it's because he's one of the only supernaturals in town that I feel like I can talk to and rely on. Or it's because—

Enough already! I internally chastise myself, racing for the door.

Jake beats me to it.

He throws it open with a wide, shit-eating grin on

his face and a mischievous twinkle in his baby-blue eyes. I want to snap at him, but...I've missed seeing him smile. Really fucking missed it.

"Well, well, well. Hello, Mr. Montgomery. What is the vice principal doing at our house on a weekend?" Jake leans against the doorjamb as if he hasn't a care in the world.

I can't see Christian's face from where I'm standing, but I hear his answer crystal clear.

"I'm here to pick up Izzy."

"Hmmm." Jake taps a finger against his chin in contemplation. "Isn't that a tad inappropriate?"

I change my mind.

I want to kill him.

But then Christian answers again, and the breath leaves me. "It probably is, but she's eighteen, and I'm only a few years older than her. And I don't even want to be a damn vice principal but was forced into the job by my father. What are they going to do? Fire me?" He scoffs and then chuckles. "Good riddance."

Jake appears stunned, but whether it's because of Christian's answer or his blunt candor eludes me.

My foster brother shakes his head, as if attempting to clear it, and then asks, "Is she your mate too? I know Hale and Gerry said—"

Oh fuck.

Nope.

Not having this conversation.

Quickly, I hurry the last few feet forward and use my hip to push Jake out of the way.

"We're not mates!" My voice is embarrassingly high-pitched.

Something in Christian's expression shifts, like a bloated storm cloud blocking the sun.

Suspicion causes my eyes to narrow. "We're not mates, right?" I repeat. "Because if we are, and you kept it from me, I would be very, very, very, very, very—"

"Very," Jake interjects pointedly.

I nod decisively. "Yes. I would be very, very, very, very, very, very—"

"Very," Jake interrupts again.

"Upset," I finish.

And angry.

And stabby.

And murderous.

And...betrayed.

I have been lied to by almost every person I care about. Even my own damn social worker kept the truth from me about who I am and where I came from. Christian was one of the only people I thought I could rely on, could trust, could talk to.

His words from my eighteenth birthday play on a loop in my head.

"It means you're mine, little human. It means you belong to the wolves."

Christian can't be my mate, can he? No. He's a lone wolf, and they don't get mates. Right?

Or is it that they don't have a pack?

Can they have a mate but not a pack?

Why the fuck isn't there a *Dummy's Guide to Pack Politics* available for me to read?

My head begins to spin, and a strange, prickling heat invades my body.

A few things occur to me in rapid succession.

Christian's interest in me.

His invitation to the barbecue.

His possessive, growled, "Mine."

His willingness to give me answers.

"No," I breathe, my voice taking on a hollow edge.

Panic flares to life in his eyes, and he holds both hands in the air as if attempting to fend off a rabid dog, one foaming at the mouth. "Izzy, please—"

"Oh shit." Jake volleys his gaze between the two of us, his blond brows nearly touching his hairline. "Is he your mate too? I was just teasing him before, but—"

"Let me explain," Christian pleads as the final pieces of the puzzle click together.

I don't like the final image it creates.

Not one fucking bit.

"You kept this from me," I manage to grit out, ice trickling into my veins.

I feel cold all over, a startling contrast to the almost blistering heat I felt moments before.

That heat...

It should've been the first indication.

I always feel as if I'm on fire when I'm around one of my so-called mates.

"You told me the truth about shifters, but that was to only keep me complacent, wasn't it? To stop me from asking more questions?"

"No, that's not true." Christian shakes his head dogmatically. "I always wanted to tell you the truth—"

"Then answer this for me." I take a single step closer, craning my neck so I can maintain eye contact. "Am I or am I not your mate?"

He opens and closes his mouth. Gaping. Floundering. Struggling to find the words.

And that...

That is the only answer I need.

Betrayal seeps into my veins, caustic and bitter, full of unencumbered resentment.

Finally, he croaks out, "It's not that simple—"

"Seems simple," Jake cuts in, anger tightening the lines on his face.

Christian's eyes sharpen on my foster brother, which infuriates me further. No one is allowed to glare at Jake. No one.

Except for me, but that's beside the point.

"Answer the question, Christian," I snap.

Jake moves back to the kitchen, no doubt to give us privacy, as I wait for Christian to respond. I can practically see the wheels turning in his head.

"It's complicated—"

"Wrong answer," I seethe, just as Jake reappears behind me.

In his hands is one of the largest steak knives we own. Without a word, he hands it to me.

Christian's eyes bulge out of his head as he focuses on the weapon.

"I know you probably have a knife on you somewhere," Jake says casually, "but this one is bigger."

"I like bigger," I tell him with a fond smile.

Jake smirks. "Baby, I can show you big—"

The growl that leaves Christian then causes the hairs on both of my arms to stand straight up. His teeth elongate into sharp-looking fangs, and fur explodes on his forehead and cheeks.

Jake appears pleased by Christian's reaction.

"I fucking knew it!" He pauses. "Actually, I didn't know it. At all. But I suspected five minutes ago, which totally counts."

"Jake?" I glance at him over my shoulder, which is the wrong thing to do, apparently.

Christian snarls fiercely and takes a single step forward. I swear he seems to broaden—his shoulders turn bulkier until they can barely fit through the door, and his chest doubles in size.

"Yeah?" Jake asks innocently.

"You should probably run."

Jake rolls his eyes then turns towards Christian. "I don't want to fuck your mate, man. Chill out."

My right eye begins to twitch. "Did you just tell the scary wolf shifter to chill out?"

He shrugs. "It's not like he can kill me. I'm already dead, remember?"

My god. The men in my life are going to kill *me* at this rate.

I squeeze the bridge of my nose and release a long-suffering sigh. "Go get Hale and Gerry please. Then stay in your room."

Jake, unable to help himself, asks, "Will you be joining me in my room? Naked, preferably. I like dem titties."

Christian's growl can probably be heard miles away, and I move to stand in front of him immediately. This... This isn't Christian. I've suspected as much from the very first growl. When I stare into his burning amber eyes, I don't see the man I've come to know. All that remains is the beast I haven't met yet.

Jake, apparently, is a damn psychopath because he laughs uproariously before practically skipping away. That's another thing I'll need to look into, but later.

"Christian?" I ask, desperately trying to pull his attention back to me.

He continues to glare in the direction Jake retreated, the fur spreading down his neck and to his arms.

I notice, belatedly, that he doesn't shift the way the others do. They transform into large wolves. But with Christian... It's like the wolf transforms into *him.*

That's the only way I can think to describe it, and it terrifies the shit out of me.

"Look at me!" I bark, discarding the knife on the entryway table and then pushing up on my tiptoes to cup his cheeks between my hands.

He tries to pull away, but I hold firm, refusing to release him. I'm still so fucking angry at him for keeping this a secret from me, but...

But I think I see why he did it.

He told me before that he's a lone wolf, and that over time, lone wolves tend to go feral.

Is this what he means by that?

Is that why he kept the mating bond a secret?

What the hell is even happening to him right now?

I remember how I comforted Reid before in the theater, and I attempt to emulate that now, infusing my voice with confidence I don't truly feel.

"Look at me, Christian Montgomery." I guide his eyes to mine. "Jake and I have never slept together, nor will we ever." I scrunch my nose in disgust. "He's practically my brother. He was just trying to punish you for keeping this a secret from me." The reminder of what he kept from me makes my hands tighten on his cheeks, my nails digging in. I force my fingers to relax, though it's surprisingly difficult. "Calm the fuck down."

Christian focuses on me, only on me, and gradually, the fur begins to recede from his skin. Then his fangs shrink back into his mouth, and his eyes return to their normal vibrant blue. He pants heavily, shock splayed across his face, but I keep my hands on his cheeks until I'm certain he's back.

"What the fuck was that?" I blurt, taking a step away, my arms falling uselessly to my sides.

Surprisingly, the answer doesn't come from Christian but from directly behind me.

Hale and Gerry stand shoulder to shoulder, their arms touching and their expressions tense.

"You already know that lone wolves tend to go feral," Hale says gravely, his eyes flicking past me to land on Christian. "It seems as if Mr. Montgomery is further along than any of us would've suspected."

A cold chill skitters down my spine. It's hard to swallow around the ball of fire residing in my throat.

"That's what it looks like when a wolf goes feral?" I whisper.

Christian gently tugs on my hand, forcing me to spin back around to face him.

"Not entirely," he confesses. "But it's about the halfway point." He swallows, and I watch his throat bob with the movement. "The first stage always revolves around shifting. It becomes harder for a lone wolf to shift into his wolf form. Then, when the shifter begins to feel a strong emotion like jealousy or lust or anger, the *wolf* is able to shift into a *human*."

"Think of the Wolf Man from the movies," Gerry interjects. "A humanoid figure with wolf-like characteristics."

"A feral wolf," I breathe in understanding.

All three men nod.

"A feral wolf," Christian agrees. "And after a while, it becomes impossible for the human to take back control at all from the wolf. It's why our kind lives out their lives in the forest. It's the only way to protect the people we care about."

Understanding dawns on me. "Is that why you didn't tell me about the mating bond?"

A deep-rooted anguish manifests in Christian's eyes, and the sight of it causes my heart to clench. I was so, so angry moments ago, but now I just feel...sad. Defeated.

"I knew that if I allowed myself to get close to you, my wolf would get closer and closer to the surface. I wouldn't be able to hold him back."

And then he'll be lost to his wolf forever...

I stumble back a step as if I've been physically shot. "But you invited me to the barbecue. You asked me to go with you. You—"

Christian matches my step backwards with one forward. His earnest blue eyes ensnare my own, and I feel like a tiny bunny staring down the notch of a hunter's bow.

"I couldn't resist you anymore, Izzy. I didn't want to." He runs a hand through his hair and then blows out a jittery breath. "I figured that if I was going to go insane, then I'd rather do it on my own time. I wanted to get to know you, even if it was just for a short while.

Maybe that makes me selfish, but I'm tired of fighting what I'm feeling. I planned on telling you the truth today, actually."

He takes another step closer until he's towering over me, but I no longer feel small and defenseless. There's so much wistful vulnerability in his eyes, so much hope, that one thing becomes abundantly clear —he's granting me all of the power.

Emotion tunnels into my throat and forms a thick ball of tension that makes it hard to breathe.

"I think this is our cue to leave," Hale whispers, and I don't know if he's talking to me or Gerry.

"And here I was thinking this would be better with popcorn," Gerry responds.

A second later, their footsteps retreat down the hall.

"You shouldn't have invited me," I whisper, wishing that each word didn't chisel away a tiny piece of my heart. "If your wolf reacts so strongly to my presence, then we need to stay away from each other. We need—"

"I don't want to," Christian responds firmly. His hands ball into fists by his sides, as if he's physically restraining himself from reaching for me. "I don't know how I was blessed with you as a mate. It's rare for a lone wolf to receive one, but not impossible." He shakes his head in confusion. "I tried to do what was best for both of us, but I don't want to pretend anymore. When you came into my office the other day and confided in me, I realized that..." He blows out a shaky breath. "I realized that I wanted to get to know you. It isn't fair that my brother and his pack are allowed to, despite not deserving you for even a second, yet I have to watch from the sidelines. I know it's selfish of me—"

"I don't think you're selfish." My heart pounds against my breastbone. "Before you returned to the school as the vice principal, you were living in the forest, correct?"

He blanches, all of the color draining from his face, but nods once. "I built a tiny cabin a few miles away from everyone."

"Because you wanted to protect the people you love?" I phrase it as a question, but I know it's the truth.

Still, Christian nods once more, the barest dip of his chin. "I wasn't sure when the wolf would take over. I needed to protect my friends and family."

"But when your father asked you to come back, you did, didn't you?"

His brows scrunch together in confusion. "How did you know that?"

"Besides what I overheard you say to Jake?" I shrug. "I suspected for a while that you didn't want to be here. I just didn't understand why you came back. Now it makes sense. Your father asked you to do something for him, didn't he?"

Shock flickers in his blue eyes, accompanied by a

myriad of other emotions I can't read, before he nods yet again.

"Can you tell me why your father asked for you to come back?" I query.

Once again, he nods.

I think I broke him.

I'm not sure he's even capable of speech at the moment.

"Okay. We can talk more in the car." I reach for my phone and slip it into my back pocket.

Christian watches me in wide-eyed disbelief as I walk past him and head towards his silver Volvo.

Confusion scrunches his brows together. "You're still coming with me?"

I pause and glance back at him. He still stands on the front porch of the house, the sunlight shining on the dark strands of his hair, making some of them appear almost blue. His leather jacket clings to his muscular shoulders but is unzipped to reveal a light-gray shirt. The color contrasts strikingly with his eyes.

"Obviously, I'm pissed you kept this a secret from me," I confess. "I hate being lied to, and I hate being played like a fool."

He looks as if he wants to say something, maybe argue, but I continue before he can get a word out.

"But unlike what happened with the others, I understand why you did it. You were trying to protect me and yourself. And...not a misguided type of protection either." I lower my voice in a piss-poor impersonation of Ashton. "*I don't want you in my world because it's dangerous and you're human and we're big, strong wolves and blah, blah, blah.*"

The corner of his lips twitches upwards. "Did my idiotic brother actually say that?"

"It was implied." I match his smile with one of my own before allowing it to fall. "I'm not saying I'm going to run off to the wedding chapel with you just yet, but we do need to talk. Set things straight."

"We do."

"Because I'm not just mates with you," I warn him, gauging his reaction carefully.

I have no idea if this will set his wolf off or not.

"I know that." His gaze remains serene.

"I'm not saying that I'm desperately in love with Ashton, Reid, Emery, or Ethan, but they are, apparently, my mates."

"I understand."

I wince before blurting out, "And I slept with my best friend, Grayson. And I also have feelings for my friend Ansel. And I kissed Reid. And I want to kiss the twins."

Oh god.

When did I develop such a bad case of verbal diarrhea?

Kill. Me. Now.

Fortunately, Christian doesn't appear upset by my proclamation. If anything, his smile widens, amusement dancing in his blue eyes.

"I've been watching you like a creeper for a while now, Izzy. I know that you have feelings for the others." He rubs at his jawline almost absently, the skin there covered by a day's worth of stubble. "I think we should all sit down and discuss things. I assume Grayson and Ansel know about the supernatural world?"

"Grayson does. Ansel just learned about it," I confess.

He nods as if he suspected as much, and I wonder if someone spilled the beans.

"I notice that you didn't mention Ashton at all. You don't want to kiss my brother?" His tone turns mocking, almost sardonic, and I have to bite my lip to keep from chuckling.

"Of course not. I honestly want to punch the little punk in the face."

Christian laughs out loud at that—a jovial, uninhibited sound that makes my chest and cheeks flush.

"Join the club, sweetheart."

My heart skips a beat at the term of endearment, but I keep my expression calm.

"It's a thirty-minute drive to the barbecue, correct?" I continue moving until I reach the passenger side of the car.

Christian, after only a moment of indecision, hurries to follow me, unlocking the car and slipping into the driver's seat.

"Yeah," he finally answers after he has the seat belt on and the car started. "Why do you ask?"

"Thirty minutes is enough time to get some answers," I respond. "I want to know everything about us, the mating bond, and why you were called back here by your father."

"That might be longer than thirty minutes, sweetheart." He blows out a breath, his hands clenching around the steering wheel.

I reach over my chest to grab my seat belt and buckle it in.

"Then take the scenic route. Because by the time we get to the barbecue, I want answers. All of them. No holding things back or keeping things from me. I already told the others this, but I'll tell you now... There are only so many times I can forgive someone for lying to me. This is your one chance, Christian. Don't blow it."

Forty-Eight

ASHTON

"So this is where the devil sleeps?"

I stiffen automatically at the sound of her voice, not turning away from my desk. I know I should be at the barbecue with the others, but I have too much on my plate to...dally with other shifters.

In front of me is every newspaper article I could find detailing a death caused by a Hunter. There were seventeen in 2020, thirteen in 2021, fourteen in 2022, eighteen in 2023, and eighty-seven in 2024. When I first noticed the dramatic increase, I was afraid my jaw had come unhinged.

What the fuck could've caused the Hunters to escalate so dramatically?

All of the deaths took place in different states. Some of the victims I knew to be werewolves, but others, I suspected, were witches, warlocks, and vampires.

The only similarity is the Hunter's mark carved onto the skin of the victims.

How can I think of barbecue and drinks and dancing when I'm on the precipice of a radical discovery?

"Is there something you want, Isabella?" I clench my jaw and reach for my pen once more. "And how did you even get into my room?"

She doesn't answer me, and my curiosity piques. I have a ton of work to do—and an incessant pounding has taken up residence in my head—but my mate is *here*. In my bedroom.

Fuck.

Slowly, I swivel in my office chair to face her, and my tongue turns to cotton in my mouth.

Isabella Martin sits on the edge of my bed, wearing nothing but lacy lingerie plucked straight out of every wet dream I've ever had...but will never admit to.

The pink bralette pushes up her breasts in a way that shouldn't be legal. Through the wisps of material, I can see her hardened pink nipples, taunting me. The frilly material ends just before her toned belly, and my gaze greedily devours all of that golden skin on display. Her matching pink panties barely cover the important bits and are attached to a garter that caresses her upper thighs the way I want my lips to.

Fuck me.

A strangled noise escapes me as she moves off the bed and sashays towards me.

"What are you doing, Isabella?" I demand, desperately trying to regain control of my senses.

I need to think with my head...and not the one that's straining against the denim of my jeans.

Keeping her gaze fixed on me, she reaches for one of her bra straps and slides it down her shoulder.

"I made a bet with the twins that I can get you down to the party." A sinful smirk pulls at the corners of her lips. "And I don't like losing."

She straddles me, her ass rubbing against my cock in a way that has me seeing stars.

Fuck. Fuck. Fuck!

Get control of yourself, Ashton!

I instinctively bring my hands to her hips—the skin warm and smooth beneath my fingertips.

"Isabella," I choke out, and she grins, leaning forward to dust a kiss against the underside of my jaw.

"Yes?" she asks airily, the question followed with another kiss to my cheek.

"We shouldn't be..."

She leans back and, grinning mischievously, reaches for the clasp of her bra. The straps slide down her arms before she slips them off and tosses the bralette away.

My mouth waters.

"Fucking hell," I breathe, feeling myself unravel.

All of my meticulous control...

Gone, replaced by a heady warmth that trills through my veins.

Izzy smirks and straightens her spine, the movement pushing out her tits.

"Do you like what you see?" she asks in a singsong, taunting voice.

Tongue-tied, I simply gape at her.

"Don't be shy, Ashton."

With another playful smile, she grabs both of my hands and guides them to her breasts. Her nipples feel like tiny pebbles beneath my palms. I squeeze both of her tits at once, loving the way they feel in my hands.

"Are you a tits man or an ass man?" she asks with feigned innocence, brushing her blonde hair back so I have an unobstructed view of the perfection in front of me.

Then her question registers.

"Huh?" As I speak, I grab her nipples between my fingers and begin to pluck them.

I want to taste them. Lick them.

Lick all of her.

She giggles, and the noise travels straight to my already aching cock.

"I think I have my answer." She pushes her breasts farther into my hands. "It's funny. I always assumed you would be an ass type of guy, but apparently, I was wrong. Who would've thought?"

She leans in even closer, and I drop my hands back

to her hips instinctively. Her sweet breath dances across my lips.

"I know about the rope in your closet," she whispers breathily.

My brain stalls, and a tiny burst of panic flares to life. Alarm bells begin to ring simultaneously.

"What? How? I don't—"

"How many girls have you tied up and fucked before?" she continues in that low, seductive voice that seems to have a direct line straight to my cock. "There's a word for that kink, isn't there?" A frown mars her pretty face before she straightens her expression out. Sharp fingernails dig into my shoulders. "Tell me, Ashton. How many girls have you tied up and fucked?"

I consider lying but decide that I've lied to her enough. I won't lie about this.

"Only one, but I didn't go through with it," I confess.

I don't even remember what the girl's name was— she was merely someone I met at a party. We kissed a little, then I tied her up the way I've wanted to since I first learned about bondage and BDSM.

I'm not an expert by any means, but I think I did a pretty good job, and she certainly seemed to like it if her moans were any indication. But before I could fuck her, something stopped me, almost like a premonition that I'd come to regret it. An innate knowledge that she wasn't the one for me.

So I got her off with my fingers and sent her on her way. That was the last time I dabbled in it.

"Where did you learn how to tie people up? A torture class?" She tilts her head to the side, and her golden hair catches in the sunlight filtering through the window.

My fingers flex on her bare hips. "Porn," I admit... then instantly wince, wishing I could shove my answer back into the confines of my mouth.

Why, oh why, did I confess that?

Izzy's fingernails scrape across my shoulders and down my biceps, and a shudder reverberates through me. "Do you watch a lot of porn?"

And just like before, I can't stop myself from answering. It's almost as if she has some sort of spell on me. Is she a siren?

"Not since I met you," I blurt.

The only material I've needed to get myself off are thoughts of her perfect body.

"I see." She leans in even closer, and I know any second now her lips will touch mine.

I close my eyes, inhaling deeply, capturing her scent, bottling it up and locking it away.

"Ashton."

"Ashton."

"Ashton! Wake the fuck up!"

I wake with a gasp, a piece of paper sticking to my cheek as I jerk upright in my desk chair.

"Holy fuck."

The familiar—and unwelcomed—voice causes my hands to clench.

Another similar voice says, "Holy fuck indeed."

"Emery. Ethan. What are you two doing in my room?"

I angrily grab the piece of paper—a printed newspaper article detailing one of the murders—and throw it back on my desk.

I feel incredibly out of sorts and confused, my brain spinning in nonstop circles.

"Were you having a sex dream?" Emery asks, sounding downright jovial by the prospect.

Ethan snickers.

"Of course not." I scoff as if the sheer idea is ridiculous, though I don't turn around.

If I do, they'll no doubt see my erection and believe it's because of my idiotic dream and not a natural part of a man's daily routine.

Keep telling yourself that.

When I close my eyes, I swear I can see Izzy's beautiful face directly in front of me, her eyes hooded and her lips parted.

But no, she would never stare at me like that—like she cares about me, wants me, loves me. I effectively severed any warm feelings she may have had in regard to me.

It's what I wanted, after all.

So why does my heart feel so heavy in my chest?

"You were moaning, brother," Emery says in a singsong voice.

"I didn't know you were capable of sex dreams," Ethan adds.

"I didn't know you were capable of even dreaming," Emery says. "Do robots dream?"

"Apparently this one does."

"Ha. Ha. Ha." Feeling as if I have myself under control, I swivel around in my chair until I can see the two goons who have encroached on my territory.

The twins stand in the doorway, so close their shoulders are nearly touching. The sight gives me pause, mainly because they haven't been able to even be in the same room as one another in months, let alone stand near each other.

"Your father sent us upstairs to get you," Emery explains when he notices my narrowed eyes. "The party's starting."

"And Desiree is waiting for us downstairs," Ethan adds softly.

All of our lips curl downwards at the reminder.

"Do we really have to pretend that we're in a relationship with Desiree the entire night?" Emery runs a hand through his spiked blond hair.

Ethan lowers his head in shame.

"Just get the girl a plate of food and call it good," I say dismissively, already returning to my work.

"You're not coming down?" Emery asks.

"I'm busy."

"You really should consider it," Ethan says softly. "They plan to release Minnie's wolf tonight. You should be here for that. We all should."

He's no doubt thinking about our future—ruling on the Council and helping to shape decisions for all shifters. It's what we're being trained for, after all. No other pack compares to ours in dominance.

"Just... Just give me a few minutes. I'll be down in a second." I begin to drum my fingers against the top of the desk.

There's a beat of silence behind me, and I imagine the twins are exchanging an eloquent look that makes words unnecessary.

Once again, that pinch in my chest returns.

When was the last time they did that?

Months?

I tried to get them to talk shortly after the accident, but all of my attempts were futile. There was too much hate, anger, and grief between the brothers. I feared they would never forgive each other.

What changed between then and now? Why are they suddenly acting like brothers?

Izzy.

It has to be her.

I curl my hands into fists and allow my nails to bite into my palms. The sting of pain grounds me, if only momentarily.

I need to stop thinking about her. Now. I made my decision, and I have to live with it. And consequently live without her. I pushed her away, made her hate us.

But what else was I to do? She was an unknown variable, and I couldn't allow her to disrupt my pack. What if she was a spy? A murderer? A Hunter?

My father told me once never to regret my decisions, that I made them for a reason, and that reason won't ever change. I've held true to that philosophy my entire life.

So why do I feel like a sack of shit?

Why does my heart feel heavy at just the thought of her?

Why do my eyes search her out whenever we're in the same room, as if I just can't help but be drawn to her?

Why do I dream about her?

And, worst of all, why is this tiny voice in the back of my head screaming at me that I fucked up?

Because if I'm wrong...

If Izzy is who she appears to be...

If she's our mate and not a spy...

I may have destroyed our pack irreparably.

Forty-Nine

IZZY

"So let me get this straight." I can't seem to wrap my head around everything Christian just told me. Some of it I heard before from Grayson, but... "Your father believes that wolf shifters are killing off other wolf shifters? That *Kain* is somehow involved?"

Christian doesn't pull his gaze from the windshield as he expertly steers his car down a dirt road.

"They're not the only supernaturals who have been killed recently." His lips purse. "My research shows me that vampires, witches, and warlocks have all seen a substantial increase in deaths over the past few months."

"And all of the murders are made to look like they've been done by Hunters?"

Christian nods. "Maybe some of them were done

by Hunters, but all of them?" A muscle twitches in his jaw. "Something doesn't add up."

I focus straight ahead, trying to process everything I was just told.

I still find it surreal that there's an entire group of humans who will actively try to kill us just because of our blood. Christian even pointed out that they would go after *me*, despite the fact I show no characteristics of a supernatural. It's disgusting.

"My father told me that the various packs have been discussing war," Christian says quietly.

I grip the seat belt over my chest. "War? With the Hunters?"

How would that even work? It's not as if Hunters wear color-coordinated clothes when making their kills. They look like any random person walking down the street.

Does this mean the shifters will attack humans at random? Anyone they think may be a threat?

"I don't know what the fuck is going on, but I don't like it. Not one bit." Christian shakes his head slightly.

"So that's why you're here?" I cautiously turn towards him, unable to help but admire the strong lines of his profile and the dark stubble grazing his chin. "Because you're helping your father investigate the deaths?"

"Before Larissa and Ali, there were only a few

deaths in the area—not enough to draw any conclusions. But my father had his suspicions and asked for my help." His long fingers tap against the steering wheel as he releases a humorless laugh. "You're the only person who knows the true reason why I'm here."

"Ashton doesn't know?"

"AJ is..." He struggles to find the right words. "He's the smartest man I know, but he's also the most oblivious. He never bothered to ask me why I was here; he simply developed his own conclusions."

"Why do you call him AJ?" I heard Christian refer to him that way before but never discovered the reason.

Christian smiles, the curve of his lips effortless. "His first name is Ashton, and his middle name is James. Our mom used to always refer to him as AJ, and I guess the nickname stuck...though our father refuses to use it. I think that's why Ashton loathes the nickname now. It reminds him too much of our mother and how things used to be."

"You told me before that Ashton is your half brother." I think back through my conversation with Hale and Gerry. "I thought that packs...combine DNA to make a child."

Christian glances at me once before refocusing on the road. The trees here are thinner, giving way to rustic log cabins and cottages. I wonder if some of the packs live here. I suppose it makes sense. If I were a wolf shifter, I would want to live somewhere deep in the forest so I don't accidentally run into a wayward hiker.

"That's true," he agrees easily, pulling the car to a stop.

Dozens of cars line the dirt street. Up ahead, a short walk away, people move about, their faces indistinguishable. Unease curls in my chest like a snake.

"But my mother had me before she met her true pack. They adopted me when I was a baby." Sadness splashes across his face, causing my chest to constrict.

"I wish you hadn't lost them," I whisper.

One of his hands rests on the center console, and I desperately want to reach for it. Squeeze it. Offer him comfort. But I resist.

"I never knew my birth father," Christian confesses. "He was a one-night stand of my mother's who died shortly before I was born. Drug overdose. My mother's packmates were the only fathers I've ever known."

Fuck it.

I place my hand over his. "I'm here for you if you ever want to talk."

"I know."

For a long moment, we simply sit there, not saying anything. Hell, we're not even looking at each other, both of our gazes fixed on the shifters in the distance.

But I've never felt more at peace.

Is this the mating bond at work? Christian? I don't know for sure, but I can't say I'm upset. Warmth envelops me from head to toe, wrapping me in a comforting embrace I don't want to escape from.

It's Christian who breaks the silence first, his tone reluctant. "We should get out of the car."

"Yeah."

Neither of us moves.

Christian licks his lips and flicks his eyes in my direction. "I really am sorry that I kept all of this from you. I know I shouldn't have—"

"You really shouldn't have," I agree, interrupting him. I give his hand a squeeze before releasing it and unhooking my seat belt. "I'm not sure if I've forgiven you completely yet. You still need to grovel."

"Grovel?" He arches an eyebrow.

When Ashton does it, he looks arrogant and pompous. When Christian does it, he just looks...cute.

Ugh. He's killing me.

"You know...get on your knees and beg for my forgiveness and all that jazz," I say, waving a hand in the air for emphasis.

His eyes heat, turning molten, and an answering blaze of warmth rushes straight to my core.

"If you want me on my knees, baby girl, all you have to do is ask."

Oh. My. God.

A flush starts at my chest, traverses up my neck, and stops at my cheeks. I feel hot all over.

Christian smirks at whatever expression he sees on my face—probably one of absolute shock and wonder—then smoothly slides out of the car. It takes me a long moment to get myself under control, to calm my rampant heartbeat until it's at a manageable level.

"That wasn't nice!" I huff, following after a grinning Christian.

"What are you talking about?" he asks with an innocence befitting the devil himself.

I pantomime strangling him, and he laughs out loud at that, the noise carefree and airy. It causes an answering smile to pull at my lips. The butterflies in my stomach begin to riot.

We walk side by side to the party, our hands so close they almost touch. Each step causes the tips of our fingers to graze. At one point, I swear Christian hooks his pinkie with mine, but when I glance in his direction, he ignores me, focusing straight ahead.

"I've never been to a werewolf party before," I whisper to Christian as we finally join the crowd I spotted from the car.

"Wolves aren't the only shifters out there," Christian tells me softly, his eyes dancing with amusement. "They're just the most common."

"But 'werewolf' sounds so much cooler than 'shifter,'" I protest.

He chuckles again. "Don't let anyone here hear you say that. Werewolf is almost considered a curse word in these parts."

My eyebrows shoot up to my hairline. "Is it really?"

Oh my god. How many times have I jokingly called one of the guys or Hale or Gerry a werewolf?

Christian winks at me. "No."

"You asshole!" I playfully swat at his shoulder as he stealthily dances away from me.

A part of me can't seem to coincide this Christian to the one at my school. Mr. Montgomery. I wonder if this was how Christian was before he discovered he was a lone wolf, before he moved out of his home and into the wilderness, before he left everyone and everything he knew behind.

A sudden sadness replaces the joy I felt only moments before.

Christian, oblivious to my change in mood, grabs my arm. "Come on. Let me introduce you to people."

The introvert in me wants to shake my head adamantly and retreat to the perimeter of the party, where I can watch and not be forced to interact. But the part of me curious about this world and the people in it allows Christian to pull me forward.

The party takes place between four houses—two on one side of the road and two on the other. All of them are rustic in appearance, seeming to be constructed out of red-brown logs.

Both adults and children alike play on the street, in the yards, and on the front porches. There's what appears to be a buffet in the front lawn of the largest house. A game of volleyball takes place on the lawn across the street. The sound of laughter fills the air.

It's...perfect.

Almost too perfect, like flipping through a catalog encouraging people to buy property in a new town.

The sight does very little to calm my rapidly growing unease.

Christian moves towards two men who are conversing a short distance from us.

"Izzy, I'm sure you know—"

"Silas, how are you?" I interrupt, recognizing the man closest to me.

His broad shoulders, scarred face, and perpetual scowl are unmistakable. I haven't seen him since my last shift at the theater, before...

A knot forms in my throat.

Silas downs his bottle of beer. "I've been better, kid."

Dark shadows distort the skin beneath his eyes.

I don't know what to say to him. Apologizing seems...wrong, somehow. I never understand why people say "I'm sorry" when something bad happens, despite having nothing to do with it. Those two words don't change anything, don't fix anything. I think an apology is designed to express sympathy towards a situation, but it just feels shallow, somehow. Insincere.

So what I say instead is, "I wish that never happened."

I could clarify what I meant—I wish Minnie never died, I wish Silas didn't lose his business, I wish

Minnie's family and friends didn't have to deal with the grief of losing a loved one—but I don't.

Silas's expression turns softer. "Me too, kid. Me too."

The second man has turned towards us at some point during the conversation, and I finally get a good look at him.

"Mr. Remington?" I ask, aghast. "You're a shifter too?"

My substitute yearbook teacher smiles sheepishly and forks a hand through his blond hair, sprinkled here and there with gray streaks.

"You'll be surprised by the number of people you know here," Christian tells me, leaning in close so his breath tickles the hair by my ear.

A shiver rumbles through me.

Both Silas and Mr. Remington stare intently at the tiny sliver of space separating me from Christian. Silas's jaw clenches, and Mr. Remington's eyes turn as dark as obsidian.

What the fuck?

Something occurs to me then, a possibility so outlandish and impossible that I have to laugh.

No, this can't be right, can it?

Ignoring Silas and Mr. Remington for the time being, I turn so I'm facing Christian completely.

"You won't get in trouble for being here with me?" I ask, making sure to keep my voice loud enough for Mr. Remington and Silas to hear.

If my theory is right...

My heart hardens, turning to stone, even as I keep a tiny smile on my face.

Christian appears confused by my question, maybe because he already assured me that he wouldn't be.

"Um...no?" He stares at me like I've lost my goddamn mind, and maybe I have.

I lower my voice to a whisper—though still loud enough for the men to overhear. "Good. I want you to fuck me again like you did on your desk at school."

Christian's eyes widen in shock, and a ferocious growl reverberates from directly behind me. Both Christian and I turn to see Mr. Remington stepping forward, his eyes glowing with the appearance of his wolf. The growl, however, came from Silas, who has begun to sprout fur on his arms and neck.

Oh my god.

Oh my god.

How could I have been so blind?

Logically, I understand how I didn't notice the similarities until just now—because I hadn't been looking for them. I didn't know that my parents weren't my true parents and that I was a wolf-witch hybrid.

But now...

I have the same nose as Mr. Remington. His is a little bigger, given the size difference between the two of us, but it's the exact same shape. And my hair color is similar to his as well. The similarities are harder to see on Silas, but they're still there.

Our eyes are the same—a bright, clear blue.

I want to believe I'm looking for connections that don't exist, but I know that's not the case. Something in the depths of my soul tells me that my theory is correct.

Mr. Remington and Silas are my fathers.

Fifty

CHRISTIAN

Something isn't right.

I know that almost immediately, without anything needing to be said.

Izzy has gone very, very still beside me, her jaw clenched and her eyes frosty. And Kyle and Silas—two of my oldest friends—are glaring at me with an almost incandescent fury, as if they wish they could peel my skin off my bones, tie the pieces together, and then use the resulting product as a rope to hang me with.

What the *fuck*?

"Is everything okay over here?" Hale hurries forward, his eyes volleying between Silas and Kyle before focusing on me and Izzy.

Trailing along after Hale is another shifter I recognize. Dane, I think his name is. Or is it Dan? I've been away from the other wolves for so long, I'm beginning to have trouble telling them apart.

Izzy's voice is glacial when she clips out, "Everything is perfect. I was just telling these two gentlemen that I'm going to fuck my vice principal because I have a lot of unresolved daddy issues."

I practically choke on my own spit.

"Izzy!" I rasp out, unsure of what else to say.

Hale's expression crumbles, something akin to understanding filling his eyes. "Oh, Izzy..."

I'm completely lost, and Silas and Kyle appear confused as well. The former's fur has receded into his skin, and the latter is no longer growling at me.

Kyle brushes at his sandy-colored hair and smiles at the two of us sheepishly. I notice that he doesn't make eye contact with Izzy.

"Sorry about that. I just get a little...protective of my students. It's hard for me to forget that I'm no longer in the classroom." He chuckles, but the noise lacks any genuine humor.

Kyle's words only serve to piss Izzy off even more. I can tell by the way the muscles begin to twitch faster in her jaw. Her hands ball into fists.

"Yeah. That's the reason." Her voice is dry as ice.

Silas doesn't justify his behavior with an explanation. He simply gives the two of us one last loaded glare before stalking towards the cooler to grab another beer.

Kyle watches his packmate warily. "And I'll apologize on his behalf. He's super protective of his employees, especially after what happened with Minnie."

"Silas always claimed that Minnie was the daughter

he never had," Dane chimes in, his voice slightly slurred from all of the alcohol he consumed. He stumbles slightly, and Kyle reaches out to keep him upright. "It's horrible what happened to her."

Izzy flinches as if she was physically struck, Hale pales, and Kyle suddenly appears as if he's going to be sick.

"I'm sorry Silas lost his...daughter." Izzy stumbles over that word. "I didn't know Minnie well, but she seemed like a good person."

Dane nods seriously, but his attention is already elsewhere. He waves at someone over Kyle's head and takes off in their direction.

"Izzy..." Hale tries again, taking a step towards my mate.

Izzy spins on her heel and calls over her shoulder, "I'm going to grab something to drink." And then, under her breath, she adds, "Hopefully something strong enough to get through the day."

I don't bother saying goodbye to Hale and Kyle as I take off after Izzy, unwilling to lose her in the crowd. Her golden hair is a glimmering beacon that captures my attention as the two of us weave through the shifters.

Someone steps in front of me, blocking my view of Izzy.

"Christian," a sweet voice says, drawing my gaze down to her face.

My throat swells shut as an indecipherable emotion arrows through me.

Lacey Heart looks exactly as I remember her—soft brown hair cascading around her shoulders in loose curls, rosy cheeks, and emerald eyes framed by thick lashes. At one point, I thought she was the most beautiful girl I've ever seen.

I first started dating Lacey when I was a freshman in high school. She was on the JV cheerleading team and always had a smile on her face. It was that smile that drew me in and demanded I get to know her. We dated for years, and I thought she was the one for me.

Then we both turned eighteen.

Lacey discovered she was the Heart of a pack—though she still has yet to find her mates—and I realized I was a lone wolf. She told me that the mating mark didn't matter, that she still loved me, that she wanted to be with me, but I knew all of her words were lies. She may have believed them to be true then and there, but I knew the second she found her mates, she would forget all about me.

For the longest time, after I retreated into the forest, I would dream of Lacey and what our life could've been like if we were normal humans. But then my dreams started changing and distorting without me even realizing it. Where her face once was, I now saw a faceless, nameless woman with flowing blonde hair.

When was the last time I even thought about Lacey?

I try to wrack my memories but realize that it's been way too long. She hasn't crossed my mind once since...

Since Izzy.

I used to dread going to these events on the off chance I would run into her, but I didn't even think about seeing her today when I invited Izzy.

"Christian." Lacey offers me a tentative smile.

Objectively, I can admit that even now, years later, she's still beautiful. But she doesn't make my heart race the way she once did, doesn't cause my hands to sweat, doesn't make me tongue-tied or weak in the knees.

"Hello, Lacey." I try to look over her shoulder for Izzy, but I can't see her any longer.

An uneasy feeling spirals through me, and I move to step around Lacey, but she blocks me.

"I feel like I haven't seen you in so long," she says with a chuckle. Red paints her cheeks as she ducks her head. "I've... I've missed you."

I finally lower my attention back to the tiny wolf shifter.

I used to love the way she stares at me—like I'm the only man in the world that she'll ever love—but now I only feel uncomfortable.

It isn't just because of the mate bond. We have free will for a reason, and if I truly loved Lacey, I would be able to be with her, regardless of my connection with Izzy.

But I've changed in my years away. Fundamentally.

Irreparably. The Christian who once lived in this town was bright-eyed and innocent. He believed that he would find a pack and live happily ever after with his mate. Hell, a part of him even believed that his pack would consist of Ashton, Emery, Ethan, and Reid. They had been his best friends growing up.

But the new Christian no longer has rose-tinted glasses on. He sees everything with unnerving clarity.

Lacey isn't right for me. I truly believe I loved her at one point, but the love inside of me has changed. I wouldn't say it's bitter or jaded, but it doesn't feel like it once did. I have walls around me now, and only one person has ever managed to break through them.

"Lacey..." I begin carefully.

Movement next to me captures my attention, and I snap out an arm, capturing Izzy around the waist before she can escape. She blinks at me in confusion, one hand holding a plate full of ribs while the other shovels the meat into her mouth. A little bit of sauce stains the corner of her full pink lips.

I can't help but smirk. "What happened to getting a drink?"

She shrugs. "A creepy man told me to try the ribs."

I frown. "A creepy man?"

"Yes. He was smiling weirdly."

"And you just...took the ribs?" I can't believe this girl.

She lifts her shoulders again. "Don't judge. I was hungry. And they looked delicious." Turning, she focuses on a perplexed-looking Lacey in front of me. "Who's this?"

She doesn't sound upset or even jealous, and I realize it's because she trusts me. A warm feeling bubbles in my chest at the prospect.

"Izzy, this is my ex-girlfriend Lacey. Lacey, this is my mate, Izzy." I can't help the masculine pride that seeps into my tone when I use the word "mate."

Both girls blink at each other.

"Mate?" Lacey whispers brokenly.

Izzy slowly rips off another chunk of meat with her teeth, not responding.

"Lacey, I'm sorry—" I begin, but she holds up a hand, stopping me.

"You don't have any reason to apologize, Chris. It's... It's wonderful that you found your mate." She offers me a wry smile that doesn't reach her eyes before turning towards Izzy. "It was lovely to meet you. Now if you'll excuse me..."

Without another word, she spins on her heel and takes off into the crowd.

Izzy waits until she's sure Lacey's out of earshot before saying, "I didn't know you had an ex-girlfriend."

I laugh out loud. "You make it sound as if I used to be a monk."

"You know that's not what I meant." She rolls her eyes. "Anyway..." She focuses on the plate in her hands before lowering her gaze to her feet. "Would it be horribly nosey for me to ask you what happened?"

"There's not much to tell. I started dating her my freshman year of high school. When I discovered I was a lone wolf, I broke things off."

Izzy frowns and finally meets my eyes. "Did you love her?"

I gauge her expression carefully, searching for any signs of jealousy or discomfort, but all I find staring back at me is genuine curiosity.

"I did," I confess, unwilling to lie to her again. "But I was a different person back then. Would we have stayed together if things had been different? I wouldn't be able to tell you. Yes, I think I loved her, but in the way a young boy loves his first girlfriend. We weren't perfect. We argued a lot and had different dreams for the future."

I used to think about this often.

Would I have stayed with Lacey if we had lived different lives?

I would like to say yes, but...

I'm honestly not sure.

A part of me believes we would've grown apart over time, when we no longer had school connecting us. But what do I know? Maybe we would've been married by now with a white picket fence and two point five children.

"And now?" Izzy takes a step closer until the tips of her shoes touch mine.

"Now"—I place my lips by her ear—"I realize I prefer blondes."

She snorts-laughs, and my heart lifts at the sound.

I lower my gaze to her pink lips. Attempting to rein in any laughter, I use my thumb to wipe away some sauce sticking to the bottom one.

Izzy's eyes widen. "Are you telling me I had barbecue sauce on my face this entire time?"

"It was cute," I insist, smirking. Then my smile fades, and I lean toward her. "I really want to kiss you right now."

She pushes up on her tiptoes until our lips are only an inch apart. The world goes still, suspended in a superficial tranquility. All of the voices fade until they're nothing but a distant murmur.

And I realize that I lied to Izzy before. Not intentionally, of course. I told Izzy I wasn't sure if Lacey and I would have remained together if things had been different, but now I know without a shadow of a doubt we wouldn't have. Lacey never made me feel like this—like I would go out of my mind if I didn't get to kiss her, touch her, caress her soft skin.

Even if I were a human, I would still choose Izzy. It isn't even a contest.

Just before our lips can touch, Izzy's gaze flicks towards something—or someone—over my shoulder. Darkness descends over her expression like bloated thunderclouds.

"Motherfucker," she hisses, taking a single step back.

I follow the direction of her gaze and scowl.

Ethan, Emery, Ashton, and Reid have finally arrived. I'm honestly surprised to see the latter. I can't remember the last time he attended one of these parties, but maybe he wanted to come and pay his respects to Minnie, his co-worker and friend.

And to see *Ashton* out and about? I wonder what my father threatened him with.

However, the appearance of the four douchebags isn't what causes anger to burn low in my chest.

It's the sight of Desiree standing between all of them, like a pampered princess being protected by her adoring knights.

Izzy's expression falls as if she's been punched in the stomach. "Are you kidding me?"

A myriad of emotions flicks across her face, all of them appearing and disappearing too quickly for me to catch. She settles on anger as she grabs my arm and tugs me towards the group.

"Izzy, what are you doing?" I whisper.

She doesn't answer as she pulls to a stop in front of my brother's pack.

Ethan and Emery both turn pale, and Reid looks away, as if it pains him to stare at Izzy for too long. Even Desiree appears upset, her mouth opening and closing as she struggles to find the words to explain herself.

Only Ashton, the apathetic asshole, doesn't react to Izzy's presence.

"Izzy, it's not what it looks like," Desiree says, stepping between the men. "My father wanted the guys to escort me to the—"

An evil smirk curls up Izzy's lips as she focuses on the twins, ignoring Desiree completely. "Remember about the bet we made back at the arcade?"

If I thought the twins were pale before, that's nothing compared to how they look now.

"Izzy, no..." Ethan breathes in horror.

Emery begins to shake his head from side to side rapidly.

Izzy's smile only grows, blossoming until it's a full-fledged grin.

Ethereal...and dangerous.

"We made a bet, and you lost. I'm cashing in on my prize."

"What bet did you make?" I ask Izzy, bemused.

"Oh, you'll see." Izzy turns to face me, and with the sunlight reflecting off her hair and a wicked grin on her face, I've never thought she looked more beautiful.

But in a scary type of way.

I shouldn't be as hard as I am right now, considering the circumstances, but god help me, I am.

"Motherfucker." Emery kicks at a rock on the ground and then takes off to...who the fuck knows where.

Ethan stares at Izzy like a kicked puppy. "Do we really have to do this here?"

"You're the one who assured me it'll grow back."

Grow back?

What the fuck?

"But..." Ethan sighs, clenches his jaw, and then nods once, fierce determination settling over his face. "All right. We deserve this."

Ethan takes off after his brother, and I watch them go with no small amount of confusion and a tiny bit of trepidation.

Desiree takes another step forward. "Izzy, I promise this isn't what it looks like—"

"Oh, I know." Izzy turns to face the other girl completely. "Emery told me about the deal his pack made with your father."

Desiree's eyebrows shoot up. "He told you about what Ethan did?"

"No, but I suspect Ethan will tell me on his own time." Izzy pauses and then asks softly, "Can we talk?"

Desiree nods. "Yeah. I think that would be a good idea."

Fifty-One

IZZY

"God, these are the best ribs of my life. I would marry the fuck out of them if I could." I moan as I use a napkin to wipe away some more sauce from my lips.

The napkin isn't as good as Christian's thumb, but beggars can't be choosers.

Desiree glances at her own plate with a crinkled nose and raised eyebrows. Hesitantly, she picks up a rib and takes a delicate bite out of the meat. I can't help but snort at how ridiculous she looks.

Like every other time I've seen her, she looks meticulous, not a strand of hair out of place. She wears a white dress that grazes her knees and a dark cardigan overtop.

"Stop laughing at me!" Desiree huffs, though her tone holds no true annoyance. "This shit is hard to eat. I don't want to spill."

"At this rate, it's going to take you five hours just to get through one rib."

Desiree carefully sets her meat back down on her paper plate and swivels on the bench to face me completely.

The two of us sit at one of the picnic tables slightly away from the rest of the party. The air has grown considerably colder in the hours since I've arrived, and a soft breeze stirs my blonde curls.

Desiree glances at her plate and then refocuses on me, her eyes slightly misty.

"Do you hate me?" she asks, and the abruptness of the question takes me off guard.

I lean back slightly and say, "If I hated you, I wouldn't be sitting here watching you attempt to eat ribs."

Desiree makes a face. "These things are a menace to society. They shouldn't be allowed to exist."

"Agree to disagree. But back to the important issue... Why do you think I hate you?"

"Maybe because you've barely talked to me since you discovered I was supposed to mate with your guys?"

A blush settles in my cheeks. "They're not my guys," I mutter.

She ignores me. "I don't want to mate them, Izzy. You have to understand that." She glances down at her hands—the nails perfectly manicured and painted a cherry red—and whispers, "I've accepted that I'm a lone wolf. It's my father who's holding out hope for me."

A tiny piece of my heart shatters at her confession. "Is there really no hope?"

I can't help but think of Christin when I ask that question. If he's fated to lose his mind to the wolf, then where does that leave us?

"There's never been a case of a lone wolf remaining sane," Desiree confesses, finally glancing up to spear me with a look. An understanding smile graces her face. "But that doesn't mean it's not possible. Stranger things have happened. I don't know Christian well, but I know that he's a fighter."

Did she see my almost-kiss with him? Christian assured me that we didn't need to be subtle, that no one here would care that he's my vice principal and mate, but I can't help but be worried. A thread of trepidation unfurls in my gut.

"How did you know...?" I blink at her in disbelief, but Desiree simply snorts and then grins.

"There's a reason I brought you to him on your eighteenth birthday. I know he's one of your mates." A fierce expression twists her face as she glares at me. "And I would've told you sooner if you didn't ignore me. You were supposed to be my friend, yet you allowed those big dickheads to get in the way."

Shame fills me. "I know. I'm sorry. It was just... hard. I didn't really know what to believe. I still don't, if I'm being honest."

"Let me cut to the chase for you." Desiree turns completely to face me and jabs a finger at my chest. "I have never and will never have feelings for your men. I knew from the very first moment I touched them that they weren't meant for me—that they'll never be meant for me. But even if I didn't know that, I wouldn't have feelings for them. Ashton has the emotional capability of a robot, Reid scares the shit out of me, Emery makes me want to become a murderer, and Ethan... Well, I think I hate Ethan least of all." She shrugs. "I just don't find him attractive."

How could she not find him attractive?

All of the guys are sexy as sin, even Ashton, as much as I hate to admit it.

Something occurs to me then.

"Desiree, do you not like...?" I trail off, unsure of how to ask the question without coming across as inconsiderate or rude. "Fuck. Sorry. It's not my place to ask."

Desiree chuckles. "I was wondering when you would ask me that." The smile gradually fades from her face, her lips compressing into a thin line. "I'm not gay, if that's what you think. But I'm not entirely straight either."

I remain silent, waiting for her to get her thoughts in order.

"For the longest time, I thought there was something wrong with me," she confesses, brushing at a loose strand of hair. "I wasn't sexually attracted to girls or guys. I mean, that can't be normal, right? I thought maybe that would change with time. I hooked up with a guy here and there, and when that didn't work, I started sleeping with girls. But I felt...nothing. I hated it, if I'm being honest."

"You're asexual," I breathe in understanding.

She licks her lower lip and nods once. "I think so. Or maybe I just haven't found the right person. I don't know yet." She shakes her head from side to side, as if trying to physically clear her thoughts. "Does that make me...weird?"

"Of course not!" I exclaim instantly. "Did someone call you weird? Who did it? I'll kill them."

Fierce indignation and protectiveness rumble through me on behalf of my friend.

Desiree offers me a soft smile. "Did you know I have a special power on top of shifting into a wolf?"

Once again, I'm blindsided by the topic change but take it in stride.

"I remember being told that some wolves have extra gifts, but I didn't know you had one."

She nods solemnly. "I can see visions of the future. And before you begin freaking out or asking me for lottery numbers, my visions are...erratic, to put it mildly. Completely random. They often happen whenever I touch someone."

I remember the way she froze when we were introduced. The way her eyes glazed over and her lips parted.

"You had a vision when we met, didn't you?" I phrase it as a question, but I already know the answer.

"I did," she says. "It was different from the others. Longer. Clearer."

"What was it of?"

"The two of us," she confesses, her cheeks pinkening. "In the vision, you were at my house, and we were talking about your mates and eating popcorn and laughing, and I never felt so content. You were my best friend, practically my sister, and I loved you with my entire heart." A single tear cascades down her cheek. "I've never had a best friend before."

"What about Mimi? Emilia?" I think of the two girls I see trailing along after Desiree in school. Both girls have become friends of mine, though Mimi is definitely more outgoing than the reserved Emilia.

"We're friends, yes, but... Is it wrong if I say that the friendships feel superficial?" Desiree tilts her head to the side. "Like, they know my shoe size and my favorite restaurant, but they don't know that I'm asexual. And I'm not sure I'd feel comfortable telling them that."

I wrap my arm around Desiree's shoulders and pull her against me. "I've been a shitty friend."

"You have," she agrees, hugging me back. She then pushes away, sniffs, and brushes daintily beneath both of her eyes, catching a few wayward tears. "But at least you have your head out of your ass now."

"I'm kind of happy we cleared the air because there's a lot I need to get off my chest."

Desiree's ears practically perk up like a dog being told her owner has a treat.

The two of us sit on the bench and chat about everything and nothing. I tell her about what Hale and Gerry said about my birth parents, and then my suspicions that Silas and Mr. Remington are my fathers. I tell her about Grayson and how he ditched me shortly after we had sex—to which she responded, "Fuck him, then. He probably has a tiny penis."

He does not, in fact, have a tiny penis.

I tell her about Ansel and Christian and even the other four wolf shifters. I express my disappointment that they've kept so many secrets from me and my fear for the future.

Desiree listens to everything I say without judgment, only understanding.

"We could run away together and become old, evil crones on the outskirts of town," she suggests once I finish.

"That's... That's actually a very tempting proposition."

She nods seriously. "We can have a bunch of black cats roaming around and set out old, creaking rocking chairs on the front porch that we can sit on when the neighborhood kids walk by. Then we can just stare at them without saying a single word and watch them run away screaming in fright."

"Damn, girl. I got actual goose bumps." I hold up my arm to show her what I mean.

"I know—" Desiree cuts off abruptly, her eyes widening. "What the fuck are they doing?"

I turn to follow the direction of her gaze, and my jaw just about hits the floor.

Emery and Ethan stand in the middle of the road, already gathering a crowd of concerned, curious, amused, and scandalized onlookers.

"Was this the bet?" Desiree asks in disbelief.

"No! I never asked them to be naked!"

Because Ethan and Emery *are* completely naked, their hands covering their junk.

And every ounce of hair on their bodies is gone.

The blond tousled curls on their heads.

Their eyebrows.

Their chests.

Their arms.

Their legs.

I wonder if they even shaved their...

Nope. Not going there.

Desiree covers her mouth with her hand as laughter bubbles free. "Oh my god."

"Is this your doing?" Christian, who has been talking with a few wolves a short distance away, comes to stand beside me, his twinkling eyes trained on the twins.

"I didn't tell them they had to come out butt-ass naked!" I insist.

"Nudity is common amongst wolves," Christian says, as if that explains everything.

It totally doesn't.

"What the fuck am I looking at?" Reid rumbles as he stomps towards our table, Ashton following a short distance behind him.

The latter doesn't even look at me.

"They were so sure they would beat me at the arcade," I say with a shrug. "I told them that if they were to lose, they would have to shave off all of their hair." When everyone turns to stare at me in shock, I shrug again. "What? Emery said it'll grow back within a couple of days."

"They look...more repulsive than usual," Desiree says, frowning.

"Like adult babies," adds Christian.

Reid simply laughs into his hands.

"Oh god. What are they doing now?" I whisper in horror, watching as Emery moves to stand on one of the picnic tables.

He removes his hands from his dick and props them on his hips.

And...yup.

He is shaved everywhere.

Oh my god.

I need to stop looking, but I can't.

My trepidation melts into heat, traversing my veins like liquid fire.

"Can I have everyone's attention?" Emery calls without any shame whatsoever.

Ethan, on the other hand, is still blushing a beet-red, attempting to cover his junk with his hands.

"You already have it," one of the shifters says, and a few laughs trickle through the crowd.

"Was this a part of the bet?" Desiree whispers to me.

I shake my head wordlessly, even as desire beats through my blood like a pulse.

"My twin and I have something to say!" Emery continues, gesturing for Ethan to join him on the table.

Ethan looks as if he'd rather stab himself in the eye than join his twin, but he eventually sighs and climbs up.

"What the fuck are they doing?" Ashton hisses.

"Hush," Desiree snaps.

"We made a mistake," Emery says. "*I* made a mistake."

He searches the crowd until his searing gaze catches my own. Time seems to stand still, and I find that I can't look away. My heart thumps unevenly in my chest, and my breath catches.

"I hurt someone I care about very much by keeping secrets from her. Lying."

Ethan clears his throat and takes a step forward, still covering his dick with his hands. "About a year ago, I did something I shouldn't have." His voice rings out clear and concise. "I won't go into the details now because it's not something you guys need to know, but I was in a lot of trouble. I made a deal to get out of it."

Shame coats each word.

"Oh my god," Desiree breathes, her gaze flicking to an older gentleman standing opposite the street.

Even from this distance, I can pick up the similarities between him and his daughter.

"What are they doing?" Ashton repeats, and this time, his voice is rife with something akin to panic.

"A lot of you think that Desiree is our mate," Emery says, taking over the conversation. "But that's a lie. She's not and will never be our mate."

Desiree's breath hitches, but it's not because of Emery's words. She's focused on her father, who is stalking through the crowd, fury painted onto every line of his face.

"We found our true mate, and she is the most caring, beautiful, amazing girl in the world." Emery's lips twitch into an adoring smile. "I don't think we'll ever be worthy of her."

"Oh my god." That seems to be the only three words I'm capable of saying.

"We're sorry," Ethan adds, and though his voice is soft, I can hear it across the distance as if he screamed. His green gaze never strays from my face. "We promise to never hurt you like that again."

Desiree's dad is close to them now, his hands balled into fists.

Emery and Ethan exchange a look, and the latter smirks evilly.

Then, as one, the two of them shift into their wolves.

Their furless, *naked* wolves.

Someone chuckles in the audience, and then that noise is followed by a few more laughs. It isn't long until the entire crowd is laughing at the guys' expense. Emery —I can tell it's him based on his personality alone— prances around in all his naked glory, his tiny tail wagging behind him. Ethan, however, comes straight to me, his head lowered in what appears to be submission.

"Oh, Ethan. What did you do?" I whisper as I tentatively reach out to touch his head.

He presses his cheek flat against my palm, his lashes fluttering shut, and I have to stop myself from grimacing. He's really, really gross like this.

"What the fuck did you do?" Ashton bellows, moving to stand beside me, his chest heaving, his eyes wild with fear. "Do you know what this means?"

Ethan's eyes snap open, and he sits, watching his packmate.

"What this means is that he broke our deal," a cool baritone rumbles from behind us.

I stiffen and slowly turn around.

"Daddy, please," Desiree begs. "Just forget about it. You know the mating wouldn't have worked anyway..."

Desiree's father turns towards his daughter, and

some of the anger in his face dissipates, replaced by desperation. "I won't allow you to go feral. I refuse."

"Mating with them won't change anything—"

"They're the strongest pack around!" her father bellows, his cheeks turning red. "They'll be able to save you. I know it. You just need to—"

"I'm sure we can come up with another solution," Ashton says smoothly, attempting to appear unruffled, but I can see the panic swirling in his eyes. I didn't think I knew Ashton well enough to notice things like that, but apparently, I do. "Perhaps monetary compensation—"

"This boy"—he jabs an angry finger in Ethan's direction—"destroyed my entire house and nearly killed me. He deserves to spend the rest of his days in prison."

Ethan flinches like he's been kicked and lowers his large wolf head, placing it on his paws. A whine emanates from his chest.

"Did he tell you what he did?" Desiree's father turns towards me, pure malice reflecting in his eyes.

"Dad, don't!" Desiree snaps.

He ignores her. "You have no idea that your mate is a drug addict, do you? An alcoholic? Did he not mention that when he was between your legs?"

"You're being fucking disgusting!" Desiree screeches, red blotches erupting on her cheeks.

"He's not a drug addict anymore," Ashton says stiffly.

"He ran his goddamn car through my living room after one of his benders. Not only did he nearly kill me, but he sent his own brother to the hospital. It's a miracle Emery was able to walk again."

"Why don't you stop talking about shit you know nothing about?" Emery growls, coming to stand on my other side.

At some point, he must've thrown on a pair of jeans, though they appear slightly too big on him, the waistband hanging low on his hips.

Ethan whines again.

"Maybe it's a good thing that Desiree won't be tied to your pack," the older man spits out. "You are all a bunch of fuckups."

"We can talk about this," Ashton tries again, keeping his voice calm and placating. "There has to be a solution—"

"Yeah, a prison sentence." He sneers down at Ethan, who whimpers and backs away. "You fucked up, boy. You fucked up real bad."

And with that, he turns on his heel and stomps back towards the party—though everyone is paying more attention to us than anything or anyone else.

Desiree curses, shoots a hopeless glance in my direction, and then hurries after him, pleading with him to listen to her.

I turn to stare down at Ethan, who tilts his head up to maintain eye contact with me. "Is that true?"

Everything starts to make sense.

I finally understand why Emery has hated Ethan for as long as I've known him.

Ethan nearly killed Emery, and not only that, but he got their pack trapped in a relationship with a woman they didn't love.

However, I don't feel any anger or hatred or annoyance when I stare down at Ethan's wolf. Only sadness. He carried this burden with him for just about a year now. It must be so incredibly tiring...and lonely.

How long has he been clean?

Did he have help along the way?

Does he have a support system in place?

Ethan continues to stare at me, his eyes unreadable, before he jumps to his feet and takes off in a run.

"Dammit!" Emery curses, taking a step as if he means to go after him.

Ashton holds up a hand to stop him. "You need to stay here and start damage control. People here find you..." His lip curls. "They find you *charming*. Use that. Rally support. I have a feeling Peter will do something sooner rather than later, and we'll need people on our side."

Peter.

That must be the man's name.

I fucking hate it.

Emery looks as if he wants to protest but nods once. "Fine."

Without a word, he disappears into the crowd.

"What's going to happen now?" I ask nervously.

Ashton pinches the bridge of his nose. "Because of the twins' idiotic proclamation, we can no longer hold up our end of the deal. That means Peter is free to take legal action against Ethan if he so desires."

"Not normal legal action," Christian adds. "They'll face the Council, and they'll decide Ethan's punishment."

A tiny bit of hope flares to life. "That's good, right? I mean, his dad is on the Council."

"His dad and packmates won't be able to vote," Reid rumbles, his tone gruff. "Conflict of interest."

"The vote will go to the second most powerful pack, which happens to be close friends of Peter's," Ashton finishes, his jaw tick-tick-ticking away like a tiny clock.

A finger of ice touches my spine, and an invisible spike spears my chest. "Fuck."

"Yeah. Fuck." Ashton scrubs a hand over his buzzed head. "He's an idiot. I don't know why he would do such a stupid thing—"

"Maybe because, unlike you, some things are more important to him than power and prestige," Christian remarks softly. "Maybe because he didn't want to lose his mate before he even had the chance to have her."

My heart thunders against my rib cage.

Ashton whirls on his older brother. "Is love more important than freedom?"

"Is that what you think the mating bond is?" Christian asks, frowning. "A cage?"

Ashton blanches as if he's been struck. "This has nothing to do with me or the mating bond but everything to do with Ethan spending the rest of his life in prison. Because you know that's what they're going to vote for—despite the fact that no one got hurt, and we repaired the house. Peter's a vindictive man. He'll want revenge for the way the twins humiliated Desiree."

"I never..." I swallow and try again. "I never would've asked them to do this for me. I swear."

Ashton turns towards me, and I swear his face softens for a fraction of a second. Then it hardens, turning to stone once more, his eyes keen knives that slice at my skin.

"I won't allow Ethan to spend the rest of his life rotting away."

"I'll see if I can talk to some of my old friends," Christian says. "Remember Bobby?"

Reid's brows furrow. "The nurse?"

"He was one of my old buddies before I...before I moved away. And he's also the son of one of the men who will be voting on Ethan's fate. I can talk to him. Try to get him to set up a meeting with his father and the rest of his pack. Make them see reason."

Reid's scowl deepens. "I can make them see reason."

His dark, threatening voice causes goose bumps to ripple up and down my arms.

"Reid, go find the twins' parents. We need to tell them what's going on. They'll know what to do,"

Ashton instructs, and I can see the wheels in his head turning, the cogs circling.

"And what are you going to do?" I ask, turning towards Ashton.

"I'm going to look for Ethan. He shouldn't be alone," Ashton says.

He begins to stalk towards the forest.

I exchange a helpless glance with first Christian and then Reid before hurrying after Ashton. "I'm coming with you."

Ashton stops abruptly. "No, you are fucking not."

He glares at me, but I hold his stare without an inkling of fear.

"Yes, I fucking am." I fold my arms over my chest and scowl. "Are you going to stand here arguing with me, or are you going to start looking?"

"You're not a wolf," Ashton snaps. "You'll just get in the way."

"I'm his mate," I counter immediately, my tone firm in its conviction.

And...I realize this is the first time I've ever acknowledged that out loud or without scorn. The rightness of that statement now seeps through my veins and surrounds me in warmth, kindling an unimaginable blaze.

Mate.

I'm his mate.

A battle wars in Ashton's eyes before he finally grits

out, "Fine," and stomps towards the forest. "But I'm not slowing down for you."

I roll my eyes. "Wouldn't dream of it."

However, despite Ashton's words, he waits for me at the edge of the forest.

I ignore him entirely.

"Do you even know where you're going?" Ashton bites out as I push away a tree branch.

It snaps back into place...hitting Ashton square in the forehead.

"I'm his mate. Of course I do," I lie, unwilling to admit that I'm completely and utterly lost.

I'm sure there is a way to find Ethan through the mate bond, but I haven't yet read my copy of *Mating Bonds for Dummies.*

"Such a liar," Ashton grumbles, and then silence descends, broken apart by the singing of crickets and the chirping of birds.

With every step, I can feel his eyes on my flesh, roaming over me in a way that makes my neck prickle. I can't fucking take it.

I pause so abruptly that Ashton nearly runs into me. I whirl around and jab a finger at his chest. "Why the fuck do you hate me?"

Shock splays across his face, momentarily replacing the impassivity I've grown accustomed to. "What?"

"Why the fuck do you hate me? No lies. No half-truths. Why. Do. You. Hate. Me?"

Fifty-Two

IZZY

A tiny wrinkle forms between both of Ashton's eyebrows. He seems genuinely surprised by my question, as if he can't fathom how I'd come to such a conclusion.

"*What*?" he demands, his tone curt.

"Why do you hate me?" I ball my hands into fists. "I have done absolutely nothing to you. Do you think I want this? God, Ashton! How much of a narcissistic asshole do you have to be to not see how fucking miserable I am?"

He seems at a loss for words. His brown eyes are abnormally wide in his face as he gapes at me.

But I don't let him get a word in.

"I came to a new town after being bounced from foster home to foster home, never staying anywhere longer than a year at a time. And then I discover that everything I thought I knew was a lie and that I'm not even human! Oh, and that apparently I have fated mates who are supposed to care about me and protect me but are instead lying assholes."

My chest is heaving, my heart racing, but I don't stop. I'm just getting fucking started.

"I don't know what you hope to accomplish with your sly comments, but it's definitely not what you're hoping for." I take a step forward, having to tilt my head up to maintain eye contact. "I don't know what the fuck the mating bond entails—at least, not exactly —but I do know I'm willing to see where it goes with Ethan, Emery, Reid, and Christian—"

"Christian?" Shock splays across his face.

"Yeah. He's my mate too." I swallow as a righteous type of anger blossoms in my chest like a noxious weed.

I am so damn sick of Ashton treating me like dirt when I've done nothing to deserve his ire. Maybe he thinks I'm a docile little girl he can push around, but he's wrong. He's so, so wrong.

"But you... You are *not* my mate."

He staggers back as if I slapped him.

"I don't want you as a mate," I continue venomously, fury blasting through me. "I understand you're a part of their pack, and I won't keep you from them, but I don't want anything to do with you."

He sucks in a sharp breath, his eyes wild.

But he doesn't say anything.

Doesn't attempt to apologize or justify his previous actions—not that I would forgive him if he did. There are only so many times I can be pushed around before I snap irreparably.

"Now that I got that off my chest, let's try to find Ethan." I spin on my heel, trying desperately to get my breathing under control.

I feel hot all over, but not the type of heat I've experienced before around my mates. This holds the bitter remnants of anger.

Ashton's quiet voice reaches me before I can take more than a few steps. "I don't hate you."

I stop, though I don't turn around. "What?"

"I don't hate you," Ashton repeats, louder this time. "I just don't trust you."

I suck in a scorching breath and whirl around. "What the fuck do you mean by that? What did I do to make it so you don't trust me?"

Annoyance crowds his features, but I have a feeling it's not aimed at me but at himself. "Nothing. You've done nothing to me." His sharp gaze flicks to my face and stays there. "If you expect me to offer an explanation for why I am the way I am, then you'll be waiting for a while. I'm not like the other men in the pack. I don't think the way they do. You were an unknown variable who had the capability of hurting my brothers." He shrugs. "I did what I had to do to protect them."

"Why did you think you needed to protect them from *me*?" I ask, folding my arms over my chest to ward off the sudden chill of the wind.

Ashton narrows his eyes on me but doesn't answer. Not that I expect him to.

I've never realized until just now how many walls he has erected around himself. And I'm tired—so damn tired—and don't have the strength to break them down. I'm not even sure I want to. Not anymore. Not after everything he's said and done to me.

Ashton grits his teeth together and turns to stare at something in the distance. "You could've been a spy sent by my father or even Desiree's dad—"

"Do you even fucking hear yourself?" I demand.

One of his eyes begins to twitch. "Excuse me?"

"Do I have to talk slower so your single brain cell will understand?" I ask scathingly. When he doesn't respond to my quip, I continue on, "I don't know what the hell is wrong with you to believe that everyone is out to get you, but I can assure you, they're not. You're pushing people away because you don't want to get hurt, but at the end of the day, you're going to end up bitter and alone."

Ashton huffs out a humorless laugh. "I'm already bitter and alone."

"And how does that make you feel?"

He doesn't answer, seemingly content to stare out over the horizon with a pensive expression on his face. I really, really want to punch him. He has a super punchable face.

"I met Tiffany two years ago." Ashton's quiet voice drags my attention—albeit unwillingly—back to him.

His eyes swarm with emotions I can't read. "Not a lot of girls take an interest in me when around the other guys. Why would they? Emery's the funny one, Ethan the smart one, and Reid the hot one, at least back then. I was just the asshole with OCD who hates ninety-nine percent of people.

"But Tiffany was different. She talked to me, got to know me, made me feel special. I didn't love her—I'm honestly not certain I'm capable of such an emotion—but she became important to me. I cared about her." Darkness rearranges his features into something unrecognizable. "But one day, when I was taking her home after football practice, she left her phone in my car. I know I shouldn't have peeked, but when I glanced at it, I saw a message from someone named Gregor. I thought, 'Surely, this couldn't be my father?'

"There were hundreds, if not thousands, of messages between Tiffany and Gregor. She told him every little detail about my life—who I hung out with, what I ate, how often I shifted into my wolf, any special abilities I may have." Raw rage causes his lip to curl before he forces his mask back into place. "I confronted her about the messages, and do you want to know what she said?" He laughs dryly and rubs a hand over his head. "She said, 'Sorry, Ashton. It wasn't personal. Just business.' That was the last time I heard from her."

Chills careen down my spine. "What happened to her?"

"She wasn't murdered or anything like that. We're

not the goddamn mafia. She just…left town. Saw no reason to stay around now that she wasn't getting paid. I thought she was my friend, but apparently, I was nothing but a job to her. And that's when I realized that everyone in this world is out to get you. You can't truly trust anyone."

My heart squeezes painfully in my chest. "That's… That's sad, Ashton."

He seems surprised by my response, physically stumbling back a step. "What?"

"One person hurts you, and you decide to spend the rest of your life alone?"

"I'm not alone," he snaps, his skin flushing red. "I have my pack."

"But for how long?" Every word I speak feels like ash on my tongue, bitter and chalky. I don't want to say this to him, but I know he needs to hear it. "There's only so many times they can forgive you."

Ashton sucks in a ragged breath but doesn't respond.

I open my mouth—to say what, I'm not entirely certain—when a loud boom ricochets through the forest. Somewhere in the distance, a building explodes outwards, tiny pieces of debris blotting out the sky.

Ashton rushes towards me. "What the fuck?"

A gun goes off.

And that's when the screaming begins.

Fifty-Three

IZZY

"Stay with me," I hiss at Ashton as I move through the trees towards the party.

For once, he doesn't argue.

The two of us stealthily weave between trunks of trees until we're at the very edge of the forest, hidden behind foliage.

For a long moment, I don't understand what I'm seeing. Then everything comes into focus, accompanied by bone-chilling terror.

The largest house—the one that had the buffet on its front lawn—has been reduced to nothing but rubble and flames. The sight of it causes my heart to clench. How many people were in that house when it... exploded? Were my mates? Desiree? Their families? Oh god.

I force myself to look away, to focus my attention on the shifters.

"My god," Ashton breathes in horror, his hand tightening around my upper arm.

I don't know when he grabbed me, but I don't have the heart or strength to push him away.

Dozens of shifters have been corralled to the center of the street where six masked gunmen surround them. All of them are tall, broad, and bedecked from head to toe in black.

"Hunters?" I whisper, making sure to keep my voice soft so the word doesn't carry.

Ashton doesn't answer, keeping his attention fixed on the gruesome sight below us.

Once again, my thoughts begin to spiral, panic digging its jagged claws deep into me.

Where are the twins? Reid? Christian? Desiree? What about Mimi and Emilia? Are they here somewhere? And where are my foster parents and my...my birth parents?

Terror compresses my chest, and my breath comes out in shallow spurts of air.

"Hey." Ashton grabs my face between his two hands and spins me so I have no choice but to face him. His brown eyes glimmer with emotion. "You need to calm the fuck down, you hear me? You are no help to anybody if you're passed out from a panic attack. So take a deep breath, pull on your big-girl panties, and help me figure out what to do. Unless you don't think you can, then you can go wait in the car."

His dogmatic words should irritate the shit out of

me, but they don't. The exact opposite, in fact. I'm suddenly more determined than ever to prove the fucker wrong.

Which was his intention in the first place.

Goddammit.

"I'm calm." I slap his hands away and then refocus on the shifters. "Why aren't they fighting back?"

There are a few dozen wolf shifters and only six gunmen. It should be an easy battle.

Ashton, his mouth pressed in a firm line, jerks his chin towards another group I didn't notice earlier. There's only one gunman that I can see, and he's surrounding...

My breath hitches, and horror trickles into my veins like a poison.

"The children," I whisper, anger rushing to the forefront of my mind and taking hold.

My body shakes with the force of my fury. The gunmen are holding the children hostage.

"They're monsters."

Ashton opens his mouth to respond but snaps it shut when one of the masked men gracefully jumps onto the longest picnic table. He holds his assault rifle loosely in his grip as he surveys the gathered wolves.

"Hello, ladies and gentlemen, and welcome to the hottest new game show around!" He has a deep accent, though I can't pinpoint where it's from. "Who should we have as our first contestant?" He taps a gloved finger to his chin before pointing at the shifters below him.

"Eeny. Meeny. Miny. Mo. You! Come on up and win a prize!"

Two of the other men surge forward and drag an unfamiliar shifter by his arms towards the picnic table. He looks to only be a few years older than me with bright-red hair. He almost resembles Dec from my school.

Could this be...?

Does Dec have a brother?

My pulse races.

"Ashton..." I whisper, but I don't know what I want to say to him, what I want to ask him.

"I know," he responds.

The man is thrown unceremoniously onto the picnic table at the leader's feet.

"Please don't hurt me," the man sobs. "Please."

"Get up," the leader says calmly.

"God, that's Sam," Ashton says in horror.

Sam.

I turn the name over and over in my head.

Sam.

"Please," Sam cries again.

Without preamble, the leader kicks Sam in the stomach, causing the other man to cry out in pain. Someone screams from the crowd, and I think I hear Dec yell something, but the roaring between my ears muffles all of their voices.

The gunmen all hoot and laugh. All...except for one. He stands near the back of the crowd, holding his gun loosely, as if he's unfamiliar with using the weapon. He twists his head away.

The leader lowers himself until he's at eye level with the sobbing shifter. "I'll ask you nicely one more time. Get. The. Fuck. Up."

Sam holds his stomach as he rocks back and forth.

"We have our first loser of the night." The leader chuckles, lifts his gun, and shoots Sam directly in the forehead.

Blood and brain splatter across the wooden table, shades of deepest red and palest pink. My stomach twists, and I place my hand over my mouth, desperate to hold in the vomit that threatens to make an appearance.

He killed Sam...

Just like that.

Fuck. Fuck. Fuck!

Screams echo through the crowd of shifters, and two large men stand up, fur sprouting on their arms. But then the man closest to the children cocks his gun and aims it at a crying little girl's face. Both men immediately fall back down, anger, regret, and grief painted across their faces.

"My god. This is bad. This is really, really bad." Terror squeezes my heart in an impenetrable vise. "We need to do something."

"What do you suppose we do?"

The question doesn't come out clipped or even sarcastic. For the first time in his life, Ashton genuinely wants my opinion. And though he tries to hide it, I can hear his fear—hear it in the way his breath hitches and the way his voice shakes. The muscles in his shoulders tremble as he grips the branch of the nearest tree, almost as if he needs it to keep himself upright.

I take a moment to push my fear away, to look at this the way I always used to do in the fighting ring. Only, instead of one opponent, I have multiple. And they have guns. And hostages. And they've already killed somebody.

Okay, think, Izzy, think.

Our best bet will be to get the shifters to fight back. If they work together, they'll be unstoppable. The gunmen won't stand a chance against so many wolves. However, no one will fight with the children's lives on the line. So...

"If we can get the children to safety, the others will be able to fight back."

Ashton turns to stare at me in disbelief. In his gaze, I can see everything he doesn't say out loud.

It's a suicide mission.

We're just two teenagers.

We won't stand a chance against a speeding bullet.

But, like me, he seems to realize that this is the only option at play. Neither of us are willing to tuck our tails and run, not with so many lives on the line. Not with our—god help me—*pack* on the line.

Determination tightens Ashton's jaw and darkens

his eyes until they're nearly obsidian. "All right. What do you suppose we do?"

"We..." My voice trails off, and I suck in a sharp breath as the scene before us changes.

A girl has been tossed onto the picnic table—a somewhat familiar girl with light-brown hair and large doe eyes.

Lacey, Christian's ex-girlfriend.

And then Christian himself appears, his arms held between two masked gunmen, his features distorted in rage and fear. His wild eyes flicker from face to face, and I know he's searching for me and his brother.

"No," I breathe in horror as they throw Christian down at the leader's feet.

He slowly pushes himself onto his knees, his back hunched, anger etched across every line of his perfect face.

Fear for him momentarily glues my feet to the ground. I can barely breathe around the spike in my heart. But then fury paves its way through me, bolstering my resolve, and I take a threatening step forward. I'll kill them all with my bare hands if I have to. This place will be a bloodbath by the time I'm done with them. I'll do whatever it takes to free Christian and—

Ashton's hand on my arm stops me, though he doesn't pull his gaze away from his older brother.

Some of my adrenaline dissipates.

Going down there right now would be suicide.

Not only for me, but for my mates, who I have no doubt will throw themselves into the line of fire trying to protect me.

Fuck.

Fuck.

Fuck!

I can't remember a time I felt so goddamn *useless*.

Focus on the plan, Izzy. Free the children, and you'll give the shifters a fighting chance. You'll give Christian *a fighting chance.*

Steel trickles down my spine.

I can do this.

I have to do this.

"Christian?" Ashton's uncharacteristically soft exclamation, rife with horror, pulls my attention to his face.

His eyes are wide, and he parts his lips, though not a sound comes out.

No. No. No.

Holding my breath, I follow the direction of Ashton's gaze, already knowing what I'm going to see.

Christian is on his knees, staring defiantly at the leader's masked face.

And a gun is pointed directly at his forehead.

Fifty-Four

CHRISTIAN

I narrow my eyes at the fucker, refusing to show fear.

"Christian!" Lacey sobs.

"You guys know each other, *non*?"

Fucker has a deep accent. Russian, I believe, though I can't say for certain. And, for all I know, the accent is fake in order for us not to uncover his true identity.

Fucker wants me to give him a reaction, wants me to respond, but I refuse to play into his little game.

And even while staring my mortality in the face, I can't help but feel relief.

Izzy isn't here.

My brother isn't here.

I would die a thousand deaths if it means the two people I love most in the world are safe.

Love.

Since when did I associate that word with Izzy? I know that she makes me smile, that I lose my breath whenever she steps into a room, that I desperately want to hear her laugh, that I look forward to those moments when she comes and visits me in my office.

Is that love?

Am I in *love* with Izzy?

I'm pulled out of my thoughts when something smacks across my face. My head jerks to the side, pain exploding in my cheek.

"Don't hurt him!" Lacey screams in anguish, and I mentally scold her for being so damn transparent.

My wolf wiggles beneath my skin, desperate to come to the surface and sink his teeth into this man's neck. It takes years of ironclad control and willpower to keep him contained. Heaven only knows what these assholes will do to the children if they thought I was a threat.

At the reminder, another wave of anger crashes over me, threatening to bury me alive.

I'm going to kill them.

And I'm going to make it hurt.

Unwittingly, I drop my gaze to the body directly beside me.

Sam.

I didn't know him too well, but he's my age. We went to school together. Played football together. Partied together.

And now he's nothing but a corpse with a bullet wound in his forehead.

I never considered anger to have a taste before, but just now, as it settles on my tongue, it reminds me of flaky ash combined with copper. Or maybe that's just because I'm biting my tongue so hard that I've ripped a hole in it.

"Who's ready to play my favorite game?" The crazy man laughs jovially. "Now, here are the rules."

Once again, I find myself staring down the barrel of a gun.

The fucker turns towards Lacey. "I'll ask you a question, darling, and if you answer how I want you to, I won't kill your little boyfriend. But if you answer incorrectly..."

The gun goes off, someone screams, and for a moment, I think I'm going to die. I just wish I got to see Izzy one last time. Hold her. Kiss her. Tell her how I feel.

But then I realize that the bullet didn't hit me but the tree directly behind me.

Holy fuck.

I try to ignore the residual panic coursing beneath my skin as I suck in a deep breath.

Lacey begins to cry harder.

"It'll be okay, Lace," I whisper to her out of the corner of my mouth.

She doesn't respond audibly, just continues to sniffle and sob.

"Now, I'm looking for someone, and I thought that she might be here." He laughs, the noise high-pitched and manic. "Where is Isabella Martin?"

Ice trickles into my veins, and I suddenly can't breathe.

Izzy?

Why are they looking for Izzy?

Unaware of the gymnastics routine my heart is putting my head through, the man keeps his attention on Lacey.

"She was here," she whispers in a shaky voice.

"I know that. Where is she now?" The gun remains steady on my head.

"Lacey, stop talking," I hiss, fear tunneling into my throat and forming a thick ball of tension that's impossible to swallow around.

Lacey turns towards me with tears in her eyes. "Christian, I love you. I won't let you die." She turns her attention back to the gunman. "I saw her go into the woods—"

"Lacey, stop."

"Over there." Lacey points a trembling finger towards where I last saw my brother and mate. "She's with another wolf shifter—Ashton."

"Lacey!" I roar, my wolf fighting to break free.

Lacey refocuses on me. "She may be your mate, but I loved you first. All I want to do is protect you."

"Mate, huh?" The masked man suddenly seems to

find me interesting. He kneels down, and all I can see is a balaclava obscuring his features from view. "You're Isabella's mate?"

I don't answer, though mentally I'm wondering how Lacey could be so fucking stupid to let something of that magnitude slip.

"I think everything is finally starting to make sense." He straightens and tilts his head to the side, studying the two of us. "You're in love with him, but he's in love with his mate. Interesting."

"Please, just let us go," Lacey sobs.

"But you were more than willing to have his mate killed in order to have him for yourself." He chuckles like the entire situation amuses him. "Do you think that he would go to you if he no longer had her? If he knew you were responsible for her death? Bitches like you never learn, do you?"

He tsks his tongue in mock disapproval before turning towards two men standing near the back of the crowd. He jerks his chin once, and the two of them head in the direction of Izzy and my brother.

No.

No.

No.

"What do you want with her?" I demand, knowing I should stay silent but unable to hold my tongue.

It feels as if an elephant is sitting on my chest and compressing my lungs. I can't breathe.

"Wouldn't you like to know?" He chuckles yet again.

Then, without any fanfare or warning, he aims his gun and shoots Lacey in the head.

Her blood explodes in all directions, wetting my cheeks and forehead. I can't move, can't think, can't breathe.

No. No. No. No. No.

Panic, horror, guilt, and a multitude of other emotions claw at me, raking their jagged talons down my spine, leaving behind deep wounds that will never heal.

No. No. No. No. No.

Lacey's dead. Izzy and Ashton are being hunted as we speak.

No. No. No. No. No.

I try with all my might to hang on to my human self, to keep my wolf contained. Because if I let him out, those children are dead. It'll be a goddamn bloodbath.

My wolf claws and howls and scratches. I can't contain him for much longer.

Please don't.

Please.

But my plea falls on deaf ears.

With a cry of anguish, I find myself being pushed out of the driver's seat and all the way into the trunk, where I'm tied up and locked away. Darkness coats the entirety of my vision, a curtain drawn shut.

And I know, without a shadow of doubt, that there will be no coming back from this.

My wolf just took control.

The man no longer exists.

Fifty-Five

IZZY

"I can't believe that bitch sold us out," Ashton growls as he hurries through the forest.

We've given up on trying to be stealthy. I can hear at least one of the gunmen behind us, rapidly approaching.

"She was scared," I reason, my breath coming out in shallow pants. "But can we talk about this when I'm not freaking the fuck out?"

We left as soon as Lacey told the gunmen where we were at. I have no idea what happened to her or to Christian, but I heard a gun go off...

Panic seizes my airway.

He has to be alive.

He *has* to be.

I refuse to accept any other alternative.

A shot rings out, but this time, it comes from

behind me, not all the way back at the party. Wood from a tree directly in front of me splinters and explodes in every direction.

"Izzy!" Ashton calls in alarm.

"I'm okay," I pant.

But the idiot turns around and hurries back to me. At the same moment, the masked man bursts forward and tackles the wolf shifter to the ground. Ashton lets out an audible "oomph" as he hits the ground.

I don't think, only react.

I jump onto the gunman's back and wrap an arm around his throat, cutting off his air. In his shock, he drops the gun, and it lands on Ashton's stomach. Thank fuck it didn't accidentally go off.

The gunman staggers to his feet with me still clinging to him like a damn spider monkey. I apply more pressure, but he rams me against a tree, loosening my grip. Rough bark scratches against my skin where my shirt has risen up.

With a snarl, I press my thumbs into his eyeballs through his balaclava.

He screams and flails, desperately trying to dislodge me, but I hold firm. Blood wets my thumbs and the fabric of his headpiece.

With a roar, the gunman grabs my leg and pulls me off of him.

I twist in the air, landing in a crouched position, and I brace myself for his next attack.

Only...it never comes.

There's a loud *bang* I feel in the hollow of my bones, reverberating through me. The gunman's head jerks backwards, and he falls to the ground, blood seeping into the forest floor around him.

Ashton slowly lowers the gun back to his side.

"Are you okay?" he asks, never taking his eyes off the now-dead man.

"Yeah. You?"

His jaw twitches, but he doesn't respond. Instead, he slings the strap of the gun over his neck and begins to move once more.

"There's still another gunman in the forest. He will no doubt come running at the sound of gunfire. We need to get moving."

"Ashton..." I don't know what to say.

He just killed a man to protect me. And though his face is impassive, an apathetic mask, I can see cracks throughout.

"Let's go," he says curtly, letting me know in no uncertain terms to drop the conversation.

And I follow.

We skirt around trees until we finally reach the other side of the forest, closest to where the gunman stands with the children. Neither of us speaks. A frigid type of tension permeates the air, lifting the hairs on both of my arms and causing my skin to ripple with goose bumps.

So far, we haven't run into the second gunman, but that doesn't mean it won't happen. There's no doubt in my mind that he heard the gunshot, and we weren't exactly being subtle when we hurried away. There's a trail of trampled leaves and smudged footprints leading directly to us.

We need to be quick but smart.

Okay, think, Izzy, think.

There's one gunman near the children, but a few more surround the adult wolf shifters. We need to take the lone gunman out first...but without alerting the others to our presence.

Ashton holds his gun up and aims it at the back of the gunman's head.

"What are you doing?" I whisper-hiss.

My breathing is slightly erratic, both because of the rapid trek through the forest and the fear pulsating through me.

"We need to take him out," Ashton replies tersely.

"Have you ever even held a gun before?" I demand, and darkness flashes in Ashton's eyes. I know he's thinking of the man he just killed, so I quickly change the subject. "Ashton, you can't take the risk, not with how close he is to the kids. What if you miss and hit one of them instead? Not to mention the fact that it'll alert every single gunman here to our location."

Ashton's entire body begins to shake, but he still doesn't lower the gun.

Through the branches and leaves, I can just barely make out the gunman pacing in front of the crying kids. He's just as tall as all the others, though not as broad. I wouldn't say he's lanky, necessarily, but something about him suggests that he's younger than the others.

"And if you kill him, who knows what the fuck will happen to Christian," I continue in a rapid-fire whisper, trying to keep the panic out of my voice.

Someone needs to remain calm, and it's apparent that person isn't going to be Ashton. I've never seen him so...unhinged before. The man has lived his life following carefully curated rules, and every single one of them has just gone up in flames.

"What if we're too late? What if he's already dead?" Ashton whispers.

"He's not dead," I snap—probably too loudly. I quickly work to moderate my volume before I alert anyone to our location. "He's not dead."

"And where's Emery? And Reid? And my father? Where did Ethan go?" Tremors rumble through his body, and a bead of sweat slides down his forehead.

"Ashton, lower the gun."

"I don't know what to do. I was supposed to protect them, but I failed. I fail at everything. I can't—"

"Ashton, lower the goddamn gun," I hiss, and my words finally seem to penetrate his downward spiral.

He inhales shakily, tears misting in his eyes, and slowly lowers the gun back to his side.

I thought I would be able to drag in a full breath now that the imminent threat is over, but I can't. There's too much at stake.

"Come on," I whisper, moving farther down the tree line until I have a better view of what's happening.

Tall trees lean together overhead, their branches knotted, but they provide a large enough hole to see out of while still remaining hidden. Now that I'm looking at everything from the side, I can spot things I didn't notice prior.

Like Hale and Gerry, huddled in the center of the shifters, matching scowls on their faces as they glare up at the picnic table.

And there, behind them, I see Mr. Remington and Silas.

Emilia and Mimi are with men and women I believe are their parents.

No Desiree.

No Emery or Reid.

I try not to let panic take root. It's a good thing that I don't see them. That could mean that they weren't around when the gunmen arrived and started rounding everyone up.

Taking a deep breath, and bracing myself for what

I'm about to see, I flick my gaze towards the picnic table.

Relief causes every muscle in my body to loosen.

Christian's alive.

He's fucking alive.

He's on his knees in the center of the table, his head lowered and his body trembling, but he's breathing. I can see the rise and fall of his chest.

But what's wrong with him?

Why isn't he moving?

Look at me, I mentally scream. *I'm here. I'm coming for you. You're safe.*

A force that seems imprinted on every corner of my soul flares to life.

Look at me.

Please look at me.

Christian doesn't lift his head.

It's only then I catch sight of the second body beside the first, her features slack in death.

Oh god.

I place my hand over my mouth to muffle my intake of breath. I'm way too close to the edge now to risk making a sound.

Lacey's dead.

Fuck. Fuck. *Fuck.*

My breathing turns thready, and I squeeze my eyelids shut and count backwards from five. When I reach one, I snap my eyes open and prepare myself for what I have to do next.

Ashton's still behind me, his face pale and eyes glazed, and I gesture for him to stay where he is. His brows arch upwards, but I'm already moving through the trees, diving behind a camping chair before anyone can see me.

I refuse to let my guard down as I crawl from chair to chair—all of them scattered haphazardly across the lawn—towards the gunman and the children. The leader continues to speak, his accented voice slashing at my skin like a thousand tiny needles.

I slowly stick my head around the chair and come face-to-face with a toddler with blonde ringlets and puffy cheeks. Her tear-filled eyes meet mine, widening in horror. I quickly place my finger to my lips, indicating for her to remain silent.

She stares at me, her mouth parted, tears cascading down her face.

I have no idea if she'll heed my request, and I don't plan to stay around long enough to find out.

Silently, I creep out from behind the chair and move towards the gunman, who has his back towards me. This may possibly be the stupidest thing I've ever done in my life, but I have to try.

Nobody else besides the kids is aware of me yet. The adult shifters are all staring intently at the picnic table-slash-stage, and the other gunmen are focusing on the shifters.

I turn towards the kids, give them what I hope is a reassuring thumbs-up, and then refocus on my target.

His back is still towards me, his attention fixed on the picnic table with the others, and I take my chance.

With an almost blistering speed, I place one hand over his mouth and my arm around his neck. I begin to drag us both backwards, his body kicking and flailing. Panic sets in—I'm not sure how much longer I can hold him—but then Ashton's there, capturing his legs, and the two of us drag the man into the forest.

When we're far enough away that no one will overhear us, Ashton hisses out, "What the fuck were you thinking?"

"Wasn't thinking," I pant out, my body shaking with both exertion and adrenaline—the latter of which is rapidly dissipating.

Damn, this fucker's heavy. And he keeps biting me. The second time he does it, I release his throat and slap him across the face from my position above him.

"Stop fucking biting me."

After removing the gun from his body, I release him, and after a moment, Ashton does as well. But before the man can even get to his feet, Ashton points the stolen gun at his forehead. I aim the second one at him as well.

I'm honestly not sure if I could shoot him. Not like this.

I've killed before, but that was self-defense.

Could I shoot someone when they're on their back with no weapons, their hands in the air?

"Take your mask off," Ashton says curtly, jerking his chin up.

The man doesn't react.

Ashton brings the gun even closer to his face. "I said, take the fucking mask off."

A wry chuckle erupts from the gunman's lips as he moves to grab the fabric. I watch him like a hawk, unsure of what other weapons he has on his body.

He pulls the balaclava over his head, the material messing up his dirty blond hair.

A familiar, grinning face stares back at me.

"Kain?" I don't know why I'm surprised, especially with what Christian told me in the car, but shock holds me immobile, cements my feet to the ground.

Ashton doesn't look too surprised either, though his eyes flash with a murderous intensity. "Tell me why I shouldn't put a bullet through your head right this fucking instant."

Kain chuckles, still keeping his hands out in front of him to show us he isn't armed. "Because you're Ashton James. You're not a killer."

Ashton's jaw tightens. "What the fuck were you doing? Who are those people? Are your brothers involved?"

I remember, belatedly, that Kain is in a pack with his older brothers.

Kain's smile merely broadens, revealing two rows of perfectly white teeth. "You're on the losing side, my man. I know you don't want to hear it, but it's the truth. The world is changing, and you can either join the movement or get left behind and die with the others." Something dark and almost manic flicks to life in the shifter's gaze. "He knows that we're the superior species. It won't be long until the world knows it as well."

"What the fuck are you going on about?" Ashton demands at the same time I ask, "Who's *he*?"

Kain's gaze shifts to me, and the expression on his face has panic jangling my nerves. "Those deaths out there? They're *your* fault. All we wanted was you. If you would've come to us, those shifters would still be alive."

"Shut the fuck up," Ashton seethes.

"He doesn't want to hurt you," Kain continues, ignoring Ashton entirely, his shrewd gaze trained on me. "He just needs you to—"

Ashton knocks him unconscious with the butt of the gun. Kain's eyes roll into the back of his head.

"Don't listen to him," Ashton tells me fiercely. "He's just trying to get into your head. It is not your fault that Sam and Lacey died, you hear me?"

Ashton glares at Kain's limp form and then leans forward to spit on him.

I jerk myself back to awareness, wiping away the sludgy remnants of Kain's words as if he physically threw them at me.

"I need to get the kids to safety. Only then will the shifters be willing to fight."

"Go." Ashton begins to remove his belt. "I'm going to secure him to a tree. We might be able to get more answers out of him later."

"Be careful."

Ashton wets his lip with a sound of regret. He doesn't meet my stare as he begins to drag Kain's limp body towards the nearest tree.

At first, I don't think he's going to acknowledge what I said, but as I begin to hurry back the way I came, I hear his voice, soft and unsure, "You too."

Fifty-Six

EMERY

"**L**et me out of this room, Reid," I snarl, balling my hands into fists.

The enormous asshole simply crosses his arms over his chest and scowls at me. "No."

One word.

One fucking word, and I want to beat the ever-loving shit out of him.

My eye begins to honest-to-god twitch.

"No?" I mimic his stance, though my hands don't uncurl.

Reid's scowl could make a lesser man piss himself.

Fortunately, I'm immune to the irritable asshole.

"GODDAMMIT, REID!" I move to push past him, slamming my shoulder into his, but the stubborn fuck-face doesn't even flinch.

The two of us are in some sort of closet in one of the houses—shelves line the walls, each one full of perfectly folded blankets and stacked pillows. Reid pulled me into it as soon as we saw the gunmen and hasn't let me leave since.

"My mate is out there!" I jab a finger at the door. "My brother! My father! My mother! My sister!"

Reid's scowl simply deepens, creating deep grooves around his mouth.

"Don't you give a shit about what happens to them?" I continue. "Don't you care about Izzy?"

That... That finally gets a reaction out of him. Anger burns to life in his hazel eyes, and his teeth audibly grind together.

But still, he doesn't respond.

I throw my hands up in the air, cursing when they ram against a shelf overhead, and then lower my head. My wolf claws at my chest in a way he has never done before. He wants to be let out, wants to be able to protect his pack, family, and mate.

I know, buddy. I know.

When Reid speaks next, his voice is gruff—raspy with suppressed emotion. "Izzy, Ashton, and Ethan ran into the woods. You know that. Those...men didn't come from the woods but the street. The three of them are safer than we are at the moment. And what do you think they would do if they saw us in danger?"

He shakes his head as if the prospect is too horrible to even consider.

Either way, he's right, and his words take the wind out of my sails. My muscles loosen and my shoulders droop. Without a word, I fall to the ground, pull my knees up to my chest, and rest my forehead between them.

"I can't lose them, man. I can't," I whisper.

I try to remember the last thing I said to Ethan, to Izzy, even to Ashton.

I spent months hating my twin—and telling him that every chance I got. But I don't hate him. Not truly. Yes, I was furious at him, but it was only because he betrayed the trust I put in him.

When he first began to struggle with addiction, I got him help, unbeknownst to our parents. Maybe that was my first mistake, but I knew Ethan wouldn't want our mom and dad worrying. He was clean. He told me he was clean.

I never should've allowed him to drive that night.

But he told me...

He promised me...

I didn't see the signs, but maybe I wasn't looking hard enough. His eyes were glazed. Sweat dotted his forehead. His hands trembled.

I nearly died that night—I probably would've if I wasn't a shifter with advanced healing—but that isn't why I spent so long harboring anger towards Ethan.

It was because of the lying. The broken trust.

I suddenly understand how Izzy feels, and it's a slap to the face.

God... Izzy. I made a mess of things with her.

Can't she see that I've been trying to do better? To *be* better?

I rub my cheek back and forth over my knee, attempting to capture a few wayward tears, and nearly choke on a laugh.

My knee...is silky soft.

As is the rest of me, thanks to the bet.

Yes, Izzy never said we had to walk around naked, nor did we have to make a public declaration, but Ethan and I felt like this was what we had to do in order to atone. Or at least, it was a step in the right direction.

"They're going to be okay, Em," Reid tells me, awkwardly patting my bald head.

He's not the best at comforting.

"Yeah." I force myself to lift my gaze, to meet his eyes. "I just have a lot of regrets, you know?"

Reid's jaw clenches. "Yeah." For a few moments, that's all he says, but then he swallows and adds, "I'm worried about them too."

I snort. "Sometimes I'm not sure if you give a shit about us anymore." When Reid frowns, I hurry to explain. "You've been different since the curse. Not that I blame you whatsoever—because what that bitch did was horrible and traumatizing—but you've been pushing everyone away."

God, I hate all of this emotional crap. Can't we just beat the shit out of each other and call it good? Next time, Reid needs to pull us into a larger room to do just that.

"I don't... I don't want to push people away anymore," Reid mutters, his words nearly inarticulate. But I hear him as if he's yelling. "Don't want to push Izzy away."

A slow grin creeps onto my face. "You like her, don't you?"

He turns away from me, his muscles flexing, and nods.

"I think we can do this," I say seriously. "Be a pack —all of us and Izzy."

"What about the others?" Reid asks.

I frown. "The others?"

"Christian, the Ansel fuck, and the vampire."

I never thought I would share my mate, my Heart, with someone other than my pack, but...

"I'm not going to stop Izzy from being happy. I care about her too much to ask her to choose." And maybe a part of me worries it won't be *us* that she chooses, if given the choice. "Besides, maybe this is what we deserve for being lying dicks to her."

"Do you think we can make this work?" Reid's voice is gruff, almost nonchalant, but his eyes spark with...hope, with a type of vulnerability I can't remember seeing from the growly, angry man before.

"Yeah." I lick my dry upper lip. "We can."

As long as we can survive today, that is.

Fifty-Seven

ANSEL

"Mom, I have some tea for you," I say, wrapping my hands around the steaming cup.

She sits at the kitchen table, dressed in a drab gray sweater and black pajama pants. Her raven-black hair is a rat's nest on the top of her head, and her brown, almond-shaped eyes are underscored by dark circles.

Still, she takes the cup of tea with a grateful smile and shakily brings it to her lips.

"I added a little bit of sugar, a little bit of honey, and a little bit of milk," I tell her, quoting her normal order verbatim.

"You're a sweet boy." Her smile falters a little bit at the edges as she focuses on the liquid. The water has just begun to turn brown. "I'm sorry you have to take care of me like this. It should be my job as your mother—"

"Mom," I interrupt, offering her a tight smile. "You're doing amazing."

A tiny bit of color enters her cheeks. "Yeah?"

"Yeah."

She seems pleased and returns her attention back to her mug and crossword puzzle. I unzip my backpack and begin grabbing out my homework assignments for the weekend.

This has been our normal Saturday routine for... well, for as long as I can remember. Saturday is the one day that Shelby has off, so I usually spend that time with my mom.

We watch cartoons in the morning, the way we used to when I was a kid and Dad was alive, then I make us a huge brunch. Mom usually naps after that while I get some chores done around the house. When she wakes up, I make her a cup of tea, and we'll both sit at the kitchen table. My mom will complete her crossword puzzles, and I'll do my homework.

As I begin my chemistry assignment, I can't help but wonder what Izzy is up to. I feel like things have been strained between us since the truth about me was revealed—and I also feel like I'm to blame for that. I needed space to wrap my head around everything. Still do, if I'm being completely honest.

I'm a warlock.

That means my birth parents were warlocks as well.

Are they still alive?

Do they live here?

Do my parents know?

Some of their cryptic comments over the years jump to the forefront of my mind, clawing at me.

I slide my gaze in Mom's direction. She's smiling serenely down at her little book of crosswords, humming something indistinguishable under her breath. Today's one of her good days. Do I dare ruin that with my questions? Yet...

Who knows when she'll be coherent enough to sit down and have a conversation with me?

My heart beats incredibly fast, pounding against my rib cage, as I set my pencil down and clear my throat. "Mom?"

"Yes, baby?" She glances up and brushes at a greasy strand of hair.

I make a mental note to have Shelby help her shower tomorrow. That is just one thing I refuse to do.

"Can I ask you some questions?" I venture tentatively, chewing on my lower lip. "And I don't want you freaking out."

My mother stares at me, wariness chasing away her initial concern. She settles back in the rickety wooden chair and crosses her arms over her chest. They're incredibly bony, almost unhealthily so. My heart pinches at the sight.

"They found you, didn't they?" she whispers, then swallows.

She couldn't mean...?

No.

No.

"You know what I am, don't you? You've always known." Shock thunders through me.

Tears fill my mother's eyes, but they don't fall. They merely hang suspended like crystalline raindrops.

"I didn't want you to get involved with them. I should've known they would find you." Her voice takes on a hollow edge. "As soon as you brought the wolves and that girl home, you were fucked."

I flinch at hearing my mom swear. She sometimes will let loose an expletive during a particularly bad outburst, but she never curses during normal, everyday conversation.

"That girl has a name," I say, a tiny bit of indignation entering my tone on Izzy's behalf.

Mother's lips purse. "I know who that is. Delaney."

Ice trickles into my veins. "No, Mom. We talked about this. That's not Delaney. That's Izzy. Or Isabella. Her mother is a woman named Helena Craft."

Mother cocks her head to the side with rigid tension. "Helena?"

"Yes, Mom. Do you know who that is?"

Her eyes glaze over, turning distant, before she nods once, the barest dip of her chin. "Yes...I know Helena. She was...kind."

My breath quickens at the revelation that my mother knew Izzy's biological mom. Maybe I can finally get her some answers.

"Everybody loved Helena," Mom continues in that

dazed, singsong voice. "She always had men following her around. One in particular worshiped the ground she walked on."

I wait with bated breath, unwilling to speak and disrupt whatever spell my mother seems to be under.

"She met...those shifters. It was the talk of the town." A timid smile curls up her lips before it falls. "Delaney wasn't happy."

"Who is Delaney?" I press gently.

"Helena's sister, of course." Mom turns towards me before immediately dropping her gaze back to her teacup. "I didn't like Delaney. She was mean."

Holy shit.

Holy. Shit.

Izzy has an aunt?

But wait...

"Why was she mean, Mom? What did she do to you?"

Tremors reverberate through her tiny frame, and she begins to shake her head from side to side, tears misting her eyes. "I did what I had to do. I did what I had to do. I did what I had to do."

"Mom." I gently but firmly place my hand over hers—the one that isn't gripping the mug for dear life. "What happened?"

Grief crowds her face. "She was never supposed to find out about you." One of her shaky hands comes up to cup my cheek. "You were my miracle baby. When your father and I found you—"

"Wait." I pull back from her palm in order to see her face better. "You found me?"

She offers me a serene smile that seems out of place at the moment. My stomach is in tight knots, and there's this incessant pounding in my head.

"You were such a cute little baby, sleeping in the car seat. I knew that you were meant to be mine."

Shock plows me over as I attempt to register her words. I turn them over and over again in my head, trying to have them make sense.

"You told me I was a foster kid," I whisper through numb lips. "You told me that I was bounced from house to house until you took me in when I was young." I don't remember anything from my foster years, but I always assumed it was because I was too young. "Mom, what did you do?"

"I had to protect you from the witches," Mom whispers shakily. "They're dangerous people, and you're an innocent child—"

"Did you..." My stomach turns in on itself. "Did you *kidnap* me?"

"We had to protect you." Mom begins to shake her head rapidly. "You were innocent—"

"Mom, answer the question. Did you kidnap me?" My tone holds more anger than I ever remember using with her.

I can barely breathe past the tightness in my throat.

"They killed your father, baby. My husband. When

you were a child, they killed him." Mom sets her mug on the table and reaches for my hands.

I pull them away before she can touch them. "Why did they kill him?"

Mom's lower lip trembles, and she shakes her head stubbornly.

"Mom, answer me. Why did they kill him? Mom!"

"Because they discovered what he was!" Mom finally screeches, more tears cascading down her face. "Because they found out he was a Hunter."

My breath leaves me. It's suddenly way too damn hot in this house.

I push away from the table on shaky legs and stumble to my feet. I wonder if this is what it's like to be drunk. I wouldn't know. I've never been drunk before.

"Ansel! Baby! What are you doing?" Mom asks in alarm as I move towards the front door.

"What the hell does it look like I'm doing?" I scream, spinning to face her.

Her eyes widen in shock at my uncharacteristic display of aggression.

"I'm leaving this fucking house!"

One of her hands flutters to her chest. "Why would you say such a thing?"

"You just confessed to me that I was kidnapped as a baby. That my adoptive father murdered people like me. What do you expect me to do?" I'm screaming now, but I don't care.

"We saved your life!" Mom cries, stumbling towards me. "You would've grown up with the witches—"

"I would've grown up with my parents!" I counter immediately.

Maybe I have siblings out there. Maybe I have grandparents or aunts and uncles.

"Tell me something, Mom, and I need you to answer me honestly." God, I don't want to ask this. It feels as if my insides are being systematically removed from my body, one organ at a time. "Are you a Hunter too?"

Mom begins to sob.

"Answer the question." This time, I don't yell. My tone is low and unyielding.

"Yes," Mom whispers through her tears. "I used to be a Hunter."

"What is wrong with you?" I ask in disgust.

I can't even look at her anymore. I don't know everything there is to know about Hunters, but I do know they kill supernaturals indiscriminately.

People like the twins, Ashton, and Reid.

People like me.

People like...Izzy.

"You don't understand..." Mom begins desperately, reaching for me, but I stealthily sidestep her extended hand.

"There's nothing to understand," I tell her tersely, grabbing my coat off the hanger and shoving it on.

I don't know where I'm going, but I just know I need to get the fuck out of this house.

"Their type are monsters—"

"Then that means I'm a monster too," I tell her stiffly.

She begins to shake her head in denial. "You're not like them."

The smile I give her then is cruel—more of a baring of teeth than anything genuine. "I'm more like them than you can ever imagine."

Mom screams my name as I yank open the door... only to come face-to-face with a somewhat familiar man. I've only seen him once before, but his dark hair, brown eyes, and sly smirk are unmistakable.

Dyson has one fist lifted as if to knock on the door, but he lowers it when he sees me.

His smile stretches. "Ansel. Just the warlock I wanted to see."

Fifty-Eight

IZZY

I remain low to the ground as I make my way back to the children. I don't know how much time I have until one of the gunmen realizes they're down a man, but I'll worry about that when it comes to it.

When I reach the tree line, I hesitate only briefly before unhooking the gun and setting it on the ground. The last thing I need to do is frighten the children—and showing up with a big-ass gun would certainly do that.

I poke my head around the nearest tree and flick my gaze towards the makeshift stage. The leader has pulled someone else onto the picnic table, though I don't recognize who it is.

And Christian...

He remains on his knees, his head lowered, his muscles shaking.

What the hell is wrong with him?

Fear for my mate twists my heart, but I force myself to focus on the task at hand. If I can get the children to safety, then the other wolves will fight back. That's the only way I can save Christian and the others.

That thought bolsters my resolve, and I direct my attention back to the kids.

Only one is looking at me—the red-faced, blonde girl I noticed before. Tears trickle down her cheeks as she stares at me.

Once again, I place one finger to my lips, indicating for her to be silent, then gesture for her to come to me.

She hesitates, biting down on her lower lip and volleying her gaze between me and the other shifters.

Come on. Come on. Come on.

I don't know how much time we have. The gunmen will certainly notice a bunch of children moving about.

The little boy next to her, maybe a few years older than the girl herself, looks in my direction. Once again, I gesture for him to come, to follow me.

The boy wipes away the snot with the back of his hand and nods once. My relief is short-lived, however, when he jumps to his feet. I shake my head and then lower myself to the ground in a crawling position.

More of the children are staring at me now, all of them crying.

I never thought I could hate Kain more than I previously did. How could he do this to these innocent children? They're going to be scarred for life—not only because they were held hostage but because people they knew died right in front of them.

I take a deep, calming breath—the last thing these kids need is to see me angry—and force a reassuring smile onto my lips.

Finally, one of the kids gathers the courage to crawl towards me. He's quickly followed by another, then another, then another. I keep one eye trained on the gunmen, making sure no one has noticed that all of the tiny hostages have made an escape.

A twig snaps from beside me, and I immediately spin towards the newcomer, my hands curled into fists. I only relax when I see that it's Ashton, his cheeks flushed from exertion and sweat on his forehead. His eyes sweep over me, almost as if he's ensuring I'm okay, before he focuses on the kids.

The blonde-haired girl throws herself at him with a cry. "Ashton!"

"It's okay, Rina. It's okay," he soothes.

He meets my gaze over the little girl's head, and I mouth, "Kain?"

"Taken care of," he responds.

I nod once and focus my attention on the sea of little faces. I count sixteen. Sixteen children who have endured unspeakable horrors. Sixteen children who will face this trauma for the rest of their lives.

Sixteen innocent children.

"Follow Ashton," I whisper to the kids, corralling them towards him.

Ashton gives me an odd look. "What are you doing?"

"I'll be right behind you," I promise.

Ashton looks as if he wants to protest, but he nods and gestures for the children to follow him. They sound like a herd of elephants traipsing through the forest, but it's okay. At least they're safe. Ashton will protect them.

Only when they're out of sight do I step out of the tree line once more.

A few of the shifters have noticed the missing children, and I can see panic, fear, and disbelief splayed across their faces. I meet Hale's eyes and nod once, silently assuring him that they're safe.

And then everything happens at once.

Hale jumps to his feet, and his clothes explode in all directions. In his place is a huge, furry wolf. He launches himself at the nearest gunman.

At first, the rest of the shifters stare on in shock, but then two more wolves join the fray. It isn't long until the street is a battlefield—though a massacre would be a better descriptor. The gunmen have no chance against a bunch of angry, ferocious wolves.

I glance towards the stage where Christian still kneels, the leader directly beside him.

Why isn't anyone going after him?

Why isn't Christian moving?

"Christian," I whisper breathlessly.

Almost as if he can hear my voice, Christian's head snaps up.

Amber eyes lock on my face.

I stagger back a step as horror trickles through my veins.

That's not...

That's not Christian.

I'm staring into the eyes of a wolf.

I wait for him to do something—maybe attack the gunman beside him or come to me—but he doesn't move. He merely remains there, staring at me, his elongated teeth cutting into his bottom lip.

Then Christian jumps to his feet with surprising agility given his size and races towards the woods.

Away from the battle.

Away from me.

My heart shatters into a million pieces.

"Christian!" I scream, my voice lost in the sounds of snarling wolves.

But one person hears me.

The leader of the gunmen turns in my direction and salutes me. He returns his attention to the battle, sweeps his gaze over his fallen comrades, and then takes off in a run in the opposite direction of Christian.

No. No. *No.* I won't let him get away.

I'm about to take off after him when someone new steps out of the woods. Someone new...but familiar.

Her dark hair stands in all directions, the inky

strands wrapped around numerous twigs and leaves. And her feet... god, her feet... Even the tops of them are dirty and covered in blood. Did she walk this entire way shoeless?

Lissa stops at the very edge of the grass, where the yard of the second largest house touches the street, and tilts her head to the side. Her glazed eyes almost appear white in the setting sun.

She opens her mouth, her jaw stretching in a way that shouldn't be normal, and begins to scream.

IZZY

I swear my eardrums explode as Lissa's scream reaches a decibel I never knew existed before.

Before me, all of the shifters fall to their knees. The wolves whimper and curl in on themselves, and the humans rock back and forth.

Something wet trickles down the sides of my face. I bring a hand to my cheek and discover it's blood.

Lissa's scream...made me bleed.

What the fuck is she?

As abruptly as it began, it stops, Lissa's lips clamping together. She sways unsteadily and then collapses onto her side, her head ricocheting off a rock.

Hale and Gerry are there almost instantly, not seeming to care about the blood cascading from their ears in a steady stream.

I seem to be the only person who wasn't knocked

off my feet by her scream. I wonder if it's because I don't exhibit any supernatural traits.

I take a moment to study all of the shifters, searching for those I recognize. I still don't see Emery, Reid, or Desiree, but I have to hope that means they're okay.

And...there. The breath leaves me when I spot Silas's broad form and Mr. Remington's sandy-colored hair. My...fathers.

I take an automatic step in their direction, wanting...I don't know. Comfort? Reassurances? Protection?

But movement in the trees captures my attention.

I immediately bend to grab the gun I discarded only to discover it's no longer there. Oh...shit. I turn to race back to Ashton and the children when something slams into my stomach and throws me over a shoulder.

Then we're running—we're running so fucking fast that the world blurs around me and I fear I'm going to throw up. I try to think of what to do, how to get out of this, but I'm dropped to the ground unceremoniously before I can come up with a solution.

The speed combined with the force in which I was dropped causes me to roll. I swear my body hits every rock, tree, and cactus along the way. Are there even cacti out here? It certainly feels as if there are. Everything hurts.

When I finally stop spinning, I find myself staring

up at the sky, a golden seam across my vision, the sun having just begun to disappear behind the horizon.

"We've been looking for you," an accented voice croons from above me.

He places a booted foot on my stomach, keeping me in place.

I remain stubbornly silent as I glare up at him.

The man reaches for the wrapping on his head and tugs it off, a wide smile on his face.

I don't recognize him whatsoever, but I do note the glowing red eyes.

"You're a...vampire," I whisper, stunned.

"You can call me Vlad." The man bows at the waist, a lock of dark hair falling forward.

I can't help but think that he certainly looks like a vampire...and like a Vlad. How stereotypical of a name. His parents must have hated him.

"This all could've been avoided if you had just been a good girl and come when I asked you to." He tsks his tongue in mock disapproval.

"So you're working with shifters now, huh? To kill other shifters?"

I can't wrap my head around that. From what I heard, shifters and vampires were—while not necessarily friendly—on cordial terms.

Vlad's grin grows, revealing razor-sharp fangs.

I wonder why I never saw Grayson's fangs before. Is it because he doesn't drink blood?

Focus, Izzy! I mentally chastise myself. I need to figure out how to get the fuck out of this.

"Can I tell you a secret?" Vlad smiles conspiratorially and cups a hand around his mouth. "This entire operation is bigger than you can even begin to wrap your pretty little head around."

I scrunch my brows together. "What do you mean?"

"Who do you think the wolves will find when they peel off the masks of their attackers?" He taps his long, dirty fingers against his legs.

I glare at him. "I don't understand."

"Did you know that if a vampire doesn't feed for long enough, they can pass as human?" he asks with feigned casualness.

He applies a tiny bit more pressure on my stomach, and a wheezing breath escapes me.

"Some of our best warriors volunteered to do that," he continues. "It took over six months, but by looking at them, you would never suspect that they were anything other than human."

Horror sluices in my veins like battery acid.

"Kain was there," I point out. "He's a shifter. He's..."

Vlad's smirk grows. "Ahhh. Yes. Young Kain. He was quite easy to capture, was he not?"

I narrow my eyes. "Of course he was. He's a little bitch who wouldn't know a clitoris from a nose."

Vlad throws his head back in laughter, which

causes his foot to dig in even deeper. I wince at the pain.

"I like you, Isabella." He wipes away imaginary tears with his pointer finger. "But you're also so incredibly naïve. Did you truly think I wouldn't notice you take Kain out? Grab the children? How stupid do you think I am?"

He leans forward until his rancid breath permeates the air around me, causing me to gag. "Everything that happened, happened because I orchestrated it. I *wanted* Kain to be taken. I *wanted* the kids to be set free. I wanted the shifters to attack the men who came with me." His smile causes glacial fear to trickle down my spine. "It's all part of his plan."

"Who are you talking about?" I whisper.

God...

If what he's saying is true...

The shifters are going to think that humans—that Hunters—attacked the party. Killed their people. Threatened their children.

And why did they want us to capture Kain? Certainly, Kain's appearance proves that there's more to this mess than what meets the eye, right?

Vlad continues to grin down at me. "And now I have the final piece of the puzzle—you."

"Me?"

"You're an extremely special girl, Isabella." Vlad reaches down as if he wants to caress my cheek, but I turn my face away, gritting my teeth.

He pauses and then straightens, much to my relief.

"I think you may have gotten the wrong person," I bite out. "I'm virtually a human."

"Your blood will suggest otherwise," he singsongs. "Besides, even if you can't do what we need you to do, you'll be able to help us get someone who will."

"That doesn't make any damn sense."

He leans over me yet again, so close I can see the darker specks of garnet in his eyes. They're truly revolting to look at. Not because of the color, but because of what they represent—all of the blood he must've consumed.

"You should be lucky you're needed, little girl, or your insolence will see you killed." He bares his teeth at me.

I grin. "Fuck. You."

What he doesn't realize is while he monologued like an old-fashioned movie villain, I crept my hand towards a fallen branch the size of my forearm. I swing it as hard as I can at his head.

As expected, it isn't enough to knock him unconscious, but it does surprise him, and he staggers back with a yelp, clutching his cheek. I nimbly jump to my feet.

"You bitch—"

I hit him again, harder this time.

And again.

And again.

And again.

Sometimes when I watch horror movies, I find myself screaming at the main character for being such a fucking idiot. For example, when they have the chance to stop the bad guy, they'll often hit them once and then run away. Hell no. You keep hitting that fucker until his legs are broken and he's unable to chase you.

Tears stream down my cheeks as I finally toss the branch to the side, certain that Vlad won't be getting up and following me anytime soon. He's still alive, but his legs look as if they've been through a meat grinder.

I spit on his unconscious form. "Fuck you."

Someone barrels through the trees from behind me, and I immediately dive for the branch and hold it up like a baseball bat.

One last gunman steps forward.

I prepare myself to have some batting practice with his head when he speaks, his rough, raspy voice curling around me like smoke.

"Gracie."

I drop the branch as shivers dance down my spine. "W-what?"

Grayson reaches for the balaclava and pulls it off, revealing a face I memorized years ago.

His dark eyebrows pull together as he glances at Vlad's unconscious form before refocusing on me with panicked urgency. "Are you okay? Did he hurt you?"

"W-what? What are you doing here? Why are you a part of this?!" I ask in disbelief.

There's no hiding the hurt in my voice either.

"I can explain," Grayson says, stepping closer and grabbing my arms. His gentle touch sends heat careening through me. "The day after we...made love, the vampires took me."

My stomach takes a nosedive. "What?"

"They wanted to know why I abandoned them." He swallows. "I didn't tell them about you, but I think they suspected. Especially if the people I was working with prior weren't Hunters but someone in the paranormal world."

"I don't understand," I say, my fingernails digging into his arms.

He's here. He's real. He's alive.

And he was apparently being held captive while I wallowed and sulked.

Guilt, anger, and sadness all war for dominance, but I push those emotions to the side and tell myself I'll sort through them at a later point.

"The other day, they pulled me out of my cell, dressed me in this ridiculous getup, and told me to wait. Then this morning, Vlad picked me up and shoved me in a truck. He told me to just fucking stand still and hold this gun. I swear I had no idea what he had planned. And when he started shooting people..." He shakes his head in disbelief. "I didn't know what the fuck to do."

"It's okay." I rush forward to wrap my arms around his waist, his steady body a contrast to my trembling one. "It's okay. It wasn't your fault."

His arms remain limply by his sides for only a second before he tightens them around me, lifting me into the air. And then we're kissing, inhaling each other. A sense of rightness and innate peace barrage me from every direction.

I shove my fingers into his dark hair, messing up the strands, as he breathes against my lips, "Mate. My mate."

I pull away to see his expression better. "Mate?"

Warmth envelops me.

A sheepish smile pulls up one corner of his mouth. "I was going to tell you the day I—"

He freezes abruptly and drops me to my feet. I spin around to follow the direction of his gaze, and my mouth goes dry.

Over twenty people stand in the forest, watching us, but it's the three in the front who capture my attention. They step forward with a gracefulness I can only hope to emulate one day.

The first one is tall and slender, perhaps a few years older than I am. Her dark-red hair cascades to just below her waist and is so straight it looks unreal. She has a heart-shaped face, stunning green eyes, and perfect pink lips curled into an enticing smile.

She studies me intently. "Is this her?"

Her voice is lyrical.

The lady on the opposite end steps forward. She's the oldest of the group, though her eyes hold a keen intelligence that belies her frail appearance. Her gray hair hangs loose and curly around her wrinkled face.

"The resemblance is uncanny," she croaks out.

The woman in the middle finally steps forward, and now that she's no longer obscured by shadows, I can see her clearly.

My breath catches, and Grayson goes still beside me.

She looks...exactly like me. An older version of me —late thirties or early forties—but those blue eyes, that blonde hair, and those full lips are unmistakable.

"Mom?" I whisper.

The woman smiles, but it doesn't reach her eyes. "I'm not your mother, child, though I am *the* Mother."

Something occurs to me then. A name I heard...

"Delaney?"

I have the pleasure of seeing shock widen the woman's eyes before she smooths out her expression.

"This is the Maiden, Soraya." Delaney points to the gorgeous redhead first. "And this is the Crone, Ara."

Ara bares yellowing teeth at me.

"You're the Trinity," I say in grim understanding.

Delaney smiles again, though her cold eyes refuse to thaw. "And you're Isabella Martin." She extends a pale, delicate hand adorned with rings. "You need to come with us."

Grayson shoulders his way in front of me. "No way in hell—"

The Crone waves her hand, and Grayson flies through the air and hits the tree with an audible *thunk*.

He struggles forward, but it's like he's held in place by an invisible wall. Anger flashes in his pale-blue eyes.

"Stop it! Let him go!" I scream at Ara.

She simply smirks, the expression somehow horrifying on her weathered face.

"We just want to talk to you," Delaney tries again.

"What does everyone want with me?" I explode. "I can't do anything! I have no magic. I can't shift into a wolf. I can't—"

"You stupid girl," the Crone rasps out. "Do you really think anyone here gives a shit about you? We all know you didn't inherit any powers. But you're the bargaining chip we need to—"

"That's enough." Delaney holds a hand up in the air, and the Crone immediately snaps her teeth together.

"It'll be easier for everyone if you just come with us," Soraya says with a soft smile. "We won't hurt the vampire."

"Let me go!" Grayson roars, fighting against the invisible restraints like a man possessed. "I swear to fuck—"

The Crone waves her hand again, and I suddenly can't hear a single word Grayson says. His lips are still moving, his eyes spewing venom, but it's like he's in a bubble.

I stare at the Crone in disbelief, and she shrugs a bony shoulder.

"What? He was swearing too much."

Soraya rolls her eyes. "You swear all the time."

"Fuck off."

Delaney turns her eyes towards the heavens as if praying for patience before refocusing on me. "You need to come with us."

"Why?" I take a step backwards, wondering if I can run.

But no. I won't leave Grayson, and there's no way he can fight off twenty-plus witches.

"Because we need your help contacting someone," Delaney says cryptically.

"I don't understand—"

"Oh, enough of this!" Soraya flicks her wrist, and my body sways to the side.

Darkness penetrates the edges of my vision, and my brain turns fuzzy, as if it's been stuffed with a thousand wet cotton balls.

But just before darkness claims me, I hear a voice whisper, "Travan will have no choice but to come."

Travan?

Who the fuck is that?

And then unconsciousness pulls me under.

Epilogue

TRAVAN

I take another drag of my cigarette before dropping it to the ground and stomping on it with my boot.

Well, well, well.

Things here have certainly gotten interesting.

I tilt my face upwards and let out a sigh. The sky above is riven with gray clouds that resemble clumps of cement. The sun has almost finished its descent entirely, though a few stubborn orange streaks cut through the darkness.

I take a deep breath—exactly as my therapist instructed me to do whenever I felt stabby—and let it out. In and out. In and out. When I finally have my emotions under control, I flick my gaze towards the unconscious vampire.

Grayson Grey.

I did my research on the little shit. Vampire assassin. Cold-blooded killer. Ruthless enemy.

My kind of man.

He'll make a fine mate for my little girl. Yes, fine indeed.

At the thought of Izzy, my blood runs cold. This time, not even my breathing exercises can keep the rage at bay.

Those witch bitches took my daughter. I watched, unable to do anything, as they knocked her unconscious, levitated her into the air, and then disappeared through the throng of trees.

I couldn't take on twenty-seven witches.

Well, I could've, but there was a good chance that Izzy would've gotten caught in the crossfire, and I wouldn't allow that to happen.

My daughter.

My fucking daughter.

A giddy, euphoric feeling bubbles in my chest. I don't quite know what it is.

Happiness, perhaps? Maybe. I can't remember the last time I was happy.

Unless you count the time I dismembered that asshole down on Canal Street in New Orleans...

A smile tugs up my lips at the memory, but I immediately squash it.

Izzy looks so much like her mother.

As always, when I think of Helena, I feel a pang in my chest—I think this particular emotion is grief, but it has been muted with time and numbed by drugs, alcohol, and death. There's a gaping chasm where my heart used to be, if I ever truly had one to begin with.

Fuck, I miss her.

Izzy's the only thing left of her memory.

I remember when I first saw Helena, back when I was in college. She looked ethereal, her golden hair curling around her shoulders like a halo and her eyes glimmering with mirth. At the time, she was dating some fuckwad, but I can't remember his name. Mike, maybe? I suppose it doesn't matter. The second she saw me, it was over between them.

I introduced her to my packmates that very day, and that night, we...well...we didn't conceive Izzy that night, but we certainly tried.

She was the light of my world, the only good thing that tethered me to sanity.

Until she was taken from me.

I squeeze my eyelids shut at the memories that threaten to assault me. Kyle and Silas begged me to stay home, but when the police called and claimed they found her body, I had to know for sure. Had to be certain it was her.

Those images will haunt me until the day I die.

We all assumed that our unborn child was killed during the...during the incident, but that wasn't true at all. Izzy's alive.

My daughter's alive.

But taken by those nasty-ass bitches—no doubt in an attempt to lure me out.

Ha. Joke's on them.

I've been here the entire time.

Of course, nobody knows that. Not even my pack-mates and brothers.

But the second a little birdy told me they found my daughter, I had to see her. Had to protect her.

It's almost an art form being a part of her life without her realizing it. I can't be too suspicious, but I also can't be too memorable. So I'll be the man at the movie theater asking for extra butter in his popcorn. The person sitting in the booth directly behind hers when she goes out to eat. The "creepy man" insisting that she try the ribs because they're to die for.

The monster following her home and killing the men who thought they could touch her.

A cold grin skates across my face at the memory. I relish the sound of their bones snapping, their blood pooling at my feet, their screams renting the air.

I wonder what the witches will taste like when I eat them.

I've been generous with them up until now, and that was due to my loyalty to Helena and her lineage. I even allowed her conniving sister to live, despite my better judgment.

But my patience has run so thin, it's practically nonexistent.

Well, I suppose I'm going to give the witches what

they want after all—me. They're more than welcome to roll out the red carpet.

"Sleep tight, little vampire," I coo to the unconscious man, kissing the tips of my fingers and then pressing them to his forehead. "Nighty night. Don't let the bedbugs bite."

I laugh uproariously and then practically prance away.

I think it's about time I let my fellow shifters know that I'm back.

Unlike them, I'm not a wolf.

I'm something...other.

Better, if I'm being completely honest.

And Izzy is too. She shares my DNA, after all. Fortunately for her, she hasn't yet learned how to tap into her powers, which is why all of the assholes are still gunning for me.

But if she ever learns what she can do...

I swagger out of the forest with a wide grin on my face. Because what isn't there to be happy about? I'm back with my family, I found my daughter, and I'm about to slaughter some witches.

I mean, I probably should feel sad about the two shifters who died, but...nah. That doesn't really concern me. They should've moved out of the way of the bullet, obviously.

I whistle as I walk through the throng of shifters. Mothers and fathers are holding their children close to their chests, crying into their hair. Hale and Gerry are leaning over a dark-haired girl. A little boy trips as he attempts to run towards an older woman who's probably his grandma.

That pinching sensation in my heart returns with a vengeance.

I never got to do any of this "parent" stuff with Izzy. Never got to teach her how to hold a blade, or how to stab a ball sac, or how to pluck out an eye, or any of the other things fathers are supposed to teach their daughters.

Maybe if I had, she would've murdered her sorry excuse for "mates" by now.

It doesn't take long for people to take notice of my presence.

An older woman flinches, terror flooding her eyes, and a father attempts to hide his children behind his legs. Someone shrieks, and someone else runs in the opposite direction. The two men covering the dead bodies with sheets—I recognize one as Gregor, the head of the Council—pause what they're doing and gape at me.

Silas and Kyle both step out of the crowd, looking a little worse for wear but alive. Silas has gone deathly still, and Kyle's face has drained of color, turning a sickly shade of white.

Kyle swallows heavily. "Oh...fuck."

I grin broadly and spread out my arms in either direction. "Daddy's home, bitches."

And the fun's just getting started.

Thank you all so much for reading. Mated by Fire is a passion project of mine. I have so much love in my heart for Izzy and her mates. Book three should release this year. Don't feel like waiting? Join my ream and be a part of the writing process. I post chapters of book three weekly. But don't worry! If you don't want to read the book on ream, it'll be coming to KU as soon as I finish writing it.

Acknowledgments

Thank you to my incredible team who made this book possible.

A special thank you to Tami, Elena, Allie, and Mindy for your support on ream.

Next, I would like to thank my editor Lindsey and my cover designer Laura. Thank you for helping me bring my vision to life.

And finally, I would like to thank you, the reader, for picking up this book and giving it a chance. I love you all.

About the Author

Katie May is a reverse harem author, a KDP All-Star winner, and an *USA Today* Bestselling Author. She lives in West Michigan with her family, cat, and adorable puppy. When not writing, she can be found reading a good book, listening to broadway musicals, or playing games. Join Katie's Gang to stay updated on all her releases! And did you know she has a TikTok? Yeah, me neither. Follow her here! But be warned... she's an awkward noodle.

Also by Katie May

Together We Fall (Apocalyptic Reverse Harem, COMPLETED)

1. The Darkness We Crave

2. The Light We Seek

3. The Storm We Face

4. The Monsters We Hunt

Beyond the Shadows (Horror Reverse Harem, COMPLETED)

1. Gangs and Ghosts

2. Guns and Graveyards

3. Gallows and Ghouls

Out of Sight (Prison Reverse Harem, COMPLETED)

1. Blindly Indicted

2. Blindly Acquitted

Kingdom of Wolves (Shifter Reverse Harem Duet, COMPLETED)

1. Torn to Bits

2. Ripped to Shreds

Tory's School for the Trouble (Bully Horror Academy
Reverse Harem, COMPLETED)

1. Between

2. Beyond

3. Beneath

The Damning (Fantasy Paranormal Reverse Harem)

1. Greed

2. Envy

3. Gluttony

4. Sloth

5. Pride

6. Lust

7. Wrath

Prodigium Academy (Horror Comedy Academy Reverse
Harem, COMPLETED)

1. Monsters

2. Roaring

3. Venom

4. Fangs

5. Blood

Kings of Grove Academy (Contemporary Academy Reverse
Harem)

1. Mania

2. Psychotic

3. Pandemonium

4. Delirium

The Death Whisper (Fantasy Reverse Harem)

1. Of Rain and Wrath

2. Of Heat and Obsession

Supernaturalette (Interactive Reverse Harem)

1. Introductions

2. First Dates

3. Group Outing

4. Game Night

5. Exes

6. Truth or Dare

7. Scavenger Hunt

8. Reveals

CO-WRITES

Afterworld Academy with Loxley Savage (Academy Fantasy Reverse Harem, COMPLETED)

1. Dearly Departed

2. Darkness Deceives

3. Defying Destiny

Darkest Flames with Ann Denton (Paranormal Reverse Harem, COMPLETED)

1. Demon Kissed

1.5. Demon Stalked

2. Demon Loved

3. Demon Sworn

Darkest Queen with Ann Denton (Paranormal Reverse Harem)

1. For Whom the Bell Tolls

Dark Temptations with Ann Denton (Monster Reverse Harem)

1. Ravaged by Monsters

2. Devoured by Monsters

3. Worshipped by Monsters

Fae Revealed with Quinn Arthurs (Paranormal Reverse Harem)

1. Courting Darkness

2. Seducing Shadows

3. Loving Demons

STAND-ALONES

Toxicity (Contemporary Reverse Harem)

Not All Heroes Wear Capes (Just Dresses) (Short Comedic Reverse Harem)

Charming Devils (Bully/Revenge Reverse Harem)

Goddess of Pain (Fantasy Reverse Harem)

Demon's Joy (Holiday Reverse Harem)

Broken Howl (Wolf Shifter Reverse Harem)

Dark Paradise (Paranormal Motorcycle Club Reverse Harm)

Ruthless as a Cheetah (Paranormal Romantic Comedy Reverse Harem)

BOXSETS

Together We Fall

www.ingramcontent.com/pod-product-compliance
Lightning Source LLC
Chambersburg PA
CBHW030331010826
48973CB00004B/955

9 798890 640369